"REBECCA IS BEGUILING. . . .

But the star, as always in Tyler's quirky world, is life itself—a daunting mix of the trivial and the profound, but always real, 'not some story floating past.' Tyler's fans will love this one."

—*The Arizona Republic*

Tyler has a "gift for showing how the small, daily events dictate a life's path. . . . She never fails to leave the reader with insights gained and new ways to view the old. She combines beautiful, incisive writing with the touching, jumbled emotions of family."

—*The Kansas City Star*

"With refreshing optimism and gentle humor, Tyler elegantly suggests that we can, in unexpected ways, glimpse all our unfulfilled destinies. Again and again, we are convinced."

—*Time Out New York*

"[A] quietly beguiling novel. Told with tenderness and humor . . . Brilliantly drawn characters . . . Anne Tyler brings yet another spectacularly flawed and wonderful family to life. . . . Her new novel displays the deceptively ordinary storytelling that grows into something quite extraordinary, which is Anne Tyler's unique gift."

—*Richmond Times-Dispatch*

"Hilarious, touching . . . An inviting, hospitable novel. Its charms are seductive. Its pleasures are many. This is Tyler at the top of her game. And as any faithful reader knows, that's high praise indeed."

—*The Sunday Patriot-News* (Harrisburg, PA)

Please turn the page for more reviews. . . .

"[A] STUNNING NEW NOVEL . . .

Tyler has a gift for creating endearing characters, but readers should find Rebecca particularly appealing, for despite the blows she takes, she bravely keeps on trying. Tyler also has a gift—genius is more like it—for unfurling intricate stories effortlessly, as if by whimsy or accident. The ease of her storytelling here is breathtaking."

—*Publishers Weekly* (boxed and starred review)

"A gifted writer can elevate the everyday to the entertaining, can transform the ordinary into the universal. In Anne Tyler's fifteenth novel, the reader can become absorbed with the storyline, woven with strands of bittersweet humor and moments of both quiet, quarrelsome drama. . . . Her novel fuses a multitude of extraordinary pieces into a brilliant whole that, observed from any angle, will reflect something of the reader."

—*The State* (Columbia, SC)

"[Tyler] tells the story in the familiar rhythms of family gossip, honest thinking, and dialogue that presents astute psychological revelation but feels like poetry. . . . Tyler's talent shines in *Back When We Were Grownups* just as brilliantly as it does in her previous works. She has turned out another fine book."

—*Huntsville Times* (AL)

"There's not a flat line in this book, not a single simple character, not a moment that isn't tapped for all its glorious possibilities. There is a party on almost every page, and there is also the party's aftermath. This is storytelling at its best and most breathtaking."

—*Book* magazine

"The pleasures and surprises are in the details, in the marvelously strange people she assembles and the painful, funny, exasperating, and moving ways they interact. Read one of her novels and you'll swear you know a family exactly like that. Or live in one."

—*American Way*

Back When We Were Grownups

Also by Anne Tyler

Back
When We Were
Grownups

Anne Tyler

Ballantine Books
New York

A Ballantine Book

Published by The Ballantine Publishing Group

Copyright © 2001 by Anne Tyler

Reader's Guide copyright © 2002 by Anne Tyler and The Ballantine

Publishing Group, a division of Random House, Inc.

www.ballantinebooks.com

Library of Congress Catalog Card Number: 2002090423

ISBN 0-345-44686-0

This edition published by arrangement with Alfred A. Knopf, Inc.

Manufactured in the United States of America

First Trade Paperback Edition: May 2002

10 9 8 7

Back When We Were Grownups

one

Once upon a time, there was a woman who discovered she had turned into the wrong person.

She was fifty-three years old by then—a grandmother. Wide and soft and dimpled, with two short wings of dry, fair hair flaring almost horizontally from a center part. Laugh lines at the corners of her eyes. A loose and colorful style of dress edging dangerously close to Bag Lady.

Give her credit: most people her age would say it was too late to make any changes. What's done is done, they would say. No use trying to alter things at this late date.

It did occur to Rebecca to say that. But she didn't.

. . .

On the day she made her discovery, she was picnicking on the North Fork River out in Baltimore County. It was a cool, sunny Sunday in early June of 1999, and her family had gathered to celebrate the engagement of Rebecca's youngest stepdaughter, NoNo Davitch.

The Davitches' cars circled the meadow like covered wagons

braced for attack. Their blankets dotted the grass, and their thermos jugs and ice chests and sports equipment crowded the picnic table. The children were playing beside the river in one noisy, tumbling group, but the adults kept themselves more separate. Alone or in twos they churned about rearranging their belongings, jockeying for spots in the sun, wandering off hither and yon in their moody Davitch manner. One of the stepdaughters was sitting by herself in her minivan. One of the sons-in-law was stretching his hamstrings over by the runners' path. The uncle was stabbing the ground repeatedly with his cane.

Goodness, what would Barry think? (Barry, the new fiancé.) He would think they disapproved of his marrying NoNo.

And he would be right.

Not that they ever behaved much differently under any conditions.

Barry had a blanket mostly to himself, because NoNo kept flitting elsewhere. The tiniest and prettiest of the Davitch girls — a little hummingbird of a person — she darted first to one sister and then another, ducking her shiny dark cap of hair and murmuring something urgent.

Murmuring, "Like him, please," maybe. Or, "At least make him feel welcome."

The first sister grew very busy rummaging through a straw hamper. The second shaded her eyes and pretended to look for the children.

Rebecca — who earned her living hosting parties, after all — felt she had no choice but to clap her hands and call, "Okay, folks!"

Languidly, they turned. She seized a baseball from the table and held it up. No, it was bigger than a baseball. A softball, then; undoubtedly the property of the son-in-law stretching his hamstrings, who taught phys ed at the local high school. It was all the same to Rebecca; she had never been the sporty type. Still: "Time for a game, everybody!" she called. "Barry? NoNo? Come on, now! We'll say this rock is home plate. Zeb, move that log over to where first base ought to be. The duffel bag can be second, and for third . . . Who's got something we can use for third?"

They groaned, but she refused to give up. "Come on, people! Show some life here! We need to exercise off all that food we're about to eat!"

In slow motion they began to obey, rising from their blankets and drifting where she pointed. She turned toward the runners' path and, "Yoo-hoo! Jeep!" she called. Jeep stopped hugging one beefy knee and squinted in her direction. "Haul yourself over here!" she ordered. "We're organizing a softball game!"

"Aw, Beck," he said, "I was hoping to get a run in." But he came plodding toward her.

While Jeep set about correcting the placement of the bases, Rebecca went to deal with the stepdaughter in the minivan. Who happened to be Jeep's wife, in fact. Rebecca hoped this wasn't one of their silly quarrels. "Sweetie!" she sang out. She waded through the weeds, scooping up armfuls of her big red bandanna-print skirt. "Patch? Roll down your window, Patch. Can you hear me? Is something the matter?"

Patch turned and gazed out at her. You could tell she must be hot. Spikes of her chopped black hair were sticking to her forehead, and her sharp, freckled face was shining with sweat. Still, she made no move to open her window. Rebecca grabbed the door handle and yanked it—luckily, just before Patch thought to push the lock down.

"Now, then!" Rebecca caroled. "What's all this about?"

Patch said, "Can't a person ever get a moment of peace in this family?"

She was thirty-seven years old but looked more like fourteen, in her striped T-shirt and skinny jeans. And acted like fourteen, too, Rebecca couldn't help thinking; but all she said was, "Come on out and join us! We're starting up a softball game."

"No, thanks."

"Pretty please?"

"For Lord's sake, Beck, don't you know how I hate this?"

"Hate it!" Rebecca cried merrily, choosing to misunderstand. "But you're wonderful at sports! The rest of us don't even know where the bases go. Poor Jeep is having to do everything."

Patch said, "I cannot for the life of me see why we should celebrate my little sister's engagement to a—to a—"

Words appeared to fail her. She clamped her arms tight across
her flat chest and faced forward again.

"To a what?" Rebecca asked her. "A nice, decent, well-spoken
man. A lawyer."

"A *corporate* lawyer. A man who brings his appointment book to
a picnic; did you notice his appointment book? Him and his yacht-
looking, country-club-looking clothes; his ridiculous yellow crew
cut; his stupid rubber-soled boating shoes. And look at how he was
sprung on us! Just sprung on us with no warning! One day it's, oh,
poor NoNo, thirty-five years old and never even been kissed so far as
anyone knew; and the next day—I swear, the very next day!—she
pops up out of the blue and announces an August wedding."

"Well, now, I just have a feeling she may have kept him secret
out of nervousness," Rebecca said. "She didn't want to look foolish,
in case the courtship came to nothing. Also, maybe she worried you
girls would be too critical."

Not without reason, she didn't add.

Patch said, "Hogwash. You know why she kept him secret: he's
been married once before. Married and divorced, with a twelve-
year-old son to boot."

"Well, these things do happen," Rebecca said drily.

"And such a pathetic son, too. Did you see?" Patch jabbed a
thumb toward the children by the river, but Rebecca didn't bother
turning. "A puny little runt of a son! And it can't have escaped your
notice that Barry has sole custody. He's had to cook for that child
and clean house, drive the car pool, help with homework . . . Of
course he wants a wife! Unpaid nanny, is more like it."

"Now, dearie, that's an insult to NoNo," Rebecca said. "Any
man in his right mind would want NoNo for her own sake."

Patch merely gave an explosive wheeze that lifted the spikes of
hair off her forehead.

"Just think," Rebecca reminded her. "Didn't I marry a divorced
man with three little girls? And see, it worked out fine! I'd be married to him still, if he had lived."

All Patch said to this was, "And how you could throw a party for them!"

"Well, of course I'd throw a party. It's an occasion!" Rebecca said. "Besides: you and Biddy asked for one, if I remember correctly."

"We asked if you planned to give one, is all, since you're so fond of engagement parties. Why, Min Foo's had three of them! They seem to be kind of a habit with you."

Rebecca opened her mouth to argue, because she was almost positive that Patch and Biddy had requested, in so many words, that she put together a picnic. But then she saw that she might have misinterpreted. Maybe they had just meant that since they knew she would be planning something, they would prefer it to be held outside. (Oh, the Davitch girls were very unsocial. "I guess you're going to insist on some kind of shindig," one of them would sigh, and then they would show up and sit around looking bored, picking at their food while Rebecca tried to jolly things along.)

Well, no matter, because Patch was finally unfolding herself from the minivan. She slammed the door behind her and said, "Let's get started, then, if you're so set on this."

"Thank you, sweetie," Rebecca said. "I just know we'll have a good time today."

Patch said, "Ha!" and marched off toward the others, leaving Rebecca to trail behind.

The softball game had begun now, at least in a halfhearted way. People were scattered across the meadow seemingly at random, with Rebecca's brother-in-law and Barry so far off in the outfield that they might not even be playing. The catcher (Biddy) was tying her shoe. The uncle leaned on his cane at an indeterminate spot near third base. Rebecca's daughter was sunbathing on first, lounging in the grass with her face tipped back and her eyes closed.

As Patch and then Rebecca came up behind home plate, Jeep was assuming the batter's stance, his barrel-shaped body set sideways to them and his bat wagging cockily. NoNo, on the pitcher's mound, crooked her arm at an awkward angle above her shoulder and released the ball. It traveled in an uncertain arc until Jeep lost patience and took a stride forward and hit a low drive past second. Hakim, Rebecca's son-in-law, watched with interest as it whizzed by. (No surprise there, since Hakim hailed from someplace Arab and had probably never seen a softball in his life.) Jeep dropped his bat and trotted to first, not disturbing Min Foo's sunbath in the least. He rounded second, receiving a beatific smile from Hakim, and headed for third. Third was manned by Biddy's . . . oh, Rebecca never knew what to call him . . . longtime companion, dear Troy, who always claimed it was while he was fumbling a pop-up fly at age five that he first realized he was gay. All he did was wave amiably as Jeep went trundling past.

By that time, Barry had managed to locate the ball. He threw it toward Biddy, but she was tying her other shoe now. It was Patch who stepped forward to intercept it, apparently without effort. Then she turned back to home plate and tagged her husband out.

Patch and Jeep might have been playing alone, for all the reaction they got. Biddy straightened up from her shoe and yawned. NoNo started clucking over a broken fingernail. Min Foo was probably unaware of what had happened, even—unless she'd been able to figure it out with her eyes closed.

"Oh," Rebecca cried, "you-all are not even trying! Where is your team spirit?"

"For that, we need more than one side," Jeep said, wiping his forehead on his shoulder. "There aren't enough of us playing."

To Rebecca, it seemed just then that there were far too many of them. Such a large and unwieldy group, they were; so cumbersome, so much work. But she said, "You're absolutely right," and turned in the direction of the river. "Kids!" she called. "Hey, kids!"

The children were hopping in an uneven line a good twenty yards away, beyond a stretch of buzzing, humming grass and alongside flowing water; so at first they didn't hear her. She had to haul up her skirt again and slog toward them, calling, "Come on, everybody! Come and play ball! You kids against us grownups!"

Now they stopped what they were doing (some version of Follow the Leader, it seemed, leaping from rock to rock) and looked over at her. Five of the six were here today—all but Dixon, the oldest, who'd gone someplace else with his girlfriend. And then there was Barry's son, what's-his-name. Peter. "Peter?" Rebecca called. "Want to play softball?"

He stood slightly apart from the others, noticeably pale-haired and white-skinned and scrawny in this company of dark, vivid Davitch children. Rebecca felt a tug of sympathy for him. She called, "You can be pitcher, if you like!"

He took a step backward and shook his head. Well, no, of course: she should have offered him the outfield. Something inconspicuous. The others, meanwhile, had broken rank and were starting toward her. "Not It, not It," the youngest child was chanting, evidently confused as to what softball was all about. Patch and Jeep's three (wouldn't you know) were vying to be first at bat. "We'll draw straws," Rebecca told them. "Come on, everybody! Winning team gets excused from cleanup after lunch."

Only Peter stayed where he was. He was balanced on a low rock, alert and motionless, giving off a chilling silence. Rebecca called, "Sweetie? Aren't you coming?"

Again he shook his head. The other children veered around her and plowed on toward the playing field, but Rebecca gathered her skirt higher and pressed forward. Long, cool grasses tickled her bare calves. A cloud of startled white butterflies fluttered around her knees. She reached the first rock, took a giant step up, and leapt to the next rock just beyond, teetering for a second before she found her footing on the slick, mossy surface. (She was wearing rope-soled espadrilles that gave her almost no traction.) So far she was still on dry land, but most of the other rocks—Peter's included—turned out to be partly submerged. This meant that the children had been disobeying instructions. They'd been warned to stay away from the river, which was unpredictably deep in some spots and wider than a two-lane highway, not to mention icy cold so early in the season.

Peter kept as still as a cornered deer; Rebecca sensed that even though she wasn't looking at him. For the moment, she was looking at the scenery. Oh, didn't a river rest your eyes! She sank into a peaceful trance, watching how the water seemed to gather itself as it traveled toward a sharp bend. It swelled up in loose, silky tangles and then it smoothed and flowed on, transparent at the edges but nearly opaque at the center, as yellow-green and sunlit as a bottle in a window. She drifted with it, dreaming. It could have been a hundred years ago. The line of dark trees on the opposite shore would have looked the same; she'd have heard the same soft, curly lapping close by, the same rushing sound farther off.

Well. Enough of this. She tore her gaze away and turned again to Peter. "I've got you now!" she told him gaily.

He took another step backward and disappeared.

For a moment, she couldn't believe what had happened. She just stood there with her mouth open. Then she looked down and saw a turmoil in the water. A small, white, big-eyed face gulping air and choking. A frantic snarl of thin, bare, flailing arms.

She jumped onto the rock he'd been standing on, skidding slightly and bruising an ankle. She plunged in waist deep and gasped. (The water was so cold it burned.) First she grabbed Peter's wrist but lost it. Then she clutched blue denim. She hitched him up by the seat of his jeans and found the time, somehow, to consider how absurd this must look: a middle-aged woman plucking a boy from a river like a sack of laundry, hoisting him aloft for one split second before her muscles registered his weight and they both went under. But she still had hold of him. She kept her grip. She fought to thrust him above the surface even while she was half sitting on the bottom. Then she was up and struggling shoreward, stumbling and falling and rising and staggering on, hauling him by his armpits. (A good thing he was so undersized or she never could have managed, adrenaline or no.) Between his coughs now he was drawing huge, rough, scraping breaths, and once or twice he gagged. She dragged him in a bobbling way across the rocks to the grass, where she dropped him. She bent double to clear her head and noticed, in that position, how her skirt was streaming with water; so she collected a handful of hem and wrung it out.

The first to reach them was Barry. He pounded up shouting, "Peter! Peter? What in hell were you *doing?*" Peter didn't answer. He was shaking and chattering, huddling into himself on the ground. Barry peeled his own windbreaker off and bundled it around him.

Meanwhile Zeb arrived—Rebecca's brother-in-law. He was followed by the children and then by the rest of the grownups, who slowed to a casual saunter once they saw that things were under control.

Zeb was a pediatrician; so Barry and Rebecca gave way to him. He squatted and asked, "Are you okay?" and Peter nodded, swiping at his nose with a sleeve of his father's windbreaker. "He's okay," Zeb announced.

Well, a layman could have done that much. "Check his lungs," Rebecca ordered.

"His lungs are fine," Zeb said, but he went on watching Peter. "How did it happen, son?" he asked.

Rebecca tensed, dreading the answer, but Peter kept silent. You couldn't tell a thing from his expression: eyes lowered, mouth pursed in a stubborn little bunch. Even before his dunking, he had had the skinned appearance of a wet cat, and now she could make out the pink of his scalp beneath his colorless hair. Periodically he swiped at his nose again in a fractious way, as if a gnat were pestering him.

"Well," Zeb said finally, and he sighed and rose to his feet. He was a gangling, bespectacled, kind-faced man, so accustomed to dealing with the children of the inner-city poor that he wore a permanent look of resignation. "Let's rustle up some dry clothes for these two," he said. "Come on, everybody. Fun's over."

As they were heading back toward the picnic—Rebecca hugging her rib cage and doing her best to stop her shivers—Barry came up beside her. "I don't know how I can ever thank you, Mrs., er, Beck," he said.

"Oh," she said, "goodness! I'm sure he would have grabbed on to a branch or something, eventually."

"Well, still: I appreciate your coming to the rescue."

For now he did, she thought. But wait till he found out that Peter never would have fallen in if not for her.

.   .   .

They didn't continue the ball game. There was talk of going home early, even; and for once, Rebecca let them argue without intervening. She sat quietly at the picnic table, cocooned in a leaf-littered blanket, while they hashed it out among themselves. Look at how blue Peter's lips were, several of the women said. He would catch his death of cold! But of course, the grandchildren wanted to stay, and the uncle—an energy miser—pointed out the waste of gas if they had driven all this way only to turn around and drive back. "Let's just eat, for mercy's sake," he said. Biddy, who had gone to a lot of trouble over the food, jumped up as if that settled things and started unpacking coolers.

By this time, Rebecca's hair had dried into its usual pup-tent shape and her blouse had changed from an icy film to a warm, damp second skin beneath her blanket. She repositioned the blanket around her waist and accepted the loan of Zeb's cardigan. Peter fared better: from the back seats and floors of various vehicles, an entire outfit was assembled. Emmy donated a sweatshirt, Danny a pair of striped baseball knickers, and Jeep two semi-white gym socks. Ignoring the curious stares of the other children, Peter stripped then and there, exposing tweaky pale dots of nipples and dingy, stretched-out underpants fraying at the edges. (This was what happened, Rebecca reflected, when a father had sole custody.) Everything was too big for him. Even Danny's knickers—and Danny was barely thirteen—hung off him in folds, clinging to him only where the wet underpants had soaked through.

It struck Rebecca as unusual that a boy that old didn't mind changing clothes in public. And there was something needful and nudging about the way he stayed so close to his father. Once they were settled on NoNo's blanket, he kept interrupting the conversation by plucking Barry's sleeve and whispering at length in his ear, as if he were not just small for his age but young for his age, too.

"Is that child all *right?*" she asked Zeb.

"Oh, sure. Just bashful, I suspect," he told her.

But a big part of Zeb's profession was soothing parents' anxieties; so she turned to Biddy. "I haven't heard him say a word to NoNo," she said. "I hope there isn't going to be some kind of step-mother problem."

Biddy said, "Well, at least he was playing with the other kids by the river. That's always a good sign."

"He wouldn't talk to us, though," one of the children spoke up. This was Emmy, a long-legged sprite pouring lemonade from a thermos. Rebecca hadn't realized she was listening. Hastily, she said, "Well, of course he wouldn't talk! Imagine meeting all of you at once! I bet he talks your ears off as soon as he feels more at home."

"He wasn't really playing, either. He was only, like, hanging around our edges."

Rebecca said, "Maybe I should give him a welcoming party. You know? The way I do for our new babies? I could, oh, set up a scavenger hunt! And all the clues could be Davitch-related, I mean things he would have to ask the other kids to—"

"He would hate it," Emmy said flatly.

Rebecca slumped in her seat.

Biddy was uncovering a tray of runny cheeses garnished with edible flowers, and a mosaic of tiny canapés studded with salmon roe, and a sunburst of snow peas filled with smoked trout and dill. Two days a week, Biddy worked as a nutritionist for a retirement community (her monthly newsletter, *What Kind of Wine Goes with Oatmeal?*, had been mentioned in the *Baltimore Sun*), but she dreamed of becoming a gourmet chef, and it showed. "Ew, what's this?" the children were forever asking, pointing to something stuffed or sculptured or wonton-encased or otherwise disguised; and today they were all the more distressed because meaty, smoky smells had started drifting down the river from somebody else's grill. "Can't we ever have hamburgers?" Joey asked.

Rebecca said, "You can get hamburgers any old place! It's only at a Davitch party you can try these, um . . . these, um . . ."

She was looking at a platter of pastry thimbles filled with what seemed to be mud. Biddy said, "Snails in phyllo cups."

Joey said, "Ew!"

"I *beg* your pardon—" Biddy began, but then Rebecca grabbed Joey around the waist and pulled him close and nuzzled his neck. "Such a persnickety," she teased him, "such a hoity-toity," while he squirmed and giggled. He smelled of fresh sweat and sunshine. "Gram!" he protested, and she released him, and he went careening off toward his cousins.

"That child needs to be taught some manners," Biddy said. "Poppy? Care for a snail?" she asked her great-uncle.

Poppy was seated on the other side of the picnic table, folding both hands on his cane and hunching forward all hungry and hopeful, but he drew back sharply and, "Oh," he said, "why, ah, not just now, I don't believe, thank you just the same."

Biddy sighed. "I don't know why I bother," she told Rebecca. "Why not just grill a batch of hot dogs, or set out a loaf of store-bought bread and a jar of peanut butter?"

Why not, in fact? Rebecca wanted to ask. It wasn't as if Biddy were catering to her own tastes, because Biddy didn't eat. She was painfully, unattractively thin, every vertebra visible down the back of her neck, even her short black ponytail skimped and stringy, her wide-legged slacks and long red sweater all but empty. Offer her a bite and she'd say, "Oh, no, I couldn't possibly," and yet she talked about food nonstop, read cookbooks the way other women read romance novels, pored over magazine photos featuring glossy, lacy salads and succulent pork roasts. "Call people to the table," she told Rebecca now. "Everything's drying out! Make them come!"—as if she herself could not be heard; as if the food were her only means of communication.

Obediently, Rebecca stood up. (She knew from long experience that this family had to be corralled; a simple shout never worked.) "Children!" she called, wading through knee-high weeds. "Lunch is on!" Her shoes were squelching wetly, and her blanket started collecting a fuzz of burrs and pollen. "Lunch, Troy! Lunch, Hakim! Come eat, everybody!"

She should wear a whistle around her neck for these occasions. She always threatened to do that, but then forgot until next time.

Patch and Jeep seemed to be having an argument. Or Patch was arguing; Jeep was just kicking the ground with one huge, cloddish running shoe, his fists stuffed in his rear pockets and his eyes on the trees in the distance. "Lunch, you two!" Rebecca sang out. She scooped up the youngest grandchild but then was thrown off balance, and her blanket sarong hobbled her so that they both fell, laughing, into a clump of sprinkly white flowers. Rebecca's daughter said, "Honestly, Mom!" and helped them to their feet.

"Sorry," Rebecca said, chastened.

Once she had been the most serene and dignified young woman. That thought came to her, suddenly. She had worn her hair in a crown of braids, and friends had complimented her on the level way she carried her head, which had made her broad figure seem almost regal. Queen Rebecca, her roommate had called her.

Well, that was all in the past now.

By the time she got back to the picnic table, Poppy had started in on the least smelly of the cheeses. "Wait, Poppy!" she told him. "We haven't drunk the toast yet!"

"Who knows whether I'll live that long?" he asked crossly, but he set down his knife. He was one of those old men who appear to curl up as they age, and his chin was practically resting on the table.

Biddy was constructing a still life of exotic fruits—kiwis and mangoes and papayas and something that looked like green hand grenades. "How pretty!" Rebecca told her, although she was fairly certain that no one would venture to eat any. She reached past Biddy for a bottle of champagne and handed it to Barry. "Could you please open this?" she asked him. (Always give guests some useful task, if you want them to feel a part of things.) Another bottle went to Zeb, and she put Patch to work unpacking the old-fashioned, shallow sherbet glasses that the Davitches still used for champagne.

"Why you bring real crystal to family picnics—" Patch began, but Rebecca said, "What better occasion, I ask you, than for my nearest and dearest?"

"Half will be in splinters before we leave here; mark my words," Patch told her.

She was still upset about the engagement, Rebecca decided. It wasn't like Patch to care if the stemware got broken. She wrapped an arm around Patch's shoulders and whispered, "Sweetie, things will work out. We have to trust NoNo's judgment! She must know what she's doing."

Unfortunately, just at that moment Barry's cell phone rang. He pulled it from a holster on his belt and said, "Hello?" Patch gave Rebecca a meaningful stare. Rebecca just smiled noncommittally and sat back down at the table.

The children were complaining about their portions of champagne. They believed they should be given as much as the grown-ups, but what did they get? A tiny drop each, barely a swallow. "Once you're legal drinking age—" Rebecca told them.

"You always let Dixon have a full glass, and he's not legal drinking age!"

"Well, Dixon's older than the rest of you, and besides, eighteen *used* to be legal."

Jeep didn't like what he'd been served, either; he preferred beer. "Didn't we bring a six-pack?" he asked. "Where's that six-pack? Geez, Patch, you know how champagne makes me burp," and he started rummaging through ice chests.

Then Poppy took it into his head to start reciting his poem. *"You're given a special welcome when you get to heaven late,"* he declaimed in a ringing voice.

This was the poem he'd written for his wife's funeral, all of thirty years ago, and he never missed a chance to quote it. As often as Rebecca had heard that opening line, she mistook it every time for a reference to the Davitches' tendency toward tardiness. So like them to be unpunctual even in death! she always thought. Although the second line dispelled that notion. *"When you're the one who's been left behind to mourn,"* Poppy went on, rolling his *r*'s.

"Yes, but, Poppy," Rebecca said gently, and she reached across the table for his hand. "This is actually more of a *joyous* occasion, you know?"

He glared at her, but he subsided. His hand had a light, hollow feel, like a dried-up locust shell, and it lay in hers without moving.

Oh, none of the others considered how every engagement on earth would have to end up, Rebecca thought. They glided right over "till death do us part."

But she squared her shoulders, and, "So!" she cried. "Barry, NoNo, tell us how you met! This has all been such a surprise!"

Barry was just replacing his phone in its holster. He looked over at NoNo, and she slipped both hands through the crook of his arm and smiled up at him. "Well," she began, in her scratchy little voice, "you know how I've always had the gift of second sight."

Her sisters nodded, but a couple of the men were heard to groan.

"Well, I'm standing in my shop one morning, and in walks Barry. Says he wants a dozen roses. 'Fine,' I say, and I turn to get them, and all at once, out of the corner of my eye, I see the strangest thing. I see me, standing next to him, and I'm wearing a white chiffon wedding dress and holding a bouquet of late-summer blooms in various shades of yellow and gold—calendulas and rudbeckia and cosmos and gerbera daisies."

Rebecca supposed it was only natural that NoNo should focus most specifically on the flowers, but even so, she couldn't help laughing. The others looked at her. "Sorry," she said.

"And then," NoNo went on, "I blink and he's alone again. Waiting at the counter and wondering what the delay is, no doubt. So I go get the roses, I bring them out, I wrap them, and all the time I'm thinking *madly*. Madly. And finally I say, 'What would you like me to put on the card?' Which is not the usual thing, of course. Usually when a customer comes in person, he doesn't bother with a card. Or if he does, he writes the message himself. But I was afraid he was married or something. I wanted to see who the roses were meant for."

"Only, *I* didn't know that wasn't the usual thing," Barry said. "I told her, 'Just write, *For Mamie with love.*'"

"And I said, 'Who is Mamie?'"

Patch stopped handing out napkins. "You didn't," she said.

"I did! I was brazen! And Barry said, 'Mamie's my secretary.' See, it happened to be Professional Secretaries Day."

"You send flowers to your secretary with *love*?" Patch asked Barry.

He shrugged. "It's just an expression," he said.

Patch looked at him a moment longer and then went back to her napkins, shaking her head.

But NoNo was oblivious. "In the meantime," she told the others, "he is taking money from his wallet, and I am thinking,

Shoot, he's paying cash! I won't find out his name! So I write on the card, *For Mamie with love, from your boss and from Elinor Davitch, who would like to get to know him better.*"

Patch sent a despairing glance toward the sky.

"Wasn't that smart?" Barry asked, beaming down at NoNo. "She figured Mamie would ask me, 'Who's this Elinor Davitch?' Which she did, sure enough. And I said, 'Who is *who*?' and Mamie showed me the card. I said, 'Well, I never! It must be that woman at Budding Genius.' And I went back there after work and asked if she'd have a drink with me."

"We hit it off immediately," NoNo said. "I knew we would. Have I ever been wrong? Remember that time I saw a big, huge belly on Patch when she was trying to get pregnant? Remember when I asked Dixon why he was wearing a Johns Hopkins T-shirt? He said, 'This is a Camp Fernwood T-shirt, Aunt NoNo, but I wish it *were* Johns Hopkins because Hopkins is my first-choice college.' And I didn't even know it! Nobody'd told me a thing!"

Patch was shaking her head again. "Ridiculous," she said in an undertone to Rebecca.

Rebecca said, "Well, she does have this uncanny way of—"

"Not that, Beck. Although how uncanny could it be, when she fulfilled her own prophecy by immediately writing that note, for Lord's sake? But do you happen to have any idea when Secretaries Day *is*?"

Rebecca said, "Um . . ."

"It's in April."

"April," Rebecca said, still not comprehending.

"That was barely two months ago! Or less; more like one month, because I think it's toward the tail end of April. NoNo's known this man just a month and now she's up and marrying him!"

Rebecca started to remind her that she wasn't marrying him till August, after all. But in the lull that had suddenly fallen—with the only sounds the distant river and the chirring of the insects—she worried NoNo was overhearing their conversation. So instead, she picked up a glass of champagne. "Time for our toast, everybody!" she cried.

One by one, they reached for glasses of their own. The children were the most enthusiastic. They raised theirs high above their heads, like people hailing taxicabs. The only exception was Peter, who sat on NoNo's blanket in a puddle of heather-gray sweatshirt and allowed his glass to dangle limply from one hand.

Rebecca drew in a deep breath and began:

> "A toast to the bunch of us gathered together
> In this glorious spring weather,
> And to Zeb for scoping out the site
> And Biddy for cooking with all her might."

Her rhyming toasts were a tradition. She had no illusions about their literary merit; she knew they were pure doggerel. (More than once, in a pinch, she'd been forced to rely on nonsense syllables— tra la la or tum dee diddle—to finish up a line.) But her family had come to expect them; so she took another breath and went on.

> "And most of all, to NoNo and Barry.
> We're so delighted they're planning to marry."

"Hear, hear," the others murmured.

Joey's glass had a bee on the rim and there was a little to-do, since Joey was deathly allergic; but eventually they did all manage to take their sips. Then Barry said, "Well, thanks, you guys," and sheepishly rubbed the top of his bristly blond crew cut.

That was the best he could do?

Oh, Rebecca always felt suspicious of the people that her loved ones fell in love with. She worried! She couldn't help it! But that was her deep, dark secret, because invariably she was the first to rush forward with a warm welcome. Now she raised her glass again. "And next!" she said.

> "Next, a toast to Peter!
> Someone new in our family!
> Nothing could be sweeter."

"Hear, hear!" they repeated, more loudly now, and Barry said, "Aww," and raised his glass to Rebecca. "That's very nice of you," he told her.

But Peter said, "*I'm* not in your family."

His speaking voice turned out to be high and thin and childish, but it managed to silence everybody.

"I've already got a family!" he said.

Rebecca said, "I didn't mean—I'm sorry! I honestly didn't mean—"

Peter scrambled to his feet, tossing aside his glass. (It sent out a spray of bright drops before it landed, intact, on the blanket.) His floppy borrowed socks nearly tripped him up, but he righted himself and started running.

Not toward the river, thank goodness. He seemed headed for Barry's car, although it was difficult to be sure. Rebecca, rising from her bench with her fingers pressed to her lips, thought he resembled one of those charred paper bits that float above a bonfire, gray and weightless, fluttering without aim. As he neared the car he glanced over his shoulder, and when he found Barry ambling behind at a nonchalant pace, he veered to the left without slowing down. In front of him was a green thicket. He plunged directly into it.

"Stop him," Zeb said suddenly.

Everybody looked at him.

"He's going toward where the river bends! He's headed for the water," Zeb said, and he set off at a lope. "Barry!" he called. "Stop him! He's about to get wet all over again!"

Barry gathered speed.

Peter entered the thicket and vanished.

A moment later, Barry vanished too.

And that is when the first intimation came to Rebecca from nowhere, brushing across her mind like the most delicate of moth wings.

How on earth did I get like this? How? How did I ever become this person who's not really me?

two

That night, she dreamed she was traveling on a train with her teenaged son.

Never mind that she had no son. Never mind that if she had, he would have been a grown man by now. In her dream, she took it for granted that this tall, quiet, gawky young boy belonged to her without question. His hair was the same fair color as hers, except that it hung in a shock to one side. He was thinner than Rebecca had ever been, but he had her gray eyes and sharp nose. And most familiar of all was some quality in his expression, something hopeful and wistful, some sense he felt a little bit outside of things. Didn't she know that feeling! She recognized immediately the shy, uncertain edginess at the corners of his mouth.

He had the window seat; she had the aisle. He was gazing out at the scenery and so was she, supposedly, but really she was seizing the chance to dwell on his dear profile. She felt a wash of love for him—the deep, pervasive, abiding love you feel for one of your own.

When she woke up she was sorry, and she tried to go back to her dream again but she couldn't.

. . .

She lay awake in the bed that she had come to as a bride, in the room that she had slept in for over thirty years. For the majority of her life, in fact; so why did she still think of this house as somebody else's? The Davitches' house, not hers. The Davitches' ornate but crumbling nineteenth-century Baltimore row house, with its two high-ceilinged parlors, front and rear, its antiquated backyard kitchen connected to the dining room by an afterthought of a passageway, its elaborate carved moldings and butterfly-parquet floors and seven sculptured marble mantelpieces overhanging seven fireplaces, five of them defunct.

The ground level provided the family's subsistence; they rented it out for parties. Christenings, graduation teas, wedding receptions, retirement dinners . . . *All of Life's Occasions from the Cradle to the Grave*, as their ad in the Yellow Pages put it. *For Your Next Important Social Event, "Experience the Charms of the Open Arms."*

Funny name for such a narrow, shutter-faced house, she'd always thought.

She'd thought it the first time she came here, nineteen years old and dressed head to toe in blue, a heavyset, timid young woman standing out on the sidewalk peering up at the shield-shaped sign. *The Open Arms, Est. 1951.* Nothing open about it at all, not that she could see. Although possibly she'd been influenced by the fact that parties of any kind whatsoever were her idea of torture.

Oh, life worked out so surprisingly, didn't it?

The flannel darkness high above her turned white and then transparent, and the birds began to sing in the poplar tree next door, and the grandfather clock downstairs gave off six mournful *dongs*. Rebecca finally got out of bed and shook her nightgown around her ankles and went over to raise the window shade. It was going to be another sunny day. Chips of blue sky showed behind the rooftops. She watched a traffic helicopter cross the space between two far-away buildings, its propeller a brisk, busy blur above its head.

This was not the master bedroom. (That had somehow gone to Poppy, after her mother-in-law died.) It was her husband's boyhood room, and traces of his boyhood enthusiasms could still be found here and there — in the half-dozen odd-colored rocks arranged on top of the bookcase, the framed display of wheat-sheaf pennies hanging on one wall, the Baltimore Colts decal plastered irremovably inside the closet door. Joe Davitch had been full of enthusiasms, even as a grown man. He'd been large in spirit and in frame, exuberant and outgoing, booming-voiced, quick to laugh, given to flinging out both hands in a gesture of wholehearted welcome.

Really it was Joe who had had the open arms.

She turned from the window and collected her clothes: an Indian blouse embroidered with peacocks, a flounced calico skirt, and the white cotton, old-lady underwear she had come to favor now that there was no one else to see it. She clutched all this to her chest and crossed the hall to the bathroom, which gave off the comforting smell of aged enamel paint and Ivory soap. The radiator was as filigreed and scrolled as a silver tea urn. The claw-footed bathtub was big enough to sleep in.

Then halfway through her shower: *bam-bam!* Poppy, knocking on the bathroom door. She squinched her face against the spray and started humming, because she wanted to go on musing about the boy in her dream. His stubby blond eyelashes. (*Her* lashes, which didn't even show unless she remembered, as she rarely did, to brush them with mascara.) His long-fingered, angular hands. (The hands were not hers, but whose, then? Whom did they remind her of?)

At some point Poppy gave up and went away, but she couldn't have said just when.

. . .

"I had the oddest dream," she told Poppy over breakfast.

"Were there any numbers in it?"

She was startled, not so much by the question as by the fact that he had heard her. Nowadays, he seemed to be absent so often. She looked at him over her coffee cup and realized, much later than she should have, that he was dressed wrong. He was wearing a pair of brown suit pants and a sleeveless undershirt but no shirt, so that his suspenders cut directly across his whiskery bare shoulders. After breakfast she would have to talk him into something more appropriate.

"If you can recall any numbers," he told her, "my friend Alex—remember Alex Ames from my teaching days?—he is always after me for numbers to play the lottery with. He wants the numbers from my dreams, but I don't have any dreams anymore."

"Sorry, no," she told him. "This was about a boy. He seemed to be my son."

"Which one?"

"Pardon?"

"Which of your sons was it?"

"Poppy," she said. "I don't have any sons."

"Then what'd you go and dream about them for?"

She sighed and took another sip of coffee.

This was a man unrelated to her—an uncle only by marriage. The brother of her late father-in-law. Yet here they were, living out their lives together like some cranky old married couple. Her mother-in-law and Joe had invited Poppy to stay for a while after his wife died, when it seemed he was about to turn into a telephone drunk. (Calling up at all hours: "Can I honestly be expected to go on without my Joycie?") Then her mother-in-law died; then Joe himself died—killed in a car wreck just six years after their wedding—and somehow, Poppy had never left. Rebecca had spent more years now with Poppy than with anyone she'd ever known; and she didn't even especially like the man, which was not to say she actively disliked him. She just thought of him as a kind of fellow boarder. It was a matter of pure happenstance that she was the one who had to listen to the state of his bowels every morning, and accompany him on his exercise walk, and ferry him to the doctor and the dentist and the physical therapist.

But he was someone to talk to, at least; so she tried again. "In my dream I was on a train," she told him, "and this boy was sitting next to me. He was, I don't know, in his early teens—that awkward, bean-pole stage just after they get their growth spurt—and it seemed to be understood that he was my son."

"Do you recall what number train it was?"

"No, and I don't know where we were going, either. Just that he and I were traveling."

And that she loved him, she wanted to say. But that would sound so theatrical, in this normal, workaday kitchen with the linoleum worn black and the chimney bricks all pocked, the checked plastic tablecloth sandy with toast crumbs, the glass-paned cupboard doors reflecting squares of yellow sunshine.

"Well," Poppy said, "I would call that a dream that was lacking in plot. In fact it's sort of uninteresting; so I'd like to switch the subject to my birthday."

"Your birthday!" She felt disoriented. "The birthday you just had?"

"The birthday coming up."

"But that's not till December!"

"Yes, December eleventh. I'm going to be one hundred."

"Well, I know that, Poppy," she said.

He didn't look it. He had hit a kind of wall in the aging process; he seemed old but not astronomically old, just slightly more shrunken than when she'd first met him. His white mustache was still bushy, and his face (unshaven, till after breakfast) bore only a few deep crevices rather than the netting of wrinkles you would expect.

"I suppose," he said, suddenly absorbed in pressing an index finger to the toast crumbs, "you're planning some big wingding for me. I mean bigger than your usual."

"Oh. Well. Yes, certainly I am!" she said. It was his averted gaze that let her know he *wanted* a wingding; that he wasn't bringing it up just to discourage the notion. "December's still pretty far away," she told him, "but when we get a bit closer, oh, I'm going to need your advice about all kinds of things!"

"I do happen to have a guest list," he said.

"Wonderful, Poppy."

She thought he meant he had a guest list *somewhere*, but he started fumbling through his trousers and finally came up with a small, fat square of folded paper. As he passed it across the table to her, the telephone rang. She rose to answer, but not before she had tucked the list in her skirt pocket and patted the pocket several times in a reassuring way.

It was NoNo on the phone. "I called to say thanks for the picnic," she said. "Barry says thanks, too. He's going to write you a note."

"Oh, honey, he doesn't have to do that," Rebecca said. She was watching Poppy, who had started eating marmalade straight from the jar. "I'm just glad you both enjoyed it."

"He really liked our family," NoNo said.

Her words hung in the air, waiting; so Rebecca said, "And we liked *him*! All of us just loved him."

Poppy raised his eyebrows at her. She turned away from him and cupped the receiver. "How's his little boy?" she asked. "He didn't catch cold, I hope."

"He's fine, I assume, but I haven't called them yet today because Barry's mornings are so frantic. If you could see how the two of them live! He has Peter wear tomorrow's clothes to bed on school nights, just to save time."

"Goodness," Rebecca said. "Now, where is Peter's mother, exactly?"

"Who knows! She went off with a bunch of Buddhists or something; lives in some kind of commune somewhere."

This was not so very different from NoNo's mother, who had abandoned her three children for a career as a New York nightclub singer. (Or would-be singer.) But Rebecca thought it wisest not to point that out. She said, "You're going to be a real help, once the two of you are married."

"Yes, I thought I would start closing my shop a little earlier, so that Peter won't be alone so many hours after school."

"What does he do now that it's summer?" Rebecca asked.

"Oh, eventually there's day camp. Till that begins, he just stays in the house. He's pretty used to fending for himself."

"Maybe he'll get to be friends with Danny. They're almost the same age, after all."

"Well . . ." NoNo said, in a doubtful tone.

Rebecca couldn't much blame her. Danny was such an athlete, with an athlete's easy confidence in his own body. The two boys seemed two different species, almost. So she didn't push it. Out of the corner of her eye she saw Poppy leaving the kitchen with the marmalade jar tucked under his arm, and she said, "I'd better go. Have a good day, sweetie!"

"Thanks, Beck," NoNo said. "And thanks again for the picnic."

Rebecca hung up and went chasing after Poppy, who could make remarkable speed for an old man with a cane.

. . .

Her dream was the kind that lingered, coloring the whole morning. Bits of it rose like dust from her pillows when she plumped them—a sense of travel, a sense of longing. When she heard the harmonica sound of a train whistle from Penn Station, she felt a little pinch of loneliness deep in her chest.

The plasterer called; then Biddy called; then a woman called about a bridal shower. (Rebecca's life was ruled by the telephone, she always said.) Each time she collected her thoughts to answer, she got that cotton-headed, almost nauseated feeling that comes from surfacing too abruptly from too heavy a sleep. More than one caller had to say, "Hello? Are you still there?"

When she opened Poppy's closet to find him a shirt, the sweetish smell of worn clothing brought back the scent of her son. When she settled on the couch to pair socks, the feel of the fuzzy upholstery reminded her of the train seat—which, she recollected, had been covered in wine-colored plush of a sort she had not seen on trains in forty years.

. . .

Her daughter dropped by to leave her two children while she went to the obstetrician. "Anyone home?" she called, and the front door banged, as it always did, against the door of the closet. (Closet, ladies' powder room, men's—all these had been crammed into one side of the foyer, not very adeptly, when the Open Arms first went into business.) Rebecca invited her in, half hoping she would refuse because the morning was getting away from her, here. But Min Foo said, "Maybe for a minute," and sent the children upstairs with their stack of videotapes. "Two whole months to go," she said, leading the way to the kitchen, "or three if this is another ten-month pregnancy, and already I've gained twenty-one pounds. I look like a cow."

Actually she looked more like a plum, or some other ripe, luscious fruit. She wore a black silk maternity dress and loops of golden chains strung with golden disks, and she walked with a slow, sultry, swaying motion that Rebecca found hypnotic. In the kitchen she sank onto a chair, her jewelry tinkling exotically. Rebecca said, "Would you like some coffee?"

"Mom! No way can I have coffee!"

"Oh, yes," Rebecca said. Such silly rules they had, nowadays. "Well, I believe there's some orange juice somewhere."

She started hunting through the refrigerator, which was filled with picnic leftovers. "I dreamed the strangest dream last night," she said over her shoulder. She shifted a plate hooded in foil. "I dreamed I had a son."

"Maybe that's a sign my baby will be a boy," Min Foo said.

This struck Rebecca as the slightest bit self-centered. "No," she said, "you weren't anywhere to be seen. And besides, he didn't have your coloring. He was a blond."

Min Foo, like her three half-sisters, was a brunette, and she had Joe's burnished olive skin and his narrow, sleepy eyes—almost Asian eyes, in her case, which was how she'd earned her nickname. Her real name was Minerva (Rebecca's choice, for this child who would be hers, she'd imagined—the same calm, quiet, bookish type she herself had once been), but Joe had taken one look at the baby in her hospital cot, at her paintbrush hair and her eyes no wider than slits, and, "Hey there, little Min Foo," he had said. She had never been anything but, from then on. So much for Minerva.

And forget about calm! Or quiet! Here she was now, all spiky and indignant: "I could have a blond baby! Certainly I could. Half my genes are yours, remember."

"Well, maybe with Lawrence you could have," Rebecca said. "But I seriously doubt you can hope for any blond genes from Hakim."

Min Foo said, "Oh."

Rebecca gave up on the orange juice and shut the fridge door as unnoticeably as possible. "Min Foo," she said. "Sweetheart. Um, once this baby is born, you won't send Hakim packing, will you?"

"Send him packing?"

"The way you did the others."

Min Foo gave her a blank, astonished stare.

"I just couldn't help but notice," Rebecca told her, "that you always divorce your husbands after you have their babies."

"Always!" Min Foo repeated. "You talk as if I'd had *fifty* husbands!"

"Well, but . . . three is not a negligible number, you have to admit."

"It's no fault of mine that I happened to hit a teensy little run of bad luck," Min Foo said. "Honestly! You make such a big deal about that. Every time I turn around, some jibing, jabbing remark. 'You're not booked this weekend, are you? Getting married or anything.' And, 'Oh, that was a gift from what's-his-name, one of Min Foo's husbands.'"

Rebecca laughed, impressed by her own wittiness, but Min Foo stayed serious. "Everything's just a joke to you," she said bitterly. "Even at our wedding reception: someone says how nice it is and you say, 'Well, it ought to be nice, as much practice as Min Foo's given me.'" She gathered the folds of her dress and stood up. "Don't bother seeing me out," she said. "I'm leaving."

"Sweetheart!"

"I'm late for my appointment, anyhow."

"Oh, all right," Rebecca said sadly, and she trailed her to the front of the house, trying to think of some parting comment that would smooth things over. But none came to her.

Her brother-in-law had a theory that Min Foo's many marriages were her way of trying on other lives. The first husband had been a professor in his sixties, and Min Foo (age twenty-one) had instantly turned into a settled faculty matron. But with the second husband, who was black and eight years her junior (*two* differences, Zeb pointed out; very efficient of her), she'd become a young slip of a girl and taken to wearing a head-wrap. Hakim, now, had her spangled with Muslim holy medals. Rebecca liked Hakim, but she was careful not to get overly invested in him. That was why she kept up the pretense that she didn't know where he was from. Of course she knew where he was from; she wasn't senile. But, "Oh, he's something, ah, Middle Eastern, I believe," she would say when asked.

Oops. Just the sort of remark that Min Foo had been objecting to.

. . .

The children were upstairs in the ex-nursery that served as the family room, watching a videotaped cartoon. You had only to look at them to guess Min Foo's whole history—Joey a freckled eight-year-old with straight black hair and blue eyes, Lateesha four years younger and decked out in tiny beaded braids, her skin the warm, soft brown of a baked potato.

"Hey, kids," Rebecca said, "who wants to help me decorate for a party?"

They didn't take their eyes from the screen, but Joey said, "What kind of party?"

"Graduation; high-school graduation. Teenagers galore! I'll need to consult with you two so I don't do anything uncool."

That got their attention, all right. Joey asked, "Are they having a DJ?"

"Certainly a DJ! He's bringing his own sound system, later this afternoon."

Joey punched the remote control and a Superman-type figure halted in mid-screen, trembling slightly. Then the two children slid off the couch and followed Rebecca downstairs. Lateesha's beads sounded like an abacus clicking. (What a jewelry-laden family Min Foo's was! Especially if you counted Joey's watch, a black rubber, digital, multi-function affair whose face was about twice the width of his wrist.)

"Biddy is doing the food," Rebecca said, "and I tried to persuade them to hire NoNo for the flowers, but they said they always use Binstock."

"*Rich* people," Joey said.

"Well, yes, I guess they must be."

They were in the kitchen now. Rebecca started pulling boxes from the cupboard beside the sink. "Look at the decorations I bought," she told the children. "Little rolled diplomas. Aren't they cute?"

But Lateesha was more attracted to a string of ancient, yellowing electric lights shaped like tiny wedding bells. "I want these," she said firmly, and Rebecca said, "Well, but . . ." and then, "Oh, well, why not? We'll pretend they're school bells." She held them up by the cord, which was the old striped, cloth-covered kind that was probably not all that safe. "These were strung across the mantel the first time I ever came here," she said.

"No, I want them high in the air."

"Well, we can do that."

They carried the boxes to the front parlor, and then Rebecca went back for a stepladder. When she returned, Joey was banging out the *Jaws* theme on the piano. "Here," she told him, opening the ladder. "You climb up and hang the bells on those hooks along the moldings." Then she gave Lateesha the little diplomas to set around, and she unfolded a crocheted cloth and spread it over the piano to hide all the stains and water rings.

"The first time I ever walked into this room," she told the children, "the bells were strung across the mantel and there was a kind of pagoda effect, a cupola effect, to the ceiling, from the twists of white crepe paper tied to the chandelier. It was my ex-roommate Amy's engagement party and her family was making a huge, huge fuss. And I had come alone—I did have a boyfriend, but he was busy that night—and I walked in and I just about walked out again. Well, you know how fancy this place can look when the bald spots are covered up. There were flowers everywhere, white and purple lilacs, so many that the house was kind of shimmering with that heavy, moth-ball perfume lilacs give off. I was bowled over! And I didn't know a soul; just Amy. She had transferred to Goucher, you see, after our freshman year at Macadam, and she had this whole set of Goucher girlfriends I had never met. So I was standing there with my mouth open, and Amy didn't notice me because she was carrying on about her engagement ring—how she had wanted platinum but her fiancé wanted gold because his mother's ring had been . . . and all at once I realized that the stereo was playing 'Band of Gold.' I thought, How appropriate! and I looked over at the DJ, who hap-pened to be Zeb, only of course I didn't know that. He was just this teenaged kid sitting behind a stereo, grinning straight into my face as if we shared a secret. He'd chosen that song on purpose! It made me laugh. And right at that moment, right while I was laughing, this man came up beside me and said, 'I see you're having a wonderful time.' And that was your grandpa."

It felt peculiar to refer to Joe as a grandpa. He had died before he turned forty. In Rebecca's mind he was forever young and hand-some, and when she tried to imagine how he would have aged she had to guess from how Zeb had aged: those wide, spare, scarecrow shoulders grown stooped, the tangle of longish black hair threaded with thick strands of gray. Although Zeb lacked Joe's expansive manner and his grace. He had always been more . . . shambling, you might say.

She lifted the lid of the piano bench and sorted through the sheet music stored inside. Even at these teenaged affairs, some rela-tive just about always ended up playing tunes for the others to sing along with. Songs from the 1950s, swing . . . She propped a folk-song collection on the music rack. She had observed that the sixties were back in favor right now.

"I bet neither one of you have ever heard 'Band of Gold,'" she told the children.

Joey, perched on the ladder, shook his head. Lateesha just set another diploma on the coffee table. "Well, it's not as if you've missed anything," Rebecca said. "A simple-minded song; it was out of date even then. With this silly chorus behind it, *baba, bababa* . . .

So there I was, laughing away, and your grandpa said, 'My name's Joe Davitch; my family owns this house, and that character flirting with you so outrageously is my kid brother, Zeb.' Which meant I had to tell him *my* name—meanwhile wondering, you know, why he was just standing there and not circulating among the other guests, because at the time I had no idea the Davitches would normally let a party sink or swim on its own. He said, 'Can I get you some champagne?' and I said, 'No, thanks, I don't drink'—I really didn't, in those days—and he said, 'We'll have to find you a ginger ale, then. Come with me,' and he took my arm and led me off to the dining room. And just as we arrived, this woman came rushing out of the kitchen passageway. Mother Davitch, that would be. Your . . . great-grandmother; goodness! She was carrying a ham on a platter and I guess we took her by surprise, because when she saw us she said, 'Oh!' and stopped short, and the ham continued on without her. Slid clear off the platter and landed at my feet. You never saw such a mess!"

This appeared to interest the children far more than their grand-parents' meeting had. Both stopped what they were doing to focus on Rebecca.

"The poor woman burst into tears," she said, exaggerating slightly in order to keep their attention. (Actually, what Mother Davitch had done was more in her usual style of just, oh, *dribbling* into tears; trembling and dissolving.) "Well, *I* didn't know what to do. I was just a big, dumb college girl! And I was worried to death about my shoes: powder-blue pumps dyed to match my dress. There was this icky pink glaze all over them. I said, 'Do you think I might have a damp cloth, please?' Mother Davitch misunderstood; she perked right up and, 'Oh,' she said, 'never mind; Joe can see to that. But I *will* let you help with the other dishes.' And that wasn't the only misunderstanding, because while she was taking me to the kitchen she started going on and on about how she wished she'd known beforehand I was coming; how supper that night was just pickups on account of the party but I was more than welcome anyway; it worried her to death that Joe never brought any girlfriends home. I said, 'Oh, um, I'm not . . .' but it didn't make the least bit of difference; she'd already got this notion in her head. Imagine what I felt! And then we came to the kitchen and there was Biddy, standing on a step stool trying to toss a salad. About five, she must have been. Yes, five: too young to do a very good job. There was more salad on the floor than in the bowl. Mother Davitch said, 'You've met Joe's oldest, haven't you?' I said, 'Oldest? His oldest . . . child?' Because underneath, I guess, I was already feeling attracted to him. Oh, I thought, he's married. Except that Mother Davitch cleared that up in no time. Told me how Joe's wife had absconded to seek her fortune and left all three of her children on Mother Davitch's hands. *Dumped* them on her, was how she put it. Right in front of Biddy. 'Dumped the whole crew on me and escaped to New York City.' But you know Biddy. Biddy spoke up cool as cream; 'Mommy's going to be a famous nightclub singer,' she said. And Mother Davitch said, 'Well, so some would have us believe,' and gave me this pointed look, but Biddy said, 'She's got this beautiful dress where the straps are made of diamonds.' 'Rhinestones,' Mother Davitch said, but Biddy told her, 'Diamonds.'"

Lateesha stopping prinking a diploma bow to ask Rebecca, "Real diamonds?"

"Well, according to Biddy they were."

Lateesha (who was not so much younger than Biddy had been, come to think of it) gave a sigh of satisfaction.

"Meanwhile," Rebecca said, "your grandpa was going back and forth with hot water and cloths, cleaning up the dining room. And finally he squatted down on the floor and started wiping my shoes off, right while I was standing there helping Biddy toss the salad."

The most memorable of the five senses, she often felt, was the sense of touch. After all these years she could still feel the heat of that damp cloth soaking through to her toes, and Joe's strong, sure dabbing motion that had reminded her of a mother cat industriously bathing her kittens. And she remembered how, once he'd finished, he rose and clasped her arm to lead her away, his warm fingers firmly pressing the bare skin above her elbow. "Where are you taking her?" Mother Davitch had cried in alarm. (For the kitchen was a disaster and that ham had so far been the only dish that had made it to the dining room.) But Joe called over his shoulder, "Don't worry; we'll be seeing her again." Even while Rebecca was wondering at this, she had felt a surge of pleasure.

"We *will* be seeing you, won't we?" he asked as they entered the rear parlor. "Are you in the Baltimore phone book?"

"Oh, I don't live in Baltimore; I live in Macadam," she told him. "I go to Macadam College."

While she spoke she had looked elsewhere, trying to give the impression that she was offering this information with no particular purpose in mind. She watched the other guests from what felt like a great distance, noticing how flighty Amy seemed and how immature and tittering the girlfriends. (Joe Davitch, Rebecca surmised, was at least in his early thirties.) The fiancé—a loud-voiced, fraternity type—was expounding on possible stag-party sites. Paul Anka was singing "Diana" on the stereo, and the DJ sent Rebecca a grin and cocked his head significantly, although she didn't know why.

"I get out toward Macadam fairly often," Joe told her. "Maybe I could look you up."

She let her eyes drift over to meet his.

He said, "Well, enjoy the party. Goodbye, Rebecca."

Then he turned and went back to the kitchen.

Rebecca just stood there for a minute, alone as when she'd first come but with a huge difference. She felt that her crown of gold braids, her blue dress, even her splotched shoes were compellingly attractive. She observed the other guests from a position of . . . power, she would almost say.

"In a way, it was love at first sight," she told the children.

Joey just said, "Huh," but Lateesha got all wide-eyed and intense. "I'm going to have love at first sight, too," she told Rebecca.

Rebecca said, "Well, I hope you do, dear heart."

. . .

Min Foo was so late getting back from the doctor's that Rebecca gave the children lunch—strawberry-jam-and-cream-cheese sandwiches. Poppy came downstairs and ate with them, although he spent most of the meal warning the children what to expect when they got old. "Step out of bed in the morning and your ankles refuse to bend," he said. "Know what that feels like? Try it sometime. Try walking not bending your ankles. I clomp to the bathroom like Frankenstein's monster. And then can't pee. A simple thing like peeing that you would take for granted. Drip, drip, drip, it finally comes—"

"Ooh, gross!" Lateesha said, screwing up her face.

Poppy ignored her. "Then getting dressed," he said. "Socks! Shoes! I have to have a special technique just for putting on my shoes. And Beck here has to tie them. It's just like being a two-year-old. 'Mom, will you tie my shoes, please?'"

The front door slammed against the closet, and Min Foo said, "Hello?"

"We're in the kitchen," Rebecca called.

Min Foo came down the passageway, rustling and jingling. "Hi, everybody," she said. "Oh, you're eating." She gave off the clinical smell of vinyl-upholstered waiting rooms and isopropyl alcohol.

"How was your checkup?" Rebecca asked.

"Dr. Fielding says I'm too fat."

"I'm sure he didn't put it *that* way," Rebecca said. "Won't you have a sandwich?"

"Mom! I say I'm too fat and you offer me something to eat. Finish up, kids; we're late for your play date."

"Can I pour you some milk? Skim, I mean," Rebecca said.

"No, thanks. We'd better hit the road."

"Try driving a car when your ankles don't bend," Poppy piped up.

"What, Poppy?" Min Foo turned to Rebecca. "I was thinking about your dream," she said.

"My dream," Rebecca echoed. In the flurry of lunch, she had started to forget her dream. Now it came back to her, but with the boy more distant now, more of an *other*. "What about it?" she asked Min Foo.

"If you dreamed you had a son, not daughters, and if the son was blond, not dark . . ." Min Foo was shepherding the children toward the front of the house, so that Rebecca had to follow her. "Well, it seems to me," she said, "that you were dreaming how things would be if you'd chosen a different fork in the road. You know what I mean? If you'd decided on some different kind of life than you have now."

This struck Rebecca as so apt, and so immediately obvious where it hadn't been before, that she stopped short. Oh, her girls could surprise her so, every now and then!

"Anyway," Min Foo was saying, "thanks for keeping the children. Kids, tell Gram goodbye."

Rebecca said, "Wait!" But then the telephone rang, and she had to turn back to the kitchen.

Poppy, who never answered the phone even when he was sitting right next to it, looked up at her from a spoonful of strawberry jam. Rebecca glared at him and lifted the receiver. "Hello," she said.

"Mrs. Davitch?"

"Yes."

"This is Katie Border's mother. The graduation party?"

"Oh, yes."

"Well, here's the problem: our daughter didn't graduate."

"Didn't graduate!"

"Can you believe it? The little minx: she never said a word. And whatever notification the school might have sent us, I guess she intercepted. So this morning I was hanging out her dress—the ceremony was set for three, her dad had arranged to come home early, both sets of grandparents had flown in over the weekend—when 'Oh,' she says, 'did I mention? I flunked chemistry.' Well, at first I didn't catch on. I mean, I failed to understand that flunking chemistry would keep her from graduating. 'Great, Katie,' I told her. 'What if you need to know chemistry later in life? If you're, I don't know, shopping for rose food or something?' And she says, bold as you please . . ."

Rebecca started silently calculating her losses. The planning, the decorations, the deposits made to the disk jockey and the bartender. Alice Farmer, the cleanup maid, would demand to be paid in full regardless, although the waiter (Biddy's son Dixon) might be more forgiving. The Borders would have to forfeit their own deposit, of course, but that didn't cover everything. And Biddy would throw a fit. Most of her dishes were perishable and not the kind you could freeze. To say nothing of all her work, and the thought she'd given the menu.

"Well, isn't it fortunate," Rebecca told Mrs. Border, "that you'd already set up this party. It sends a message, don't you think?"

"'Mom,' she said to me . . . Message?"

"When your daughter must be feeling so disheartened, so discouraged with herself. But here's this wonderful party to show her how much you love her."

"Oh, Mrs. Davitch, I can't imagine—"

"And a message to your friends, as well. A sort of statement."

"My friends! I don't know how I'll face them. They're all going to feel so sorry for me. Behind my back they'll be telling each other—"

"Mrs. Border, have you ever stopped to consider what a marvelous purpose a party serves? Think about it! At a moment when you and your daughter would normally not be speaking, when you know she must feel ashamed in front of the world at large and the world is surely wondering what to say to *you*, why, everyone's thrown together in a gigantic celebration. Everyone's forced to hug, and kiss, and toast the other graduates, and announce to everyone else that what matters is you all love each other. It's like that scientific discovery they made a few years back; remember? They discovered that if you fake a smile, your smile muscles somehow trigger some reaction in the brain and you'll start feeling the way you pretended to feel, happy and relaxed. Remember?"

"Well . . ."

"Imagine if you hadn't had the foresight to schedule this party! Because we've been booked for months and months ahead, this time of year. You'd call and say, 'Do you have an evening this week when we could throw a little fete for our daughter? She's experiencing such, um . . . low self-esteem'—yes, that's the term: 'self-esteem'—'and we want to show her we love her.' I would have to say, 'Sorry, Mrs. Border—'"

"And it's true it's going to be hard to cancel our guests," Mrs. Border said. "If I had any hope of reaching just their answering machines I'd start telephoning this instant, but you know how people tend to pick up the receiver precisely when you don't want to talk. I'd be forced to make all these complicated excuses."

"Oh! It would be so difficult!" Rebecca told her.

"I did consider tacking a note to your front door, saying the party had been postponed due to unforeseen circumstances. Cowardly, I admit, but—"

"And also wasteful!" Rebecca said. "Wasting that once-in-a-lifetime opportunity to create a memory that will last long, long after your daughter's made up her chemistry credits and graduated and gone on to college and you've forgotten all about her momentary little setback."

She stopped for air, and Mrs. Border said, "I guess we do have to remember what's important here."

"Absolutely," Rebecca said. She squared her shoulders. "Oh, one thing I'd meant to call you about: when shall I expect Binstock to bring the flowers?"

"Well, they promised them for three o'clock, but now I don't know if—"

"Three is fine," Rebecca said smoothly. "I'll make sure to be here. See you this evening, Mrs. Border."

"Well . . . so . . . well, yes, I suppose," Mrs. Border said.

Rebecca hung up and sank into a chair.

"Way to go, Beck," Poppy said, setting aside the jam jar.

"I'm exhausted," she told him.

And also . . . what was it she felt? Compromised. She was a fraud.

Yet when Poppy asked, "Isn't it time for my nap?" she found herself once again putting on her hostess act. "You are absolutely right!" she told him, all zip and vigor. "Look at that clock! Let me help you to your room." And she rose to slide his chair back.

He was light as milkweed, these days. He tilted against her and breathed rapidly and shallowly, clutching his cane in his free hand but relying on her for support. "There's also the question of aches," he announced when they reached the stairs. His breath smelled like strawberries. "Take inventory at any given moment and you have to say your back aches, your shoulders ache, your knees are stiff, your neck has a crick—"

"The moral of the story is, stop taking inventory," Rebecca told him. "Don't think about it. Put your mind on something else."

"Easy for you to say. You're still in your forties."

"My forties! I'm fifty-three," she said.

"You are?"

She helped him up another step.

"How did that happen so *fast?*" he asked.

Rebecca laughed.

After she had deposited him in his room, she crossed the hall to the family room. Superman had grown tired of pausing and the screen had reverted to a television commercial—a woman asking why her hardwood floors were so dull. Rebecca switched it off and sat down at the little spinet desk to write checks. The window washers, the gas and electric, the man who had patched the front stoop . . .

Gradually, her pen grew slower. She took longer and longer to reach for each new bill, until finally she came to a halt and just sat staring into space.

. . .

"I see you're having a wonderful time," Joe Davitch had said.

His very first remark to her.

Wasn't it strange how certain moments, now and then—certain turning points in a life—contained the curled and waiting seeds of everything that would follow? *I see you're having a wonderful time:* Joe's view of her forever after, his unwavering belief that she was a natural-born celebrator. And look at her answer: "Yes!" she'd said. "Thanks!" Or something of the sort. In a loud and energetic tone so as to be heard above the stereo. And from that day forth she seemed to have confirmed his view, although really she had been the very opposite sort of person, muted and retiring, deeply absorbed in her studies, the only child of a widow in little Church Valley, Virginia, and engaged-to-be-engaged to her high-school sweetheart.

She had swerved onto a whole different fork in the road. (As Min Foo would put it.)

For one brief, wistful moment, Rebecca entertained the notion of turning back, retracing her steps to where the fork had first branched. Church Valley still existed, after all. Her mother was still alive. Although the high-school sweetheart, no doubt, had found somebody else to marry by now. She pictured herself returning in the dress that she had worn to that party—powder blue, scoop-necked, short-sleeved—and the powder-blue pumps still faintly splotched with ham glaze. Carrying the witty (as she'd thought then) patent leather pocketbook shaped to resemble a workman's lunch box, although it, too, was powder blue.

In those days, everything had matched. There had not been any surprises.

.   .   .

"Hello-o-o!" Biddy called, and the clatter of catering trays followed the slam of the door. Then Binstock arrived with the flowers, and a woman phoned to arrange an office cocktail party, and the plasterer showed up to mend the hole in the dining-room ceiling.

Life went on, in other words.

Rebecca spread a bright cloth across the dining-room table and set one of Binstock's arrangements in the center. "Pretty," the plasterer said, peering down from his ladder. He had promised, cross his heart, not to create any mess, but already Rebecca could see several white flecks on the carpet. "Rick—" she said, and he said, "I know! I know! It'll all be vacuumed up again; trust me."

Sad when your plasterer's such a fixture that he knows what you're going to say before you say it.

Biddy was trying to fit her trays into the refrigerator. "What *is* all this?" she asked Rebecca. "It looks like you're planning to feed the Red Army."

"Those are leftovers from the picnic."

For cooking, Biddy always wore surgical scrubs—a full tunic and baggy green pants that hid her skinny figure. She had her pony-tail balled hygienically into a hairnet. She said, "Could you fetch me the cake stand? The glass one, with the pedestal."

"Oh, I hope you haven't put any writing on the cake."

"Just *Congratulations, Katie.*"

"Well, Katie flunked her chemistry course."

Biddy shut the fridge door and gave Rebecca a look.

"Could we peel off the *Congratulations*?" Rebecca asked. "Just leave *Katie*?"

"Not without any traces, we couldn't."

"At least they didn't cancel," Rebecca said, lifting down the cake stand from an overhead shelf. "I had to talk mighty fast, as you can imagine. Where's the cake?"

"In that tin by the stove."

The tin was a rusty white metal box that had belonged to Mother Davitch. Rebecca took the lid off and peered inside. "Maybe we could cover it with another layer of chocolate," she said.

"I don't have any chocolate. Do you?"

"I have peanut butter."

But all she got for that was another look.

Sometimes Rebecca wondered what Biddy really thought of her. What any of her stepdaughters thought of her, in fact. Of course there'd been a few of those you're-not-my-mother scenes at the start. ("You cow!" Patch had shouted once. "You big old frumpy fat cow; just wait till my mama gets back!") By now, though, all three seemed cordial and even affectionate, in an offhand sort of way. When Biddy went through that terrible time at age twenty—losing her fiancé to an asthma attack and discovering she was preg-nant just two days later—she had come straightaway to Rebecca; not to her mother. She had told Rebecca the whole situation and asked for her advice. But then she had ignored it. Not only had she made up her mind to keep the baby; but the following week she'd returned to debate moving in with her fiancé's homosexual brother and then she had ignored that advice as well. "Do *what*?" Rebecca had said. "Um, Biddy, it's awfully nice of Troy to make the offer, but please, think about this. It's not fair to either one of you. You'll want to meet a new man someday, whether or not you can picture that now, and it won't be all that easy if you're installed in another man's house. And you know that Troy will eventually find someone of his own. This is a mistake, believe me!"

Biddy had not believed her. She'd promptly moved in with Troy.

Well, okay: Rebecca had no idea how they'd worked things out between them, but she had to admit they appeared to be a very contented couple. And Dixon could not have asked for a better father.

Still, wouldn't you think that Biddy could have considered Rebecca's words? Or pretended to, at least, for half a minute?

The doorbell rang, and Rebecca went to answer it. A stylish, small-boned woman in her forties stood on the stoop, dressed in a tailored beige pantsuit and tiny boots. "Mrs. Davitch?" she said.

"Yes."

"I'm Susan Arnette. Here to talk to your food person?"

"Oh. Right," Rebecca said. She'd forgotten she'd set up the meeting. "Come on in, won't you?"

She was conscious, all at once, of her own outfit. It was too loose and too wrinkled and cluttered, she realized.

On their way to the rear parlor, Mrs. Arnette hung back to ooh and ah. "Those cornices!" she said. "Look at that fretwork!"

"Yes, actually the place dates from . . . originally belonged to . . ." Rebecca recited for the thousandth time.

Just once she'd like to counter with, "Those rattly panes! Look at that dry rot!"

She seated Mrs. Arnette on the couch and went to call Biddy, who was bringing in the cake to set on the dining-room table. ("Yum," Rick volunteered.) Biddy followed her to the parlor, wiping her palms on the seat of her scrubs. "This is Mrs. Arnette," Rebecca told her. "She wants to discuss the food for her parents' fiftieth anniversary. Mrs. Arnette, Biddy Davitch."

Then she tactfully withdrew—returned to the dining room. "How's it coming along?" she asked Rick, using her loudest, liveliest voice so that she wouldn't seem to be eavesdropping. Although she was, of course. (Mrs. Arnette had mentioned that she might have her maid do the food, instead; so Biddy would need to scramble.) Rick said, "Oh, just finishing up." Rebecca pulled out a chair and sat down to watch him work. There was something satisfying about the sweep of his trowel across the ceiling. All that was left of the hole was a patch of shinier white. White dust littered his hair, which was as woolly and thick as a Persian-lamb hat; but he had managed to confine most of his mess to his drop cloth. "See there?" he said. "Mr. Neatness."

"Good for you, Rick."

Mrs. Arnette seemed to be telling Biddy about her parents' troubled marriage. "In fact it's kind of a miracle that they are still together," she said. "Twice that I can recollect, Mom has packed her belongings and gone off to live with her sister."

"Do they have any allergies or aversions?" Biddy asked.

"What? Aversions?"

"Lots of times my older clients take against hot spices, for instance."

Mrs. Arnette said, "No, not as far as I . . . Why, once Mom stayed away two years, back when I was in college. Which might mean this is not their fiftieth anniversary after all, come to think of it. Would you say it still counts as fifty years?"

"The baby artichokes, for example," Biddy said. "I serve them with a very spicy curry sauce."

Oh, Biddy just *hid* behind food. It was exasperating. Rick, however, was a whole different story: a shameless gossip, as so many workmen seemed to be. "Of course it counts," he told Rebecca, wiping his trowel on a cloth. "Remember when me and Deena split for six months and got back together? We still considered that year a full year of marriage, though." He shouted toward the parlor, "You would only subtract those two years if the separation was court-decreed!"

A slight pause followed, and then Mrs. Arnette lowered her voice and asked about prices.

. . .

Rebecca phoned the roofer; then the appliance man; then the exterminator. (This house would be the death of her.) Then a woman called to complain about the food at her husband's business party. It had all been so foreign, she said. Rebecca said, "Foreign?"

"It was almost . . . vegetarian!"

"Well, I'm sorry," Rebecca told her, "but my stepdaughter does attempt to keep up with the latest trends in . . ."

She didn't have to think, even, as she spoke. She'd been fielding calls like this from the early days of her marriage, because the Davitches were notoriously mistrustful of the telephone. (Even Joe, to her amazement—Joe who had phoned so persistently while they were courting.) Whenever the phone rang, they spent an inordinate time debating: "Who can it be?" "It's not for me." "Well, *I'm* not expecting anyone." "You get it." "No, it's your turn." Often, the caller hung up before they got around to answering. They dreaded placing calls, as well, and would put them off for days. Monday, *Phone liquor store*, the kitchen calendar read; Tuesday, *Phone liquor store*; Wednesday, *Phone liquor store*; till on Thursday, maybe, or Friday Rebecca would step in—inexperienced though she was, a young and tentative bride with no management skills whatsoever— and phone the liquor store herself. She became, by default, the telephone person. By now it was automatic: "Needless to say, we are very concerned that our guests feel satisfied with our . . ."

She hung up just as Poppy was starting down the stairs from his nap. She heard the tap of his cane and went to help him. "Here," he said when he saw her, and he paused to search his pockets. "Wait, now; wait, now, I know I put it . . ." He pulled out another folded square of paper. "Room rates," he said.

Rebecca thought at first he'd said "roommates." "For me?" she asked, puzzled.

"So you can send a list of hotels with the invitations."

"Um . . ."

"The invitations to my birthday party, Beck! Where is your mind, these days?"

"Oh. Your birthday party."

"You know my second cousins will want to come, Lucy out in

Chicago and Keith in Detroit. And other people; there must be other out-of-towners, as soon as I think of their names. You'd never have the space for everybody to stay at the house."

"You telephoned all these hotels yourself?" Rebecca asked. She had unfolded the square of paper and was studying the list—a column of names and numbers printed laboriously with a skippy ballpoint pen. "When did you *do* this?" she asked.

"After I woke up from my nap. Can we go on our walk now?"

"Yes, of course." And she refolded the paper and tucked it into her pocket, where it rustled against the list he'd given her earlier.

This spring had been so unseasonably cool that Poppy, from habit, wore his gray V-necked cardigan; but Rebecca didn't bother with a sweater herself. She had let in enough of the outside world today to know that the weather had turned warm. When they stepped through the door, she told Poppy, "Feel that!" and he tipped his head back and closed his eyes and said, "Ah." Buttery June sunshine lit his face. The saplings lining the street were a vivid new green, and even above the traffic Rebecca could hear a few birds.

Funny how walking slowly could tire your muscles more quickly than walking fast. She resisted the impulse to point that out to Poppy, though; he would take it for a complaint. Instead she commented on the scenery, which presented itself inch by inch as they proceeded. "Oh, what a pity, they've boarded up the blue-gable house."

"Pretty soon the Open Arms will be the only place *not* boarded up," Poppy said.

It was true: this peaceful old street, once the height of elegance, was taking on a sort of toothless look. The house next door had turned into a meditation center, with a banner bearing a mandala flying above the front stoop. Around the corner, dignified mansions sported signs for bail bondsmen, palmists, and cut-rate car insurance. A place with an imposing columned porch was undergoing some kind of remodeling, and when they stopped to investigate they found a placard in the window announcing the arrival of a body-piercing parlor.

"It never reverses, you notice," Poppy said.

"Pardon?"

"Never changes back into something better."

"No."

"Of course when Joe first started the Open Arms, people were none too happy. They claimed he was bringing the neighborhood down."

"Well, he didn't have a choice!" Rebecca said. "His father died! How else could he support the family?"

"What he originally set out to do," Poppy said, "he wanted to make it a tourist home. You remember tourist homes. Now they're called bed-and-breakfasts and they're considered very tony, but back then, oh, his mother had a fit. She said, 'I can't be changing strangers' bedsheets! Letting all and sundry spend the night under my roof. Whatever would the neighbors say?' As I recall, Joe had gone and bought an old sign from some kind of salvage place. *HOTEL NO VACANCY*, it said. With the *NO* removable, for whenever they had a room free. But, 'Over my dead body!' his mother said. It was Zeb who thought up giving parties instead. Even that kind of went against Liddy's grain. Better than the Hotel No Vacancy, though, she had to admit."

Rebecca smiled. "This is the first I've heard of that," she said.

"Oh, you don't know everything, Miss Beck."

She took his arm, and they resumed walking. They were overtaken by others, more able-bodied: a boy on Rollerblades, two girls leading a little dust mop of a dog, a middle-aged couple carrying plastic bags of groceries. The couple stayed just slightly ahead; they weren't talking, but there was something sympathetic and companionable about the way they kept in step with each other, their shoulders gently touching.

Sometimes Rebecca had to fight down the feeling that life had treated her unfairly.

As if he had read her mind, Poppy asked, "Do you ever think of Joe anymore?"

"Naturally I think of him!" she said, almost offended.

"But can you hear his voice in your head still? Or get a flash of how he looked at some certain, particular moment, as if he were still here?"

She tightened her hold on his arm. She said, "Yes, I've had that happen."

"Joycie used to say to me, 'Oh, hell's bells!' Remember how she'd say that? I hear it sometimes just when I'm about to fall asleep. 'Oh, hell's bells!' in that kind of squawking way she had, just as clear! Just as real! Like she's there in the bedroom. My heart will start pounding."

"Yes, I know," Rebecca said.

With her, it was the pressure of Joe's hand on the small of her back, guiding her across a street.

"Then I say, 'Joycie, if you're going to appear from beyond and give me a message, couldn't it be something more useful than "Hell's bells?"'"

Rebecca laughed, and they turned at the end of the block and started back toward home.

.   .   .

Patch dropped by with her youngest—Meredith, aged seven— and asked if she could leave her while she and Jeep went to a ball game. "Certainly," Rebecca said. "She can help with the party." She had to shout, because the disk jockey had arrived and was testing his equipment. Deep, throbbing bass notes shook the floorboards. Patch said, "She hasn't . . . !" something, something, and Rebecca shouted, "What? Hasn't what?"

"Hasn't eaten yet!" Patch said too loudly, speaking into a sudden lull. "Time just got away from us, somehow."

"That's okay; we haven't either," Rebecca told her. "I'll give her supper."

Then the music took over again; so Patch waved instead of saying goodbye.

Back in the kitchen, Rebecca put Merrie to work peeling hard-cooked eggs. "We're eating upstairs in the family room," she said.

"The party tonight's extra early." Deftly, she removed the plastic wrap from one of the catering trays and stole three miniature sandwiches. Then she rearranged the others to cover the gaps. Merrie, meanwhile, picked off tiny fragments of eggshell, catching her lower lip between her teeth. She was standing on the step stool, which made Rebecca think of Biddy tossing the salad so many years ago. Although Merrie looked nothing like Biddy. (She was a carbon copy of Patch, all muscle and bone in sausage-skin bicycling shorts.) But everything else was the same: the ivory metal stool with its corrugated rubber treads, and the chipped and stained sink, and the cupboards so layered with paint that their doors could never quite close.

"I had this really weird dream last night," Rebecca told Merrie. (And why was it she just then thought of it?) "I dreamed I was on a train with my teenaged son."

All Merrie said to this was, "*We* went on a train. Me and Emmy and Mama. We went on a train to Washington last week. But Danny stayed at home because it was only us girls."

So Rebecca changed to her grandma voice and said, "Oh, what fun! What did you see? Tell me all about it!"

She loved these children, every last one of them. They had added more to her life than she could have imagined. But sometimes it was very tiring to have to speak in her grandma voice.

She set plates and silver on a tray, poured three glasses of milk, and piled some fruit in a bowl, meanwhile listening to Merrie's Washington saga. In the back of her mind, though, her son continued traveling. He gazed out at the scenery while Rebecca studied his hands—those oddly familiar hands with the squared-off thumb joints, a pink Band-Aid wrapping one finger.

Upstairs in the family room, Poppy sat in semi-dark watching a game show. (He had a thing about turning lights on needlessly.) "The answer is Napoleon, you fool!" he was muttering as Rebecca entered. "Don't they educate people anymore?" Still focusing on the screen, he lowered the foot of his recliner so Rebecca could unfold a snack table in front of him. "There," he said. "Look at that. Now that woman is six points ahead and he stands to lose it all."

The woman he was referring to was jumping up and down and clapping her hands and squealing. Game shows selected their guests on the basis of their pep, Rebecca had heard. Like cheerleaders—the same criterion. This woman had a cheerleader ponytail, even, which flew up with a kind of geyser effect each time she bounced to earth.

Poppy said, "You ought to go on this show, Beck."

"Me?"

"You'd be a natural for it."

Rebecca turned to stare at him, but he was watching the screen and he didn't notice.

. . .

Katie Border—Katie the non-graduate—wore white eyelet and a wreath of daisies, just as if she had graduated after all. "My, don't you look lovely!" Rebecca shouted above the music, but Katie just said, "Um . . ." Rebecca followed her eyes and saw, of course, Dixon.

Girls' eyes were always on Dixon. He was eighteen years old and six feet tall, black-haired and brown-eyed and coolly, casually elegant even in his white waiter's coat. But he seemed indifferent to his conquests—had, in fact, a long-term sweetheart, disappointingly plain-faced—and never responded to the girls who fluttered around him at parties. Now he was lowering a tray of stuffed mushrooms onto Merrie's outstretched palms. While Katie, as if pulled by strings, started drifting toward him, he tracked Merrie's progress through the crowd. Merrie seemed awfully unsteady on her feet, Rebecca noticed. Why, she was wearing high-heeled shoes. What on earth . . . ? Also a great long string of colored wooden beads, Rebecca's beads, actually, which were dangling in the mushrooms. Rebecca stifled a laugh and turned to catch the last of something Mr. Border was saying. "The what?" she asked. "Oh, the cornices, yes . . ."

Merrie tottered past an elderly couple sitting on a love seat, past a woman in a brocade dress with an armored-looking bosom, past two business-suited men, and she didn't offer food to any of them, although one of the men seemed about to make a grab. She reached her goal—four teenaged girls, all in white—and gazed up raptly, adoringly, with the tray held out in front of her. Then Dixon approached, and the girls turned in unison and melted in his direction. Merrie asked, "Stuffed mushrooms?"

"Now, Harold here makes a wonderful martini," Rebecca told Mr. Border. "Or if you'd prefer something nonalcoholic . . . Oh, you're right, this is definitely an occasion for strong drink! Let's ask him to fix you one, shall we?"

A light touch on Mr. Border's elbow, a quick, bright smile toward Harold. A tilt of the head for Dixon: *Could you pry Merrie away from those girls and start her circulating, please?*

At a perfect party, Rebecca would be unnecessary. The drinks would flow, the trays would magically stay full, the guests would mingle freely, nobody would be standing forlornly in a corner. Then Rebecca could retreat to the kitchen, or maybe steal upstairs a while to rest her feet. But there were no perfect parties. That was something a social misfit like Rebecca knew instinctively; while the Davitches, bless their hearts, hadn't had an inkling. Not even Joe. (Looming up beside her to announce, so mistakenly, "I see you're having a wonderful time.")

In the Davitches' view, the Open Arms existed simply to provide a physical space, sometimes with food and drink as well if the customer was misguided enough not to hire an outside caterer. What they hadn't understood was that almost more important was an invisible oiling of the gears, so to speak: pointing one person toward the liquor and another person away from it, finding a chair for an elderly aunt or loading her plate or fetching her sweater, calming an overexcited child, signaling to the DJ to lower the volume, hushing the crowd for the toasts, stepping in to fill an awkward silence. Yes, a large part of Rebecca's job had to do with noise, really. You shouldn't have too much noise, but neither should you have too little, and she often felt that her main function was keeping a party's sound level at a certain larky, lilting babble, even if it meant that she was forced to babble herself.

Won't you have a petit four? Oh, how can you say such a thing? If anything, you're *under*weight! Of course, let me show you the way. The light switch is on your right, just inside the . . . Why don't I freshen that drink for you? All right, everybody, gather round! I've been told we have a real musician with us tonight! Diet tonic water? Why, certainly! I'll run get some from the . . . Whose little girl are *you*? And isn't that a pretty dress! Welcome! Many happy returns! Congratulations! Best wishes!

I see you're having a wonderful time.

. . .

"I'm thinking of taking a trip," she told Zeb on the phone.

Often, after she was in bed, the two of them would go over their respective days together—their minor triumphs and their petty irritations. She knew that was pathetic. Most people had husbands or wives whom they could bore with such things. All Rebecca had was her kid brother-in-law—although "kid" was probably not the right term for a middle-aged bachelor doctor.

Tonight's party had been such a success that she hadn't had the heart to break it up at the designated hour. Now she worried she was calling Zeb too late, but he said no, he was reading. He said, "A trip would do you good. A real rest. Maybe a cruise."

"I don't mean that kind of trip," she said. "I thought I might go see my mother. Just an overnight stay. Would you be willing to come to the house and spend the night with Poppy sometime?"

"Well, sure, whenever you like. Is your mother okay?"

"She's fine," Rebecca said. "But I was thinking I'd like to go home and sort of . . . reconnoiter. Check out my roots." She gave a light laugh.

"Zeb," she said, "do you ever get the feeling you've changed into a whole different person?"

Probably he didn't (he was living in the city where he'd been born, doing what he had planned to do since childhood), but he seemed to give her question serious thought. "Hmm," he said. "Well . . ."

"I mean, look at me!" she told him. "I'm a professional party-giver! I never read anymore, or discuss important issues, or go to cultural events. I don't even have any friends."

"You've got friends," Zeb said. "You've got me; you've got the girls—"

"Those are relatives. And everyone else I know is some kind of repairman."

"You can have friends who are relatives. You can have repair-man friends."

"But what happened to the people I knew in college? Or in high school? Amy Darrow—the girl who had her engagement party the night I met Joe, remember? Whatever happened to Amy? I didn't even go to her wedding! By then I was married myself and all three girls had chicken pox."

"I'm sure you could track her down if you tried."

"I should get myself a dog," Rebecca said.

Zeb snorted.

She said, "If I had a dog to walk, it would be easier to meet people."

"You don't want a dog," Zeb told her.

"Well, it's true they're a lot of trouble," she said. She traced the stitching across her top sheet. "They need to be fed and watered and taken to the vet and such."

"They're as demanding as toddlers," Zeb said.

"Besides, I don't even like dogs."

"Then you certainly don't want one."

"They bark at night, and chew things."

"Rebecca. *Forget* the dog."

"But how will I make friends, then?" she asked him. She knew she was being ridiculous, but she couldn't seem to drop the subject once she'd gotten hold of it. "I'm not good at starting conversations with some stranger on the street."

"You could just walk around with a leash and an empty collar."

"What? How would that help?"

"You'd see someone and she'd ask, 'Excuse me, where's your dog?' And you'd say, 'Oh, no! My dog! I must have lost him! Could you please help me look for him?'"

"Then the two of us could go on walking, getting to know each other—"

"You'd have to be careful, though, not to let that person catch you doing the same thing to someone else the next day. She'd spot you up ahead of her, you'd be dragging your empty collar, you'd be saying to someone new, 'Oh, no! My dog! I must have lost him!'"

By now Rebecca had the giggles, and Zeb was laughing too.

Eventually, though, she said, "Well." She sighed. "I should let you sleep. I'll check with you again as soon as I figure out when I can leave."

"Any time," Zeb told her.

Then they said good night, and she hung up and lay back on her pillow.

The best way to travel to Church Valley was by car. Although it was possible, too, to take a bus. She could do that if she didn't mind a transfer. What was not possible was a train, but somehow, even so, she pictured going by train. She pictured sitting in an aisle seat, next to the son who would have been hers if only she had continued with the life she had begun.

three

"As soon as I sort my belongings I'm moving to a retirement home," Rebecca's mother said. "I already know which one. It's just that I need to get my belongings sorted first."

They were sitting in Rebecca's mother's living room — Rebecca in an armchair, her mother on the couch. Her mother wore her usual outfit of pastel polyester top and dark, skinny knit slacks with the creases stitched down the front. She was eighty-seven years old — a little cornhusk doll, straw-colored and drily rustling. Rebecca had outweighed her since late childhood, but she had always considered her to be a sturdy woman. It came as a shock to picture her in a retirement home. "What's made you think of moving?" she asked. "Are you having any health problems?"

"No, not a one. But Church Valley isn't like when you lived here, Rebecca. After they built that mall out where the duck farm used to be, why, seems we just got hollow at the center. Downtown isn't even downtown anymore. So I signed up for a unit at Havenhurst, but I don't know when I'll get to go there with all these belongings to sort."

Rebecca glanced around her. She didn't see any evidence that her mother had started yet. Not that there was much to do — this was a small house, fastidiously tidy—but every object had the glued-down appearance of something that had stayed in the same position for decades. Two hurricane lamps were spaced symmetrically on the mantel, an Oriental vase was centered in the front window, and the table at Rebecca's elbow bore a shrinelike arrangement of three gilt-framed photos, a candy dish, and a bowl of faded silk flowers. If she were to pick up, say, her parents' wedding photo and set it down again, she knew her mother would be over in two seconds to re-adjust its location by a fraction of an inch.

"Maybe I could help," she said.

"Oh, no, thank you," her mother said. "I won't forget what happened when your Aunt Ida tried to help. It took me days to undo what she'd done! And some things I could never undo. For instance, she threw away an entire sheet of postage stamps; three-cent postage stamps. I wasn't aware of it at the time because I was out of the room, fixing her a snack. That's how it is when people try to help: they need snacks and cups of tea, and before you know it you've gone to more trouble than if they'd stayed at home. I brought out a plate of those peppermint patties that she's always been so fond of, and then she told me she was on a diet. I said, 'What do you mean, a diet? I've been nagging you all your life to diet and it didn't do the least bit of good; so why would you take it into your head now that you're in your eighties?' And Ida said—"

"But the stamps . . ." Rebecca prodded her. Then she wondered why she'd bothered, since even the stamps were not the point of the conversation.

"The thing is, I didn't know she'd thrown them out. There I was in the kitchen, waiting on her hand and foot, and meanwhile Ida was in the living room merrily discarding my stamps. When I went to look for them later in the week, I couldn't find them. I phoned her. I said, 'Ida, what did you do with those stamps?' 'What stamps?' she asked, innocent as an angel. 'That sheet of stamps in my desk drawer,' I said. 'There's not a thing in that drawer now but dried-up ballpoint pens with advertising on them.' And Ida said, 'I hope I didn't throw them away.' 'Throw them away!' I told her."

Rebecca said, "Well, luckily they were—"

"I said, 'Where did you throw them away?' and she said, 'Now I'm not saying for certain that I did, you understand.' 'Where?' I said, and she said, 'The recycling sack under the sink, maybe?' I said, 'No.' I said, 'You didn't.' I said, 'You couldn't have.' Because I'd gotten rid of that sack on paper collection day."

"Luckily," Rebecca said, "they were only three-cent stamps."

"A *hundred* three-cent stamps, might I add. What we're saying is, my sister threw away three dollars. And I told her as much. 'Fine, I'll pay you back,' she said. 'Next time I come over to visit, I'll bring three dollar bills.' Which is so exactly like her, isn't it? I said, 'Now, what on earth will that accomplish? You'd still have wasted three dollars, and all for nothing. We might as well have burned it; that money's simply gone. Turned to paper soup in the recycling plant.'"

Rebecca started jiggling one foot.

"So I'll just do my sorting on my own," her mother told her. "Never let it be said that I'm unable to learn from experience."

And she tucked her chin in modestly and gazed down at her lap, while Rebecca recrossed her legs and started jiggling the other foot.

.   .   .

It had taken her more than a month to find the time for this trip, and now they were in the full bloom of summer—a Thursday in mid-July. When they set out on a walk to Ida's after lunch, the town appeared to be liquefied by the heat, all wavery and smeared like something behind antique window glass. The clay path leading down to the river was baked as hard as linoleum, and the foot-bridge's black metal railing burned Rebecca's hand. The river itself—wide but shallow, pebble-bottomed—seemed sluggish and exhausted, its sound less a rush than a series of slow glugs. Rebecca paused halfway across to study it. "The funniest thing," she told her mother. "Lately, I've started loving rivers."

"Loving them!"

"I've always *liked* them, of course; but I look at a river now and it just satisfies my eyes, you know? It seems to me so . . . old-fashioned."

"Maybe you should move back here, then."

"Well . . ."

"Why not? The girls are grown; you've got no responsibilities."

"Only the Open Arms," Rebecca said.

"The what? Oh, the Open Arms. Well, that's the Davitches' business; not yours."

"No, actually, it's mine," Rebecca said. This was a startling thought, for some reason. She said, "It's how I make my money, what little of it there is. How would I make any money in Church Valley?"

"I'm sure you'd find something or other," her mother said.

"Besides, I've got Poppy to think of."

"Poppy! Is that old man still alive?"

"Of course he's still alive. Next December he'll be a hundred. I'm planning a gigantic hundredth-birthday party for him," Rebecca said. Then she stopped to reflect upon the oddly boastful note that seemed to have crept into her voice.

"What I'd do," her mother said, as if Rebecca hadn't spoken, "is put my house in your name instead of selling it. Let you move right in. Leave you most of the furnishings, even."

Rebecca said, "Oh, I suspect you'll need to sell your house in order to afford the retirement home."

"I'm not getting but a little studio unit. The least expensive model. I can pay for it out of my pension."

She had worked for nearly thirty years in the basement of the county courthouse, keeping track of old documents. Rebecca didn't suppose that her pension was very large. She said gently, "Thanks anyhow, Mother."

But as they climbed the steep path on the other side of the river, approaching her aunt's part of town, she briefly entertained a fantasy of returning here to live. She imagined her routine: each day crossing the river for her meager supply of groceries, stopping first at the library the way she used to as a child. She had been the kind of child a librarian would love, she saw now, so pale and polite and considerate, careful to check that her hands were spotless before reverently selecting yet another Louisa May Alcott book. This was in the late fifties, when other children were turning to TV, but Rebecca—pudgy even then and stodgily dressed, her father dead and her mother several years older than any of her classmates' mothers—was not in step with most other children. She had always been the town's Bright Girl. ("Brain" was the term they used.) She tended to stay on the fringe of things, observing from a distance, and she had noticed that what she observed was often outside the normal frame of vision. It was as if she didn't *have* a frame of vision, so that during the Christmas pageant her attention might be caught by some small personal drama in the audience while everybody else was watching the stage. But she was not unhappy. She had had several friends, and in high school she'd had a boyfriend. And she was good at amusing herself when she was alone. In fact she'd been very content with things just the way they were; her set-apart position had felt comfortable, and restful.

When she grew up and left for college, the librarian gave her a going-away gift: a leather-bound blank book entitled A *Reader's Life List*. But Rebecca used only the first few pages, because college was when everything changed.

College was when she met Joe.

She said, "I don't suppose Miss Bolt still works at the library, does she?"

"Good heavens," her mother said, "I haven't thought of Miss Bolt in ages. I'm sure she must have passed on. Anyway, now they use volunteers, and the library isn't open but three half-days a week."

It was ludicrous to imagine moving back here. Rebecca didn't know a soul.

But when she pointed that out—"See there? To me Church Valley's all strangers"—her mother said, "Oh, piffle. You know Aunt Ida. You know the Finches. And Abbie Field and Sherry and the Nolan twins."

"Do you still see all of them?"

"Well, of course! This town is very close-knit."

She must mean the older people in town, though, for it was clear that she didn't recognize the various teenagers and young mothers they met walking along Grove Street. She threaded her way between them without so much as a glance; and for all the attention they paid her, she might have been invisible.

Aunt Ida lived above Gates Drugstore. Arnold Gates, the pharmacist, had been her husband, and after his death she'd sold the drugstore but arranged to continue living in the four little rooms upstairs. Nobody would have guessed she was Rebecca's mother's sister. She tended to put on weight, and she dyed her hair a metallic red, and she wore frilly, too-young dresses and bright makeup. Today she was all in pink—pink strappy sandals and pink toenails, even—with some kind of gauzy pink ruching knotted around her throat. And her apartment was as cluttered as her clothing. "Now, let me clear you a path," she said as they entered. "Oh, my, what is this doing here?"—referring to a Raggedy Ann doll grinning from the carpet. A reasonable question, since Ida had no children or grandchildren. (The great tragedy of her life, she always said.) But then, she was forever opening her doors to other people's offspring.

When Rebecca was a very small girl, she had nourished a secret daydream that her parents would painlessly die and she could go live with her aunt. Ida was so welcoming and easygoing; her household seemed capable of limitless expansion, and almost any time Rebecca dropped in she found somebody staying a week or two—a toddler whose mother was sick, or Arnold Gates's ne'er-do-well nephew, or, on one memorable occasion, three members of a Polish wrestling team visiting Church Valley High on some kind of sports exchange program. When Rebecca's father actually did die (felled by a stroke just after her ninth birthday), she had felt so guilty that she'd avoided her aunt for months. And besides, her mother needed her at home.

"Well, come on in where I can look at you," Ida was saying. "Oh, my! I would never have the courage to wear plaid with paisley, but on you it's so artistic."

Rebecca's mother, moving an armload of magazines so she could settle in a rocker, said, "You didn't tell me they were painting the hardware store, Ida. We passed it and it just about hit me in the face. Oxblood, I would call it; or, no, more like magenta. I said to

Rebecca, I said, 'What a pushy color!' And then of course the Wool-worth's; Rebecca's not been here since they closed the Woolworth's, and I can't even remember the store that used to be next to it, can you? I was trying to think. Not the jeweler's; that was across the street. Not the pet supply. Well, I know it will come to me eventually. Wait! No, not the shoe repair . . ."

"Sit right here; move the cat," Ida told Rebecca. "Look at what I've made you! Froot Loop Bark Candy, it's called. I got the recipe out of the paper. Isn't it pretty? The bright spots come from the Froot Loops and the lighter spots are colored-marshmallow bits. I tried them out first on the neighbors' little boy; he was staying here a while because, oh, it's such a sad story . . ."

"A fingernail place!" Rebecca's mother said. "That's what it was! Can you imagine a place devoted to nothing but fingernails? No wonder it closed!"

Rebecca took a bite from her piece of candy, which looked more like some kind of novelty toilet soap. As soon as she could get her teeth unstuck, she asked her aunt, "Is that Percival?"

She meant the cat—a fat gray tabby. "Why, no, dear," Ida said, "that's Daisy. Percival died last Christmastime."

"Oh, I'm sorry to hear it."

"Yes, I had to have him put to sleep on account of kidney trouble. I wanted Dr. More to do it before he retired; you know he'd tended Percival ever since kittenhood."

"I myself," Rebecca's mother said, "have never had a professional manicure in my life and I don't believe my nails are any the worse for it. Who knows what you could pick up in such a place? Sharing instruments with strangers—files and clippers and scissors and such."

"Dr. More retired at the end of the year when he turned sixty-five," Ida told Rebecca. "He said he was moving to Florida."

"Well, he should know," Rebecca's mother said smartly.

There was a sudden silence, as if the sisters had surprised themselves with this momentary convergence in their conversation. Then Ida sat forward, clasping her plump, ringed hands, and said, "How long will you be with us, Rebecca?"

"Just until tomorrow. I've left Poppy with Zeb overnight, but I should be back in time to give him lunch."

"And tell us about NoNo! I'm so thrilled that she's engaged."

This was what Rebecca loved about her aunt. Her mother had not inquired after NoNo, or Patch or Biddy either; they weren't blood relations. Her only question had concerned her "real" grand-daughter, Min Foo—how her pregnancy was proceeding—and she had worn a pinched and remote expression as she asked, because she had disapproved of Min Foo ever since her second marriage, the one to LaVon. But Ida seemed equally attached to all four girls, and still sent each of them a dollar bill in a Hallmark card for their birth-days. "Your mother says NoNo isn't planning much of a wedding," she said now, "but I hope she'll change her mind. Is she thinking she's too old? She's not too old! Nowadays lots of people don't get married till their forties. And she's waited so long for Mr. Right; all the more reason to celebrate."

"Oh, she's celebrating, for sure," Rebecca said. "Along with you two, I trust," she added, sending them each a glance. Ida beamed and nodded. Rebecca's mother gazed thoughtfully at a rainbow afghan on the floor. "What she means is, she doesn't want anything formal. And that's partly because of her age but more, I think, because Barry's been married before."

"Well, what has that got to do with the price of eggs in China?" Ida asked.

"Tea," Rebecca's mother said.

"What?"

"*Tea* in China."

"The bride is the one who counts," Ida said. "You tell her so, Rebecca. Tell her to have a long white dress, a veil—the works. Flower girls, attendants . . . Tell her Barry should have a best man. Maybe his son, if he's old enough. Is he old enough?"

"He's twelve."

"That's plenty old enough!"

"Well, maybe," Rebecca said. "He's kind of a young twelve, though."

"How does he get along with NoNo?"

"All right, I guess. It's hard to say. He's very quiet. At our Fourth of July barbeque, he just sat in a corner and read a book."

"Well, he's going to love you-all once he gets to know you," Ida said.

She passed the candy again, but this time Rebecca and her mother both refused. Ida herself was the only one who took a second piece. "Law," she said, licking each finger daintily, "it seems like yesterday we three were planning *your* wedding! You made the prettiest bride."

"Well, I certainly had a pretty dress," Rebecca said, because the dress had been sewn by her mother and Ida, working almost around the clock. (She'd given them two weeks' notice.)

"We took down all your measurements and then you lost eight pounds, remember? We got to Baltimore the day of the wedding and found you just a shadow of your former self. Right up till time for the ceremony we had to baste and pin and tuck . . . You'd turned into a skeleton! I guess it was bridal jitters."

Rebecca had been nowhere near a skeleton; just slightly less fat than usual. And that was due to pure happiness, not to jitters. She had been so extravagantly happy! She hadn't been able to eat or sleep. She had walked around in a trance.

Yet that wedding had made a great many people unhappy. The boyfriend whom she'd jilted, needless to say; but also her mother and Ida, who had never so much as heard Joe's name before she stunned them with her news on an unannounced trip home. "Wait: I thought you were marrying Will," her mother had said. And, "You've known this person *how* long? He makes his living doing *what*?" And finally, "I just have to point out, Rebecca, that this is mighty convenient for him. A case where a man is so needful, where a wife would be so useful. Three little girls to take care of! And their mother nowhere in sight! I guess he *would* want to marry!"

Rebecca had accused her mother of doubting that anyone could love her. She had left the house in tears, slamming the door behind her, vowing not to return. "I never said . . . !" her mother called, trailing her down the driveway. "I only meant . . . Couldn't you first have a long engagement? What's your hurry?"

A question asked as well by people at Macadam—her faculty advisor and her history professor. Why sacrifice a college degree, they said, to marry a near-stranger thirteen years her senior? Why not wait till she graduated?

And on Joe's side, there were his daughters. Oh, his mother was ecstatic; you'd think the whole romance was her idea. And the other adults seemed delighted. But his daughters were stony-faced and resistant. They left Rebecca's chirpy remarks hanging foolishly in midair, and they found a million reasons to mention "our mama" in her presence. More than once, in those two weeks before the wedding, they had made Rebecca cry.

So many tears, now that she looked back! It hadn't been pure happiness after all. Part of that time, she'd been miserable.

But always there was Joe.

He drew her close and she pressed her face against his ropy brown throat. He called her his corn-fed girl, his creamy one, his beautiful blond milkmaid. (All those dairy-type references.) He wiped her eyes with his handkerchief that carried his smell of warm toast.

So was it the happiness or the misery that had made her lose those eight pounds?

Which, anyway, she had regained soon enough after the wedding.

Her mother and Aunt Ida were on the next subject by now—or the next two subjects. Her mother was saying that lately it seemed any chair she sat in was a struggle to get out of, and Ida was saying simultaneously that it wasn't only her vet who had retired but her doctor as well, and also her podiatrist, both of them replaced by mere whippersnapper youngsters. There was a pause, and then Ida said, "Old again"—announcing yet another convergence of topics. And they sighed and started off their next two conversational paths.

. . .

For supper her mother served chicken salad and peas. She spent a long time on her preparations, because she believed in taking no shortcuts. First she had to disjoint a hen and poach it, then make her own mayonnaise with a little hand-cranked eggbeater. Rebecca was not allowed to help because, her mother said, she tended to be too slapdash. "You can set the table, though," she said, as if offering a gift, but then she did it over again after Rebecca had finished—squaring the place mats and straightening the silver. Rebecca gave up and sat down to watch while her mother ran water into a pitcher and emptied it three times before finally letting it fill.

"I was wondering," Rebecca said. "Instead of moving to Havenhurst, why not invite Aunt Ida to live here with you? She's alone and you're alone. Wouldn't it make sense?"

"Goodness, no, she talks too much," her mother said. "Besides, it's not that I want to live *with* somebody. I just don't want to live by myself."

Rebecca laughed, but she understood what her mother meant.

"Also, Ida's so messy," her mother said. "And more difficult to get along with than you might suppose. Did you try her Froot Loop candy? It was sweet enough to give me an earache! Yet she turned down those peppermint patties at my house. Well, I know why she turned them down. She wasn't on any diet; no, sir. She just prides herself on being the generous one. She doesn't like to switch roles. It interferes with her theory of the universe, that I should be the one to bring her a plate of goodies."

Meanwhile, she was putting away the napkins that Rebecca had set out and bringing forth others—neither better nor worse, just different. Rebecca smiled to herself.

After they had finished their meal (which was, as always, bland and pallid-tasting, so underseasoned that no amount of salt seemed able to set things right), they watched the news on the huge old black-and-white TV in the living room. "Oh, honestly," her mother kept telling the announcer. "Oh, for gracious sake." She plucked irritably at the crease in her slacks. "Look at that," she said when a group of congressmen appeared on the screen. "Children are running the country now. Every one of those men is younger than I am."

"Well, but . . ." Rebecca said. She hesitated. She said, "Everyone just about everywhere's younger than you are, by now."

"Yes, I'm aware of that, thank you," her mother said. "But it's more noticeable, somehow, when they're the government. You know? If I thought about it long enough—the whole U.S. in these people's hands—I wouldn't be able to sleep at night."

"For me," Rebecca said, "it's just the opposite. Those men are younger than I am, too; at least a lot of them are. But I look at their gray hair and I think, '*Old* guys,' as if I didn't realize that I'm getting old myself."

"You don't know the half of it," her mother said. "Fifty-three! A mere child."

The congressmen faded away and a throng of soldiers appeared, wearing antique uniforms but sauntering across a field in a distinctly modern, offhand manner. They were reenacting one of the major battles of the Civil War, a reporter explained. Every attempt had been made to ensure that their equipment was authentic, although of course they were not using live ammunition.

"Men," Rebecca's mother said. "If they can't find any good reason to fight, they have to make one up."

The clock on the mantel struck the quarter hour, playing part of a hymn in golden-throated notes. One of the men fell down on a hillock of grass.

"Do you remember your paper on Robert E. Lee?" her mother asked.

"Yes, of course."

"You invented this whole new theory about why he chose to side with the South. Remember? Your professor was thrilled."

"Professor Lundgren," Rebecca recalled. She hadn't thought of him in years—his high, veined forehead and translucent hair.

"Come see him in his office, he said. He had such big plans for you! That's when you decided to change your major to history."

Rebecca said, "Oh, well." She was afraid they might be working around to how she'd dropped out of college. "No great loss, really," she said. "I don't think it was history that interested me so much as . . . tracking down the clues, you know? Like a kind of detective story. Coming across that book no one else had bothered to read; it was the first time I'd seen the fun of independent research."

"He wanted you to expand your paper into an honors project. But before you even got started, bang! Joe Davitch hove into view."

"Oh, well."

"And poor Will Allenby; poor Will," her mother said, making a sudden right-angle turn. "He never even knew what hit him! One day you two were as good as engaged, and the next day you'd married a man nobody knew from Adam."

"It wasn't the next *day*," Rebecca said. "It wasn't quite as sudden as that."

"It was as far as anybody hereabouts could tell."

Fair enough, Rebecca supposed. It was true that she had kept Joe a secret. But at the start it had seemed so innocent—just a casual visit when he happened to be passing through Macadam. (Though if it had really been that casual, why had she not mentioned it to Will?) He had taken her for a sandwich at a diner just off campus, entertained her with a couple of funny stories about his work. The party the evening before, he said, had been a wedding reception where the bridal couple's mothers had nearly come to blows. "We all know perfectly well," the groom's mother had shouted, "why your daughter is getting married in a dress with an umpire waistline!" Rebecca had laughed, and Joe had sat back and watched her with a fond, considering smile that made her wonder, suddenly, whether they already knew each other from some earlier time in her life that she had simply forgotten. But no, she surely would have remembered this larger-than-life man with the complicated upper lip that reminded her of a cursive letter M. "You were laughing the first night I saw you, too," he told her. "You were enjoying the party more than anyone else in the room."

She didn't contradict him.

Everything might have turned out differently if she had.

He said he had started the Open Arms in 1951, when he'd left college for financial reasons after his father—an ironically uninsured insurance agent—had died without warning. "So is that . . .

what you *do*?" Rebecca asked him. "I mean, is that your whole profession?"

"Yes, there you have it," he said. "Nothing in my life but parties, parties, parties."

She glanced at him, thinking she had detected a certain edge in his voice. But then he went on to give a very amusing account of a christening celebration where a child had dropped the baby into the punch bowl, and she decided she'd been imagining things.

She did tell him about Will Allenby. Or she alluded to him, at least: she said, "my date and I," when discussing a movie she'd seen. Granted, she didn't use the term *boyfriend*. But that would have been sort of tactless, wouldn't it? Sort of bragging and inconsiderate.

Will Allenby was long-boned and slender and self-contained, with a cloud of yellow curls and an expression of luminous sweetness. He attended Macadam too—certainly not by coincidence—and they were planning to marry as soon as they graduated. This was in the 1960s, when half their classmates seemed to be sleeping with the other half, but they themselves were waiting till after their wedding. At the end of every evening, they kissed and kissed and kissed, clinging to each other, trembling, but then they parted company—Will to go off to his dorm, Rebecca to hers. "Au revoir," Will always said, because using the word *goodbye*, he claimed, would make him too sad. Rebecca found this incredibly romantic, especially when he remembered to gargle that first *r* the way the French did.

None of this came up in her conversation with Joe at the diner, however, or in any of their other conversations. For there *were* other conversations. He telephoned two days later to solicit her advice about a Sweet Sixteen party. Rebecca had never been Sweet Sixteen herself (she'd been sixteen-going-on-forty, she felt), but nobody would have guessed it from her flood of helpful suggestions. And when he dropped by the following week on his way to a linen outlet, although Macadam wasn't really on his way at all, wouldn't her friends have been surprised to see how readily she slid into his car to accompany him, and how authoritatively she coached him on his selection of cocktail napkins, embroidered guest towels, and stenciled table runners!

"I find myself in Macadam" became his regular excuse, although Macadam was nearly an hour's drive from Baltimore, over near D.C. "I find myself in Macadam and I wondered if you'd like to . . ." Grab a cup of coffee. Hunt a book in the college bookstore. Help select new stemware. In the course of three weeks he visited seven times, and after every visit, her first act was to return to her room and check her own face in the mirror. Her pink cheeks and her shining eyes, still a bit damp from laughter, and her heavy crown of braids. Was this how Joe Davitch saw her?

She spent an hour, once, doodling what looked like birds in flight—those shorthand double tildes that children fill the skies of their drawings with—before she admitted to herself that she was trying to capture the shape of his upper lip.

It was inevitable that Will should find out. His roommate reported seeing her with "some man" in downtown Macadam. Rebecca said, "Oh, for goodness sake. That was only Joe Davitch! He's thirty-three years old. He's nothing but a friend."

Noticing, meanwhile, how she treasured the excuse to utter his name.

Although she believed that she meant what she said: she wasn't in love with Joe. It was more that she was *swept along* by him, was how she put it to herself. She fell into this giddy mood whenever she was with him—laughing so uncontrollably, acting so lighthearted. *Acting* lighthearted. It wasn't her true nature.

Once when they were taking a drive she developed such a case of the giggles that she popped a button on the waistband of her skirt. (They were listening to a ball game and he began impersonating one of those chatty sports commentators—inventing human-interest stories about the players because, he said, baseball was so slow-moving that they'd both die of boredom otherwise. "How's that pitcher coming along with potty-training his kid, do you know?" he asked his imaginary colleague.) And once he brought his three daughters with him, and Rebecca, as easily as breathing, rallied them around and raced them to the little pond behind the gym, ducking into the cafeteria for stale rolls as they passed. "Look!" she called when they reached the pond. "Fish! Who wants to feed them?" The children stared at her silently—stolid Biddy, who seemed to have no recollection of meeting her before, and belligerent Patch and wary little NoNo. Eventually, though, they accepted the rolls and tossed them into the water. Rebecca said, "Wonderful!" and clapped her hands together. Joe stood slightly apart, smiling his fond smile at her.

With his thumbs hooked in his jeans pockets.

His beautifully hinged pelvic bones.

His narrow, dark-brown eyes watching only Rebecca.

.   .   .

He telephoned one Wednesday afternoon and invited her to supper at his house the following evening. "My mother wants to make it up to you," he said. "She's ashamed of falling apart the night you first came here."

Rebecca hesitated. She felt imposed upon, for some reason. She almost wished she hadn't answered the phone.

"Please say yes," he told her. "Mom's worried you'll think she *always* drops hams on her guests' shoes."

So she laughed and said, "Well, all right."

She was sorry, though, the minute she hung up. What did she imagine she was *doing*?

And she didn't have an inkling what to wear. First she put on something that would have been suitable for church—a beige shirtwaist, conservative—but at the last minute she switched to an embroidered peasant dress with a drawstring neckline because Joe had once asked admiringly if she were of Swedish descent. (She wasn't.) The skirt was very full and she realized, too late to change yet again, that it made her hips look even wider than they were. "She has such a pretty face," she imagined Mrs. Davitch saying behind her back, with the rest of the remark understood: *It's a pity she's so heavy.*

The car she drove was her roommate's—a Volkswagen Beetle. She had told her roommate she was going to dinner with the family of a friend. "Family friends," it might have sounded like. (None of her girlfriends knew about Joe. She had not confided in anyone; she didn't want to give him, oh, *meaning*. Importance.) She propped the directions on the passenger seat, although she felt fairly confident about finding the Open Arms a second time, and she drove with the radio off, both hands clasping the wheel, her expression calm and impassive. It was all right to be doing this. She was completely blameless. The Davitches honestly, truly were just the family of a friend.

Joe was the one who answered the doorbell, but his mother was right behind him. "Welcome, honey!" she cried, and she pressed her soft cheek to Rebecca's. Her hair was set in finger waves so crisp they made a sizzling sound. "And happy birthday!" she added.

Rebecca said, "Birthday?"

"Oh, I know it's not till Saturday, but we're generally booked on Saturdays so Thursdays are when we always have our family celebrations."

Rebecca looked at Joe, who was grinning. "I peeked at your driver's license," he said. "The seventh of May. You'll be twenty."

Had he also seen what she weighed? was her immediate thought.

"When *I* turned twenty I already had a two-year-old," Mrs. Davitch said. "But I don't know; young women nowadays are more focused on careers, I'm afraid."

This time the Open Arms seemed less grand, perhaps because there was no crush of guests to hide the flaws. The floorboards creaked under Rebecca's feet, and the couch in the front parlor had a slumped and burdened look, and the crystal chandeliers were dull with dust. Draped across the mantel was a pale-blue satin swag reading *BIRTHDAY GREETINGS* in silver spangles, some of which had flaked off to glitter on the hearth below. Rebecca said, "Oh, you shouldn't have," but Mrs. Davitch said, "Anything for you, dear one!"

Rebecca had the same eerie feeling that Joe's fond smile often gave her. Did this woman know her from somewhere?

Then here came the kid brother, bounding into the room like a puppy. Zeb? Yes, that was his name. Wearing a suit too short in the sleeves and a clumsily knotted tie. Before he could shake her hand—while he was stumbling over the rug on his way to greet her—the front door flew open with a slamming sound. "It's only us!" a woman trilled. A heavily rouged, brassy blonde in a fluid black jersey dress, and a gray-haired man with a handlebar mustache. The man was unexpectedly familiar. He had passed the hors d'oeuvres at Amy's party, Rebecca realized; only then he'd been wearing a waiter's white coat and now he was in a maroon smoking jacket with quilted lapels. "Meet Aunt Joyce," Joe told Rebecca, "and Poppy, my uncle. Folks, this is Rebecca."

"Look at you!" Aunt Joyce said, hugging her tightly. "You're every bit as pretty as Joe told us!" She stepped back to pat her husband's shoulder. "Poppy here is Joe's father's brother; I don't know if you know. He and Joe's father were identical twins, so if you want to see what Joe's father looked like—"

"Well, I'm planning to show her the album after dinner," Mrs. Davitch said. "Would you believe I've finally brought that album up to date? I spent half this afternoon pasting pictures in, just so Beck could get to know the family."

Rebecca (who had never been called Beck in her life, or any other nickname) felt a combination of pleasure and panic. This situation seemed to be rushing on without her—Zeb saying, "Geez, Mom, you're not going to show her those old photos! They're so embarrassing!" while Poppy told Aunt Joyce, "Number one, we were not identical twins; we were fraternal. And number two, we looked nothing alike. Nothing whatsoever."

"Oh, lovey, you just don't want to admit you aren't unique," Aunt Joyce said. "Get used to it! How about you?" she asked Rebecca. "Do you have any brothers and sisters?"

"Well, no—"

"Isn't that a coincidence!" Mrs. Davitch broke in. "Joe was very nearly an only child too. I couldn't get pregnant again for ages no matter how hard I tried, which explains why I have one son thirty-three and another just barely sixteen."

"Great, Mom," Zeb groaned. "Let her know how old I am, why don't you."

"Well, it's not a state secret, Zeb. Poppy, could you pass the dip around? I'm going to check on dinner."

"Why doesn't Zeb pass the dip?" Aunt Joyce asked Mrs. Davitch. "Poppy's not on duty tonight."

"I didn't say he was, did I? I only asked if he'd help."

"Be glad to," Poppy told her, bending for the tray on the coffee table. But Aunt Joyce seized his arm and then wheeled on Mrs. Davitch to say, "Just because he fills in sometimes in a pinch doesn't mean he has to spend a family night waiting tables, Liddy Davitch."

"Now, Joycie," Poppy began, while Mrs. Davitch's chin started wobbling and she said, "Oh, that's so unfair of you!"

"Would you ask your doctor to check your appendix if you met him socially?"

"That is so uncalled for!"

"I'll just pass it myself, why don't I?" Rebecca suggested, and she stepped between the two women to lift the tray. (Celery sticks and carrot sticks that had been sliced too far ahead of time, from the looks of them, with a bowl of sour-cream-and-onion-soup-mix dip at the center.) "Have some," she told Zeb, who happened to be standing practically on top of her. Zeb seized a carrot stick, dropped it, and stooped to retrieve it. "Joe?" she said. "Celery? Carrots?"

"Thanks," he told her, but he stood smiling down at her without taking a thing. Rebecca flushed and moved on, finally.

Mrs. Davitch said, "Well, aren't you nice." She dabbed beneath her eyes with her index fingers and gave Rebecca a watery smile. Then Poppy asked, "Drinks, everybody?" and went over to the cocktail cart. This time, Aunt Joyce raised no objection.

Within the next half hour, several more people arrived—two male cousins, another uncle, and a middle-aged woman named Iris, her relationship to the others never specified. Each of them walked in without knocking, slamming the front door into the closet door, and each seemed to know all about Rebecca. "Did you find a summer job yet?" one of the cousins asked, and Iris said, "*I* majored in history, too; I expect Joe will have mentioned." They filled the rear parlor, the women perching on the very edge of the couch with their knees set all at the same angle like a chorus line; and they talked about people Rebecca didn't know, but they kept sending her complicitous smiles so that she felt included.

Dinner, when it was finally served (much too late, after some apparent crisis in the kitchen) was roast beef and mashed potatoes and salad. The roast was dry, the potatoes lumpy, the salad leaves transparent with store-bought dressing. Mrs. Davitch acknowledged all this with a moaning sort of laugh, but her guests said everything was fine. They spent most of the meal arguing about another cousin—an absent cousin—who either had or had not said something rude to Mrs. Davitch about her husband's death. Mrs. Davitch was of the opinion that his remark had been very hurtful, but Aunt Joyce pointed out that suicide was suicide and she might as well face up to the fact. Mrs. Davitch set her fork down and covered her eyes with one hand.

Rebecca hadn't known that Joe's father was a suicide. She looked across the table at Joe, but he appeared to be concentrating on his meal.

Dessert was a chocolate layer cake blazing with twenty candles, the top layer slightly askew and held in place with toothpicks. For that, the little girls were summoned from upstairs—all three in pajamas and squinting crossly from an evening of watching TV in the dark. "Give Beck a birthday kiss, now," Aunt Joyce ordered, and they hung back at first but eventually obeyed, each leaving a tiny star of dampness on Rebecca's cheek. Then everybody sang "Happy Birthday," while Rebecca gazed around the table and pretended that she belonged here—that she was the much-loved member of a large and boisterous family, just as she had yearned to be when she was a child.

Later all the adults settled once more in the parlor, and Mrs. Davitch laid the photo album across Rebecca's knees so that everyone could explain just who was who. Here was Mrs. Davitch herself, unrecognizably girlish in flared khaki shorts from the forties. Here was Mr. Davitch, with Joe's broad smile but, yes, perhaps a slightly shadowed look around the eyes. Here was baby Zeb chewing on a teething ring, and here a teenaged Joe—nudge, nudge—in a very loud houndstooth sports coat with shoulders sharp as wings. No attempt had been made at chronological order: the present-day Aunt Joyce, overblown and dumpy, was followed by Aunt Joyce in a willowy, wasp-waisted bridal gown. And there wasn't a sign of Joe's ex-wife, although several shots of his children had had someone scissored out of them.

Rebecca sat very straight-backed, and she refrained from touching a picture even when asking a question about it. She didn't want anyone to think that she was presuming. She knew she was a guest here, she meant. She knew these colorful relatives weren't hers.

But when Joe walked her out to the car at the end of the evening, he said, "Everybody felt you were like a member of the family. You fit right in, they told me."

"Well, they were very hospitable," she said.

"They think I ought to marry you."

"What?"

"I'd told them ahead that I wanted to."

She stopped at the curb and turned to him. "Joe —" she said.

"I know," he said.

All at once she grew conscious of the stillness of the evening, the absence of any traffic, the hushing sound of new leaves on the little tree beside them. When he took a step toward her, she thought he meant to kiss her, and she knew she would kiss him back. Instead, though, he slowly, solemnly, carefully tied the drawstring at her neckline.

Why did that make her knees go limp?

She gave a shaky laugh and turned to get into her car. "Well," she said, "thanks for dinner. Goodbye."

"Goodbye," he said.

He closed her door so gently behind her that she thought at first it wasn't latched. But it was.

. . .

Friday, there was no word of him. Well, thank goodness. Friday evening she and Will went to the movies. Saturday they shared a pizza for her birthday, and Will gave her a locket with his photograph inside. She kept thinking Joe would pop up somewhere. She walked self-consciously, keeping her head high. But he never appeared.

Sunday, Will's mother and Rebecca's met them for brunch at Myrtle's Family Restaurant. It was a tradition, once a month or so, since Macadam was an easy drive from Church Valley. At the end of the meal, Rebecca's mother said it was her turn to pay. The bill was not very large, but Rebecca felt a pang when her mother pulled her worn cloth coin purse from her pocketbook. Later, as they were walking back to campus, Rebecca asked Will, "Why don't *we* ever pay for brunch?"

"Oh, well, you know how our moms like to give us a little treat," he said.

It was the word *moms* that got her—that weak and childish word falling from his lips. "Oh," she said, "I'm so sick of this eternal . . . studentness! Each thing in its own time, every stage of our lives waiting for the proper, reasonable moment!"

Will said, "Pardon?"

Didn't he seem so young, all at once! So loosely constructed, and narrow through the jaw! So half-baked, really.

"Rebecca?" he asked. "Is something the matter?"

"No," she said. "I'm just tired, I guess."

It occurred to her that she led an absolutely motionless existence. There was nothing to look forward to in it. Nothing whatsoever.

. . .

Monday evening, as usual, they met in the library to study. Rebecca arrived first, and a few minutes later Will sat down at her table and opened his leather briefcase. Shuffle, shuffle, his notes emerged, and two textbooks arrived with a thud, followed by a loose-leaf binder, followed by a great array of pens and pencils. His red ballpoint for editing, black fountain pen for composing, lead pencil for notes in borrowed books, and blue ballpoint for the books that he owned. Each one he aligned precisely with the others at the head of his place. Watching made Rebecca feel itchy.

He opened his loose-leaf binder and smoothed a page that was already smooth.

On April 19, 1861, Rebecca forced herself to read, *troops were ordered transferred from* . . .

Something made her glance toward the library door—a flash of movement. She looked through the center windowpane and found Joe Davitch's laughing eyes. She scraped her chair back. Will set an index finger on his page and raised his head. "Goodbye, Will," she told him.

"Huh?" he asked. "You're leaving? So soon? I still have work to do!"

"That's all right; stay where you are."

"Oh. Well. Okay. So, um . . . au revoir, I guess."

"No," she said. "Goodbye."

And then she walked out the door and into Joe Davitch's arms.

.   .   .

Or that was how she described it to her grandchildren, years later.

Gliding over the complications: the second, third, and fourth goodbye scenes that Will thickheadedly seemed to require; the loose ends left behind at school with exams not taken, spring semester incomplete; the general dismay when she moved, bag and baggage, to the Open Arms' third floor two weeks before the wedding. "Oh, I know this person must be very attractive," her mother said on the phone. "Very handsome and good-looking; I can just imagine. Probably has no end of charm. But I have to ask you this, Rebecca: do you realize what you're getting into? We're talking about the man who'll be holding your hand when you die. Or you'll be holding his hand when he dies. Is that something you have considered?"

"Die?" Rebecca said.

"No, I thought not," her mother said grimly.

Then at another point—at several other points: "And what about poor Will? What about his mother? How on earth will I ever face Maud Allenby again?"

She probably *hadn't* faced Maud Allenby again, Rebecca thought now. She probably crossed the street to avoid her, even after all these years. She turned from an aspirin commercial to ask, "Do you ever see Mrs. Allenby?"

"She passed away," her mother said, not taking her eyes from the screen. "I thought I told you."

Rebecca said, "Oh!" She did seem to recollect that she had heard that.

"But we'd stopped keeping company long before," her mother said. "It just never was the same after you jilted Will."

"Well, I'm sure he managed to survive it," Rebecca told her.

"Maybe. Maybe not. I wouldn't have any idea. I don't know where he settled, what he's doing, whether he ever remarried . . ."

Rebecca waited for her mother to correct herself, but she didn't; so finally she said, "He couldn't *re*marry; he wasn't married in the first place."

"The fact of the matter is," her mother said, "Will Allenby was your true soul's companion. I still believe that. The two of you had so much in common; you were so much in love; you understood each other so well. Maud and I talked about it often. 'Aren't they compatible?' I used to say. 'It's just as if they knew each other from some previous incarnation. They're both such old, wise souls,' I said. 'They belong together, those two.'"

Rebecca turned to look at her.

"You became a whole different person after you jilted Will," her mother said.

. . .

Rebecca's girlhood room still had the same furniture—a twin bed with a white-and-gilt "French provincial" headboard, a low bureau with an attached oval mirror, and a nightstand topped with a doily. But all personal traces of her had vanished long ago, and when she walked in with her overnight bag she could just as well have been entering a hotel room. It didn't even smell like her anymore. Not that she was certain what her own smell was; but this smell was her mother's, clean but musty, unused.

What kept her mother going, these days? Her life seemed so stagnant: the tea-and-toast breakfast, the few dishes washed and dried afterward, the bedclothes pulled up, the carpet sweeper rolled across an already immaculate carpet . . .

Well, what kept anyone going? Who was Rebecca to talk?

The telephone rang—the turquoise Princess phone with a rotary dial that still sat on the nightstand—and a moment later she heard a tapping on her door. "Rebecca?" her mother called. "It's Joe's brother."

"Oh, thanks," she said, and she picked up the receiver.

She assumed it was something routine until she heard the thin blade of distress in his voice. "I'm sorry as hell to bother you—" he started right in.

"What's the matter?"

"The basement: it's filling with water. But there hasn't been a drop of rain; I don't know what—"

"Which part of the basement?"

"The part over by the window."

"Darn," she said. "It's the main drain again."

"What does that mean? What should I do?"

"Are you upstairs?" she asked him.

"Yes, I'm in the family room. I don't know what happened! I went down to put my laundry in the dryer; I'd done a little wash earlier. And all at once I was walking in water. There was this horrible sloshing sound! It was like something in a nightmare!"

Rebecca tried not to let her amusement show in her voice. "Now, Zeb," she said, "this is not all that much of a problem. It's the tree next door's roots clogging up the drain line, that's all. Mr. Burdick will have it fixed in no time."

"This late at night?"

"No, we'll have to wait till morning. But you should call him now to let him know we need him. Go over to my desk, get my little leather address book—"

"What if the water keeps rising?"

"It won't. Just don't turn on any more faucets than you can help, and try not to flush any toilets. I'll start out extra early tomorrow so I can be there when Mr. Burdick arrives."

"I'm awfully sorry, Rebecca. I wanted you to have a worry-free visit."

"I *am* worry-free," she said. "And you should be, too. This is not a serious problem. Just call Mr. Burdick—John Burdick & Sons."

"Well," Zeb said. "All right."

She could tell he was reassured. His voice had returned to its usual level rumble.

"How's Poppy doing?" she asked him.

"He's okay. He's gone to bed. He asked me twice what time you were coming home."

"Tell him, oh, say, nine a.m. And tell Mr. Burdick, too. I don't want him getting there before me."

"Okay, Rebecca. Thanks."

"Good night, Zeb."

She hung up and reached for the alarm clock, an old Baby Ben that had been allowed to run down. First she wound it, and then she set the alarm for 6:00.

Any time now, she was convinced, that house was going to end up a heap of rubble. Only she knew all its hidden ailments. She remembered the day she'd moved in—the shock of the upstairs with its fake-wood-grain metal bedsteads and rickety pressboard bookshelves. The casual guest would never suspect how the windows stuck, and the faucets dripped, and the walls appeared to be suffering from some sort of skin disease. From a distance, the place looked so imposing.

If her very first meeting with Joe had foretold her role in his life forever after, she thought as she undressed, hadn't it also foretold her role in the Open Arms? For it seemed the place was *always* beset by disasters, both physical and social, and Rebecca was always, by default, coming to the rescue. Not that she'd had any aptitude for it. She wasn't much of a cook; she couldn't hammer a nail straight; she'd been a wallflower from birth. But gradually, she had learned. She'd become more take-charge, almost bossy. "Have you grown taller?" her mother asked on one of her rare visits. "There's something different." Rebecca hadn't grown an inch, but she agreed there was something different. She felt she took up more space. Her voice sounded louder now, even to her, and her laugh had acquired a ha-ha sound while before, it had been mere breath.

Standing naked in this room where she had spent her childhood, slipping her nightgown over her head and letting it fall to her ankles, she thought how her past self would have gasped at the sight of her. The old Rebecca would never have known the woman she saw in the mirror, with the hair like a heap of cornflakes and the ramshackle face. She would have been put off by the slipshod, heedless way this woman strode toward her bed.

She folded the spread back and whacked it flat.

Surprisingly, she had no trouble getting to sleep. She turned once, tossed aside her blanket, turned again, and Poppy was celebrating his birthday. The Open Arms was packed with guests, all the women in hoopskirts and the men in Confederate gray. But Rebecca had on the chambray smock spotted with bleach that she wore for heavy cleaning. She glanced down at herself and, "Oh, fiddle!" she said, in a flirty Southern voice like Scarlett O'Hara's. Then she saw that one of the guests was Will Allenby. He walked over to her, smiling, holding his hat in his hand. He wasn't one day older than the very last time she had seen him: twenty. His chest was paved with medals and his riding pants stretched taut over his long thighs.

She opened her eyes in the dark and felt a deep ache of regret.

four

Now she began to lead a whole other life—an imaginary, might-have-been life flowing almost constantly underneath the surface of her day-to-day existence.

If she had not attended Amy's engagement party that long-ago evening, if Zeb had not made her laugh so that she seemed, for one brief moment, to be a joyous and outgoing person, if Joe Davitch had not walked up to her and said, "I see you're having a wonderful time," why, no doubt she would have stayed on in college.

Graduated with honors.

Married Will Allenby.

Dear Will Allenby, with his airy yellow curls and serene, contemplative smile, his nearly transparent eyes that seemed lit from within. She was startled to discover him complete and detailed in her mind, as if all these years he had been poised to step forward the very first instant she recollected his existence. He used to have a habit of raking his fingers through his hair whenever he was caught up in some intellectual discussion, and now she could see so clearly those agile, knuckly fingers (like the fingers of the son in her dream!) and the electric look of his hair. She recalled how he had loved listening to Bach, hated girls who giggled, and claimed an almost physical allergy to the color red.

Peculiar memories popped up out of nowhere: a high-school assembly, for instance, where the World's Fastest Typist had given a demonstration. Plump and bald and expressionless, he had sat behind a tiny metal stenographic desk, facing his audience but gazing over their heads while his typewriter, seemingly of its own accord, chattered away without pause and spat sheets of paper onto the floor. Will had muttered under his breath during the whole performance. What did this prove? he kept asking Rebecca. The man's assistant—a leggy blonde dressed in what appeared to be a carhop's uniform—scooped up each page and proclaimed it to be perfect, one hundred percent accurate, x many words per minute; but why should they believe her? From this distance, the pages could be blank. Rebecca had tried to hush him, but Will had persisted. "This is outrageous!" he had said in a piercing whisper. "They're wasting our valuable learning time!" She had grown annoyed with him; she had moved her arm away from where it was touching his. Now she liked remembering that. Cataloguing his flaws brought him back to her more convincingly. She dwelt upon his overlarge teeth, which she used to feel pressing knobbily behind his lips when they kissed; the puppy-dog clumsiness of his hugs; and the affectation (as she saw it now) of his "Au revoir" at the end of every evening.

It was true they had never slept together, but they'd talked about it endlessly. Why it was better to wait; how maybe it was silly to wait; what were the pros and cons. Will had a book called *Married Love* that he'd ordered from the back of a magazine. He had perused it from cover to cover and studied all the diagrams—the fallopian tubes like orchid stems and the Missionary Position. He read aloud from it to Rebecca and she listened with what she hoped was an expression of mild interest, her head slightly tilted and her eyes on a point in midair. (Although inwardly, of course, she was riveted by every word, and found it almost beyond belief that the married couples of her acquaintance could spend hours together engaged in any other activity.) Oh, she and Joe had had a very happy sex life, but now she was sorry she had missed the experience of figuring it all out with someone equally unskilled. Will would have been so scientific about it! So focused, so comically intense!

She used to write *Will Allenby* on her notebooks, and W.A.+ R.H. And, in very small, secretive letters, *Rebecca Allenby*. It had bothered her that a voice break was required between those two adjacent *a*'s. *Rebecca Holmes Allenby*, she had amended. *Mrs. Willard Allenby*.

She supposed that they would have married immediately after college. That was one of the steps in their life plan. They would have moved to some larger and more prestigious university where the two of them could pursue their Ph.D.'s—Will's in physics, Rebecca's in American history. She could visualize their apartment as concretely as if that, too, were a memory: a comfortably shabby flat in some faculty widow's house just off campus, with brick-and-board bookcases, Chianti-bottle candlesticks, and a batik bedspread. Their meals would be very simple—bread and soup, say, on a cleared space among the books on the kitchen table. And every night after supper they would take a walk, just the two of them, hand in hand, learnedly discussing their respective research projects. The town they walked through seemed to be Baltimore and yet not Baltimore, the way places are in dreams. It was cleaner and more organized, and it smelled of fresh-grated nutmeg as Baltimore used to do before the spice factory moved to the suburbs. Also, there was no traffic. The only sound was the tapping of their shoes on the empty sidewalk.

Her true real life, was how she thought of this scenario. As opposed to her fake real life, with its tumult of drop-in relatives and party guests and repairmen. Gradually, she sank so deeply into her true real life that she grew remote and strange, and it took her minutes, sometimes, to pull herself together when she was asked a question. But nobody seemed to notice.

. . .

At the moment, her fake real life revolved around NoNo's wedding. This was set for the twelfth of August—a Thursday, so as not to interfere with any paying events. NoNo kept insisting that it shouldn't be a big deal, but even so there was the guest list to be seen to, the arrangements to be made for Barry's family, the food to be discussed with Biddy. If Rebecca had had her way they would have scheduled a rehearsal, too, but so far the couple hadn't even found a minister. (Neither of them belonged to any kind of church.) "Never mind," NoNo kept saying, "I'm sure it will all work out"—an assumption that seemed foolhardy when you considered she had grown up in the Open Arms. And then she announced, out of the blue, that all she really cared about was the garden. "The what?" Rebecca asked.

"The garden. Did I mention that I wanted an outdoor wedding?"

Rebecca's jaw dropped.

For starters, they didn't have a garden. They had a scratchy little three-foot plot of rosebushes at the front of the house, for show, and a slightly larger plot of mostly weeds at the back of the house that ended where the kitchen building began. And since it was the hottest and driest summer in living memory, the weeds were not even green. They were a parched and frizzled beige, and the azaleas under the dining-room window had turned into dead brown twigs. Besides which, who in her right mind would want an outdoor wedding when the average heat index was a hundred and five degrees?

But NoNo said, "I *am* a florist, after all," as if that explained everything.

"Well, then," Rebecca said, "maybe, as a florist, you can tell me how to get a halfway decent garden inside of two weeks."

"Don't you have that lawn-mowing boy? Rock, or Stone, or whoever?"

"Brick," Rebecca said. "He hasn't been here since early July. There's nothing for him to mow."

"I'm sure he can think of something. Lay down sod, bring in a few container plants . . ."

Rebecca had always considered NoNo to be the easiest, the most compliant and obliging of the four Davitch girls. But now she wasn't so certain.

And then came the food issue. All at once, NoNo decided she didn't want Biddy to cater. This was after Biddy had planned out her menu and lined up a non-family wait staff. NoNo said she would hate to make Biddy work on her sister's wedding day. Biddy said, "I'd work *before* the day. That was going to be my gift to you and Barry. I wouldn't have to lift a finger during the actual wedding. I would show up in a dressy dress and behave like a regular guest."

"I was thinking about the people who catered that shower last weekend," NoNo said in a musing tone. "The Guilty Party, their name was. I have a copy of their menu."

Biddy looked over at Rebecca. She said, "You just so happen to have a copy of their menu."

"They do such nice, straightforward, uncomplicated food," NoNo said.

Biddy's eyes grew pink, and she turned and flounced out of the kitchen. A moment later, they heard the front door slam. All NoNo said was, "Hm-hm-hm!"—a little three-note humming sound—as she poured herself another cup of coffee.

Oh, Rebecca didn't look forward to this wedding in the least.

And the worst of it, from her own point of view, was that Tina was attending. NoNo's mother, Joe's ex-wife, all the way from England, where she lived now. Because she had so far to come, she arrived three days ahead of time. A whole caravan of cars went to meet her at the airport—Biddy and Troy, Patch and Jeep, NoNo and Barry, and every available child—but even so, several pieces of her luggage had to ride back in people's laps. She traveled like a movie star, with one suitcase devoted to shoes and another to cosmetics. And she didn't carry a thing herself but sailed ahead of her struggling bearers, bestowing a smile to her right and her left as she entered the house. "Rachel, dear!" she cried. Rebecca said, "Rebecca," and let herself be engulfed in a perfumed embrace. "What a sweet outfit!" Tina told her. Rebecca had given some thought to her outfit—a plain white blouse that she had gone so far as to iron and a conservative, non-Bag-Lady, navy A-line skirt—but now she saw that what she most resembled was an overweight flight attendant. Tina, on the other hand, looked gorgeous. She was tall and slim, with masses of auburn hair piled on top of her head, and all her features were stunningly exaggerated: large, long-lashed eyes, pillowy red lips, confident prow of a nose. Her blurry, clinging dress could have gone straight to the wedding, but Rebecca knew, from earlier occasions, that Tina's attire at the wedding would outshine the bride's. It was obvious that she was nearly sixty, but she made sixty seem sophisticated and sexy.

Rebecca sank into a depression, all at once. She folded her arms across her stomach and watched bleakly as Tina dove into her luggage, pulling forth lavish presents for every member of the family. (Her second husband—ex-husband, now—was a very wealthy man.) French colognes, Irish crystal, a genuine badger shaving brush for Poppy, a regiment of lead soldiers for her new grandson . . . and for Rebecca, an apron. "Thanks," Rebecca said tonelessly, but her voice was lost among the others.

It had occurred to her, often, that the way to win your family's worshipful devotion was to abandon them. Look at how Tina's daughters clustered around her! The men acted bashful and smitten—especially Barry, who was meeting her for the first time—and the children were dumbstruck. Even Min Foo, no relation at all, wore a look of breathless expectancy when she arrived. "Minerva, darling!" Tina cried, sweeping her into her arms, and then she gave her a pair of carved ivory chopsticks for her chignon. Tina never used nicknames; it was always Minerva, Bridget, Patricia, Elinor with her. Rebecca supposed that was significant. Distance was the key, here: the distant, alluring mystery woman whose edges had not been worn dull by the constant minor abrasions of daily contact.

"Well," Rebecca said, "I guess I'll go see to dinner."

Nobody offered to help.

In the kitchen, Alice Farmer was slicing tomatoes. Her angular, blue-black face was generally unreadable, but there was no mistaking the sardonic arch of her eyebrows. "Come to hide out, have you," she said. (She'd been working here long enough to have witnessed several of Tina's visits.)

"I've a good mind to eat at a Burger King," Rebecca told her. "Let them get their own damn dinner."

Alice Farmer gave a whistling hiss of a laugh and handed her a bag of corn to shuck.

Rebecca wondered how Joe would have behaved in this situation. She had never had the chance to observe him and Tina together. (The two women had first met at his funeral—probably a bizarre encounter, although Rebecca had been too numb with grief to notice.) Of course she had quizzed him about Tina while they were courting. "I suppose she's very attractive," she had ventured, and Joe had said, "Sure, if that's the type you go for."

"And she must have a beautiful voice."

"Tina? She's got a crow's voice."

"But if she's a nightclub singer . . ."

"*So-called* singer. *Quote-unquote* singer."

She had felt a wave of relief that must have been visible, for Joe had smiled at her and said, "Have you been fretting your head about her?"

"You did choose to marry her," she reminded him.

"She did happen to be pregnant, Beck."

"Well . . ."

"Do you think we'd have married if she weren't? Either one of us? We were miserable together. At the end of that third pregnancy, she was counting the days till she delivered so she could leave."

But now Rebecca heard the girls' laughter clear back here in the kitchen—louder than usual, and merrier. You would think they'd had the world's most doting mother.

She unraveled the tassels from an ear of corn and let herself return to her true real life, where she and Will had one child between them, one biological child. A boy, let's say. (Girls were so complex.) A boy like the one on the train. They would have named him something dignified: Ethan, or Tristram. Something that couldn't easily be shortened. He would be a solemn type even when he was very young—a watchful, focused baby, content to sit for long periods of time studying his surroundings. A quiet toddler. An inquisitive little boy. The kind who might take a clock apart out of scientific curiosity. "Tristram! What have you done?" she would ask, coming upon a heap of sprocketed innards. But she would feel secretly proud of him.

She would buy him—she and Will would buy him—books about dinosaurs, and Atlantis, and the boyhood of Thomas Edison. Maybe they would pick up an old music box at a thrift shop, and later a toaster or radio, something broken that he could tinker with and eventually get to working, much to everyone's amazement.

He would probably have a little trouble making friends. Oh, she might as well face up to the fact! Nobody was perfect. His grade-school teachers would send home reports: A's on his academic subjects but a C or D in phys ed, and a note to the effect that he lacked team spirit. That he worked poorly on group projects. That he experienced some minor difficulty in getting along with his peers.

She would go in for a conference and nod and look concerned, and then try not to show her pleasure when the teacher finished up by saying, "Apart from that, of course, your son is a real joy. None of my other students is as bright or creative as Tristram."

"Yes, well, he's always been very . . ." she would murmur. With her eyes modestly lowered.

In high school his sole companion would be a boy obsessed with computers. The two would spend whole weekends shut up in Tristram's room, constructing something incomprehensible out of electrical wire and a disemboweled television set. She would knock and offer cookies; Tristram would say, "Huh? Oh. Thanks." Then she would stand in his doorway a while breathing in the smells of machine oil and sweaty sneakers. It wouldn't bother her a bit that he paid her no attention. She knew he had reached the stage where he had to start pulling away from her.

She knew that underneath, he would always love her.

"Hand me them corn ears, will you?" Alice Farmer said. "Miz Davitch? Pot's on the boil. Could you please hand me the corn?"

Rebecca merely blinked at her.

. . .

There were so many people at dinner that the children had to eat separately. This caused several different arguments, because some of the children—the ones in their teens—felt they were old enough to eat with the grownups. And it didn't help a bit that Tina kept saying, "Of course you're old enough! Come sit next to me." Rebecca had to step in, finally. "Tina," she said, "this table seats twelve, and that's how many adults we have. I'm putting all seven of the children in the kitchen."

Tina shrugged and gave the teenagers a pouchy-lipped look of commiseration. Then she patted the chair to her right and said, "Oh, well, Barry, *you* sit next to me, then. And Hakim on my other side." (The two best-looking men in the room, wouldn't you know.) "Seven grandchildren!" she told Rebecca. "You and I could practically start a baseball team!"

Half of Rebecca felt flattered; there was a certain confiding, intimate quality to Tina that she always found seductive. But the other half wanted to point out that Tina had no right at all to claim Min Foo's two children. She gave her a bland smile and then deliberately seated herself between her own favorites, Troy and Zeb, although her usual spot was next to Poppy. Poppy was down near the end, repeatedly asking if someone would please turn off the lights in the parlor. Nobody volunteered, though. They were all vying for Tina's attention, the girls addressing her as "Mother" more often than was needed, forming their lips around the word in a self-conscious and unskilled manner.

It was pathetic to recollect that once, when Rebecca was first married, she had suggested to the girls that they call her "Mom." "But you're not our mom," they had said. "That would be a lie." Oh, children were such sticklers for the absolute, literal truth. (The other day, introducing Peter to the plumber, Rebecca had said, "Meet my future stepdaughter's stepson; I mean my stepdaughter's future stepson. My stepgrandson-to-be, I mean." Mr. Burdick's eyes had widened. No doubt he'd thought her unwelcoming, not to simply call the boy her grandson. But Rebecca knew from experience that Peter might all too well have contradicted her outright and made her look like a fraud.)

Alice Farmer sailed in, stately and important, holding a platter of crab cakes high above her head. "Why, Alice," Tina said. "Are you still with us?" This gave Rebecca a twist of wicked satisfaction, because Alice Farmer hated being addressed by anything but her whole name. It was one of her quirks. Alice Farmer set the platter in front of Rebecca and sent Tina a long, flat stare beneath half-shuttered lids before she left the room.

"If I were Tina, I'd hire myself a taster before the next course," Zeb murmured out of the side of his mouth. But Tina had blithely moved on, by now, to the subject of the wedding. She was asking Barry how he and NoNo had met, where he had proposed, what kind of ceremony they planned. Her questions were delivered with that falling intonation that the English use—"Won't it be dreadfully *hot* in the garden"—and at some stage during her years abroad she seemed to have lost the knack of pronouncing her r's. "God-den," was what she said. Rebecca resolved to stop being so critical. "Could I offer you a crab cake," she asked Troy, but unfortunately the question came out with that same downward note at the end. Troy gave a sputter of a laugh. Rebecca plopped a crab cake onto his plate, pointedly avoiding his eyes.

"We've finally found a minister," Barry was telling Tina. "NoNo and I were in a restaurant the other night, talking about who we could get to marry us, and our waitress said, 'Why, I could do that.' Turns out she has some kind of certificate she sent away for through the mail. Perfectly legal, she says. A really nice lady. Says she'll do it for free."

This was news to Rebecca. All she'd heard was that the officiator would be a woman. She had pictured someone magisterial, wearing a flowing black robe like Sandra What's-It on the Supreme Court bench. Now a whole new image popped up: a person in a dingy pink nylon uniform and a hairnet.

"Well, and why not," Tina said cheerfully. "It's all a big charade, anyhow. Isn't it," she asked Hakim. He gave her a dazzled smile. "Just a primitive tribal ritual," she went on, "meant to make us forget we're merely propagating the species. When I think what I could have accomplished if I hadn't bothered with marriage! It's enough to make me weep."

"What," Zeb said politely.

"Pardon?"

"What could you have accomplished?"

"Well, you'll have to ask my voice teacher that. She was devastated when I married Joe. Absolutely devastated. 'My dear,' she said, 'you are throwing away a God-given talent, purely to enter an institution invented by males for their own benefit.' And she was right; I know that now. Oh," she said, turning a radiant smile on Hakim, "women may find marriage useful during that little childbearing phase. But then as the years go by, they need their husbands less and less while their husbands need them more and more. Men expect all that listening and marveling and yes-darling-aren't-you-amazing, those balanced meals and clean sheets and waxed floors, and then the blood-pressure monitoring and the low-sodium diet, and the hand-holding when they retire and can't think what to do with themselves. And the wives, meanwhile, start longing to get free. They start running off to their ladies' luncheons and their women's book-club meetings and their girls-only wilderness trips."

"Great, Tina," Zeb said. "You certainly know the right thing to say to a bridal couple."

The others laughed—some a bit uncertainly, Rebecca thought. But Tina lifted her chin and told him, "I don't notice *you've* been in any rush to marry."

"No, I guess I haven't," he said. "I'm still waiting for Rebecca."

Rebecca sent him a grateful smile, but Tina did not appear to have heard. "Seriously, though," she told the others. "You have to admit that love is a waste. It's expensive, it's inconvenient, it's time-consuming, it's messy . . ."

They laughed again, more easily now. They must have decided she was joking. That Tina: such a card.

But Rebecca didn't think she was joking. Or not entirely. She suspected Tina was expressing exactly what she felt.

The funny thing was that she felt that way herself, at certain moments. She gazed around her at this tangle of relatives and in-laws, the children tumbling in from the kitchen to complain about some injustice, Poppy announcing his birthday party for the thousandth time, Peter slouching wretchedly on the fringes of the group . . .

And she thought what a clean, simple life she would have led if it weren't for love.

. . . .

Phone photographer, she reminded herself before she went to sleep. *Phone NoNo to ask what music she wants. Pick up Poppy's suit from the cleaner.*

She knew she should switch on the lamp and make a list, but she was too tired. Instead, she tried to envision the list on the ceiling above her bed—a mnemonic device that never really worked. *Ask Dixon if he could drive Alice Farmer home after the wedding,* she added. She slid her left foot to a cooler spot on the sheet. *Find out whether Barry . . .*

Then she lost track of her thoughts and lay staring into the dark.

It made her might-have-been existence more real to imagine also the negatives. Will, for instance, would probably have been a workaholic. He was just the type to stay late at the lab and converse in monosyllables when his mind was on his research. There she'd be, serving him a gourmet dinner, wearing something enticing, brushing the back of his neck with her fingers as she poured his wine, and he would say, "You know? I think I've figured out where I went wrong in that last experiment."

As for Tristram: he would never quite outgrow his social inept-ness. She and Will would always worry about him a little. Although professionally he would be very successful, doing something scientific that she couldn't pretend to understand, she didn't suppose he would marry till relatively late. He tended to develop inappropriate crushes on shallow, bubbly blondes who didn't return his interest.

(You had to be able to see beyond his earnest, shy, fumbling manner.) Like his father, he would seem a bit removed from his own culture.

Oh, it wasn't always easy, Rebecca would tell her friends.

. . .

"I can't believe you're going to let Poppy give a toast at the wedding," Tina said. "He's not in earshot, is he."

"No, he's up in his room," Rebecca told her. "He had breakfast hours ago."

She was hoping to make a point—it was after 9 a.m.—but Tina let it pass right over her head. "The man's a total loss!" she said. "He seems to have about one-sixteenth of his mind left, every cell of it devoted to the savoring of sweets."

Rebecca had never heard anyone use the word *savoring* in casual conversation. She wondered if Tina would spell it in the British way, with an *our*. She spent so long considering this—standing at the kitchen stove, watching a pat of butter melt and begin to sizzle—that Tina gave a cluck of impatience and reached past her for the egg carton. "My God, it's some kind of cruel joke," she said when she had lifted the lid. She was looking down at a double row of eggshells. Rebecca always put the shells back in the carton when she was cooking. In fact, she'd assumed that everyone did. This was what happened when people came to stay: they forced you to view your life from outside, to realize that there was, come to think of it, something faintly mocking about a carton full of empty shells. But two eggs remained intact, and she plucked those out and rapped them against the rim of the skillet.

"As for that birthday party," Tina said, "I don't know how you can even consider it! He'd forget you'd thrown it, anyway, half a minute later. And think of the conversation: round and round, the same subjects over and over. All his guests would go mad."

Rebecca, too, suspected that Poppy might not remember the party afterward. Her hard work would come to nothing. But she said, "That's okay; we'll remind him."

"Simpler just not to do it and tell him you had."

"Also," Rebecca said, dreamily stirring the eggs, "it can be kind of interesting when he repeats himself. New details come out, different slants on the old stories. Sometimes I end up learning something."

"For what *that's* worth," Tina said. "He always was a bit of a bore, even when Aunt Joyce was alive; but now, good God! I guess she covered up for him more than we imagined."

"Well, who knows? Maybe we'd say the same thing in reverse if *he'd* been the one who died," Rebecca said. "Maybe the two of them together made a unit that worked, and whichever one of them went first would have left the other, oh, just . . . lopsided and lame."

There was a short silence, during which Rebecca turned off the burner and carried the skillet over to the table. She dished the eggs onto Tina's plate, set the skillet in the sink, and asked, "Coffee? Tea?"

Only then, turning from the sink, did she notice how intently Tina was studying her. "What," she said.

Tina said, "Oh, nothing." She settled at the table, scooping her long skirt beneath her. (Like someone in an old movie, she wore a full-length satin dressing gown to breakfast.) "Coffee, please," she said. Then she said, "You must have felt sort of lopsided yourself, all these years."

"Well," Rebecca said.

"You don't have any, shall we say, man friend, I suppose."

"Oh, no," Rebecca said. She poured a cup of coffee and set it in front of Tina.

"Quite right: why would you want one," Tina told her. "Such a nuisance, they are."

This struck Rebecca as unexpectedly kind. She sat down opposite Tina and said, "It isn't that, exactly—"

"And after baby-sitting Joe Davitch!" Tina said. "No wonder you need a rest. God, the Davitches in general: a bunch of mopers. They could really weigh a person down."

"Oh, well, I wouldn't—"

"Any time I think of his mother, I picture her on the verge of tears. You know how her chin would pock up. How her lower lip would quiver. It's ironic that her profession was throwing parties. I mean, just because your house has fourteen-foot ceilings doesn't automatically make you a social butterfly, does it. I'll never forget what I heard her tell an old friend once. 'I like you, Ginny,' she said, 'but do we actually have to *get together*?'"

Rebecca smiled, hearing her mother-in-law's plaintive little voice echoing across the years.

"And Joe's father taking those pills," Tina said. "Not even leaving a note behind. There must have been some sort of depressive chromosome or something, descending from both branches."

"Well, but *sometimes* they were happy," Rebecca said, because she was thinking, just then, of her twentieth-birthday party, all those people singing to her around the table.

"And then Aunt Alma, his father's sister," Tina said, "forever checking into Sheppard Pratt for little rest cures. Or how about Cousin Ed! Walking in front of that bus."

Rebecca hated it when Tina showed off her inside knowledge of the Davitches. She herself had never heard of Cousin Ed, and she had thought Aunt Alma's rest cures were a secret that Mother Davitch had confided to her alone. She said, "Yes, but in any family—"

"And the way Joe drove: those crazy left turns. Tell me those weren't suicidal! Directly into the path of oncoming traffic. More than once I ducked under the dashboard; I bet you had that experience. Or did he do that only with me."

No, he had done it with Rebecca.

When they were courting, it hadn't alarmed her. She had been so trusting, back then. She remembered riding blissfully next to him, cradling his right hand in her lap as he made a dashing one-handed swerve across two lanes of speeding cars. But later she grew more anxious—especially after Min Foo was born. They had even had a couple of quarrels about it. "Who's behind the wheel, here: you or me?" he had said, and she had said, "Yes, but my life's at stake too, after all; mine and the children's. I have a right to object!"

"You don't think that's the behavior of someone who wanted to do himself in?" Tina asked now.

For once there was a question mark, American-style, at the end of her sentence. But even so, Rebecca didn't answer.

"In any event," Tina said finally, "at least he didn't take you along the night of the accident." She glanced around the table. "I don't suppose there's orange juice."

"I may have some in the fridge," Rebecca said, not moving.

"Ah."

Tina waited for a moment. Then she said, "Why don't I fetch it," and she slid back her chair and stood up. Her dressing gown made a sound like sand running through a sieve as she crossed the linoleum.

It was true that Rebecca had sometimes sensed some other quality, a glimmer of something like desperation, lying just beneath the surface of Joe's exuberance. On occasion she had thought she detected a hollow note in his voice, a forced heartiness as he welcomed guests. Or was it just that in any marriage, you end up knowing more than you should about the other person? (The inner meaning of that sudden hitch to the shoulders, or that flicker in one temple.) Once or twice, after a party, she had found him slumped in the darkened front parlor, staring into space. "Joe?" she had asked. "Aren't you coming to bed?" and he'd given his head a sharp shake and struggled to his feet.

She had felt at certain moments—but not always! not for long stretches!—that she was dragging him through an invisible swamp, and Joe was hanging back while she herself, to compensate, grew quicker and more energetic. *See how easy it is? We'll get through this in no time!*

Through Mother Davitch's stroke, and Aunt Joyce's death, and Poppy's moving in with them. Through the constant threat of financial failure—blank squares on the appointment book, painful calls from creditors. Through Mother Davitch's death, too, and the time they nearly lost Patch to appendicitis.

But through the good things, as well. Min Foo's birth. The older girls' gradual adjustment to Rebecca. Zeb's admission to medical school. The little pleasures of everyday life, like a perfectly weightless snowfall on a clear December night, or the sound of the children's jump-rope chants outside on a summer evening.

"Yeah, sure, sweetheart," Joe said when she pointed these out, and he would sling an arm around her and draw her close. Even then, though, she might catch a certain clouded look in his eyes, as if he were listening to some private voice that Rebecca couldn't hear.

She did believe he loved her. But she couldn't help feeling, sometimes, that he loved that private voice more.

Had she been a disappointment to him? That was her greatest fear. Consider how he had first seen her: the girl enjoying the party more than anyone else in the room. He had clung to that image obstinately, no doubt hoping that her happiness was contagious. And it hadn't been. And besides, she was really no more or less happy than most other people she knew.

"This place is like a time machine," Tina said out of the blue.

Rebecca started, wondering if her head was so transparent. But Tina was drifting obliviously around the kitchen. "Same old round-edged sink as when *I* was living here, only maybe a mite yellower. Same sticky wooden cabinets. Same scummy little plastic drinking glasses." She raised her glass of orange juice, demonstrating. "Same baggy, rusty screen door," she added, turning to gaze through it. "Why! It appears that some young man is carpeting your backyard."

"Really?" Rebecca said. She stood up and went over to check. Sure enough, Brick Allen—bronzed and muscular, wearing shorts and boots and nothing else—was unrolling what appeared to be a bristly green stair runner. "It's grass," she told Tina. "We're putting it in for the wedding."

"How American. An instant lawn," Tina said. She opened the door and called out, "Very impressive!"

Brick raised his head to see who was speaking. He took in Tina—her shimmering robe, the cant of her hip as she leaned against the doorframe—and then he said, "Well, thanks. I've been working out with weights."

There was the briefest pause, and then Tina gave a husky laugh and turned to include Rebecca. But Rebecca didn't laugh back.

She was thinking that if she'd been wise, she would have granted as much significance to Joe's behavior that first night as he had granted to hers. *Goodbye,* he had said. Just that easily.

Not *Au revoir,* but *Goodbye.*

.   .   .

Imagine she was walking down the street one day and who should round the corner but Will Allenby. He would look the same as always, except older. (As an afterthought, she grayed his hair and etched two faint but attractive lines at the corners of his mouth.) "Rebecca?" he would say. He would stop. He would look at her. "Rebecca Holmes?"

Conveniently, he would not have married; or he would have married but found the woman lacking in some way, just never quite up to his memories of Rebecca, and now he was divorced and living nearby—say in one of those luxury high-rise condos overlooking the harbor. Oh, it wasn't so far-fetched!

Might-have-been slid imperceptibly into could-still-be—a much more satisfying fantasy. He would invite her for an intimate supper. She would show up with a bottle of wine and he would seat her at a table next to the picture window, with the boat lights twinkling like stars below them and the Domino Sugars sign glowing in the distance. "So tell me, Will—" she would begin, but he would put his hand over hers and say, "Don't we know each other well enough not to bother with small talk?"

And he was right; they did. They fit together perfectly, both of them so serious and cerebral and nonsocial, content to spend their evenings reading on the couch. Sometimes they would go to plays or concerts. She hadn't been to a concert in years! It would be wonderful to walk down the aisle holding somebody's arm; to have him remove her coat in a sheltering, cherishing way after they were seated; to feel his shoulder pressed against hers as they listened to the music.

"Where's Beck?" the girls would ask each other.

"I think she's out on a date."

"A date!"

At that moment she would walk in the door, smiling a mysterious smile, her lips a little squashed-looking as if someone had been kissing her.

. . .

Macadam College had a vast selection of telephone numbers now, where once there had been only one. "Administration? Admissions? Alumni?" the operator offered. Rebecca said, "Alumni," in a voice that was already shaky. And when she reached the Alumni Office, she felt her heart speeding up. "I'd like to have an address for one of my old classmates," she said, gripping the receiver too tightly. She was relieved when she was transferred to another desk. It gave her a moment to compose herself.

Tina had taken her daughters to lunch, and Poppy was having his nap. This would be Rebecca's one chance all day for privacy. She was sitting on the edge of her bed, about two inches of it, with her head bent close to the receiver and her free hand cupped protectively around her mouth.

An older woman asked, "May I help you?"

"Yes, please," Rebecca said. "I'd like an address for someone from the Class of '68. A Willard Allenby."

This took so much breath (which she seemed to have very little of) that she ended with a gasp. Thank heaven, she thought, the next wait would no doubt be longer. But instantly the woman said, "*Dr.* Allenby?"

"Why, yes, I suppose he—"

"Dr. Allenby is right here!"

Rebecca made a sound distressingly like a squawk. "Right here at Macadam, I mean," the woman told her. "He's head of the physics department."

Rebecca said, "Oh!" in a voice that was still not quite right.

Mercifully, the woman said, "Wait till I get the directory." She dropped the receiver with a clatter.

Rebecca cleared her throat and sat up straighter. She noticed that her ceiling fan was trailing wisps of dust as it spun — rags of dust, actual streamers of dust.

"Here it is," the woman said. "Four hundred Linden Street."

Rebecca switched the receiver to her left hand and wrote down the address. Her handwriting was as wavery as Poppy's. She wrote down the telephone numbers for Will's office and his home — evidently Macadam was still enough of a backwater not to be paranoid about such things — and then she said, "Thanks so much!" in what she hoped was a breezy tone. "Bye!" And she hung up.

Linden Street was where the full professors lived — the settled, tenured professors with good salaries and established families.

Will must have a family.

How could she have supposed he was still alone at that library table, his books still spread around him?

She tore the page off her memo pad and folded it over and over until it was a tiny paper stick. For one irrational moment, she had an urge to chew it up and swallow it, but instead she tucked it out of sight underneath the telephone. Then she rose, smoothing her skirt, and went back downstairs.

. . .

By the afternoon before the wedding, Tina had become just the slightest bit less popular with her daughters. This always happened, Rebecca remembered now. Feelings would get hurt, misunderstandings would arise — the usual untidiness that came from rubbing elbows over a period of days. Patch, for instance, felt that Tina wasn't being nice enough to Jeep. Not only that; she was being *too* nice to Barry. It turned out that Patch had entertained high hopes for Tina's derailing the wedding. In her woman-of-the-world way, she would see Barry for the cad he was and then, by some magic, persuade NoNo not to marry him. Instead, Patch said, Tina had *cozied up* to him; she had made a fool of herself over him; she had behaved just shockingly, linking elbows with him at every opportunity and laughing her throaty laugh directly into his face, not even acknowledging the chair that Jeep pulled out for her at the table but deliberately choosing another chair, far away from Jeep and next to Barry. "Barry, of all people!" Patch told Rebecca. (She had stopped by for just a moment to drop off her youngest.) "We're talking about a man who makes calls on his cell phone during dinner. Calls his own answering machine to leave himself a message. 'Don't forget my dress shoes in the back closet,' he says. Right in the middle of a joke Jeep was telling!"

"Oh, honey, Barry didn't mean . . . Your mother didn't mean any harm," Rebecca said.

Although she couldn't help feeling guiltily pleased.

Then Tina suggested to Peter that he go along on the honeymoon. "Think about it," she told him. "They're planning to leave you in this mausoleum over the weekend with Rebecca. Practically a stranger! I don't know about *you*, but I would never stand for such a thing. The three of you are a family now, tell them. You deserve to come too."

It was unlikely he'd have followed her instructions—he just smiled uncertainly at his shoes and then slid a glance toward his father—but NoNo took offense anyhow. "You don't know the first thing about it," she told Tina in a low, trembling voice. "Barry and I have three days only, three short days, Friday, Saturday, Sunday; that's all I'm asking, and now you have the nerve to say—"

"All right! All right! Never mind me!" Tina said, holding up both jeweled hands. "I'm just the fly on the wall, here."

Then she turned back to Peter and gave him a sympathetic, I-tried-my-best shrug.

This scene took place in the family room upstairs, because downstairs they had a paying event. A man had engaged the entire public space—both parlors and the dining room—just so he could propose to the woman he loved. Evidently the Open Arms was where they had first met, at some sort of charity function. The details, he had said, he would leave to Rebecca, but he wanted this to be a grand and formal occasion with a tuxedoed waiter, a four-course dinner, and a strolling violinist. So Rebecca hired Dixon, who looked elegant in his rented tux although, sad to say, he had started growing one of those skinny jawline beards that seemed more trouble than shaving; and she asked Biddy to do the food and Emmy to play the piano, since she didn't know any violinists. Emmy was diligent if not inspired; she sat at the old upright, wearing a tank top and a miniskirt and approximately fifteen earrings, and plunked out Chopin études while the couple sipped champagne on the front-parlor sofa. The man was gray-haired and portly, his cherubic face shining with sweat even though the air-conditioning was cranked so high that you could hardly hear Emmy's playing. The woman was gray-haired as well but very pretty in a soft, genteel way, and she wore a trim navy dress and tiny navy pumps with straps across the insteps. Rebecca was able to observe all this because she kept inventing excuses to go down and check how they were doing. First she stepped in to welcome them, and then to say that hors d'oeuvres would be served in the other parlor (since it seemed a shame not to employ all the space they had hired), and then to announce dinner. She had the impression that the woman couldn't think what to make of the situation. Upon arrival she had asked where the other guests were, and now she kept giving Rebecca anxious, searching smiles as if she were hard of hearing, although plainly she was not.

"This is a huge mistake," Biddy whispered, slicing hearts of palm in the kitchen. "Such an unprivate proposal. What if she says no? I'll die. I'll burst out crying."

She was serving a meal with a valentine motif: everything pink or heart-shaped or referring to hearts in some way. The main course would be beef heart. Talk about mistake! Rebecca thought. But of course she kept that to herself.

When she returned to the family room, she found NoNo flipping angrily through a magazine while Tina told Barry the story of her own proposal from the Englishman. "We were staying at the country house of friends of his," she said, "and one evening over drinks our host said, 'Tina, darling, I wonder if you could fancy linking up with Nelson, here.' That was Nelson's notion of a proposal. He was scared to ask me himself, he said later. Wouldn't you think I'd have been warned off by that! The man had no backbone whatever. I'm surprised he could sit upright in a chair."

She said nothing about how Joe had proposed, Rebecca noticed.

Peter and Poppy were watching a sitcom on TV. Or Poppy was watching. Peter wore a tense, fixed expression, and a sudden roar of canned laughter didn't cause even a smile to cross his face. "Want to come downstairs and help with the dinner?" Rebecca asked him.

He rose so dutifully that she hurried to say, "Not that you have to or anything."

"Go on, son; I'll be down in a minute," Barry told him. "We've got to be leaving pretty soon anyway. Big day tomorrow, hey, guy?"

Peter gave him a wan smile and trailed Rebecca out of the room.

What on earth would she do with this child for a whole weekend?

In the kitchen, Biddy was moaning over the coeur à la crème she'd just unmolded. "Beautiful!" Rebecca told her, but Biddy wailed, "How can you say that? It's a fiasco!"

She must be referring to the slight indentation at the center. "Camouflage it," Rebecca said briskly. "Didn't I see some strawberries somewhere?"

"This is all NoNo's fault," Biddy said. "She's made me lose my confidence. First she says I can cater the wedding and then she says I can't, and then she says, oh, if it means so much she'll let me do it after all; and ever since then, I swear, everything I've made has come out wrong in some way. Look at this! It's an embarrassment!"

Meanwhile, she was just standing there. It was Rebecca who located the strawberries. "Here," she told Peter. "Fill in that place in the middle and put some more around the edges."

Peter first wiped his palms on the seat of his jeans, and then he took the bowl from her and started gingerly, meticulously placing the berries just so.

"Not much of an appetite out there," Dixon said, walking in with two plates that looked untouched. "Do you think that's a good sign, or bad? I'm pretty sure he hasn't proposed yet, because all they're talking about is some movie they've both seen."

"It's my cooking," Biddy said gloomily. "I knew I'd overseasoned that beef heart."

Rebecca said, "We should have asked if he planned to give her a ring. Then we could have put it in the dessert or something and he'd be *forced* to propose."

"A ring! Isn't she too old for a ring?" Dixon asked.

"With my luck, she'd just eat it," Biddy said.

Rebecca said, "Now, Biddy, you're being silly. This is a lovely meal, the beef heart is lovely, and Peter is doing such a nice job with the berries!"

Her voice cracked on a high note, but nobody was paying any attention anyhow. Except, perhaps, for Peter, who took on a full-cheeked look of pride when she complimented his work. He stepped back from the counter and cocked his head, appraising the dessert with narrowed eyes. Then he stepped forward again and added one more berry precisely in the center.

"You should have seen your father propose," Biddy told Dixon. "He really and truly got down on his knees."

"I didn't know that!" Rebecca said—more to encourage the change of subject than anything else. "And what did he say, exactly?"

"He said, 'Well, I suppose you can guess what I want to ask you.' And I said, 'Well, and I suppose you can guess what I would answer, too.'"

Rebecca laughed, but Dixon stayed very sober and alert, his eyes fixed on his mother's face. (He could never hear enough about his father.)

"It didn't occur to me till this instant that he didn't actually ask," Biddy said. "And I didn't actually answer, either." She shook her head. "Bring a serving spoon with you when you carry in the dessert," she told Dixon. "Let them dish it out themselves. The more privacy the better."

Then she started bustling around, scraping plates and wiping counters.

Rebecca would have liked to know how Troy had proposed, if *propose* was the proper word. Did he say, "Biddy, Dixon Senior may be dead but Dixon Junior is on the way, and I've always wanted a child to raise"? Or had it been more romantic? ("I do prefer men in general, Biddy, but I prefer you in particular and now I'd like to take care of you.") Well, at least the arrangement seemed a success, contrary to all predictions. Rebecca was everlastingly grateful to Troy for sticking by Biddy so loyally and providing Dixon with some warmth in his life. Who could say for sure that it didn't work just as well as a regular marriage?

Barry came into the kitchen, jingling his keys in his pocket, and told Peter it was time to leave. "Any errands I can run in the morning, call me," he told Rebecca.

"Well, thank you, Barry. Have a good night."

She looked past him and saw NoNo just behind him, her purse clutched to her chest. "Sweetie?" Rebecca said.

NoNo didn't answer, but she came to stand beside Barry. Her head barely reached his shoulder—her dark, shiny cap of hair resembling an upside-down flower. She was such a little elf. Ridiculously, Rebecca's eyes filled with tears. "Oh, sweetie," she said. "You're getting married! You're all grown up! Oh, I know—" and she gave a laugh. "I know you've been grown up for ages, but, oh, here you are! About to be a wife!"

She reached out her arms, and NoNo stepped into them. They stood there hugging for a moment with NoNo's purse pressed bulkily between them. Rebecca heard a sniff as delicate as a cat's sneeze. She patted NoNo's sharp shoulder blades and drank in her familiar smell—the rainy, limp smell of fresh violets.

From the passageway, Dixon said, "*Hot* dog!" He burst into the kitchen, and Rebecca and NoNo drew apart. "Well, he did it," he said.

"Did what?" Rebecca asked.

"He proposed, Gram. Wake up!"

Then he described in detail how it had happened: the man taking hold of the serving spoon but setting it back down, swallowing so loudly that Dixon could hear it from where he stood. "I could tell that something was up," he said, "so I got out of there. Walked out but then stopped just around the corner; so I heard him say, 'Vivian, I know you must wonder why I asked you here all by yourself, and you probably think I'm a fool,' he said. 'Lord, I must look like such a fool, but I didn't know how else to . . . Vivian,' the guy said, 'look. I really, really need you to marry me.'"

Biddy made a clucking sound, and Barry said, "Well, gee, he could have come up with something a little more romantic."

"What did *she* say?" Rebecca asked. "Did you hear?"

"She said, 'Steven, I'd be honored to marry you.'"

NoNo clapped her hands, and even Peter started grinning. Rebecca said, "Well, thank heaven. I'm so relieved."

Although she also felt a little sad that her moment with NoNo had been cut short. Oh, nothing in this family ever flowed from start to finish without interruption. Their lives were a kind of crazy quilt of unrelated incidents—always some other family to consider, some strangers getting married or retired or promoted. (Even her own wedding had taken place at an earlier hour than she'd wanted because of an anniversary party scheduled for that night.)

When she was a girl, she had imagined her future as a single, harmonious picture. But what she had ended up with was more like the view in one of those multi-lensed optical toys that Lateesha was so fond of: dozens of tiny *chips* of pictures, each interfering with the others.

She saw Barry and Peter and NoNo out the back door, kissing Barry and Peter politely on the cheek and giving NoNo another hug. Biddy hugged NoNo too. Apparently she'd recovered from her hurt feelings. "Nighty-night, hon," she said. "Get your beauty sleep, you hear?"

Then she and Rebecca set up the coffee tray.

"But don't take it in quite yet," Rebecca told Dixon. "Let them have a little time together on their own."

It was some consolation, at least, to arrange that for somebody else.

.   .   .

She closed her bedroom door because Poppy and Tina were still up watching TV, and she sat down on the bed and drew the stick of paper from underneath the phone.

301, his area code was. She lifted the receiver and dialed it. Then she paused. Then she hung up.

It was nearly ten o'clock. Maybe he was asleep already. In the old days he'd been a night owl, but that could very well have changed.

Maybe his wife would answer. "Will, darling!" she would carol. "Some woman wanting to speak to you, darling!"

Or, "Dr. Allenby's working late tonight," in a forbidding tone. "Who's calling, please?"

Rebecca lifted the receiver again, but this time she punched in his office number—the first three digits of it, at least, after which she paused so long that a voice came on the line saying her call could not go through as dialed. Even the recording—that impersonal, singsong "We're sorry"—caused her heart to race, and she slammed the receiver back down. "You're an idiot," she said out loud. She rose abruptly and left the bedroom. "Ninny," she told the mirror in the bathroom. "Silly moron," she said as she yanked her toothbrush from its holder.

"What say, Beck?" Poppy called.

"Nothing, Poppy. Never mind."

.   .   .

The big surprise was, the wedding went wonderfully.

NoNo was a vision in her white chiffon dress, with her giant yellow-and-gold bouquet, and Barry made a very handsome bridegroom, and Peter, wearing his first grownup suit, seemed touchingly dignified. The backyard was more or less presentable, if you ignored the sort of wide-wale effect produced by the strips of sod that had not had time to meld together yet; and the dead azaleas (which would have to wait to be replaced by professional nurserymen) had been cunningly costumed in billows of white netting—a solution proposed by NoNo herself, although even she had not foreseen that the netting would attract a flock of tiny yellow butterflies so decorative that they might have been sewn on by an inventive designer.

It was too hot, anyway, for the guests to venture outside for long. Until the ceremony began they stayed in the house, which Alice Farmer had cleaned and polished to a fare-thee-well. Nobody would have known that a curtain rod had torn itself loose from the wall in a cloud of plaster dust only that morning. Barry's family—his brother and sister-in-law, plus a couple of cousins—kept admiring this and that, asking if the dining-room fireplace actually functioned (it didn't) and if the people in the portraits were actual ancestors (they weren't). Most of the Davitches arrived not too scandalously late and stayed on their best behavior throughout, never once bickering or stalking off in a huff; and the grandchildren were models of deportment. It was true that Rebecca's mother and aunt—in town just for the day, since neither one of them liked sleeping in strange beds—kept to the edges of the gathering, Rebecca's mother wearing her characteristic who-are-these-people expression. But at least they came; at least they each accepted a glass of wine, and conversed agreeably when spoken to, and Aunt Ida was heard to observe that she hadn't seen such a beautiful bride in donkey's ears. ("Years," Rebecca's mother said. "What?" Aunt Ida asked. "Donkey's *years*, Ida." But Aunt Ida was already turning away to flash her sweetest and most winning smile at Peter.) Also, Tina's hot-pink gown was put to shame by Alice Farmer's sequined turquoise cocktail dress with matching feather tiara. Rebecca found this immensely gratifying.

As for the waitress who officiated, she was nothing like what Rebecca had feared. Demeter, her name was, and she was at least partly Greek, with one of those strong, noble Greek faces. She wore a simple black dress and carried herself as if she were supporting an entablature. Granted, Rebecca still wished they'd rehearsed. The "Wedding March," for instance—played on the piano by Emmy and relayed to the backyard via Min Foo's baby monitor—continued all the way through to the end while the couple stood sweating in the hot sun waiting for her to finish; and then Demeter asked, "Who gives this woman . . . ?" which no one had thought to prepare for. Rebecca was just opening her mouth to say that she did, in order to move things along, when Tina finally said, "Oh! Me." But she was repositioning her corsage at the time, so that it seemed she was merely sort of *tossing off* the bride.

Well, these things happen. What mattered was that Barry and NoNo really appeared to enjoy their own wedding. As soon as the ceremony was finished, they moved back indoors and Zeb took over the stereo and people started dancing. Rebecca watched from the sidelines, smiling. She was wearing a red silk dress with a many-tiered skirt, and she felt like a gypsy queen. Everything that Biddy's waiters offered her, she accepted—little canapés and stuffed pastry shells and several glasses of champagne. All of it tasted delicious. And the cake, when they wheeled it out, was a work of art: six layers, each decorated with a different kind of sugar flower to reflect NoNo's profession. Unfortunately it listed to the right somewhat, but Barry and NoNo cleverly solved that problem by listing to the right themselves, arm in arm, when they posed behind it for the photographer.

The best thing about being stepmother of the bride was that Rebecca didn't have to think up one of her rhymes. Troy offered the first toast—a nice little rumination about what couples learn from each other as they travel together through life. "From Biddy I have learned caretaking," he said. "Feeding, nurturing, nourishing," and he raised his glass to Biddy across the room, which made Rebecca a little teary because she had never before considered what Biddy had brought to Troy; it had always been the other way around. Then Barry's brother delivered a humorous speech about Barry's improved taste in women, and then Poppy struggled up from the couch to propose *his* toast, although he got confused and started reciting his poem instead. He was partway through it before Rebecca realized what was going on. (*"If you weep away the days, or you try not to weep, or can't,"* he was intoning, *"And pace the floor all night and sleep at dawn . . ."*)

"Poppy," she called. "Wait." He paused, lips still parted, and turned so blindly in her direction that it stabbed her heart. She threaded her way through the crowd and came up and hugged his nearest arm to her breast. "A toast to NoNo and Barry," she whispered into his tufted ear. "Long life and happiness."

"Eh?" he mumbled. "Oh." He turned to the others. "Long life and happiness," he echoed. Then he seemed to collect himself, and in a stronger voice he added, "May your marriage be as happy as Joyce's and mine was!"

Everybody clapped, and Rebecca squeezed his arm tighter and kissed his cheek.

"I got a little mixed up," he told her as she helped him sit down. "But it was just for a second, there. I don't think anyone noticed."

"Not a soul," she assured him. "Can I bring you a piece of cake?"

"I believe it was hearing the vows that took me back," he said. "Seems like only yesterday *I* was saying those vows."

"I know, Poppy."

"People imagine that missing a loved one works kind of like missing cigarettes," he said. "The first day is really hard but the next day is less hard and so forth, easier and easier the longer you go on. But instead it's like missing water. Every day, you notice the person's absence more."

"I know."

"But I surely never meant to spoil NoNo's wedding."

"You didn't spoil it! You were fine," Rebecca said. She caught a waiter's attention and beckoned him over. "Look," she told Poppy, lifting a plate of cake from the tray. "Fondant icing! Your favorite."

"Ah, yes," he said, brightening.

The photographer—just a college boy, a friend of Dixon's—snapped Poppy's photo as he raised the first forkful to his mouth. "I *think* I got that," he told Rebecca.

Then Zeb came up and invited her to dance. The stereo was playing "Band of Gold." "Where did *that* come from?" she asked as she stepped into his arms.

"It's one of those 1950s collections," he said. "Looked like good slow-dance music." He steered her into Min Foo by accident and murmured, "Sorry." Min Foo was so pregnant by now that Hakim had to hold her practically at arm's length, leaning across her belly to set his cheek against hers. It made Rebecca laugh. Zeb drew back to smile at her. "You're having fun, aren't you," he said.

"Yes," she said, "I am."

In fact she might have been tipsy, because everything made her laugh, after that. She laughed when Tina waltzed by clinging firmly to Peter, who wore the shocked, frozen look of a hijacking victim. She laughed when Alice Farmer, whose church forbade dancing, started swaying her head to the beat so enthusiastically that her feathers must be setting up a breeze. She laughed when "Band of Gold" switched abruptly to "Sixteen Tons" and everyone came to a stop and looked helplessly at everyone else. Then Dixon's friend herded them outside for a huge group photograph. "Could the people not related by blood get over on the left end?" he asked. "Just in case, you know. Because I'm not absolutely sure I can fit you all into the picture."

"How ingenious: a pre-cropped photo," Zeb murmured, and Rebecca laughed till her cheeks ached.

Yes, she had to admit that the wedding went much better than she had expected.

. . .

Alone in her room, with everyone else in the house fast asleep and the champagne giving her courage, she sat on the edge of the bed and dialed Will Allenby's home number.

The phone at the other end rang twice and then gave a click. "Dr. Allenby," a man said. A man; not a boy. He had the worn, slightly furry voice of somebody middle-aged. She recognized the Church Valley accent, though, that turned *Allenby* into *Allen-bih*.

"Will?" she said.

"Laura?"

"Who?"

There was a sharp silence, during which she longed to hang up.

But finally she said, "This is Rebecca Holmes Davitch, Will. Do you remember me?"

"Rebecca?"

She waited.

"Rebecca," he said dully.

"I hope you weren't asleep!"

"No . . ."

"Just tell me if you were! I know it's late!"

It seemed she could not get rid of this insanely manic tone. She grimaced to herself. "In fact," she said, "maybe I should call another time. Yes, why don't I do that? Okay! Bye!"

She hung up and doubled over, burying her face in her lap. It felt to her as if something in her chest had started bleeding.

f i v e

The house had a post-wedding atmosphere: crumbs ground into the carpet, paper napkins splotching the grass, soiled white satin ribbons drooping listlessly from the mantel. Peter returned to his room after breakfast and shut the door and remained there. Tina left for the airport with a skeleton crew of luggage bearers, her hair a sickly pink in the morning light. Alice Farmer washed stemware so silently and morosely that she might have been hung over, except that she didn't drink.

The telephone kept ringing in a jarring way, and each time Rebecca answered, the cold, smooth weight of the receiver brought back last night's call to Will. She felt battered and damaged and mortified. It was all that she could do not to hang up in mid-conversation.

". . . only thinking of the baby," Patch was saying at the other end of the line. "It's not *my* fault Min Foo's so sensitive. I just mentioned it for the baby's sake."

Mentioned what? Rebecca had lost track.

"Face it: Fatima's a terrible name! And has anybody considered what they'd be bound to call her for short?"

Rebecca caught sight of what seemed to be a wine stain on the Redial button. Focusing her eyes required a great amount of effort, she noticed.

"Beck? Are you there? Did you hear me?"

"Yes, well . . . maybe it will be a boy," Rebecca said.

"NoNo has decided it's a girl," Patch told her. "Min Foo's not even considering boys' names anymore, which is very shortsighted in my opinion because NoNo isn't half as clairvoyant as she thinks she is."

Rebecca started kneading her forehead.

"Otherwise, why would she marry a man like Barry Sanborn?"

"This all seems so pointless," Rebecca said after a pause.

"Well, pardon *me*," Patch snapped, and she slammed down the receiver.

Rebecca wondered where Patch found the energy for so much indignation.

At noon she set out leftovers and called Poppy and Peter to lunch. It wasn't a sociable meal. Poppy kept stealing glances at a magazine lying open beside his plate. Peter concentrated on his food, peeling every last strip of fat from his ham and separating the carrot shreds from his salad before he ate it.

Then Poppy went off for his nap, but when Peter started toward the stairs Rebecca slung an arm around his shoulders, even though it meant she practically had to body-block him first. "How about you and me going out for ice cream?" she asked. "Get ourselves a little fresh air."

"No, thanks," he said, standing limp within her embrace.

"Want me to phone Patch? See if she can bring Danny over?"

"No, thanks."

"Or a game, then. Some kind of board game."

She saw him prepare to say no again, but she pressed on. "Monopoly? Checkers? Clue? We don't want to tell your dad you didn't do one thing all the while he was gone, do we?"

Peter said, "I don't care."

"He would blame *me*. He'd think I wasn't a good—" She started to say "baby-sitter" but changed it at the last minute. "Wasn't a good hostess! I kept you locked in your room on bread and water his whole entire honeymoon!"

A faint smile thinned Peter's lips, but he said nothing.

Oh, Lord, she thought, life was so wearing. Still, she forced herself to persist. "Scrabble? Parcheesi?" she asked, giving his shoulders a squeeze. "We've got them all!"

"Well, Scrabble, maybe," he said finally.

"Scrabble. Oh, you'll regret this, young man. It so happens I'm the world champion of Scrabble."

So they went upstairs to the family room, Rebecca chortling and rubbing her hands together and making a general fool of herself, and settled on the couch with the Scrabble board between them. Peter remained fairly quiet, but he did seem interested once things got under way. He turned out to be the type who took the game very seriously—less from any competitive spirit, she surmised, than because he was a perfectionist. He would peer at the board for minutes on end, reach toward his tiles but draw back, frown and say, "Hmm," consult the dictionary and shake his head and return to his study of the board. This suited Rebecca just fine. She could brood to her heart's content.

Who was this Laura person? What was she to Will?

"Guess this is about as much as I can do," Peter said. He set an *oxy* in front of *moron*, which earned him sixty points because of a triple-word square.

Rebecca said, "Heavens." Even allowing for his looking it up in the dictionary, she was impressed. Peter just shrugged and reached for the scorepad. He was wearing a polo shirt—long-sleeved! in this heat!—tucked conscientiously into his shorts, which looked like two bunchy skirts above his skinny legs. The poor child was such a waif, Rebecca thought. She sent him a sudden smile, one that she really meant, and he surprised her by smiling back before he wrote his score down.

While she was debating her own choice of words—none of them half as clever as Peter's—Poppy wandered in from his nap. He still had his magazine, which he dangled at his side with one finger marking a page. "You remember NoNo's wedding cake," he said, standing over the Scrabble board.

"I remember," Rebecca said.

"You know how it kind of tilted."

"Yes."

"Well, I don't feel that cakes are Biddy's strong point."

"No, I guess they're not," Rebecca said.

"So do you think it would hurt her feelings if somebody else made my birthday cake?"

"Not in the least, I'm sure," she said, although in fact she wasn't sure at all.

He wandered out again with his magazine—*Hospitality Monthly*, she saw. She sighed and set down an N and an O to spell *nor*. "Sorry, it's all I could come up with," she told Peter. "I wish I hadn't promised Poppy this party. He'll forget it before the balloons have shriveled; maybe the instant it's over."

She watched Peter total her score. His nails were so deeply bitten that the fingertips gripping the pen resembled little pink erasers.

"Last Monday," she said, "he nagged me all afternoon to take him to see his friend Mr. Ames, and I kept saying, 'I took you this morning, Poppy, remember? You've been, already; you brought him a scratch-off lottery ticket. You and he sat on his porch while I went grocery-shopping.' He'd say, 'Oh, yes, my mistake,' but then not ten minutes later he'd start nagging me again."

Peter set the scorepad aside. "He could enjoy the party while it was happening, though," he said. "Even if he did forget it later."

"Yes, well . . ." She thought that over. "I guess I want points," she told him. And then, when she saw his puzzled glance toward the game board: "Points for giving the party, I mean. I want him to credit me afterwards for doing it."

He said, "Oh," and went back to his rack of tiles.

"As for the cake," she said, "I think botched cakes are a Davitch tradition. You should have seen *my* wedding cake! Mother Davitch didn't bake it long enough and it was all soupy in the middle. The bride figurine on top fell into this sort of sinkhole, waist deep."

Peter moved a letter from the middle of his rack to the end. A Z, she couldn't help seeing. The lucky devil.

The bride had been ivory plastic, she recalled, with a pinpoint-sized dot of red lipstick and two little beady brown eyes. A matte black, scallop-edged hairdo had been painted onto her head. And the groom had been blue-eyed and blond—nothing at all like Joe.

The telephone rang. She reached for the receiver. "Hello," she said.

"Ah, may I speak to Rebecca, please."

She grew extremely still.

The furred voice, the Church Valley accent. The leisurely, drawn-out vowels, with *I* sounding not much different from *Ah.*

"This is Rebecca," she said.

"Um, Rebecca, this is Will Allenby."

"Will! How did you find out my number?"

"I looked at my Caller ID."

That Will had Caller ID was a shock. It seemed she had been picturing him still living in the sixties.

"You hung up on me so fast," he was saying. "Thank goodness for modern inventions, I guess."

What did he want, anyhow? Why had he called her back?

It made things all the eerier that he said, at that very moment, "So. What did you call me for?"

"Oh, I . . ." She smoothed her skirt across her lap with her free hand. "I happened to be at home," she said, "home in Church Valley, I mean, and Mother and I got to talking about old times and I don't know, I just all at once thought, I wonder where Will ever got to!"

"Not so very far, as you can see," he said. He gave a short laugh. "I'm right here where you left me." Then he hastened to say, "Where we went to college, that is. Well, I haven't been here the whole time. I did go away for my doctorate. But now I teach at Macadam."

"That's wonderful, Will."

"In fact, I'm head of my department."

"Congratulations."

"Yes, I can't complain. Can't complain at all. Really I've done very well. Been very fortunate."

"I'm glad to hear it," she said.

"Last year they nearly made me a dean, except they decided in the end that they ought to bring in an outsider."

"Isn't that nice," she said. "And are you . . . do you . . . I mean, I suppose you must be married, and all."

"Well, I used to be."

"Oh."

"I married an ex-student of mine. An English major; beautiful girl. She was once even offered a modeling job, although of course she didn't accept it."

"I see."

"But we're, um, divorced, at present."

"Oh, I'm so sorry," she said, feeling a quick surge of pleasure.

"Don't be sorry! Really! I'm doing just fine. Getting along just dandy."

Had he always phrased things so stuffily? She couldn't tell if it was his age or his natural manner; she had forgotten now how he had spoken when he was young.

"And what about you?" he was asking. "I know *you're* married, right?"

"I'm a widow."

"A widow," he said slowly.

He seemed so unfamiliar with the word, she wondered for an instant whether she had made it up. It did sound peculiar, suddenly—almost African. (Or was that just because it reminded her of that song, "Wimoweh," that the Weavers used to sing?)

"Well, please allow me to offer my condolences," he was saying.

"Thank you."

"Was this . . . ah, something recent?"

"No, my husband died a long time ago," she told him.

The phrase "my husband" struck her all at once as tactless. She rushed on, so as to make it less noticeable. "I'd only been married six years," she said. "I was left with four little girls—his three and one of my own."

Peter glanced up from the board, just then, where he was laying out something that seemed to interconnect with almost every existing word. He gave her an oddly searching look, as if what she had said was new to him.

"That must have been hard," Will was saying on the phone.

She gripped the receiver more tightly and asked, "Would you like to get together, ever?"

Oops. Too sudden. Too direct, too pushy; she could tell by his hesitation.

"Or else not," she said. "I mean, I realize you must lead a very busy life."

"Well, not *inordinately* busy . . ."

"So, then, maybe we should get together and catch up! I'm just over in Baltimore, you know."

He said nothing. She plowed on. "Would you like to, say, meet someplace? Meet for a drink?"

"I'm afraid I'm not much of a drinker," he said.

He didn't drink at all, was what he meant. Church Valley people didn't, by and large. She gave it one last try. She said, "Or maybe a bite to eat; how about it?"

"A bite to eat," he said thoughtfully.

"I could come to Macadam, if you like."

"Well, that's a possibility."

Something about the lingering way he said it—his ostentatious reluctance—made her more confident. She saw now that as the injured party, he required wooing. And sure enough, his next words were, "I do happen to be free this evening."

"This evening? Oh, I'm sorry; this evening I have an . . . event."

"Tomorrow, then?"

"Tomorrow I have a tea-dance," she told him. "And something Sunday, too, I'm afraid, but Monday's good! Monday would be perfect!"

He waited a beat before he said, "All right, then. Monday."

Maybe if she phoned right now, she could get a hair appointment Monday morning. Maybe she could buy a new dress; maybe even lose a little weight. She said, "What's a good place? Do you still like Myrtle's?"

"Myrtle's?"

"Myrtle's Family Restaurant?"

"Oh, Myrtle's is long gone. I'd forgotten about Myrtle's," he said. "But I believe there's something catty-corner from where Myrtle's used to be. The Oak Tree, the Elm Tree—some such name. I don't know how good it is, though. I've never eaten there."

"Well, at least I'll be able to find it," she told him. "Shall we say seven o'clock?"

"Seven o'clock. All right."

She said, "I'm really looking forward to it."

"Well, fine," he said.

He didn't say that *he* was looking forward to it.

When she had hung up, she let out a long breath. "That was my very first boyfriend," she told Peter.

He raised his eyes again from the Scrabble board.

"My only boyfriend, not counting Joe Davitch," she said.

Then she plopped down two tiles to make another three-point word, and she didn't even apologize.

.   .   .

Saturday morning she dropped Peter off at Patch's house, after which she drove to a giant shopping mall. She forged grimly through each clothing store fingering fabrics, holding dresses under her chin in front of mirrors, and twice even trying things on. It appeared that without her noticing, the fashion world had been edging back toward the skimpy styles of the seventies. All she found were off-the-shoulder necklines, tight cap sleeves, and skirts that showed her underwear seams. In the mirrors she looked sweaty and unhappy. By noon she was still empty-handed, and she couldn't spend any more time because the dining-room ceiling at home had dropped another chunk of plaster and Rick Saccone had agreed to come fix it before the tea-dance.

"Peter's just finishing lunch," Patch said when Rebecca arrived to pick him up. Then she lowered her voice. "This was not a big success. The kids tried to get him involved, but all he wanted to do was read his book. It wasn't their fault, I swear."

"Never mind," Rebecca told her. "He read all through breakfast, too." She was navigating Patch's foyer, which was the usual jumble of sports equipment—gloves, bats, lacrosse sticks, and every conceivable size of ball. "Peter?" she called. "Ready to go?"

"Stay and have a sandwich with us," Patch said.

"I can't; Rick's coming."

"Not again!"

Anyway, Rebecca planned to skip lunch. The memory was still vivid of how she had looked in those dresses she'd tried on: the material strained taut across the broad mound of her stomach.

Peter emerged from the kitchen reading his book as he walked—some old science fiction paperback he'd found in the guest room—and during the drive home he continued reading, in spite of her attempts to start a conversation. "How was lunch?" she asked him.

"It was okay," he said, with his eyes still on the page.

"How'd you get along with Danny?"

"We got along okay."

But then on Eutaw Street he looked over at her to ask, "If you were offered a trip on a time machine, would you take it?"

"Well, certainly!" she said. "I'd have to be crazy not to!"

"Would you go to the past?" he asked. "Or the future?"

"Oh, the future, of course! I'd like to know what's going to happen."

"Yeah, me too," he said.

"My grandchildren, for instance. How will they turn out? What's that funny Lateesha going to do with her life? She's such a little character. And Dixon: I just have this feeling Dixon's going to amount to something."

"I'd also like to know if scientists ever discover the Universal Theory," Peter said.

Rebecca laughed.

He said, "What's funny?"

She said, "Oh, nothing," and he went back to his book.

. . .

As soon as they reached home, she went upstairs to her closet and took out all her dresses and piled them on the bed. One by one she tried them on, standing sideways to the mirror and surveying herself critically.

She had never aimed for the emaciated look; it wasn't that. In fact, some part of her had always wanted softness and abundance — the Aunt Ida look. (Which may have been why she had slipped off every diet she'd ever attempted: the first pounds she lost invariably seemed to come from her cheeks, and her face would turn prim and prunish like her mother's.) The problem was, soft and abundant women were seen to their best advantage when naked. It wasn't her fault clothes had belts to bulge over, and buttonholes that stretched and gaped!

When Rick showed up to fix the ceiling, she met him at the door in an eggplant-colored gauze caftan that wafted unrestricted from neck to ankle. But she could tell from the way his eyebrows rose that it was a little too noticeable. "I'm having dinner with my high-school sweetheart Monday," she explained, "and I'm nervous as a cat. I guess this won't do, huh?"

"Well," he said cautiously, "the *color's* nice . . ."

"Oh."

He said, "What about those harem pants you had on that time I was patching the bathroom?"

"I can't wear pants to a restaurant!"

"Why not?" he asked. He heaved his ladder over the doorjamb. "Now, me: I have dinner with my high-school sweetheart every evening."

"You do?"

"I'm married to her."

"Deena was your high-school sweetheart? I didn't know that!"

"I thought I'd told you."

"I'd have remembered if you had," she said.

After she saw him into the dining room she went upstairs again, this time to the hall cedar closet where she stored items she couldn't quite bring herself to throw away. There she found what she was hunting: the powder-blue dress she had worn the night she met Joe. So she must have worn it with Will, too, on some occasion or other. (It wasn't as if she had owned that many clothes.) But it would barely cover her crotch; she could tell by holding it up against her. "Would you believe it?" she asked Peter. He was heading into the family room with his book. "I actually used to go out in public in this! It reminds me of that Mother Goose rhyme where the old woman wakes from a nap and discovers her skirts were cut off."

"Is that what you're wearing to the tea-dance?" he asked her.

"No, honey, I don't suppose I'll ever again wear it in all my life," she said. "I just hang on to it because it's what I met your grandpa in; stepgrandpa."

"Well, the *color's* nice."

She laughed and turned back to the closet.

It was silly to worry about her appearance. This wasn't a date, for heaven's sake! This was two middle-aged ex-classmates catching up with each other. Having a bite to eat and then, no doubt, parting for good, because the chances were they had nothing at all to talk about anymore.

When she hung the blue dress in its place, a wistful, sweet, lilac scent drifted from its folds. But she supposed it was just the smell of aged fabric. It couldn't be Amy's engagement party, after all these years.

. . .

On Sunday afternoon, NoNo and Barry came back from their honeymoon. NoNo had a toasted look while Barry, who was fairer-skinned, had turned a ruddy pink with a brighter patch across his nose. (They'd borrowed a friend's beach cottage in Ocean City.)

NoNo made a big fuss over Peter, kissing him hello and asking about his weekend, offering him his choice of restaurants for tonight's first meal as a family. Peter dug a toe into the carpet and mumbled that it would be nice to eat at home. NoNo said, "Oh. At home," her forehead cross-hatched with worry because she had never had the slightest talent as a cook. But Barry said, "Great. I'll grill some steaks." Then he and Peter went upstairs for Peter's belongings.

As soon as they were gone, Rebecca said, "I've been meaning to ask you, NoNo. Do you still go to that book club of yours?"

"Mm-hmm," NoNo said. "Why?"

"I was thinking how wonderful that must be, having people to talk with seriously. I wish *I* belonged to something like that. It seems I never get involved in any intellectual conversations anymore."

NoNo was examining her wedding ring, turning her left hand gracefully this way and that.

"So," Rebecca said. "Do you think maybe I could join?"

"Join?" NoNo said. She let her hand drop. "Join my book club? But . . . this is a group of all women. You know?"

"Well, I'm a woman," Rebecca said with a feathery laugh.

"I mean, it's like a, practically group therapy. You wouldn't believe the subjects we get onto, sometimes! Emotional issues, and relationships and such. I just think it would feel awfully funny to have a relative there. I mean *any* relative; my sisters, too, I mean. I'm not trying to be—"

"No, of course not. I wasn't using my head," Rebecca said. "Goodness! That *would* be awkward!"

Then Barry and Peter came clattering down the stairs, and she looked up at them with a big, false smile and asked if they had everything.

It probably wouldn't have been the right kind of book club, anyway. She could talk about emotional issues any old time; it seemed she was always doing that, with every passing repairman.

.   .   .

Monday afternoon at two—the first available appointment— she got her hair washed and set at Martelle's Maison of Beauty, but she came home and shampooed thoroughly under a beating shower because Martelle had been having an off day and gave her a headful of frizz. So she ended up with her usual look: the two beige fans at her temples. She put on a long blue flowered skirt, a lighter-blue tunic from Pakistan dotted around the neckline with tiny mirrors, and dark-blue panty hose to make her ankles look thinner. After checking her reflection she wound a red-and-white paisley scarf several times around her throat, although the temperature was in the eighties. Then she stepped into a pair of red pumps. (She had heard somewhere that men found red shoes provocative.)

Last of all, she blotted her face with powder, brushed her eyelashes with mascara, and applied a coat of lipstick the same shade of red as her shoes. But she wiped most of the lipstick off again, because she decided it made her look garish.

After that she sat down in the rear parlor, since it was only four-thirty and she didn't have to leave until six. She folded her hands in her lap and did nothing, gazing straight ahead and trying to remember not to touch her eyes so that she wouldn't end up looking like a raccoon. From time to time Poppy poked his head in and stared at her, but mercifully, he asked no questions. She had set out a cold supper earlier and told him to eat when he liked. Around five-thirty she heard a chair scrape across the kitchen linoleum, followed by the clinking of cutlery against china, and she thought of going out to keep him company but instead she continued sitting there. For one thing, she felt the need to hang on to her composure. For another, talking to Poppy would wear away what was left of her lipstick.

At ten till six she made one last trip to the bathroom, and then she gave Poppy a wave from the kitchen doorway. "Night-night," she said, taking care to use no words that required pressing her lips together. By now it was 5:55. Recalling her grandchildren's superstition about clocks, she made a wish. She wished for dignity, was all. Just let her get through this evening without appearing foolish. She took her purse from the hall radiator and walked out the front door.

It was a muggy, heavy evening, cloudy but without a hope of rain to cool things off. When she got into her car, a blast of stored-up heat instantly dampened her powder. She started the engine and switched on the air-conditioning, which made her hair fly every which way. All her primping had been for nothing. She gave a despairing glance toward the rearview mirror before she pulled into the street.

Her car was an '84 Chevy, rust-speckled and noisy and given to swaying dizzily on sharp curves. (She was always threatening to turn it into a planter.) It was littered front and back with her grandchildren's odds and ends—their fast-food bags, soft-drink cans, old comic books, and crumpled, graying gym socks. Now she wished she had thought to clean it. She felt a brief flash of resentment: she used to keep her things so nice, before she met up with the Davitches.

At first, the drive was no different from one she might take any day. She passed the same tall, stern old houses, most of them transformed into offices or shops or cheap apartments. She veered south into a stretch of Laundromats, Chinese restaurants, liquor stores, boarded-up grocery stores. Rush hour was practically over, and she slid easily through a series of intersections. She stopped at a red light where a boy was peddling cellophane tubes of single, imprisoned-looking roses. At the next light a cadaverous man in a winter jacket held up a placard saying he was hungry, sick, tired, and sad. A child approached with a dirty rag and a bottle of Windex, but Rebecca shook her head.

Then she was driving through the frayed hem of the city, through a wasteland of broken-paned factories and tarp-covered mountains of tires. No doubt there was some high-speed, multi-lane road to Macadam these days, but she turned onto the old one. The scenery grew more spacious—weedy and brambly and shrubby. She was sorry to find, though, that the rolling pastures of her girlhood had been replaced by housing developments. The developments had an established, dowdy look to them; she could tell they weren't brand-new. Above-ground pools crowded nearly every backyard. A bridge was spray-painted with valentines and *Trust Jesus* and, in childishly crooked letters, *I Still Like Larry.* A long, low, brick elementary school sent a Dreamsicle-colored sunset glaring back from its picture windows.

Just beyond the railroad crossing she turned right, and several miles later she came upon a tasteful black-and-brass sign reading *Macadam*. (In her day there'd been a huge billboard: *ENTER-ING MACADAM, HOME OF MACADAM COLLEGE AND LYON INDUSTRIES, INC. "You Can Rely on Lyon for All Your Janitorial Supplies."*) She passed the eastern edge of the campus—Federal-style brick buildings under large old craggy trees, just as she remembered. The town itself, though, had changed, and not for the better. It seemed scrappier, more chopped up, a hodge-podge of hastily constructed fast-food joints and tattoo parlors and taverns. And Myrtle's (when she found it, after two wrong turns) had become a CD store. Posters for various rock groups filled the window, although the white stucco above it still bore the ghost of the old name where the letters had been pried off.

It felt to her as if a bowling ball had come to rest in the pit of her stomach. Her heartbeat lurched and stammered.

Catty-corner from the CD store was the Maple Tree (neither Oak nor Elm), looking out of place with its richly varnished door and forest-green awning. She parked almost squarely in front of it. First she craned toward the rearview mirror and patted her hair down, checked her lipstick, and arranged her features into more lilt-ing, upward angles. Then she picked up her purse and got out, plucking at the back of her skirt where it seemed glued to her thighs. Her watch read ten minutes till seven; so probably Will wasn't here yet. Still, just in case, she made sure to step light-footedly as she approached the entrance.

Inside, the semi-darkness and the smell of musty carpet com-bined to make her feel that she had walked into a closet of stored woolens. A girl with long blond hair stood waiting with an armful of menus. "*Good* evening!" she trilled.

Rebecca said, "I'm meeting someone, but I don't suppose he's—"

"Would that be him?"

She followed the girl's eyes. In the dimness she could barely make out the dozen or so tables, but she saw that two of them were occupied—one by a dressed-up young couple, the other by a skinny old man. "No," she said.

And then she said, "Oh."

He was sitting by the window, his beaky profile silhouetted against the dark curtain and his hair a radiant cloud of wild white corkscrews. When she started walking toward him (leading the hostess, now, instead of following), he sent her a glance, and she could tell that he was equally uncertain. He hesitated, then half stood, then hesitated again before rising to his full height. "Rebecca?" he said.

She said, "Hello, Will."

She held out her hand, and he took it. (This must surely be the first time they had shaken each other's hand.) His fingers were as knuckly and wiry as ever, but there was a difference in the texture of his skin, a kind of graininess that she saw in his face, too, now that she was close enough—a sandy look to his cheeks, a trio of fine lines straining across his forehead. His lips, which had once been very full and sculptured, were thinner and more sharply defined. He was wearing a wilted suit jacket over an open-necked white shirt—elderly clothes, sagging off his bony frame in a slack and elderly way.

She settled in the chair opposite him, and he sat back down. "What happened to your long golden braid?" he asked her.

She raised a hand to her head. "My . . . ?" she said. "Oh. I cut it off. It was too much trouble to take care of."

A menu arrived on her plate, and another on Will's. The hostess said, "May I tell Marvin what you're having to drink?"

"Who's Marvin?" Will asked.

"Iced tea for me," Rebecca said, although she could have used something stronger.

Will said, "Just water, please."

"Sparkling, or still?"

"Pardon?"

"Tap," Rebecca volunteered. (That much she felt sure of, although the question would not even have been thought of in their dating days.)

As soon as the hostess had left, Will turned back to Rebecca, plainly expecting her to begin the conversation. Instead, she spent some time placing her purse just so on her left, then unfolding her napkin in slow motion and smoothing it across her lap.

Why was she acting so gracious, she wondered—so matronly, so controlled?

It was the way she behaved with strangers. Really, he was a stranger.

But she said, "It's wonderful to see you, Will!"

He blinked. (She may have been a bit loud.) He said, "Yes, me too. For me to see *you*, I mean."

There was a pause.

"And all except for the braid, you look exactly the same," he added.

"Yes, fat as ever!" she said, laughing brightly.

He cleared his throat. She rearranged her napkin.

"I took the Poe Highway over here," she said. "Goodness, things have changed! So many new housing developments, or new to me, at least, and Macadam looks *very* different. I doubt I'd even—"

A young man dressed in black set their drinks in front of them. "So," he said, whipping out a pad and pen. "Decided what you're having?"

Rebecca said, "Not quite yet, thanks," but Will said, "Oh, sorry, wait a minute, let's see, what am I—"

He took a pair of rimless glasses from his breast pocket and hooked them over his ears. (Now he seemed downright ancient. She could draw back from him and imagine that she had never seen him before.) "You go first," he told Rebecca.

She said, "Well, I . . . The salmon, I guess." It was the first thing her eyes landed on.

Will was peering at his menu. "Salmon, veal, rib roast . . ." he said, his index finger traveling down the page. "Ah, maybe the rib roast."

"And how would you like that cooked, sir?" the waiter asked.

"Medium, please. No, better make it well done."

"Well done it is," the waiter said, writing on his pad.

"On second thought," Will told him, "I believe I'll have the Award-Winning Swordfish."

"Swordfish," the waiter said. He scratched out what he'd written.

"But without the Caramelized Onion Sauce," Will said. "Unless . . ." he said. He beetled his snarly white eyebrows. "Would it still be the actual Award-Winning Swordfish if it didn't have the sauce?"

"It wouldn't be the *actual* Award-Winning Swordfish in any case, sir," the waiter said, "because that one was eaten by the judges."

Rebecca laughed, but Will just said, "All right, then, no sauce. And no dressing on the salad." He looked across at her. "I'm trying to watch my cholesterol."

This surprised her at least as much as his having Caller ID. Mentally, she supposed, she had sealed him in amber—imagined him still a college boy wolfing down milk shakes and burgers.

"I'm not used to eating out much," Will told her once the waiter was gone. "Generally I cook at home. I make my famous chili. You remember my chili."

"Oh! Your chili," she said. She did remember, she realized. Or at least she remembered Will chopping onions into tiny, uniform squares, and Mrs. Allenby tut-tutting at the red spatters across her clean stovetop.

"My particular recipe constitutes a completely balanced meal," Will was saying. "I mix up a double batch every Sunday afternoon, and I divide it into seven containers and that's what I eat all week."

"All week?"

"Now I'll have an extra container on hand because of this evening. I'm not sure yet how I'll deal with that."

"But don't you get awfully bored, eating the same meal every night?"

"Not a bit," he said. "Or if I do, what of it? I've never understood this country's phobia about boredom. Why should we be constantly diverted and entertained? I prefer to *sink into* my life, even into the tedious parts. Sometimes I like to sit and just stare into space. I don't require newness just for newness' sake."

"Well . . . you're right, I guess," Rebecca said. "Goodness! *I* don't know why we mind boredom so much."

"I have my lunches in the college cafeteria. Spinach salad and yogurt."

"That sounds extremely healthful," she told him.

The waiter set a basket of breads between them, and Rebecca selected a roll and put it on her bread plate. Then she reached for the butter. The silence was that obvious kind where every gesture becomes important. The slightest turn of her wrist seemed almost to make a noise.

"So," she said finally, "I gather you've adjusted to living on your own, then."

"Yes, I can't complain. I rent a very nice apartment over on Linden Street."

"An apartment," she repeated. (Cancel that image of the tenured-professor's house.)

"In the home of Mrs. Flick. You remember Dr. Flick of the English department, don't you? She started renting out her top floor after he died. I have a good-sized living room, dining room, kitchenette, bedroom, and study. The study can double as a guest room if my daughter ever wants to stay over."

"Oh, Will, you have a daughter?"

"Seventeen years old—a senior in high school. Beatrice, her name is."

Beatrice! Rebecca was struck dumb with admiration. Beatrice would be a female version of Tristram. Rebecca pictured her in a modest muslin dress from the nineteenth century, although she knew that was unlikely. She pictured Beatrice and her father joined in some scholarly endeavor—Beatrice reading aloud while Will nodded soberly in his rocking chair by the fire.

"But that's nothing compared to you," Will was saying.

"Me?"

"You have *four* daughters, you mentioned."

"Oh, yes, I'm way ahead of you!" She took a gulp of iced tea—too big a gulp; she nearly choked. "I've got grandchildren, even! Six. I mean seven. Because my husband's three girls were older, you know; his girls from his previous marriage."

"And how did he happen to pass away? If you don't mind my asking."

His delicate wording, along with the clumsy look of his mouth as he spoke—a sort of crumpled look, as if he had too many teeth—made her feel the need to set him at ease. "He died in a car wreck," she said forthrightly. "It was very sudden. Well, a car wreck is always sudden, of course. But I was so unprepared! And so young! I was twenty-six years old. And his girls had just barely gotten to where they admitted I existed."

"Couldn't you have sent them to their relatives? They must have had some, someplace."

"Well, only their mother."

"Their mother!" Will said.

"But she'd remarried; she lived in England. Sending the children to her would . . . In fact, the subject never came up."

Will shook his head. "Personally," he said, "I would find that situation intolerable."

This hurt her feelings, for some reason. She knew he meant to sympathize, but she couldn't help imagining a note of judgment in his voice. She said, "Everything ended up fine, though! Just fine! I've managed very well. I run a little business out of my home, hosting parties. Joe started that—my husband. And the girls are all grown up now. You should meet them! It's this huge, big, jumbled family; nothing like what you and I were used to when we were children. Oh, isn't it amazing, how life turns out? Could you have imagined we'd be sitting here, waiting for swordfish and salmon, back when we were eating pancakes at Myrtle's Family Restaurant?"

On cue, the waiter set their plates in front of them—Will's swordfish starkly naked, Rebecca's salmon buried beneath a conglomeration of capers, mushrooms, sun-dried tomatoes, black and green olives, and pine nuts. Two salads arrived, Rebecca's smothered in blue cheese dressing. "Fresh-ground pepper?" the waiter asked, brandishing what looked like a mammoth chess piece. Will shook his head. To make up for him, Rebecca said, "Yes, please!" even though she was longing for the two of them to be left alone. One twist of the grinder and she said, "Okay! Thanks!" Finally, the waiter walked off.

"Where was I? Myrtle's Family Restaurant," Rebecca said. She speared an olive. "Oh, doesn't it seem long ago? But of course, it *was* long ago. And yet, in another way . . . I can remember just like yesterday that time in ninth grade when we went to the drive-in movie. I had such a crush on you, and you thought we were just friends. You thought I was only this kid you'd gone to nursery school with."

The olive had a pit, she discovered as she bit down. She removed it with a thumb and forefinger and hid it under her roll. Luckily, Will's eyes were on his plate and he didn't seem to notice.

"A bunch of us went to the movies," she said, "in Ben Biddix's older brother's pickup truck. Remember? Ben paid his brother five dollars to take us since none of us could drive yet. And we all sat out on that grassy spot down in front of the screen—do you remember this?"

Will shook his head.

"It was you and me and the Nolan twins and Ben and his brother and Nita Soames, who was going out with Ben's brother at the time. In fact I think she eventually married him. The night was really clear and warm with a balmy breeze, a kind of *promising* breeze, you know that kind? You were sitting next to me and I put my hand down flat in the grass, hoping to seem nonchalant, and then I inched it a little closer to your hand and waited, and then a little closer; so finally just the sides of our hands were barely touching, or maybe not even touching but warming each other, sort of—"

"You broke my heart," Will said.

All this time he'd gone on gazing at his plate, keeping his face so impassive that she wasn't sure he was listening. And she wasn't sure even now, because there she was, magically transported to that starlit evening in 1960 when everything was poised to begin, and meanwhile he had leapt forward to the very end of the story. She set down her fork. The olive was sitting high in her throat like a thick, heavy stone.

"You never gave me the slightest warning," Will said. He took hold of both sides of the table. "I thought everything was fine. I trusted you. Then one day you said goodbye and walked out, not a word about why. Got married two weeks later. I had to hear it from my mother. 'Did you know about this person?' she asked me. 'He must have been in the picture for quite some time,' she told me. 'Rebecca can't have been dating him only two weeks, I shouldn't think.'"

As he spoke, he leaned toward her until he was hugging the table between his sprawling arms. It made Rebecca see, at long last, that this really was Will Allenby—a lanky, big-eared giraffe of a boy who never had quite learned how to manage his own limbs. Those were his startling eyes, whose clear blue light she only now detected underneath the shelter of his thatched brows. And his wide, sharp shoulders, and his boxy Adam's apple bobbing in his neck. Looking at him was like looking at changeable taffeta—back and forth between the generic old man and the specific young Will. Which made it all the worse that he sounded so bitter.

She said, "Will. I'm sorry. I know I didn't treat you well. But it wasn't anything I planned! I was just . . . overwhelmed! Swept off my feet by a fully grown man, someone who already had his life in order, was already *living* his life, while you and I were still . . . but I never meant to hurt you. I hope you can believe that."

The waiter said, "Is everything to your liking, folks?"

"Yes, delicious," Rebecca said. "Then afterwards," she told Will, "after I was married and settled, I know I should have written or something. Offered more of an explanation. But everything started moving so fast! Everything was so chaotic! I had the three little girls to take care of and more and more of the business falling on my shoulders; I was living in that crowded house with my ailing mother-in-law and an uncle-in-law in mourning and a very adolescent brother-in-law; and then my own baby came along. There wasn't a moment to think, even, let alone write you a letter! It seemed I got onto a whole different path, got farther and farther away from my original self. But just this summer I sort of . . . woke up. I looked around me; I said, Who have I turned into? What's become of me? Why am I behaving like this? I'm an impostor in my own life! Or another way I could put it is, it's *not* my own life. It's somebody else's. And that's the reason I phoned you."

Will straightened slowly in his seat until he was upright again. He said, "I guess you thought you could waltz on back as if you'd never left."

"I didn't think that!"

"You thought I'd say, 'Oh, sure, Rebecca, I forgive you. I've forgotten all about what you did. Let's go back to the old days.'"

"I never thought any such thing," she said.

But she had, in fact. Secretly, she had fantasized that he might say he'd never stopped loving her. Now that seemed conceited, and self-deluding, and shameful.

She slid back her chair and stood up in a rush, bruising both of her thighs against the underside of the table. "Sorry," she told him. "I can see this has been a mistake."

She collected her purse and walked out. He didn't try to stop her.

. . .

All the way home she talked to herself, and shook her head, and blinked back angry tears. "How could I have been so stupid?" she asked. "So outspoken? So forward?" She turned the air-conditioning higher. Her face was filmed with a layer of sweat as slick and tight as shrink-wrap. "But why did he say he'd meet me, if that was the way he felt? Why did he phone me back, even? Oh," she wailed, "and I should have paid half of the dinner check!" She risked a glance toward the rearview mirror. She decided that her two fans of hair made her look like a Texas longhorn.

Baltimore was solid and familiar and reassuring, its buildings twinkling with safety lights. She rolled her window down and breathed in the sooty petroleum smell, which struck her as refreshing. And the windows of the Open Arms, when she pulled up, glowed so kindly. She parked and unfolded herself from the car. Her skirt was as wrinkled as wastepaper. The colors of her outfit—red, white, and blue, for Lord's sake!—reminded her of that cheap disposable picnic ware intended for the Fourth of July.

She climbed the front steps and unlocked the door. "I'm home!" she called.

"Hah?" Poppy said from upstairs. She heard laughter on the TV—a sound that ordinarily grated against her nerves, but tonight she found it cozy.

She went straight to the kitchen and set down her purse and looked for something to eat. Standing in front of the open fridge, she devoured two chicken legs, the last of a pasta salad, and several cherry tomatoes. She polished off a container of coleslaw and half a jar of crab-apple rings left over from Thanksgiving. She was so hungry she felt hollow. It seemed no amount of food could ever fill her.

Early on the last Wednesday morning in August, Joey and Lateesha rang Rebecca's doorbell. Lateesha was carrying the pink crib pillow she never slept without, and both children wore knapsacks. Behind them stood Hakim—a considerable distance behind, all the way out on the curb, almost back in his car already. "I take Min Foo to the hospital!" he shouted. "The pains are five minutes apart!"

"All right! Good luck!" Rebecca said, and she blew a kiss to Min Foo. "Just remind yourself, sweetheart, you're going to get a baby out of this!"

Min Foo said, "What? Well, *yes*. The kids haven't had breakfast yet, Mom."

"I'll see to it," Rebecca promised, laying an arm around each child.

As soon as the car had driven off, she led the children upstairs to the third-floor guest room. "Isn't this exciting?" she asked as she helped Lateesha shuck her knapsack. "By lunchtime, I bet, you'll have a brand-new brother or sister!"

They didn't seem all that thrilled. They had the bleary, befuddled look of sleepers awakened too suddenly, and they followed her back down to the kitchen in a shuffling silence. When she set out toast and jam, Lateesha's eyes filled with tears. "The jam's got dots!" she said. "It's got dots that will stick in my teeth!"

"Those are raspberry seeds, dummy," Joey said.

"Joey called me a dummy!"

"Now, now," Rebecca said. "Never mind; I'll find you some nice grape jelly."

Then Poppy came down wanting *his* breakfast, and he needed the situation explained to him several times. "Min Foo's having a baby? I thought she was divorced," he said.

"She was, Poppy, but then she married Hakim, remember?"

"Hakim! Good glory, not another black man!"

"No, Poppy, he's Arab. What a way to talk," Rebecca said, sending a glance toward Lateesha. But Lateesha was absorbed in spreading grape jelly precisely to the edges of her toast, and she seemed oblivious.

After breakfast, Rebecca made up the two beds in the guest room and propped Lateesha's pink pillow against one headboard. This had probably once been a servant's room. It was small and stuffy, with an oppressively low ceiling and a single narrow window. In one corner stood a dark wooden bookcase crammed with curling paperbacks, faded textbooks from the girls' school days, and the histories and biographies that Rebecca used to read in college. She used to get crushes, almost, on people like Mahatma Gandhi and Abraham Lincoln. She would study them in depth, try to learn every detail of their lives in much the same way that her roommate studied the lives of movie stars.

And she had once been so political! She had picketed the Macadam cafeteria on behalf of its underpaid workers; she had marched against the war in Vietnam; she had plastered the door of her dorm room with anti-nuclear stickers. Now she could barely bring herself to vote. All she read in the newspaper was Ann Landers and her horoscope. Her eyes slid over Kosovo and Rwanda and hurried on.

It occurred to her that so far, the only step she'd taken toward retrieving that old Rebecca was to try and reconnect with the old

Rebecca's boyfriend. Like some fluff-headed girl from the fifties, she had assumed she would reach her goal by riding a man's coattails.

Just as well that she had failed, she told herself. (Although still, more than two weeks later, the memory of her dinner with Will continued to pinch her pride.)

The telephone rang and she flew downstairs, calling, "Get that, somebody! Answer the phone!" because she thought it might be Hakim. But it was only the man from Second Eden, arranging to come replace the dead azaleas in the backyard. "Now, I don't want to do it quite yet," he said, "because it's still kind of warm. Could turn downright hot again, even, and I always advise waiting till—"

"My daughter's having a baby; could you get off the line?" she said.

"Oh! Sorry."

"Not that I mean to be rude," she said, instantly feeling guilty. "It's just, you know how it is when one of your children—"

"Ma'am. Believe me. *My* daughter had twins. Me and my wife sat in that waiting room twenty-one hours."

"Twenty-one hours!"

"The nurses kept saying, 'You-all might want to go home and come back,' but we said, 'No, sir. No, indeed. No way, José. Not on your life,' we said, and it got to be suppertime, got to be dark, got to be the next morning—"

"I have to get off the line," Rebecca told him. She hung up, and then felt guilty all over again.

It seemed she always developed a stomachache when one of the girls was in labor. Unconsciously, she would spend the duration holding in her abdominal muscles. It made her wonder how the nurses in delivery rooms survived.

As luck would have it, no party had been scheduled for that evening. The Open Arms was going through a slow spell. But to keep the children amused, she hauled out all the candleholders and set them on the dining-room table. Then she unloaded a mammoth shopping bag of fresh candles. "Put in any color you like," she said. "After that you can light them for a minute, just so they'll lose that new look. Only while I'm in the room, though; you understand?"

She watched Joey choose a taper striped red and white like a barber pole—a bit Christmassy, but never mind. She said, "Now that fall's on the way, we can start using candles at parties again. I always hate to give them up over the summer, but it's true they have a sort of warming effect psychologically, even if they don't produce that much actual heat."

The telephone in the kitchen bleeped once and fell silent. Rebecca paused for several seconds, but no rings followed.

"When I was a little girl," she went on, "my Aunt Ida gave me this beautiful, tall white candle with a kind of frill of white lace running up it in a spiral. I thought it was the most elegant thing I'd ever seen in my life. I saved it in my bureau drawer for some momentous event, although I can't imagine now what that would have been. I mean, I was only eight years old. Not a whole lot of momentous events happen when you're eight. And Aunt Ida would ask me, now and then, 'Have you ever burned that candle?' I'd say, 'No, not yet. I'm saving it,' I'd say. Then one day, oh, maybe three or four years later, I came across it in my drawer. It had turned all yellow and warped; it was practically a C shape, and the lace was coming off in crumbles. I'd never seen it burning, and now I never would. So ever since that time, I light my candles any chance I get. I light them by the dozens, all over every room, at every party from September through May. *Multitudes* of candles."

She handed each child a box of matches, and they started lighting the candles that marched the length of the table—tapers and pillars and votive lights, white and colored and striped and gilded, blazing in the dim room like a skyful of stars.

. . .

It was after one o'clock when Hakim finally called. "I have a son!" he said. "He is huge: eight pounds ten ounces. Is looking just like me. Min Foo is feeling fine and sending all her love."

"What's his name?" Rebecca asked.

"We have no name. NoNo said that it would only be a girl."

"Oh. Right," Rebecca said.

She let the children telephone their aunts and all their friends to spread the news, and after that she hauled out her decorating supplies and the three of them made a poster reading *WELCOME HOME, MOM AND LITTLE BROTHER*. Then Poppy came down from his nap and they all drank a ginger-ale toast in Mother Davitch's sherbet glasses. Poppy seemed to have the impression that the baby was Rebecca's, but he got that straightened out in due course.

When Hakim called again, in the late afternoon, Rebecca drove the children to the hospital for a visit. "You two are lucky," she told them on the way. "It used to be they wouldn't let children visit before they were twelve. Your aunts didn't see your mother till I brought her home from the hospital."

Hard to believe that had been thirty-two years ago. To Rebecca, it seemed as vivid as last week: the nearly imperceptible weight of that tiny body, the warmth of that downy head nestling in the crook of her neck as she climbed the front steps, and the three little girls in the doorway, goggle-eyed and awed, reaching out reverently to touch the baby's foot.

When she was handed her new grandson in the hospital room—another modern development, no plate-glass window between them—she had a moment of confusion where it seemed he was Min Foo. He had Min Foo's paintbrush hair and caraway-seed eyes, and he peered curiously up at Rebecca as if he thought he might know her from somewhere. "Look," she told the children. "He's saying, 'Who are *you?* What kind of people have I ended up with, here? How am I going to like living on this planet?'"

She hoped they didn't notice the ridiculous break in her voice.

. . .

When they got home again, bringing carry-out chicken and French fries for supper, they found Poppy playing solitaire on the coffee table in the front parlor. "I couldn't stand it up in the family room," he told them, "because that telephone kept ringing, ringing, ringing. Durn thing nearly rang my ear off."

"Did you answer it?" Rebecca asked.

"No," he said, "I let them leave a message. Yammer, yammer away on that benighted machine of yours."

But when she went upstairs to check, she found only three messages. "Well, this here's Alice Farmer," was the first. "I know you don't plan on no parties this weekend but I want to come in anyhow because I need the money. My brother's girl Berenice is turning twenty. You remember Berenice, who's afflicted with eating disorder . . ." Then she sort of wandered off, still talking but growing fainter.

The second message was a long pause and a click.

The third, recorded one minute after the second, was, "Rebecca, um, it's Will."

She drew back sharply.

"I was just afraid you might have gotten the wrong idea," he said. "I don't know why you felt you had to rush off like that. You didn't even eat your salmon! The waiter asked if anything was wrong. I'm afraid you might have misunderstood me. Could you please call me back, please?"

She frowned at the machine for a moment. Then she pressed the Delete button.

. . .

Thursday morning she took the children to the zoo, where they spent some time commiserating with the dusty, panting lions. From there they went to the hospital. The baby was off getting circumcised, with Hakim (a cardiologist) watching from the sidelines and no doubt wringing his hands, and Min Foo was sitting up in bed doing a crossword puzzle; so Rebecca took a short walk in order to give the children a private visit with their mother. She stopped at the nursery window, where rows of infants lay in their cots like little wrapped burritos, and then she went back to the room. The baby had returned in a state of outrage and was being soothed and cooed over. Lateesha was sucking her thumb, which she hadn't done in some time. Rebecca suggested to the children that they go home and have a picnic lunch in the backyard.

In the afternoon LaVon came by, Lateesha's father, and carried the children off to watch his jazz band practice. (He was actually a fourth-grade teacher, but he had hopes of someday becoming a professional musician.) When he brought them back he stayed for Thursday-night supper; so Rebecca thought of his appearance as sort of a mixed blessing. Not that she wasn't pleased to see him. He was a funny, charming, high-spirited young man, inclined toward African-print shirts and wild hairdos, so full of energy that he all but danced even when he was standing still. But Hakim was at supper too, and he tended to act somewhat bristly around his predecessor. Also, Min Foo would hear about this and throw a fit. "Why are you so nice to LaVon?" she'd be bound to ask. "Don't you understand that he's out of the picture now?" To which Rebecca would answer, "I can't turn my feelings off like a faucet, honey, every time you choose to dump another husband."

Although she did turn her feelings *on*, in a way, because she had always sworn that she would welcome newcomers to the family. She had promised herself that, Aunt Ida–like, she would declare her door to be permanently ajar, and she had kept her promise so faithfully that now she couldn't say for certain whether she truly loved her sons-in-law or merely thought she did.

Anyhow, what difference did it make? They were good husbands, all of them—including Troy, the non-husband. Good husbands and good fathers. (Well, maybe except for Joey's father, the antique Professor Drake, who had moved to some Greek island after his banishment and ceased all communication.) She smiled now to see how comfortably LaVon tipped back in his chair as he argued some musical issue with Troy, who taught theory at the Peabody Conservatory. Poppy was interrupting to say that nothing remotely worth listening to had been written after 1820. "My favorite composer is Haydn," he said. "It's true I used to think he was sort of music-boxy, but that was before I went to a concert and heard him play in person."

"In . . . what?" LaVon asked, not having been exposed lately to Poppy and his lapses.

Rebecca hastened to tinkle a fork against her iced-tea glass. "Okay, everybody!" she said. "Time to propose a toast to Abdul!"

That was the name the parents had finally chosen for the new baby: Abdul Abdulazim. Rebecca liked pronouncing it. "To Abdul Abdulazim!" she said now. "His arrival makes us beam." Abdul's father, Hakim Abdulazim (whose name was even more fun to pronounce) sat up straighter and raised his chin proudly. "It's such a pleasure to have a new boy," Rebecca chanted, "Let's hope he's as nice as Lateesha and Joey!"

Hakim lifted his glass, and so did the two children, but the others just murmured, "Cheers," and went on with their conversations. They heard so many toasts, after all. Rebecca could sympathize. It seemed she was constantly mustering enthusiasm for her family's engagements and weddings and births, their children's straight A's and starring roles and graduations. Sometimes, for lack of any other reason, she proposed a toast to Thursday. "To Thursday once again, and so many of us together! To good food and good talk, and lovely summer weather!" (Or spring weather, or fall, or winter weather.) And that was not even counting all those professional events—her clients' Christmases and New Years, their business promotions and mergers and retirements, their everlasting anniversaries and confirmations and bar mitzvahs and bridal showers.

Well. She squared her shoulders and turned to Hakim. "Now, about the baby-welcoming," she said.

He looked worried. "This is what?" he asked.

"The party we give our new babies. It's kind of a Davitch tradition," she told him. "The idea came from one time when I was waiting for one of the girls at the airport and I saw this huge, happy, noisy crowd carrying balloons and placards and video cameras and regular cameras and flowers and wrapped gifts, and then the plane landed and a woman walked in with a tiny little button of a baby,

Korean I think or Chinese, and the crowd started cheering and this couple stepped forward and the wife held out her arms and the woman gave her the baby and . . . I've always felt sort of cheated that we haven't had any adoptions in our family. Adoption is more sudden than pregnancy, don't you think? It's more dramatic. So I said, 'Why don't we welcome *our* babies like that?' And that's what we've done ever since."

Hakim blinked. Rebecca wondered, sometimes, exactly how good his English was. "Well, anyhow," she said, "all I need from you two is a date. We can do it this weekend, if you like. The Open Arms isn't booked. Or would you prefer just a Thursday? A normal family Thursday?"

"I will ask Min Foo," he said. But he still looked worried.

It wasn't a huge gathering tonight—just nine around the table. As usual, Troy and Biddy and Zeb were present—Biddy because she used Thursdays to experiment with new recipes, and Zeb because (Rebecca suspected) this was his only chance for a home-cooked meal. He would go home laden down with leftovers, she always made certain. It used to be that NoNo had been a regular too, but since the wedding they'd hardly seen her. Well, that was as it should be, of course. She was establishing her own traditions now.

Last week, NoNo had phoned Rebecca and asked how people formed car pools. Peter's school was due to reopen and she would be in charge of his transportation. "Do I put an ad in the paper?" she'd asked. "Tack a note to a bulletin board? Or what?"

"You get hold of the school directory . . ." Rebecca began. She spoke slowly; she was trying to cast her mind back. "You look up all the students who live near you . . ."

"I asked Peter who lived near us and he said he didn't think anyone. But I'm not sure he knows. It doesn't seem to me that he has any friends."

"None at all?" Rebecca said.

"Well, he never gets any phone calls, at least."

"Maybe boys just *don't* phone," Rebecca told her.

"Oh, you're right; maybe they don't."

"It's not as if you or I have had much experience with boys."

"You're right," NoNo said again, and her voice turned thin and quavery. "I'm really not equipped for this, you know?"

"Oh, sweetheart, you'll do fine," Rebecca had said. "Don't worry for an instant. Just call Patch or Min Foo and ask *them* about car pools, why don't you."

Now she leaned across the table to Joey. "Joey," she said, "do you ever talk on the phone?"

"I talk with you, Gram."

"With your friends, I mean. Do you ever get on the phone and talk with them in the evening?"

"Well, sure, if I need to know about a homework assignment or something."

"But not just to talk for no reason."

"No reason! Then why would I call?"

"Aha," Rebecca said. She told Zeb, "NoNo thinks Peter doesn't have any friends because nobody ever phones him."

"He'll be okay. Just give him time," Zeb said. Which was probably what he told every parent who walked into his office, Rebecca reflected. He was helping Lateesha cut her pork chop, and he didn't even look up as he spoke.

"This spinach dish—" Biddy was announcing. "Could I have people's attention, please? This spinach dish contains a tiny bit of nutmeg, but the point is that you're not supposed to taste it. It's only meant to enhance the flavor of the spinach. Does anyone taste any nutmeg?"

Hard to tell, for as usual, the others were too busy arguing and interrupting each other. "*I* think it's delicious," Rebecca told her.

But Biddy said, "I don't know why I bother making the effort," just as if no one had spoken. She snatched up the spinach dish and marched back to the kitchen.

Rebecca looked down at her plate for a second, and when she looked up again she found Zeb watching her. He said, "It's just that you always say things are delicious. She didn't mean any harm."

"Well, I know that," Rebecca said.

Then she said, "More pork chops, anyone? Who'd like another pork chop?" and the moment passed.

. . .

On Friday Min Foo and the baby went home, and Rebecca dropped the two children off along with a bag of groceries. From there she drove directly to a bookstore. "Do you have any books on Robert E. Lee?" she asked a salesclerk.

"Try Biography, over by the window."

"Thank you."

She crossed the store, pausing once or twice when something in another section caught her eye—a children's book on ballet, which was Merrie's current passion, and a collection of Holy Land photos that would make a very good birthday present for Alice Farmer. In Biography she found three books about Lee, one of them a paperback. She plucked that from the shelf and studied the portrait on the cover: Lee's square-cut beard and disappointed gaze. He wasn't someone she particularly admired. It was only that he represented the first and last extensive scholarly research she had ever undertaken. She had barely assembled her reference materials, was just starting to feel caught up in the project, when Joe Davitch walked into her life. Now the sight of Lee's face brought back a swarm of memories: the musty smell of the Macadam College library; the sweetly rounded o's of her history professor, who came from Minnesota; and the thrilling crispness of brand-new textbooks and spiral-bound notebooks purchased from the school store.

A couple of feet away, a severe-looking woman with a tight bun of white hair selected a hardback and showed it to a girl in a miniskirt—her granddaughter, most likely. "Now, this would be a good choice," she said. "The life of Charles Lindbergh."

"But it's, like, humongous," the granddaughter said. "I'd totally never finish it before the start of classes."

The woman somehow managed to grow taller as she stood there. "May I inquire," she said icily, "what kind of voice that is you're using?"

Rebecca knew exactly what kind of voice it was. She'd heard Dixon call it a surfer-girl voice. (Though why it should be needed in Baltimore, Maryland, and how that shallow, breathy tone could be advantageous—did it carry more easily over the sound of the waves, or what?—she couldn't say.) But the granddaughter didn't seem to have heard. "And besides," she went on, "he's, like, a guy. Guys' biographies suck."

"I *beg* your pardon," the woman said, growing even taller.

"Well. Sorry, Grandma," the girl said meekly.

The woman sniffed and replaced the book on the shelf.

Rebecca was impressed. Imagine having such authority! She herself might have drifted into a string of *likes* and *totally*s right along with the granddaughter, hardly noticing what she was doing. She had no sense of definition, was the problem. No wonder she'd ended up a whole different person!

She bought not only the Lee paperback but the two hardbacks as well, although she couldn't afford them. When she set them on the counter, the salesclerk asked, "Will that be all?" and Rebecca said, "Yes. It will," in a firm, declarative manner that (she realized too late) exactly duplicated the white-haired woman's.

. . .

Some days were telephone days and other days were not. Did it work that way for everyone? Some days Rebecca's phone rang non-stop, one caller tumbling over the heels of another, and other days you wouldn't know she owned a phone.

On this particular afternoon the painter called; then the dentist's office; then the man who inspected the furnace. Poppy's physical therapist wanted to reschedule. Patch wanted to complain about Jeep. Min Foo wanted to list possible dates for the baby-welcoming.

A Mrs. Allen called to arrange for her husband's fiftieth-birthday party. "This would be, oh, maybe sixty guests," she said. "Or sixty-five. Let's play it safe and say seventy."

Rebecca wondered why people couldn't figure these things out before they got on the line. But she said, "Seventy. All right."

"It's going to be a surprise."

"Really," Rebecca said.

She should have let that go, but in all good conscience, she

couldn't. "If you want my honest opinion," she said, "surprise parties are guaranteed disasters. Is what *I* would call them."

This made the plumber, flat on his back beneath the kitchen
sink, snort and mutter, "Amen to that!" But Mrs. Allen was unde-
terred. "I'm thinking just drinks and canapés," she went on blithely.
"Sit-down dinners are so stuffy, don't you agree?"

The Open Arms could not have managed a sit-down dinner for
seventy; so Rebecca certainly did agree. They settled on the date
and the deposit fee, after which she prepared to say goodbye, but
Mrs. Allen moved on next to the subject of her husband's midlife
crisis. (His decision to try a hair transplant, his drastic weight-loss
diet, his purchase of a sixteen-hundred-dollar set of golf clubs
although that was cheaper, she supposed, than taking up with some
dolly half his age.) Rebecca tiptoed across the kitchen, stretching
the telephone cord to its limit, and turned the timer dial on the
stove till it started dinging. "Oops! Gotta go!" she cried, and she
hung up. "Some people think the phone is some kind of . . .
hobby," she told the plumber.

He said, "You ought to check out *my* house. You know my
daughter? Felicia?" Then the phone rang again.

Rebecca sighed and reached for the receiver. "Hello," she said.

Will Allenby said, "Rebecca?"

She said, "Oh."

"Don't hang up!"

"I wasn't going to hang up," she told him.

Although a part of her would have liked to. It was only curiosity
that stopped her.

He said, "I just wanted to apologize for the other evening."

"That's quite all right," she said stiffly.

"I never meant for the conversation to go that way, believe me. I
don't know how it happened."

The odd thing was, the apology made her feel humiliated all
over again. But she said, "Really, don't give it a thought. I've forgotten it completely. Thanks for calling, though."

"Wait!"

She waited.

"Please," he said. "Could we just talk a little bit? Could you just listen?"

"Well," she said, "all right. I guess so."

"I seem to be in . . . something of a sorry state, Rebecca. Lately it's been all I can do just to get up in the morning. I get up; I look in the mirror; I think, Oh, God, it's the same old, same old me, and I want to crawl back into bed and stay there forever."

Rebecca held very still, as if he could observe how attentively she was listening.

He said, "The fact of the matter is, the divorce was my wife's idea, not mine. I'm not even sure what went wrong there! One day she just announced that she wanted me to move out. And of course she kept our daughter with her. I can understand that; what do I know about teenaged girls? But we both agreed that I'd still have lots of contact. I would see my daughter regularly, any day I liked, back and forth between our two places. Now whenever I phone, though, Beatrice is busy. I ask her to come for supper and she says she's got a friend over, or she's made other plans. She never has any time to get together."

"Well, she's seventeen!" Rebecca said. "Of course she doesn't have time."

"I tell her to bring the friend along and she says her friend wouldn't feel comfortable in my apartment."

"You know how teenagers are. They're constitutionally ashamed of their parents. It isn't personal."

"No," Will said, "there's more to it than that. I can't explain it. It seems I'm just . . . destined not to have anyone in my life. Here I am, all alone in this old lady's dead-quiet house, and it feels so natural; that's the worst of it. It feels like my natural state. What did you expect? I ask myself. Did you imagine someone would actually want to stay with you forever? You should thank your lucky stars you ever got married at all. It's as if I'm lacking some talent that everyone else takes for granted."

"Now, Will, you're just plain wrong about that," Rebecca said.

"Okay," he said. "Then tell me."

"Tell you what?"

"Tell me why you broke up with me."

"We've been through that! When Joe Davitch came along—"

"No, I want the real reason. I want you to be honest."

"I *am* being honest!" she said.

"Don't insult my intelligence, Rebecca."

She felt stung. She said, "I can see this is going nowhere; so I'm going to hang up now. Goodbye."

And without waiting for his answer, she put the receiver back on the hook.

The plumber was packing his tools away more noisily than seemed necessary, with lots of clanks and rattles and many exaggerated grunts as he reached for various wrenches. She suspected he felt embarrassed for her. "What a nuisance!" she said gaily. "These people who stay on the phone forever; I just never know how to get off, do you?"

The plumber said, "Sort of persistent type, was he?"

Then he cocked his head at her and waited, looking expectant, but Rebecca just said, "Right," and asked if he'd fixed the leak.

She wished she hadn't ended the call so abruptly. She was beginning to get that awful torn feeling she always had after saying something hurtful to somebody.

For the rest of the afternoon the telephone was silent, but at suppertime, there was the usual flurry of telemarketers. Also another call from the Second Eden man. "Those azaleas I told you we had, they're a teensy bit off from the color I said. They're more like a, what would you say, not a pink, not a red, not orange—"

"I couldn't care less what color they are. Any color. Fine," she said, and she hung up and returned to the table. "If I could undo one modern invention," she told Poppy, "I believe it would be the telephone."

"Why, I would choose the zipper," he said.

Rebecca stared at him a moment, but before she could pursue the subject, the telephone rang again. Mrs. Allen had forgotten to mention that her husband didn't eat red meat. Then a moment later, she called back: he didn't eat chicken, either.

"Why don't you let that machine of yours pick up?" Poppy asked Rebecca.

A reasonable enough question. She didn't tell him that she kept thinking each call might be Will Allenby.

The evening seemed to be the time for wrong numbers. Three different people phoned by mistake, one of them several times in succession—a Slavic-sounding woman who wanted to argue the issue. "Wrong number! No! This is not wrong number! I telephone my daughter! Bring her on!"

At nine o'clock, Rebecca went off to bed with one of her Robert E. Lee books. It began with Lee's genealogy, which she found dull. She made herself continue, though. The thought came to her (on a whole separate track in her brain, while the first track continued cataloguing Lee's great-grandparents) that over the years, she had gradually given up reading anything difficult. Even a newspaper article, the briefest little piece: if the first line didn't grab her, she turned the page. It was something like her attitude toward exercise. Whenever she grew the least bit tired or out of breath, she quit. "I figure my body's trying to tell me something," she would say jokingly to Patch. (For invariably, it was Patch who urged her into these fitness efforts.) "If it's sending me such a clear message, how can I ignore it?"

When Lee's great-grandparents gave way to his grandparents, she put down her book and phoned Zeb. "What are you doing?" she asked when he answered.

"I'm reading about the harmful effects of night-lights."

"Night-lights!"

"Evidently, children who've been raised with night-lights in their rooms end up having vision problems. Their eyes don't get enough rest, is the hypothesis."

"Or maybe," Rebecca said, "the children didn't see well to begin with, and there's some biological connection between fear of the dark and bad eyesight; ever thought of that?"

"Hmm."

"Maybe their bad eyesight *caused* their fear of the dark. The chair that looks like a monster, for instance."

"This subject appears to have really gripped your imagination," Zeb told her.

"Yes, well . . ."

She glanced at her clock radio. It was almost 10 p.m. Anybody phoning this late would think, *Who can she be talking to?*

She must be so popular! he would think.

"I've been making some resolutions," she told Zeb. "From now on, I'm reading two books a week, serious books that I have to work at. Also, I'm joining a gym. I plan to get into shape, for once."

"Now, what would you want to do that for? You're fine the way you are."

"No, I'm not! I'm a slug. You of all people, a doctor . . . Or maybe I should take up jogging. That would be less expensive. Except jogging's affected by weather. Half the time the weather would be too hot, or it would be raining. I would feel so conspicuous, jogging with an umbrella."

"Rebecca. Joggers don't carry umbrellas."

"How do they stay dry, then?" she asked him. But she was just being silly now, trying to get him to laugh.

After they said goodbye, she instantly sobered. The torn feeling seemed to have grown more pronounced, spreading its ragged edges deep inside her. She sat upright against her pillows and fixed her gaze on the phone. But no one else called.

.   .   .

The time that was finally settled on for the baby-welcoming was Labor Day. Another picnic lunch on the North Fork River, was the plan, except that Hurricane Dennis moved through the area over the weekend and they changed it to an indoor event.

The general theme turned out to be medical emergencies. First Joey was stung by a bee that had somehow found its way into the front parlor, and he had to be rushed off for a shot because he was allergic. Min Foo and Hakim, of course, were the ones who took him, along with the guest of honor since Min Foo was breast-feeding. This made the whole occasion sort of pointless. (Although still the Open Arms was a seething mass of Davitches, quarreling and laughing and shouting above the racket, children chasing each other around the dining-room table, Biddy pressing food on people, Troy and Jeep exchanging hair-raising childbirth stories.) Then Patch's youngest two got into some kind of shoving match—not a very serious one, but Merrie bruised her crazy bone and had to be carried off, howling, to the kitchen for ice. "It wasn't *my* fault," Danny said. "She's the one who was acting so damn piggish."

Rebecca tried to grow taller. "I *beg* your pardon," she said.

Danny, raising his voice, said, "It wasn't *my* fault; she's the one who was acting so damn piggish!"

Rebecca briefly closed her eyes. She opened them to find Poppy standing in front of her, swaying slightly. "Beck," he said, "I don't feel so good."

"What's the matter?"

"I've got this pain."

"Where?" she asked.

"Here," he said, and he clutched a handful of his shirtfront.

His face, she saw now, was a grayish white. All his features seemed to have sharpened. "Sit down," she told him. "Zeb? Where's Zeb? Somebody get Zeb! Hurry!"

She was leading Poppy toward the sofa as she spoke, half supporting him, noticing how alarmingly lightweight he was. She thought that he was trembling; then she thought it might be she who was trembling. He, in fact, seemed curiously calm, and made a point of positioning his cane just so along the inside edge of the sofa before he lay down. He laced his fingers across his diaphragm and closed his eyes. Rebecca said, "Zeb?"

"Zeb went with Joey and them," a child offered.

"He did?"

"In case Joey needed first aid on the way."

"Call an ambulance," Rebecca ordered. "Poppy? Is the pain, let's see, radiating down your left arm?"

He thought it over. "It could be," he said.

"Somebody call an ambulance!"

Then there was the question of who would go along. Half a

dozen people offered, including Danny, who wanted to see what an ambulance ride was like, and Alice Farmer, who felt that Poppy needed her prayers. "Beck would be enough," Poppy said with his eyes still closed. "I don't believe I care for a lot of clucking and wailing." His lids were like bits of waxed paper that had been crumpled and then smoothed out.

Rebecca rushed off for her purse and Poppy's Medicare card. His room, with its smell of cough drops and stale clothing, the bedspread drawn clumsily over the pillow, seemed emptier than was natural. She snatched his billfold from the bureau and hurried downstairs.

Two ambulance men were already loading Poppy onto a stretcher. They had arrived without sirens, or maybe she just hadn't heard them over the hubbub. (Everyone seemed to be issuing orders, and a couple of children were crying.) "What's the matter with him?" she asked the men. "Is he going to be all right?" They brushed past her with the stretcher and she trotted close behind, clasping Poppy's frail ankle beneath the blanket until they reached the front door and she had to let go. Luckily it wasn't raining at the moment, although the sidewalks were wet and everyone had to step carefully.

Inside the ambulance, which was crammed with a reassuring array of dials and gauges and stainless steel machinery, Rebecca sat on a little seat beside the stretcher and took hold of Poppy's ankle again—the only part of him not hooked up to wires in some way. This time they turned on the sirens. The driver spoke into a sort of intercom while he drove, relaying Poppy's name, age, and Social Security number as Rebecca supplied them, and the other man monitored Poppy. "Is this a heart attack?" Rebecca asked, and the man said, "Too soon to tell."

Poppy said, "But I haven't had my hundredth-birthday party yet!"

"Oh, Poppy," she said. "You'll have your party! I promise."

She felt close to tears, which surprised her, because hadn't she always chafed at Poppy's presence in her life, and resented how she'd had no choice in the matter, and even, on occasion, allowed herself to fantasize his death? But apparently you grow to love whom you're handed. It seemed shocking—a scandal, an atrocity—that such a thin, gray, warm-ankled person might just stop being, as easily as that.

Poppy glared at the ceiling and chewed his mustache.

Once they'd reached the hospital, Rebecca was directed to a desk to answer questions while the ambulance men wheeled Poppy through a set of swinging doors. "I've already answered everything!" she told a nurse. (*Was* she a nurse? Hard to know, nowadays, with these teddy-bear-print smocks and baggy pants.) The woman patted her arm and said, "You can see your loved one in just a few minutes."

Rebecca didn't like the sound of that *loved one.*

She answered the questions all over again, signed several forms, and then chose a chair as far as possible from anybody else. The room had the scrappy, exhausted look of a place where people had sat too long and then left in too much of a hurry. Empty Styrofoam cups—one of them scalloped with bite marks around the rim—dotted the tables; the magazines had been read into ruffles; a blue-jeaned man lay sleeping on an orange vinyl couch patched here and there with duct tape. Near the window, a family argued about who should go back home and walk the dog. A woman spoke urgently into a pay phone. Another woman tore something from a magazine inch by inch, trying to make no sound, while her husband yawned aloud and stretched his legs out until he was nearly diagonal in his seat.

Just yesterday Rebecca had snapped Poppy's head off. He'd been complaining about his exercises—"Why you make me go through these boring, baby arm bends every morning . . ." he'd said—and she had said, "Fine, then; quit doing them. See if *I* care when your elbows rust solid." And last week she had refused to take him to visit his friend, Mr. Ames. Worse than refused: she had said she would but kept putting it off, hoping Poppy would forget, and eventually he had stopped asking her, perhaps because he forgot but perhaps because he had simply lost hope. It broke her heart, now, to think of that.

She watched a skeletal man on crutches shuffle through the room, guided by some kind of aide—a round-faced young girl who kept an arm around his waist. He was speaking to her in a peevish drone: "They shoot you with their needles, wrench you every which way, make you stay perfectly still for hours on end . . . Then they force you to drink all these gallons of water after. Say, 'With our patients who get a dye, we like to encourage the fluids.' Which gave me quite a start, seeing as how what I heard was, 'With our patients who're *going to die* . . .'"

The girl laughed softly and squeezed his waist with such apparent affection that Rebecca wondered for a moment whether she was a relative. But no: more likely just one of those low-level, underpaid hospital employees who showed more genuine care than many physicians. She was opening a door now and shepherding him through it, one hand placed gently at the small of his back.

This was where they'd brought Patch when her appendix burst. Although the place had been remodeled since then, perhaps more than once. And NoNo when she broke her wrist. Or maybe not; that might have been Union Memorial. Oh, all those accidents, childhood illnesses, frantic late-night rides . . . Rebecca ought to publish a rating chart for Baltimore emergency rooms.

Joe had been taken here, too, but they'd moved him to Intensive Care before she arrived. She had spent four days and three nights in the Intensive Care waiting room—a much smaller space, with its own uniquely dread-filled atmosphere. Once an hour she had been allowed to come in and grip Joe's unresponsive hand for five minutes before they made her leave again. Upon her return to the waiting room, total strangers would ask, "Did he speak to you? Did he open his eyes?" and she would ask the same of them when they returned from *their* relatives. They had grown as close as family through fear and grief and endless hours of just sitting. Although now, she couldn't recall what those people had looked like, even.

A woman dressed in aqua scrubs called, "Mrs. Davitch? Is there a Mrs. Davitch?"

"Here I am," she said, standing up.

"You can come on back now."

Rebecca collected her purse and followed the woman through the swinging doors, down a linoleum-floored corridor. "How is he?" she asked, but the woman said, "Doing just fine!" so promptly that Rebecca suspected she had no idea. They entered a large, uncannily quiet area where doctors were going about their business without any appearance of haste, thoughtfully studying clipboards or conferring at a central desk. Curtained cubicles lined three walls, and the woman slid one curtain back to expose Poppy's yellow-soled feet poking forth from his stretcher. "Company!" she sang out, and then she left, her jogging shoes squeaking as she turned to close the curtain behind her.

Rebecca walked around to Poppy's head and found him wide awake, scowling at the machine that chirped and blinked beside him. "How're you feeling?" she asked him.

"How do you expect I'd feel? With all this commotion going on."

"Is the chest pain any better?"

"Some."

"What have they done so far?"

"Punctured about six veins for blood. Gave me an EKG. Went off and left me lying here in the very worst position for somebody subject to backache."

He was wearing a pastel hospital gown that made him look frivolous and pathetic. An IV needle was attached to the back of one hand. She covered the other hand with her own, and he allowed it. He closed his eyes and said, "It's okay with me if you stay."

"I'll be right here," she told him.

She kept her hand on top of his, shifting her weight from time to time when her legs started to tire. There was a chair over near the curtain, but she didn't want to risk disturbing him.

If this turned out to be Poppy's deathbed, heaven forbid, how strange that she should be standing beside it! Ninety-nine years ago, when he had come into the world, nobody could have foreseen that an overweight college dropout from Church Valley, Virginia—not even a Davitch, strictly speaking—would be the one to hold his hand as he left it.

Well, that was the case with nearly everybody, she supposed. Lord only knew who would be attending *her* deathbed.

The curtain rattled back, and all at once, there was Zeb—a comfort to behold, with his long, kind, homely face and smudged glasses. "How're you doing?" he asked her.

"Well, I'm fine, but Poppy, here . . ."

Poppy opened his eyes and said, "I believe they're trying to finish me off."

"Nope. They're letting you go," Zeb told him. He was peering now at the chirpy machine. "Turns out it's indigestion."

"It is?"

"I just spoke with the resident."

"Oh! Indigestion!" Rebecca cried. It was such a wonderful word, she felt the need to say it herself.

"I hear you had three cupcakes at the baby-welcoming," Zeb told Poppy.

"Well, what if I did? I've eaten far more, many a time."

"They're going to bring you an antacid. That should help," Zeb said. "It may take a while to spring you, hospitals being what they are, but sooner or later, we'll get you out." He looked over at Rebecca and said, "We should let them know at home. They're pretty worried."

"Did Joey get his shot?"

"He did, and he's back at the party making up for lost time."

"I'll go telephone," she said. She bent to kiss Poppy's cheek and told him, "I'm glad it wasn't serious."

"Well, I don't know what the world is coming to," Poppy said, "if a man can't eat three measly cupcakes without folks calling an ambulance."

She patted his shoulder and walked out, feeling lighter than air.

During the period she'd spent with Poppy, the waiting room had acquired a whole different population. The blue-jeaned man had vanished from the couch. A boy in a yellow raincoat sat slumped in front of the TV. An elderly woman stared into space and bit her lip. Rebecca felt a distant, detached pity. When she dropped her coins in the pay phone and called home, she tried to keep her voice low so that none of them would hear what a lucky person she was.

. . .

By the time they got back to the Open Arms, it was evening and all the guests had gone home except for Biddy. She was tidying up in the kitchen. "Have some green-tea soufflé," she told them. "There's a ton of it left over, because none of the others would eat it. I shouldn't have let on what kind it was. 'Green tea!' they said. 'What's wrong with chocolate?' Oh, you had a phone call, Beck. Somebody named Will Allenby."

Rebecca froze.

"'Green tea is for drinking,' they said, and I said, 'Listen.' I said, 'If you-all were not so prejudiced—'"

"What did he want?" Rebecca asked.

"Pardon?"

"What did Will Allenby want?"

"Just for you to call him back, I think. He said you would know his number. How are you feeling, Poppy? Are you still having chest pains?"

"Pains? Oh, pains," Poppy said. He was dishing out the soufflé, piling it into a bowl he had taken from the cabinet. "I don't know why everybody had to get so excited," he said. "I told them all along, I said—"

"I guess I'll be going to bed now," Rebecca broke in.

Everyone looked at her.

"Good night," she said, and she walked out, leaving a startled silence behind her.

She climbed the stairs, went straight to her room, and sat on the edge of her bed. Felt for the little stick of paper under her telephone. Held it up to the soft yellow light shining in from the hall.

It meant something, she supposed, that she hadn't thrown away his number.

He answered after several rings, just when she was starting to think he might be asleep. But his voice was alert. "Dr. Allenby speaking."

"Hello, Will. This is Rebecca."

But of course he already knew that, if he had looked at his Caller ID. So when he said, "Oh! Rebecca!" in a voice spiked with stagy surprise, it made her smile. She said, "I hope I didn't wake you."

"No, no! Goodness, no! No, I'm just . . . I was just . . ." There was some kind of scrambling sound, a rustle, a clink, something falling over. "I was just sitting here," he said, out of breath. "Gosh, thanks for calling back."

"Well. That's okay."

He cleared his throat.

"Actually," he said, "it occurred to me that you might have misinterpreted my question."

"Your question?"

"What I asked on the phone last time. About why you broke up with me. See, it wasn't a . . . reproach. It wasn't meant rhetorically. I really did want you to tell me where it was I went wrong."

Rebecca said, "Will—"

"No, no, never mind! I withdraw that. I realize I'm being tedious. Don't hang up!"

She started to speak, but then stopped. Anything she could think of to say seemed a mistake. In fact, speech in general seemed a mistake. It struck her all at once that dealing with other human beings was an awful lot of work.

"I'll tell you what," she said finally. "Let's start over."

"Start over?"

She said, "Maybe you would like to come here for dinner some night."

She heard a caught breath, a kind of exclamation point in the airwaves. Then he said, "I would love to come to dinner."

"Are you free, um . . ." She cursed tomorrow's engagement party—the first Open Arms event in over a week. "Are you free Wednesday?"

"Wednesday would be wonderful."

"Fine, let's say six p.m. Now, here's how to get to my house."

She gave the directions with such assurance that she probably took him aback, because he responded with a meek "All right . . . all right . . ." And after she had finished, there seemed nothing more to talk about. "Till Wednesday, then!" she told him.

"Yes, all right . . . goodbye," he said.

She tried to remember, after she had hung up, whether in the old days he had said *goodbye* at the end of telephone calls. He surely couldn't have avoided the word altogether, could he?

Then she went on to try and remember their first meeting, since recently, first meetings had begun to seem so significant. But it was lost in the mists of childhood. They had probably met in kindergarten, or perhaps some play group in the little park by the river. Really, Will had just always been there.

Which had its own significance, she thought.

Outside, a wind was blowing up, buckling the warped black screens and wafting the gauze curtains almost horizontal. The air smelled of rain and damp earth. The room took on an eerie, greenish glow. A door slammed somewhere downstairs, and Rebecca felt almost afloat with the sense of possibility.

Y

ou'll never in a million years guess who I've asked to dinner," Rebecca told her mother on the phone.

"Who's that, dear?"

"Oh, nobody but Will Allenby."

"Will Allenby! Are you serious? My stars! How did *this* come about?"

"We just happened to talk on the phone a little while ago."

"My Lord in heaven! Tell me everything," her mother ordered. "Every last detail."

"There's nothing to tell, really. I had supper with him a few weeks back, and tomorrow night he's coming to my house. He's living in Macadam. He's head of the physics department."

"Is he single? Or what."

"He's divorced."

"Divorced! Poor Will; who'd have thought? Though divorced is much better than widowed, of course."

"How do you figure that?" Rebecca asked.

"Well: if they're divorced, they're mad at their ex-wife and so they put her out of their minds. If they're widowed, they go on mourning. They feel guilty about remarrying."

"Who said anything about remarrying?" Rebecca asked. "We're just having a meal together."

"Yes, but, you never can tell. One thing leads to another, you know! And you and he have all that shared past. It's not as if you're strangers. Oh, I'd love it if you married Will!"

"Mother," Rebecca said. "Let's not jump to conclusions. I'm sorry now I mentioned it."

Why *had* she mentioned it, in fact? Almost the instant she woke up this morning, she'd had it in her mind to call her mother and tell her the news. It was like some kind of offering—a mouse she could lay at her mother's feet. *See there? I'm still the old Rebecca after all!*

"What does he look like?" her mother was asking. "Is he as good-looking as he used to be?"

"Yes, but he's older, of course. His hair is white."

"That's okay! What do you care! None of us is getting any younger. Oh. Rebecca. Do you want to hear an amazing co-incidence? Would you believe I ran into his mother's sister-in-law just last weekend at the Kmart? And this is not someone I see every day. Or every year, even! In fact, I'm surprised I recog-nized her. *You* must have known her. Katie, or Kathy; something like that. Was it Katie? No, Kathy. No, Katie. She was married to Will's mother's brother, Norman, before he died, and they used to live on Merchant Street in this darling little cottage that always made me think of a doll's house. Do you remember that house?"

Rebecca sighed and said, "No."

"Well, it was next door to the Saddlers' place. You remember the Saddlers' place, the one with all the chimneys."

"No, I don't think I do."

"You must! It had two chimneys in the middle, and one more at each—"

"I remember."

"You just finished saying you didn't."

"Mother. What difference does it make?" Rebecca asked. "This is a house next to another house that I don't remember either, where somebody I never met used to live before her husband died."

"I'm sure you did meet her, dear. She must surely have been at the Allenbys' many a time when you were visiting."

"All right," Rebecca said, "I met her. What did she say?"

"What did she say about what?"

"About anything. When you ran into her at the Kmart."

"Oh, we didn't actually speak. I was afraid she wouldn't know me. I just swiveled my eyes in another direction and made like I didn't see her."

Rebecca began massaging her left temple.

"So who did he marry?" her mother asked.

"Who did who marry?" Rebecca asked, contrarily.

"Will, of course. My goodness! Who have we been talking about, here?"

"He married an ex-student of his."

"Was the divorce his idea, or hers?"

"Hers, I believe," Rebecca said.

"Oh, dear. Well, never mind. We'll just hope for the best."

"What is *that* supposed to mean?" Rebecca asked.

"Never mind! What are you planning to wear, do you know?"

"I hadn't thought," Rebecca said.

"I was reading somewhere just the other day that the color brown is the most flattering to any type of figure."

"I don't own anything brown," Rebecca said.

"You still have time to go shopping!"

"I have to hang up," Rebecca said. "Talk to you later, Mother."

.   .   .

It wasn't true that she'd given no thought as to what she would wear. Throughout the night—even in her sleep, it seemed—she had mentally reviewed her wardrobe, and she had settled, finally, on the eggplant-colored caftan. By midafternoon Wednesday, she had already put it on. She had already set the table, placed candles around the dining room, and added the finishing touches to the food—everything cold, so that she wouldn't have to be off in the kitchen for any length of time. In the front parlor, the cushions were plumped and more candles stood about in groups. She had opened all the windows, even those on the street side, to whisk away any trace of cooking smells.

Absurd to make such a to-do. Absurd.

Promptly at five-thirty, Zeb arrived to pick up Poppy. He had promised to keep him occupied for the evening. "I thought we'd try that new steakhouse," he told Rebecca, "and then maybe go to a movie. That would put us back here at, oh, nine-thirty or ten. Is that okay with you?"

In fact, it seemed a bit early. What if she and Will were to linger over coffee? What if they returned to the parlor after supper and started . . . Well, not that they'd be doing anything very private, of course, but what if they just wanted to talk without other people listening? She couldn't say this to Zeb, though, because he'd already rearranged his schedule to help her out. "That'll be fine," she told him. "It's good of you to take him, Zeb."

He said, "Jesus, it's the least I can do. So. Is this a . . . what. Is this an actual date you're having?"

"No, no! Mercy," she said. "I'm much too old to be dating."

"Is that right," he said mildly, and then he called, "Poppy? You ready?"

Poppy emerged from the rear of the house, patting all his pockets with the hand that wasn't holding his cane. Every pocket rustled. He had taken to insisting, lately, on bringing a supply of candy bars on his outings. Evidently he feared being caught in some emergency situation with no source of sweets. "I'm all set," he announced. "Going to have a boys' night out," he told Rebecca.

"Good, Poppy. Enjoy yourselves, you two."

As soon as she had closed the door behind them, she raced up the stairs to her bedroom. She had decided that the caftan was too informal. It might even be mistaken for sleepwear. She changed into a silk blouse and a floor-length hostess skirt, and she switched her clunky leather sandals to daintier ones, high-heeled.

Her room looked ransacked. Cast-off clothes littered the bed, and half a dozen pairs of shoes were strewn across the floor. In the mirror, her face had the bright-eyed, hectic expression of someone who'd been nipping at the sherry.

Well before six, the doorbell rang. It was so early that she feared a drop-in family visitor. But no, when she opened the door, there stood Will, practically invisible behind a gigantic plant of some kind. "Oh! You shouldn't have," she said.

"I know I'm early," he told her. "I allowed a little extra time in case I got lost."

"That's all right! Let's see, maybe you could set that here on the floor by the . . . Isn't it unusual!"

In fact, the plant was bizarre. Three feet tall, at least, with monstrous, lumpy, dark-green leaves speckled a sulphur yellow, it loomed from a red-rimmed white bowl that reminded her of a chamber pot. Once Will had set it down, it blocked nearly all the light from the foyer window. "What is it called?" she asked.

Will spread his arms helplessly. "I don't know," he said. "They told me it was impossible to kill, was all."

"Oh, good."

His white curls and lined forehead shocked her all over again. (In her mind, she seemed to keep returning him to his youth.) His palms were dusted with potting soil. He was wearing faded jeans with a short-sleeved, gray plaid shirt, and on his feet were mammoth jogging shoes. He must have seen her glance at the shoes, because he said, "I guess I should have dressed up more."

"Nonsense! *I'm* not dressed up."

She led him into the parlor, walking as quietly as possible so he wouldn't notice her heels. "Have a seat," she said. "Can I offer you something to drink?"

"No, thanks."

He sat down on the sofa, first carefully tweaking the knees of his jeans as if they had a crease, which they didn't. Then he gazed around him at the crystal chandelier, the damask draperies, the Oriental carpet. "This is really very . . . This is quite a place," he said.

"Yes, well, don't let it fool you," she told him. She chose to settle not on the sofa beside him but in the wing chair to his left, to her own surprise. Then she tugged her skirt up a bit so it wouldn't seem floor-length, but when she remembered she was wearing knee-high nylons she lowered it again. "Any minute now," she said, "I expect the roof to fall in."

"Is that picture above the mantel an ancestor of your husband's?"

He was referring to a portrait of a woman in a hoopskirt, with an obstinate, thick-necked look to her. "No," Rebecca said, "I think they bought it at a garage sale."

"Well, still, it's . . . the whole place is very impressive."

"Tell me, Will," she said. "Have you kept in touch with any of our old college friends?"

She had thought up this topic ahead of time. It seemed a neutral one, and certain to fill several minutes, at least. But he just said, "No, not really."

"Your roommate, for instance? Don Grant? Or Horace what's-his-name?"

"No."

"Oh. Well, me neither," she said. "But I was assuming that in my case, it was because of . . . *you* know. Because of dropping out and getting married and all."

"I've never been very sociable," Will told her. He didn't seem to have his mind on what he was saying; he was still gazing around the room. He said, "This house must have quite a—"

The doorbell rang. He looked at her. "Quite a history," he said. And then, when she didn't move, "I believe your doorbell rang."

"Oh," she said. "Right."

She rose and went to answer it.

Mr. Quint, from Second Eden, scraped his perfectly dry feet on the mat before he stepped into the foyer. "Just wanted to let you know I've set my men to working out back," he told her. "I did say we'd be—What is *that*?"

He meant Will's plant. He drew back as if he thought it might bite.

Rebecca said, "I'm not sure, exactly. Wouldn't that be your department?"

"Mine? Lord, no. I've never seen anything like it." He kept on staring at it in a perplexed and worried way even as he picked up where he had left off. "I did say we'd be here by noon, but we've been running a tad bit late today."

"That's okay," she told him. To be honest, she had forgotten he was coming.

"We can finish up before dark, I'm just about certain. You want to take a peek at them azaleas I was talking about?"

"No, I'm sure they'll be fine."

"Not that they've got any blossoms this time of year anyhow, but there's these little hang tags, you know? With color photos on them."

"It doesn't matter. Really."

"Or why don't I just pull off a tag and bring it in to show you? I'll go round back right now and fetch it."

"I don't *care* about it!" she said.

"Oh."

"I have company."

"Suit yourself," he said. "As long as you don't come running to me after you see them in bloom."

He still had his eyes on the plant as he turned to leave.

In the parlor, she found Will standing at the piano. He pressed one chipped, crackled key until a note plinked out.

"I know it's a little flat," she said. (In high school, Will had been famous for having perfect pitch.)

He said, "Oh, well."

"Our guests seem to like that sort of honky-tonk sound—that dance-hall, tinny, plunky sound. At every party, just about, someone will sit down to play."

Will closed the piano lid. He said, "You used to be so shy at parties."

Probably this was just a meaningless remark, but she read it as an accusation. How could she have changed so much when he had remained the same? he might be asking. She said, "I'm no different now! I promise. It's just, you know, when parties are your livelihood—"

The telephone rang.

She said, "Why don't we let the machine get that."

There was a second ring. A third.

Too late, she recollected that the machine was not turned on. The telephone kept ringing, and Will kept looking at her.

"So!" she said. "I should go see to our supper. Would you like to come out to the kitchen?"

"Certainly," Will said. "Can I help?"

"No, no. Just keep me company," she said.

The phone shut up, finally. Rebecca led the way through the rear parlor and the dining room, where Will began to lag behind. She turned to find him studying another portrait—the one that hung over the sideboard. "Was this your husband?" he asked her.

"Why, no," she said. Was he joking? The man in the portrait wore a frock coat and fitted trousers, and he carried a shiny top hat in one gloved hand. "I'll show you what my husband looked like," she said. "I've got an old snapshot on the fridge." And they continued down the passageway to the kitchen.

What she hadn't realized was that the snapshot she had in mind—Joe on some long-ago beach trip, holding up a fresh-caught crab and laughing in the sunlight—had gradually become buried beneath a shingling of later snapshots. Photos tended to live in the imagination, she thought; she hadn't actually looked at this one for years, although she could still visualize every detail. She had to weasel it out from under the others, and once Will had seen it ("Ah, yes," was all he said), he went on to peer at the rest. "That's Dixon in the cap and gown," she explained. "My grandson, at his high-school graduation party. And this . . ." She pointed toward a picture partly obscured by a magnet shaped like a bagel. "This is NoNo, my youngest stepdaughter, at her wedding. Doesn't she look beautiful? Biddy is the oldest; that's her standing next to LaVon, my former son-in-law. They were celebrating Lateesha's baby-welcoming, I think. And then Patch, she's our athlete. A gym teacher; can you imagine? I believe this must have been taken when her girls' lacrosse team won the—well, listen to me, rattling on! And I bet you must be starving to death."

She spun away to unwrap the platter of cold chicken on the

counter. Will followed at her heels, his hands jammed awkwardly in his rear pockets. He said, "It's true you always wanted ten children."

"Who, me?"

"You said that being an only child was so, what did you say, so pitiful. You wanted a big, jolly *crew* of children."

"I did?"

She stopped to stare at him, with a serving fork poised over the chicken.

"And you would have all these traditions, you said—all these family rituals, those big Christmases and Thanksgivings that other families had."

She said, "I don't remember that."

"Well, it seems you ended up with it, anyhow."

"I don't remember a bit of that," she told him. "Could you bring in the bread basket, please?"

He picked the basket up and followed her back to the dining room. "Pretty," he said of the table.

She flushed. She thought now she might have overdone things. "Oh," she said, setting down the platter, "it's no big deal. You can sit facing the window. I'll go get the salad."

But when she returned, he was still standing. He waited till she had lit the candles, and then he pulled out her chair for her. His hand on her chair was so close that she could feel its warmth through the fabric of her blouse. In a sudden fit of daring, she leaned back imperceptibly until her shoulder was pressing against his fingers. But he drew away as if he hadn't noticed and went around to his side of the table.

Or maybe he *had* noticed, and was deliberately rebuffing her.

"What's happening in your backyard?" he asked as he sat down.

"My . . . ?" She twisted around to look through the open window behind her. "Oh, those are the nurserymen. They're putting in some azaleas."

He said, "This is like running a *plantation* or something. Do you employ a large staff?"

"No, just . . . well, a woman who helps with the cleanup, sometimes, if it's a big party." She passed him the chicken.

"And what is your role at these parties? You provide the entertainment? Magicians for children's birthdays and such?"

"No, it's really just the physical space. Although we do offer catering, if the customer wants it."

She hated how chatty and informative she sounded, like someone delivering an advertising spiel. Was this all they could find to talk about? They seemed to do much better on the telephone than in person.

She forked a drumstick onto her plate. "I was wondering," she said. (Preplanned topic number two.) "Is your daughter like *you* were at her age?"

"No," Will said. "She's bewildering."

Rebecca laughed, but he gazed back at her glumly. He said, "I never have understood the first thing about her. I didn't understand her when she was a baby and I understand her even less now that she's an adolescent."

"Oh, well, adolescents," Rebecca said, waving a hand. "Who does understand them?" She helped herself to a roll.

"Laura seems to. Her mother."

"Really?"

She waited to hear more, but the person who spoke next was one of the workers in the backyard. "Now, this here is my advice," he said. His words were punctuated by the chuffing sound of a pickax. "Never, ever agree to stay overnight at a woman's place. No matter how she begs and pleads, you have her stay at your place, or else a motel or a buddy's place. Because you really got no way of knowing when her boyfriend might get out of jail. This one gal, she says her boyfriend couldn't never in a million years get out, and like a fool I believe her. I say okay, I'll sleep over, and what do you think happens? Next morning there's a knock on the door. 'Oh,' she says. 'Who can that be?' Steps up naked as a jaybird to look through the little peephole and then comes squawking back to me, 'Lord Almighty, it's him!' I says, 'Woman?' I says, 'Woman, didn't you swear and declare that he was locked up good?'"

Will said, "Of course, Laura's considerably younger than I am. I suppose it's only natural she would have a better understanding of adolescents."

Rebecca refocused her thoughts. "How much younger?" she asked.

"She's thirty-eight; I'm fifty-three."

"So, let's see . . . fifteen years. Well, with Joe and me it was almost that much: thirteen and a half."

Outside the window, the nurseryman was saying, "I walk past him in the hall; say, 'How you doing,' and keep on going. 'How you doing,' he says back, and I walk on down the stairs just easy-like and careless-like, but all the time the back of my neck is tingling; know how it will do? Waiting for that knife between the shoulder blades."

"Man, you was *lucky*," another voice said. "How come you put any stock in what a woman tells you?"

"This chicken is delicious," Will said.

Rebecca said, "Thank you. Won't you have some salad?"

"Thanks."

"The thing about women is, they want what they want when they wants it," the first man said. "They don't mind what they might have to do to get it. They'll do anything. They won't be stopped. They call you on the phone, and they come by your place of work, and they look you up at the house and try to mess with you. You tell them, 'Gal, hey, cut me some slack,' but they just, man, they just steamroll on and can't nothing turn them aside."

"But you were so mature for your age," Will was saying.

Rebecca said, "Excuse me?"

"You were so serious. So involved in your studies. Laura, on the other hand . . ." He shrugged. He was stirring his salad around rather than eating it, she saw. (This was a recipe of Biddy's, involving charred yellow beets. It might have been too gourmet.) "Well, I should have known," he said. "The way we met: she enrolled in my introductory physics class but decided it wasn't relevant to her life. She came to get permission to drop the course and I persuaded her not to. That was our first conversation."

"Aha! See there?" Rebecca crowed, pointing her fork at him.

Then she glanced toward the window and lowered her voice. "You're bearing out my theory about prophetic moments."

"Pathetic?" Will asked.

"Prophetic. Moments that predict a couple's future. See: at the very start of your courtship, she was threatening to leave you."

"But I thought it was just a normal student interview. I had no idea that that was the start of our courtship."

"No, of course not. That's how prophetic moments work," Rebecca told him. "You don't suspect that's what they are at the time they're taking place."

"It does seem I should have heard some kind of alarm going off," Will said. "This was the course I was always so proud of, the one where I showed beginning students that physics could be an adventure."

Rebecca said, "Oh, what a shame."

"And she never did really take to the subject," Will said sadly. "She stayed on after I convinced her but dropped the course second semester; switched to ecology instead to finish up her science requirement. Ecology! A pretend sort of science. But all I thought at the time was, now I could ask her out. I must have been blind as a bat."

"*She* must have been blind, to think physics was irrelevant," Rebecca said.

"Well, that's where the two of you differ," Will told her. "Laura's a more superficial type of person. What matters most to her are material things. Clothing, makeup, hairstyles, jewelry . . . On every possible occasion, including Easter, she expected me to give her a gift of jewelry."

"Really!" Rebecca said. This was getting interesting. "What kind of jewelry?"

"Oh . . . I don't know."

"I mean, important jewelry, like diamonds? Or just a new charm for her bracelet or something."

He stopped stirring his salad and looked at her.

"Well," she said hastily, "some women are like that, I guess."

"She owned so many shoes that a closet company had to come build a special rack in her closet."

"Gracious!"

Rebecca owned a lot of shoes herself. Not that she was a spendthrift. These were very cheap shoes, purchased on sale or at discount stores. But they seemed to have a way of not fitting quite right a short while after she bought them, and so she was always buying more. Mentally, now, she began discarding the extras. Those brown suede clogs, for instance: she could easily get rid of those. She had worn them exactly once and discovered that her heels hung half an inch over the backs, although she could have sworn they'd fit perfectly when she first tried them on.

"Plus another thing is, they're so jealous," the nurseryman was saying. He grunted, and then she heard the thud of a rock or a root stob as he heaved it aside. "They phone you all the time and they ask you what you was doing if you take a minute to answer. They show up at your door and check out you're not cheating on them. This one guy I know, he had to move to Arizona finally just to get shed of this woman who was always on his tail."

"It's more than a fellow can handle, sometimes," the second man agreed.

Rebecca slid her chair back and rose to shut the window. She tried to make no noise, but she had a glimpse of two startled faces looking directly into her eyes before she turned away. When she had reseated herself, smoothing her skirt beneath her, she said, "You know, I've always regretted not completing my education."

"You could do that now," Will told her.

"Well, yes. Yes, I could! In fact, I've just started reading a biography of Robert E. Lee."

"Lee," Will said consideringly.

"Remember, how I had this new theory about Lee's real reason for deciding to cast his lot with the South? And the other day I thought, I should go on with my research anyhow, just out of sheer curiosity."

"Well, there you have it," Will told her. "Laura's got no curiosity whatsoever."

Rebecca clucked. The telephone rang.

He said, "Don't you want to answer that?"

"No, never mind."

She waited till the ringing stopped, which seemed to take forever. Then she said, "So she isn't a scholar."

"Who isn't?"

"Laura."

"No, not in the least."

She hoped he would elaborate, but just then the phone started ringing again.

"You certainly get a lot of calls," Will told her.

"Yes," she said. She sighed. "Won't you have more chicken?"

"No, thanks, I couldn't eat another bite."

Her own plate was nearly untouched. Even so, she removed her napkin from her lap and prepared to slide her chair back. "I'll go make us some coffee," she said. "Would you prefer regular, or decaf?"

"Neither, thanks."

"I can have it ready in a jiff."

He said, "I never was in the habit of coffee, you may remember."

She didn't remember, actually. She remembered only that he hadn't liked sweets—unusual, in a young man. But when she said, "I purposely did not fix a dessert," he said, "Oh, that's all right," as if he thought she was apologizing.

"I mean, I didn't suppose you'd want one."

"No, really, I'm fine."

She gave up. "Well," she said, "shall we go into the parlor, then, where it's comfortable?"

Instead of answering, he leaned toward her. The movement was so sudden that she wondered, for a second, whether he had a stomachache. "Rebecca," he said, "it's occurred to me that this was providential."

"Was . . . what?"

"That first night you telephoned, I had just about hit bottom. It was so incredibly providential that you called me when you did, Rebecca."

He reached across the table and gripped one of her hands. Unfortunately, it was the hand that held her scrunched-up napkin. Also, she felt an instantaneous, nearly overwhelming urge to wriggle her fingers frantically, like some kind of undersea creature. She forced them to stay motionless, although the urge was so intense that she was almost vibrating. At the same time she had to remember to make her eyes look wider than they normally were, and to keep her head raised high so that the cushion of flesh beneath her chin would not reveal itself.

Then the front door slammed against the closet, and Zeb called out, "We're home!"

He had promised they wouldn't be back till ten! Or nine-thirty, at the earliest! But here came Poppy's cane tip-tapping through the two parlors, following Zeb's softer tread. Will withdrew his hand.

"In the old days, ice-cream places offered unlimited samples," Poppy was saying. "Any kind of flavor you liked—eggnog, pistachio, rum raisin—on little wooden spoons for you to try before you committed yourself."

They arrived in the dining-room doorway. "Well, hi, there!" Zeb exclaimed, in what struck Rebecca as an artificial tone of voice.

"What are *you* doing here?" she asked him coolly.

"We stopped for ice cream after supper and Poppy was so displeased with the service, he said he'd just as soon have his dessert here at home."

He was looking not at her but at Will, who had turned partway around in his seat to see him. Rebecca still had a distant hope of avoiding introductions—if Zeb and Poppy would only retire tactfully to the kitchen, while she and Will moved into the front parlor—but now Will rose and held out his hand. "How do you do," he said. "I'm Will Allenby."

"I'm Zeb, Rebecca's brother-in-law," Zeb said, shaking his hand. With his poor posture and his dingy, wire-rimmed glasses, his strings of oily gray hair hanging over his forehead, he seemed almost ugly tonight. "This is my uncle, Paul Davitch," he said. "Sorry to barge in like this."

"I thought you two were going to a movie," Rebecca told him.

"We were *considering* a movie," Poppy said, "but after the ice-cream fiasco I just didn't have the heart for it." He stood poised in the doorway, pivoting his cane with both hands as if he thought he was Fred Astaire.

"What fiasco was that?" Will asked him politely. (Too politely, in Rebecca's opinion.)

"I told the girl at the counter I'd like a little taste of butterscotch ripple," Poppy said, "and she gave me one and it was weak, just very frail and weak in flavor. So I said, 'Well, I believe I'll sample the coffee nugget next,' and she said, 'Sir!' in this smart-aleck tone—not a respectful 'sir' by any manner of means. 'Sir, if we gave out unlimited samples we wouldn't have any product left to sell, now, would we.'"

Will clicked his tongue.

"Back in my day, folks were more accommodating," Poppy said.

"Mine too," Will told him.

"So we thought we'd come on home and see what *you*-all's dessert was."

"We're not having any dessert," Rebecca said. "I didn't make one."

"I'll go look in the freezer, then. Check what flavors of ice cream we've got. Want some ice cream . . . um?" he asked Will.

"That'd be great," Will said, and he sat down again.

Rebecca slumped in her seat.

Poppy set off for the kitchen, humming something tuneless. He was leaning on his cane hardly at all, for once. He had a jaunty lilt to his walk that struck Rebecca as infuriating.

"So!" Zeb said chummily. He pulled out the chair next to Will. "You knew our Rebecca back when she was in high school, I hear."

"*Our* Rebecca?" she demanded.

"Oh, way before high school," Will said. "I knew her in nursery school. I knew her when she was too young for any kind of school."

"I bet she was quite something when she was a little kid."

"She was cute, all right," Will said.

Rebecca rolled her eyes.

"Well: cute," Zeb said. "She was cute even when *we* met her.

Showed up that very first evening in a blue dress and matching blue shoes, carrying a purse that was shaped like a workman's lunch box."

Rebecca would not have expected him to remember that. She hoped he wouldn't mention some other things he might remember—like that twentieth-birthday party, which had taken place when she and Will were supposedly still a couple.

Before Zeb could say any more, though, the front door slammed open again. "Beck?" NoNo called. "Are you home?"

"Out here," Zeb called, and he cocked his head at Rebecca—trying to imply, no doubt, that now he wasn't the only one who'd interrupted her evening.

Rebecca just glared at him.

NoNo had Peter with her. She was wearing her work clothes—a green smock with a yellow trowel embroidered on the pocket—and she looked tired and out of sorts. "Where *were* you?" she asked Rebecca. "I've been phoning and phoning all evening, and nobody ever answered and the machine wouldn't pick up."

"I was entertaining," Rebecca said pointedly.

This didn't faze NoNo for an instant. "Anyway," she went on, "Peter wants to ask you—"

Rebecca said, "Will, I'd like you to meet my stepdaughter, NoNo Sanborn, and her stepson, Peter. This is Will Allenby."

"Oh. Hi," NoNo said. Will had stood up again when she entered, but they were too far apart to shake hands. "Peter wants to ask you something," she told Rebecca.

"Will was my high-school boyfriend," Rebecca said.

It seemed important to make this clear, although she wasn't sure just why.

NoNo gave Will a second glance and said, "Really? Well. Nice to meet you." Then she turned to Peter. "Tell Beck what you wanted to ask her," she ordered.

Peter said, "Um, at my school they have this, what-do-you-call . . ."

He had combed his hair flat with water, or maybe one of those newfangled gels. He had a skinned-back, pale, nervous look, and when he laced his fingers together Rebecca could hear his knuckles crack. "It's kind of like a, well, maybe, exhibit; an exhibit of these projects we've been working on, and the thing of it is . . ."

He gazed imploringly at NoNo. She smiled at him and nodded several times.

"I don't know why they do this," he said, "but they call the exhibit Grandparents' Day, and they have us invite all our grandparents."

Rebecca was so anxious for him that she was nodding along with NoNo, willing him to get through this. But Will said, "Isn't that great!"

Everybody looked at him.

"That he's inviting you to Grandparents' Day," Will explained to Rebecca.

Peter said, "Well, I'm not . . . I know she's not *really* my grandma. I mean, she wouldn't have to come if she didn't want to. But since my dad's parents are dead and all, and we don't get to see my mom's parents much; we don't see them ever, in fact—"

"I would love to come," Rebecca told him.

"You would?"

"I'd be honored. When is it?"

"It's not till Friday the twenty-fourth, but we have to get our slips signed by tomorrow so the teachers will know for sure—"

"This school of his is driving me crazy," NoNo told the room at large. "Last night at a quarter till ten, I swear, some woman telephoned saying I should send four dozen cookies into class with him this morning. And now this grandparent thing—would somebody please clue them in? What about kids like Peter, who don't happen to *have* grandparents available at the drop of a hat?"

"Peter has me, though," Rebecca said, "and I'm looking forward to it enormously."

He gave her a grateful smile, and his shoulders lost some of their tightness.

Then Poppy was back with the ice cream—a half-gallon drum tucked under his arm, a scoop in his free hand. "Vanilla," he said bitterly. "You'd think there would be something a little more imaginative. Oh, hello, NoNo. Hello, youngster." He set the carton and the scoop in front of Zeb. "Good to see you again," he told Will.

"Well . . . thanks."

"Been keeping busy lately? Still enjoying your work?"

Will glanced across at Rebecca. She gave a slight movement of her eyebrows that amounted to a shrug, and he turned back to Poppy and said, "Yes, I enjoy my work very much."

"Don't count on that lasting forever," Poppy told him. "Me, I got burned out in the end. Too many students asking, 'Will we be tested on this, or not?' And you knew if you said, 'Not,' they'd figure it wasn't worth writing down, even. No sense of joy in learning for its own sake, is my diagnosis."

He must have taken Will for one of his old teaching colleagues, but Will couldn't have known that. He looked again at Rebecca. Perversely, she refused to come to his rescue. "Uh, you're probably right," he said finally.

"Too durn much TV, is what *I* tell folks."

Why did Poppy insist on speaking in that homespun way? Rebecca wondered for the first time. He was an educated man; he had a college degree. She sent him her narrowest, meanest look, which he ignored.

"Rebecca," Zeb said, brandishing the scoop, "will you be having ice cream?"

"No, I will not," she said in a forbidding tone.

"Five servings, then," he said cheerfully. "Because I know *you* will, NoNo, and—"

"I've put you on the guest list for my birthday party," Poppy told Will, "but I don't suppose Beck has sent the invitations yet. I'm turning a hundred years old in December."

"A hundred!" Will exclaimed.

By now, Rebecca's annoyance had spread even to Will. She disliked the counterfeit note of admiration in his voice, and the eager way he reached for the bowl Zeb passed him. Zeb himself, she thought, was behaving like a barbarian, licking ice cream off his knuckles before he dug the scoop back into the carton; and NoNo and Peter had pulled out two chairs as if they had every right to horn in whenever they wanted. As for Poppy: he was beyond forgiveness. "It's my fondest wish," he was telling Will, "that I'll be able to say I've seen two centuries change over: the nineteenth and the twentieth. Not that I consciously remember when the nineteenth changed, of course, but I was there, I can say! I was there!"

"That's amazing," Will said.

And as he lifted his spoon he opened his mouth to expose his large, square, wolfish teeth, unattractively yellowed now with age.

. . .

By the time they'd finished their ice cream, Rebecca had revised all her expectations of the evening. This was just another family melee with an extra person added, and she heartily wished it were over. She was tired of acting nicer than her true self. Wouldn't it come as a relief to be alone, finally! To be upstairs in the family room, playing a game of solitaire! She longed to kick her shoes off, and let her stomach stick out, and allow her face to go slack.

None of the others, though, seemed in any hurry to go. Zeb was telling Will about his work; Poppy was repeating the ice-cream incident to Peter; NoNo was asking Rebecca what kind of plant that was in the foyer. "It's not an anthurium, although it's certainly grotesque enough; too big to be a pilea, in spite of those warty leaves . . ."

"Ask Will. He's the one who brought it."

". . . surely can't be a dracaena, though it does have that mottled, diseased look of the *Dracaena godseffiana* . . ."

When NoNo and Peter finally rose to leave, Rebecca stood up too and said, "Yes, it *is* late, isn't it. I can hardly keep my eyes open."

Even Will couldn't miss that. He untangled himself from his chair and said, "Ah. All right. So, I guess . . ."

Everybody waited, but he just stood there. It was Zeb who completed his sentence for him. "I guess we should *all* be going," he said helpfully.

Then they headed in a group toward the door, leaving Poppy alone at the table scraping out the ice-cream carton.

Outside, Rebecca folded her arms across her bosom and

watched as Zeb climbed into his car (a Volvo so old it had the humpbacked shape of the earliest models) and NoNo and Peter walked on down the street to NoNo's minivan. "Good night," NoNo called back, her voice floating across the twilight, and "Good night," Zeb called.

But Will stayed next to Rebecca, and so she was forced to say, finally, "Well, I should be going in now."

"You used to have this long cloak," he told her. "Do you remember that?"

"Cloak," she repeated.

"It was a color called champagne. Your mom and your aunt sewed it for you the year we started college. I can see you in that cloak to this day. It matched your hair exactly. You wore your hair coiled in a braid on top of your head. You wore that cloak and these soft brown boots that crumpled around your ankles. You looked like somebody out of King Arthur's time, I often thought; or Robin Hood's. Very self-possessed and calm."

Rebecca still faced the street, but she was listening.

"I guess this sounds presumptuous," he said, "but I can't help feeling that that woman in the cloak is who you really are, and I'm the only person who knows it. I feel that I can *see* you, in a way other people can't. I don't mean to sound presumptuous."

She turned to look at him. With the streetlight shining behind him, she couldn't tell what his expression was. She had to rely more on feeling than on sight—feeling the steady focus of his regard, and then his dear, familiar warmth as he stepped forward to hug her. They clung together for maybe a minute, like people consoling each other for some loss. Then he pulled away and said, "I'll call you! I'll call tomorrow! Thanks for supper!"

He plunged off down the street, clanging against a garbage can as he hurtled around the corner and disappeared.

Rebecca stood there for some time after he had gone. She was shivering slightly, even on this hot summer night, and she felt happy but also dismayed, and bashful, and confused.

At that moment, it seemed she actually had managed to become her girlhood self again.

eight

You wouldn't call it a courtship. What would you call it? Just say they, oh, started arranging to get together now and then. Go shopping for a book Will had heard of. Grill steaks in Rebecca's backyard. (But with Poppy there too, of course, wanting a steak of his own, and Biddy happening by later as they were sitting around the table.) These certainly weren't anyone's notion of romantic assignations.

Still, Rebecca let herself think sometimes: might it be possible, after all, to return to that place where her life had forked and choose the other branch now? Even this late in the journey? Even after she had used up the branch she had first chosen?

It seemed like cheating. Like having her cake and eating it too.

She remembered things he did not; he remembered things she did not. Their past was a bolt of fabric they had scissored up and divided between them. He had no recollection, for instance, of the World's Fastest Typist. "Why would they have wasted our time with a typist, for heaven's sake?" he asked, and she told him, triumphantly, "That's exactly what you said when you were seventeen!"

He remembered that she used to recite poetry on their dates, although she couldn't believe she would ever have been so mawkish. That she'd kept a scrapbook of thought-provoking quotations from her reading; that she'd worshiped Joan Baez's singing; that she'd very nearly committed to heart *The Feminine Mystique*. All of which sounded to her like some completely unrelated person—*she*, rather than *I*.

And did he recall, she wondered, a night when they'd been studying late at his house, and his mother had gone to bed, and they had decided to take a catnap on the sofa? It was the first time they had lain down together. The length of his body pressed against hers had felt so good and so *needed*; his quick, hot breaths had sent a sort of ruffle up her spine. Now she couldn't say who had finally brought things to a halt. Both of them, perhaps.

But this was not one of the memories she mentioned to Will. No, they weren't yet familiar enough for that. At the moment they were still very restrained with each other, very circumspect and proper. When they met, he would kiss her lightly on the lips (his mouth not one she recognized), and when they sat in her family room, he would let one arm rest along the back of the couch behind her. Both of them were well aware that somebody might walk in on them at any moment. *Comfortably* aware, Rebecca might have said. Secure in the knowledge. Poppy would call, "Beck?" or the telephone would ring, or the front door would slam open, and the two of them would separate slightly, looking elsewhere, clearing their throats. At the end of a visit they hugged goodbye. Rebecca looked forward to those hugs. It seemed that her skin felt thirsty for them.

Her family—the few family members who'd met him— appeared to believe that Will was just another of her strays, like that electrician whose marriage had been breaking up the whole time he was wiring the house for air-conditioning. "Oh, hi," they would say offhandedly, and then they would rattle on about whatever had brought them here. Rebecca found this slightly insulting. Did they feel she wasn't *capable* of romance? All they seemed to notice was that she had grown less available to them. The Friday after she went with Will to a lecture at Johns Hopkins: "Where were you?" they demanded. "We came to dinner last night and Poppy was all by himself. It was Thursday! You weren't here!"

"There's no law that says I have to stay home every Thursday of my life," she told them. Although, as a matter of fact, she had simply forgotten what day of the week it was. Oh, she was very absent-minded lately, very muzzy and distracted. She lost her place in conversations, failed to answer when people asked her questions. Everybody who wasn't Will struck her as irrelevant. "Really," she would murmur, and, "Isn't that interesting," but inwardly she was saying, *Get on with it!* and, *What difference does it make?*

While the rest of her world blurred and swam, Will grew steadily more distinct. Parts of him flashed across her vision at inappropriate moments: the authoritative curl of his fingers around his car keys, the stirringly beautiful drape of his sports coat across the back of his shoulders. His most casual remarks came back to her unbidden, weighted with significance. She replayed her own remarks and longed to change them—to make them more intelligent, more original, more alluring.

When he asked her, for instance, why she had never remarried, she had answered fliply, "Nobody ever proposed." Which happened to be true, but there was more to it than that. A few men *had* made tentative moves in her direction, she should have told him, but she had felt oddly indifferent; she had felt a kind of fatigue. It had all seemed like so much trouble. (And the men, to be perfectly honest, had not persisted unduly.) Now Will would suppose that no one had found her attractive. She tried to bring it up again, hoping for a second chance. "Have you ever noticed," she asked him, "how what you look for in a person changes as you get older? When I was young, I wanted somebody *other*—the most wildly other type possible. I guess that's what drew me to Joe. But then as I got older, why, it began to seem so wearying to go out with somebody different. Maybe that's why parents are always telling their daughters to date that nice boy from their church, while the daughters are pining for motorcyclists that later on they wouldn't glance at."

"Motorcyclists?" Will asked. This was over the telephone, but she could almost see the bafflement crossing his forehead.

"I mean, after a while that kind of . . . bridging just seems like so much work. I gave up wanting to bother with it."

"But, Rebecca," Will said. "What are you saying? Are you trying to tell me something? Because look at you and me: we're totally different."

"We are?" she asked. And then she said, "Oh, well, maybe now it might *seem* we are. I can see why you might think that. But don't forget, I used to be much more introspective. I don't know what became of that! Sometimes I hear you talk about the old days, about the way we lived our lives then and the subjects that used to interest us, and I think, Oh, yes, that was back when we were grownups. Well, you still are a grownup; even more so. But me: it seems to me that I've been traveling in reverse. I know less now than I did when I was in high school. I'm trying to remedy that. I hope it's not too late."

"I just meant that you're more outgoing," Will told her.

"I'm not outgoing! It's only how I act on the surface, because of the Open Arms."

"Ah," he said.

But she could tell that he wasn't convinced.

It was easier to talk on the telephone than face to face, she noticed. On the telephone they might say almost anything, but when they met they grew self-conscious. Also, his physical reality often came as a surprise. Who was this craggy, white-haired man? He was very appealing to look at, but who *was* he? Over the course of the evening she would adjust to this new version of him, but the next time they spoke on the telephone, she seemed to have conjured up the original Will all over again. "Hello, Rebecca," he would say, and back came his lopsided boyhood smile, a cloud-gray sweater he had worn in junior high, and his springy corkscrew curls the color of wild honey.

· · ·

She took out subscriptions to the *New York Times, The New Yorker,* and the *New York Review of Books.* ("Just what city do you imagine we're living in?" Poppy asked when he heard.) She walked to the Enoch Pratt Library to request a copy of the memoir that she had written about in college. It turned out to be something they had to send away for through Interlibrary Loan, but she did have a long, absorbing talk with the reference librarian—a woman who seemed a real kindred spirit. Then she went home and finished reading her first Lee biography, after which she launched immediately into the second.

It emerged that Lee had felt emancipation would come about on its own, in the natural course of events. He wrote this in a letter to his wife. "Well, I never," Rebecca told Poppy. "I had no idea Lee was such a rationalizer."

"Lee who?" Poppy asked.

"*General* Lee. Robert E. When I was a girl, I thought I was going to rewrite his chapter in history. I could not believe he would have chosen which side to fight on purely out of personal loyalty."

"Well?" Poppy said. "What better reason?"

"How about principle? Even a wrongheaded, evil principle?"

"Robert E. Lee was one of your Virginia types," Poppy said. "All the principle he cared for was his own little bit of acreage."

"Not according to this memoir I came across in college," she told him.

"Oh, well, college," Poppy said. Then, as if he'd proved his point, he returned to his own reading—a multicolored magazine, surely not the *New York Review.* He was making notes on a memo pad with a promotional ballpoint pen from Ridgepole Roofers. The article he was consulting, she saw, was called "Ten Ways to Shake Up a Party." She sighed and looked down at her book again. Lee's wife gazed mournfully from the left page, Lee himself from the right. Rebecca caught herself wondering what kind of sex life they'd had.

.   .   .

Rebecca's mother telephoned. She had been much more atten-
tive lately—all sly questions and perky alertness, like a girlfriend
hoping for confidences. "You're home!" she said. "I thought you'd
be out."

She didn't say why, in that case, she had bothered to call.

Rebecca said, "How are you, Mother?"

"I'm fine. How about you? No date tonight?"

"No date."

"What did you do *last* night?"

"Sat home with Poppy," Rebecca said perversely. In fact, she'd
seen Will in the afternoon, but her mother hadn't asked about the
afternoon.

"Well, I just wanted to tell you that Sherry Hardy knows all
about Will's ex-wife."

"Have you been talking to Sherry Hardy about my private business?" Rebecca demanded.

"Just who you're going out with, is all. I really don't remember
how the subject chanced to come up."

Rebecca groaned.

Her mother said, "Sherry's second cousin went to Will's wedding. She told Sherry that his wife seemed way too young for him."

"Well, she was a former student of his. You knew that."

"She was pretty but unlikable, according to the cousin. A dis-
contented type. You could see it in the corners of her mouth. All
during the reception, she poked fun at how stodgy Will was. At one
point he made some comment that was the least little bit professor-
sounding, and the bride told everybody, 'Will is my *first* husband,
needless to say.' Only joking, of course, but when you consider how
things turned out . . ."

Rebecca, who had been listening more closely than she would
admit, felt a stab of pity. Will could never have held his own against
that kind of woman! But she just said, "Well, that's all water over the
bridge now."

"Dam," her mother said.

"Pardon?"

"Water over the dam."

"Whatever."

"The ceremony was Catholic, or maybe just High Episcopal. This cousin wasn't quite sure. She said there was a lot of kneeling going on. When Will was defining what a homophone was, he used *feted* and *fetid* as his examples."

Rebecca said, "He used what?"

"*F-E-T-E-D* and *F-E-T-I-D*. That was the comment that struck his ex-wife-to-be as professor-sounding."

"Why was he defining a homophone at his wedding?" Rebecca asked.

"Oh, you know how these subjects come up . . . I really couldn't say."

"Well, anyhow—"

"Also *liken* and *lichen*."

"Excuse me?"

"*L-I-K-E-N* and *L-I-C-H-E-N*."

"What on earth?"

But then her mother asked when Rebecca planned to bring Will for a visit—a prospect that seemed filled with possibilities for disaster—and Rebecca shifted her focus to inventing reasons not to.

After she had hung up, though, she started picturing Will at his wedding. She saw his fine-boned, serious face surrounded by laughing young guests, and she felt such a deep sense of injury on his behalf that it was almost physical.

Yesterday afternoon, he had come over to watch a movie with her—something subtitled, black-and-white, very difficult to follow, that she had driven all the way to Video Americain to rent. And Zeb had stopped by, as often happened on Sundays, and he and Poppy got to reminiscing about old times at the Open Arms. Zeb, in particular, could pull out any number of horror tales. The wedding ceremony where Mother Davitch started sobbing and couldn't stop, the Easter morning when Joe hid six dozen raw eggs that he thought were cooked, the after-prom breakfast they forgot to put on the calendar . . .

"Can you imagine where we'd be if Rebecca hadn't shown up?" Zeb asked Will. "We all thanked our lucky stars. She turned out to be awfully good for the business."

Will had pulled his gaze from the screen. "Rebecca, good at business?" he'd said.

"Good *for* business, actually. If not for her, we'd have long ago gone under."

"Oh, for heaven's sake," Rebecca had said. "Why are you talking this way? The first time I helped with a party, I let fly a champagne cork straight into some woman's bosom."

"Right! I'd forgotten. Most comical picture," Zeb had told Will. "Rebecca pops off the cork and crumples to the floor in mortification, so it looked as if she were the one who'd been hit. Meanwhile the woman with the bosom goes on talking, completely unaware. Falsies, was my considered opinion. I was very observant about such things in those days."

"We never let on to my mother-in-law," Rebecca said. "When she saw me on the floor she said, 'Dearie? Are you all right?' and I just said, 'Yes, fine,' and got up and poured the champagne."

She and Zeb had started laughing, while Will looked from one to the other with a tentative smile that seemed prepared to broaden as soon as he got the joke. "So," he'd said finally, "I gather you were still living at home then, Zeb."

"Lord, yes," Zeb had said, taking off his glasses to wipe his eyes. "Yes, I was still a kid when Joe and Rebecca married. The whole experience scarred me for life: seeing Rebecca walk out of their bedroom every morning all rosy and contented."

Rebecca had instantly sobered. She'd said, "Stop talking rubbish, Zeb."

It wasn't like him to be cruel. She had glanced toward Will to see how he was taking it, but his gaze was fixed on the movie again. His head was craned forward earnestly and his long, articulated fingers were cupping his bony knees.

Stodgy, she thought now. Wasn't that the word the wedding guest had used? Well, Rebecca knew he was stodgy! She knew his literal cast of mind, his reliance on routine, his almost laughable pompousness. (That "Dr. Allenby speaking" when he answered the phone.) The thing was, to her those traits were endearing. More than that: she felt partly responsible for them. Any time she saw him looking lost and ill at ease, she was reminded all over again that she had once abandoned him.

Which was why, yesterday afternoon, she had openly, pointedly, brazenly reached for his nearest hand and clasped it in her own.

. . .

She completely forgot about Grandparents' Day. What was the matter with her? She made plans to go to D.C. with Will and visit a museum; Fridays he had no classes. When Peter called to remind her, she went into a secret flurry. "Oh!" she said. "Right. Tomorrow morning at . . . what time did you say? I've got it on my calendar."

So she had to phone Will and cancel, because she couldn't break her promise to a child—especially Peter. (Not that she wasn't tempted.) Will was very understanding about it. Still, she felt regretful and, to be honest, more than a little put upon. When NoNo said, the next morning, "You're awfully nice to do this," Rebecca wanted to tell her, "You don't know the half of it!" But she didn't, of course. What she said was, "Oh, I've been looking forward to it for weeks now!"

They were standing on NoNo's front porch, waiting for Peter to run back upstairs for his knapsack. "He's so disorganized," NoNo said. She was dressed in her florist's smock, her purse already slung over her shoulder. "I tell you, mornings in this house are chaos. Find it?" she asked Peter. "All right, have a good day; I'll pick you up this afternoon."

She kissed the top of his head, which meant she had to rise on tiptoe because (Rebecca realized) Peter had recently undergone one of those dramatic growth spurts that seemed to strike boys overnight. His trousers were so short that they showed two inches of ankle, and his blazer sleeves exposed his wrist bones, which looked like small ivory cabinet knobs. "You're getting to be taller than I am!" Rebecca told him as they walked toward her car.

He smiled faintly, hitching his knapsack higher on his back and sending her a sidelong glance from under his long lashes. "Next month I'm turning thirteen," he said, and she fancied she could detect a new croakiness to his voice.

His school was on the other side of the city. No wonder NoNo complained about the drive, Rebecca thought as she maneuvered through the rush-hour traffic, the crossing guards and gaggles of children on every corner, the sullen-looking workers waiting in clumps at bus stops. This was not a time of day when Rebecca was ordinarily out in the world. "How about your car pool?" she asked Peter. "Am I supposed to pick up anybody else?"

"They're all riding with their grandparents," he said.

"Oh, yes."

"This one guy? T. R. Murphy? He's got a matched set."

"Matched set of what?" Rebecca asked.

"Grandparents. Mother's mother, mother's father. Father's mother, father's father."

"Lucky!" she said.

"Dick Abrams is coming with *eight* grandparents, but they don't really count because a lot of them are steps."

"I see."

"I don't mean stepgrandparents aren't okay," he said, shooting a worried look at her.

"No, I know you don't."

"They're going to have to ride in three cars to get there. Really they could fit in two, but one set isn't speaking to one of the other sets."

"This is fascinating," Rebecca said.

"Oh, and, um . . ." he said.

He drummed his fingers on his knees for a moment and stared out the side window. Rebecca waited.

"Um, would it be all right if I called you Gram?" he asked. "Just for today?"

"Why, sweetie, you can call me that every day!"

"Okay," he said. And then, "So! Do you think that during our lifetime, people will start traveling by dematerialization and rematerialization?"

"Well, I wouldn't mind trying it this morning," she told him.

This was intended as a joke, but when he didn't laugh, she said, "I suppose they might, in theory. With all that could go wrong, though, imagine the lawsuits they could end up with."

"Lawsuits! Right!" he said. "Gosh!"

She reflected that Peter was something like a yo-yo—popping up unexpectedly in sudden bursts of enthusiasm, subsiding and then popping up again with no warning. She smiled at him, but he was watching the street and he didn't notice.

In the entrance hall of his school—a stone building covered with ivy that looked arranged, rather than free-growing—they were met by a young woman passing out self-stick labels and felt-tip pens. *Hi!* the labels read. *My grandson is* _____. Rebecca wrote *Peter Sanborn* and returned the pen to the woman. The instant she had affixed the label to the front of her blouse, a small, bald man in a suit stepped up to her. "Peter Sanborn!" he cried.

"Yes?"

She was expecting him to offer some compliment on Peter's project, but instead he seized her hand and said, "I want you to know that we have taken his stepmother's complaint very, very seriously and we do understand her concerns."

"Her concerns?"

"Naturally it's an issue, at this time when families are so often fragmented. With all the working mothers, though, grandparents seemed the logical solution. It never occurred to us that . . . But now that Mrs. Sanborn's alerted us, we have fully prepared ourselves for every possible contingency. In a case where a child lacks grandparents, we offer one on loan."

Rebecca gave a startled guffaw. The man peered solemnly into her face. "Students have been encouraged to apply at the office," he told her. "Strictest confidence is guaranteed."

"That should reassure my daughter no end," Rebecca told him.

"My own mother is one of the names on file," he said.

"And then there's always Dick Abrams," she couldn't resist adding.

"Abrams?"

"He has *eight* grandparents. Surely he should be asked to share the wealth."

"Oh, ah, I don't feel we could—"

"Just something to consider," she told him, and she withdrew her hand.

"What's gotten *into* NoNo?" she asked Peter as they moved through the crowd. "Patch, I might expect it of, but NoNo, acting so contentious all of a sudden!"

"That was our principal," Peter said. "NoNo telephoned him last week."

"Well, isn't that always the way! No sooner do you get your children nicely pigeonholed than they turn around and surprise you."

They were walking down a wide corridor, traveling in a swarm of gray-haired women, a sprinkling of gray-haired men, and an underlayer of boys in navy blazers. Two boys near Rebecca were trying to step on each other's shoes. They elbowed and wrestled and stumbled into passersby while the middle-aged woman accompanying them sailed on serenely. One of them fell into Peter, but Peter just moved aside and the boy didn't apologize. Rebecca had the impression that Peter didn't know all that many of his schoolmates. She felt a familiar clenching of her shoulders, a sort of mother-bear response; she wanted to hug him close and snarl at the other children. But Peter showed no sign of discomfort. He seemed intent on maneuvering them toward the double doors ahead, which opened into a gigantic, echoing gymnasium filled with felt-draped tables and fabric screens.

Rebecca had not thought to ask what type of exhibit this would be. She had expected science projects, since she'd spent a number of long, dull hours at science fairs in the past. But this appeared more art-related. Paintings were tacked to the screens; sculptures and clumsy ceramic vases and abstract wire constructions stood on the tables. Each had a name next to it, lettered in grade-school print on a rectangle of white poster board, and already some of the grand-parents were saying, "Did *you* do this?" and, "Oh, my, isn't this something!"

"Which is yours?" Rebecca asked Peter.

Instead of answering, he turned sideways to slip through a cluster of women. He rounded the first aisle and stopped short at the head of the second.

There, in a glass box the size of a large aquarium, a sort of oil derrick made of brightly colored rods and sockets and toothed wheels pivoted up and down, allowing a series of blue marbles to roll the length of its spine and land in a metal saucer. Each marble was a slightly different size and rang out a different note on the scale: *do, re, mi* . . . From the saucer the marbles traveled through a convoluted tube and returned to their starting point, where they rolled down to land once again—*do, re, mi, fa, sol, la, ti, DO!*, over and over, delicate musical *plinks!* that could be heard, she belatedly realized, throughout the gym. What caused the marbles' return, she couldn't imagine. She was mystified, and awestruck, and captivated. She could have stood there forever, rapt, and other people must have felt the same because quite a crowd had gathered, none of them in any hurry to move on.

"Peter!" she said. "This is wonderful!"

Peter tilted his head and studied the contraption critically, his hands deep in his pockets, his back angled forward beneath the weight of his knapsack.

"This is . . . I don't know how you did it! It's amazing! What do your teachers say?" she asked him.

"I think they kind of liked it."

"Is there a motor, or what?"

"That's a secret."

"Oh, don't tell me, then. I'll just view it as a miracle."

"But I *will* give you a hint," he said. "Think about those toy birds that bob into a drinking glass."

"Ah," she said, none the wiser.

He said, "Would you like to see the other projects?"

"No," she said, "I believe I'll just stay here and admire this one."

He grimaced and looked at the ceiling, implying, *Grandmothers! What can you do?* But she could tell he was pleased.

. . .

She phoned Will as soon as she got home; she felt stretched like a band of elastic until she heard his voice at the other end of the line. "I'm back," she told him. "Did you go to D.C. without me?"

"Oh, no, I would never do that."

"You should have," she said. Although she was happy he hadn't. "How was your grandson's exhibit?"

"It was marvelous! I wish you could have seen it."

"I wish I could have too," he said.

She let herself picture that, for a moment: Will at her side on Grandparents' Day. Finally, finally, she would not have to show up everywhere alone. But he was asking her something. Asking her to dinner.

She said, "Dinner? At your place?"

"I thought maybe you might like to meet my daughter."

"I would love to meet your daughter," she said.

Already her mind was racing through possible outfits, possible topics of conversation—choosing who to *be*, really, for this very important encounter.

He said, "How about tomorrow night?"

"Tomorrow? Saturday? Oh."

She didn't have to explain. He sighed and said, "I know. A party."

"But I could do it Sunday," she told him.

"All right: Sunday. I'm assuming she'll be free then. Let's make it early. Six o'clock, since it's a school night."

"Can I bring a dish?"

"No, just yourself," Will said in a memorized way.

She refrained from asking him *which* self.

Later, talking on the phone to NoNo, she happened to let slip that she would be meeting Will's daughter. "You'd think it would be no big deal," she said, "after meeting you three girls. But I can't help feeling nervous, a little."

"Oh, well, I'm sure you'll do fine," NoNo said absently. "*Whose* daughter is this, again?"

"Will Allenby. He was with me a couple of weeks ago when you and Peter stopped by after dinner."

"Oh, yes," NoNo said.

"But I was forgetting! Peter! Peter's the reason I called! NoNo, that boy is a genius."

"Yes, everyone tells me he's bright," NoNo said. "I only wish he could drive."

"Did you see his project?"

"Are you kidding? I watched him construct it, every wheel and gear of it."

"I'm not sure whether it's art, or science, or music," Rebecca said. "Maybe all three. It's astounding!"

"I was the one who had to ferry him to the back of beyond for his supplies," NoNo told her. "Barry was away attending a conference, wouldn't you know."

"Oh, honey," Rebecca said, "I realize it must be hard, but I wish you could enjoy this boy. He's going to be grown and gone in a flash! And then you'll discover you miss him."

"Easy for you to say," NoNo told her bitterly. "You don't have the least idea what it's like, being saddled with somebody else's kid when you're basically still on your honeymoon."

Rebecca said, "Is that so."

It was one of those moments when she really did, literally, have to bite her tongue in order not to say more.

.   .   .

Sunday morning, she called Will twice to ask what she should wear. The first time, he said, "Anything. Or maybe—but no, just anything." Which was why she called the second time: that little hitch in his voice. She called back a minute later and said, "Will. You can tell me. Was there something special that you thought I ought to be wearing?"

"Oh, no."

"Something I ought *not* to be wearing?"

"Well, I don't know. Maybe just . . . something not too hippie," he said.

"Hippie," she said.

For a second, she felt hurt. She thought he was referring to the size of her hips. But he went on to say, "It's only that a few of your clothes tend to be sort of . . . striking, and I would like Beatrice to focus on you more as a person."

"Oh," she said. "Well, sure. In that case."

So she wore her flight-attendant outfit—tailored white blouse and navy skirt. Actual stockings. Actual leather pumps. And she battened down the wings of her hair with two plain silver barrettes that one or another granddaughter had left in the third-floor bathroom.

This time the drive to Macadam was more familiar, and therefore it seemed shorter. The swimming pools' vivid turquoise color reminded her of a type of hard candy she used to favor. *Trust Jesus*, she read. *I Still Like Larry*. The stop sign on the corner of Will's street had a sticker that said *EATING ANIMALS* plastered underneath.

The house he lived in—the late Professor Flick's house—was a white clapboard Colonial gone yellow around the edges. Hurricane Floyd had swept the state the week before, and evidently no one had bothered cleaning the front yard since. Rebecca had to thread her way through small branches and broken twigs and clumps of wet leaves on the walk. One branch was such a booby trap, lying in wait at ankle height, that she felt compelled to pick it up and heave it into the grass. So she arrived with damp, dirty hands, which she tried to scrub with a screw of tissue from her purse before she pressed the doorbell.

Once she had been buzzed in, she crossed a foyer crammed with antiques and climbed a carpeted staircase, rising into a steadily intensifying smell of lamb stew. It must have drifted up from Mrs.

Flick's kitchen, though, because when Will opened his door, just off the second-floor landing, nothing but the cold gray scent of newspapers floated out to her. Gazing past him, she saw newspapers everywhere—stacks of them on the chairs, the tables, the windowsills, the floor. "Come in! Come in! Have a seat," Will said, but there was nowhere to sit. He said, "Oh," as if he'd just realized. "Here, I'll . . ." He tore around the room, scooping up armloads of papers and piling them in a corner. "I keep thinking I should hire a cleaning service," he said. Rebecca didn't tell him that a cleaning service wouldn't have helped. She sat down and looked around her.

The walls were bare, marked with crumbling nail holes and the ghosts of old picture frames. The windows were curtainless, tall and narrow, letting in a bleached white light. She was sitting in one of those canvas butterfly slings from the sixties, and she would bet that the other pieces came from that era too. Will must have raided his garage or attic before he moved here, unearthing remnants of his student days—a cheap blond coffee table, a matted orange shag rug, a wheeled, adjustable chair meant for an office desk.

"Maybe you could give me some decorating tips," he said, and he smiled at her hopefully, showing all his teeth.

Rebecca smiled back. "Is Beatrice not here yet?" she asked.

"No, but I expect her any—oh, I'm sorry! What can I bring you to drink?"

"What do you have?" she asked.

"Water, milk . . ."

"Water, please."

He left the room. He was wearing slippers, she saw, folded down in back beneath his heels, although otherwise he was neatly dressed in khakis and a white shirt. She could glimpse no more than a sliver of the room adjoining this one—wallpapered with dark, ugly flowers—but she gathered it was a dining room. She heard a faucet running, and then he returned, holding a pink aluminum tumbler. "Here," he said, giving it to her. When their hands accidentally touched, she was reminded that he hadn't kissed her hello. He must be anxious. He started raking his fingers through his hair in that agitated way he had, and instead of sitting down himself, he remained standing in front of her. She took a swallow of water. It was room temperature, tasting of chlorine and something sharp, like mildew. She set the tumbler on the floor beside her chair and rose and wrapped her arms around his neck. "What—?" he said, stepping back, looking toward the door even though it was closed.

She didn't let him go. She tightened her hold and said, "Don't worry; everything will be fine. You'll see."

"Oh, you don't know Beatrice," he said, still eyeing the door.

"We're going to have such fun!"

"I'm serving this nutritious grain dish because she's vegetarian, and I think I might not have cooked it enough."

The buzzer rang, making him start. Rebecca dropped her arms, and he went to press a button next to the light switch. "Oh, God," he said. He raked his fingers through his hair some more. He turned back to her and said, "Also, I used chicken broth. Don't tell Beatrice."

"My lips are sealed," Rebecca said.

"It was what the recipe called for, and I wasn't sure I could omit it."

"Next time, I'll give you the name of a powder you can substitute," she told him.

She felt peculiarly unconcerned, as if she were playing a part in a play—the part of somebody knowledgeable and efficient. While Will tucked his shirt more securely into his khakis, she just stood waiting, not so much as glancing down at her own clothes. (At least she knew she couldn't be taken for a hippie.)

Slow footsteps climbed toward them. Will flung open the door. "Hi, there, Beatrice!" he said, in a sprightly voice that Rebecca had never heard him use before.

The person who walked in was small and tidily constructed, of no determinate gender, dressed entirely in black leather although it was a warm evening. Her skin was a stark, chalky white and her barbs of black hair had a dead look, as if they'd been dyed. She endured a brief clasp from Will—less a hug than a momentary spasm of his arm around her shoulders—and then she turned and surveyed Rebecca coolly. She had a gold stud in her nose and a thin gold ring in one eyebrow—the kind of thing that always made Rebecca feel she should diplomatically avert her gaze. Not one feature in this girl's face brought Will to mind.

Rebecca said, "Hello, Beatrice. I'm Rebecca."

Beatrice turned back to Will. "You told me to be here at six," she said, "so here I am."

"Well, thank you, Bee. I'm awfully glad you came."

"Are we eating supper, or not? Because I have things to do."

Will looked over at Rebecca. She smiled at him encouragingly. He looked at Beatrice. "Wouldn't you like to sit around a while first?" he asked. "Have a little talk?"

"Talk? Talk about what? Is there something you want to tell me?"

"No, just—"

"Who *is* this lady, anyhow? I don't get it."

Will tugged violently at a handful of his hair. Rebecca was the one who answered. "I'm an old, old friend of your father's," she said. "He and I grew up together."

This earned her another cool stare, from head to foot. All at once, Rebecca was less confident of her outfit.

"So," Beatrice said, "I guess you're going to tell me next you've fallen madly in love or something."

Will said, "Beatrice!" in an explosion of pent-up breath.

"Well, it's true we've . . . fallen in *fond*, I guess," Rebecca said. "But really I just came here tonight to meet you."

"Okay: we've met," Beatrice said. "Can I go now?" she asked her father.

"Go?" he said. "But you haven't eaten!"

"All right. If you insist, let's eat," she said.

Will sent Rebecca another look. She said, "Yes! Why don't we."

Anyhow, there weren't enough cleared chairs for the three of them to sit in the living room.

They went out to the dining room, Will leading the way. The table was incongruously elegant—a dark, varnished oval on a

pedestal of lion paws—but the chairs were the folding metal kind
you'd see in church fellowship halls, and a dozen cardboard boxes
partially blocked the window. Will said, "You two sit down and I'll
bring the food." Then he disappeared behind a swinging door.

"Well!" Rebecca said. "Where's your usual seat?" Because she
wasn't about to make the mistake of displacing Beatrice.

But Beatrice said, "I don't have one," and pulled out the chair at
the head of the table.

Rebecca chose the chair to Beatrice's right. She took some time
settling herself, unfolding her napkin (paper) and spreading it in her
lap. Three green glass plates had been laid directly on the table,
each with a rust-specked knife and fork to its left. Reflexively,
Rebecca started to switch her knife to the other side. Then she
thought better of it and left it where it was.

"When your dad was your age," she told Beatrice, "his entire
aim in life was to get his driver's license." This was one of her preplanned topics—something to break the ice. "He was the only boy
in our class who wasn't driving yet. He kept failing the road test. Has
he told you that?"

"No, but it doesn't surprise me," Beatrice said. She seemed
more affable now. She had picked up her plate and was holding it in
front of her face, either checking her reflection or peering through
it. "He's such a klutz," she said, setting the plate back down. "Every
time he goes anywhere, just about, he comes back with a dented
fender or something."

"Well, he's thinking," Rebecca defended him. "He's got his
mind on more intellectual matters."

Beatrice merely raised her eyebrows. Rebecca wondered if that
was painful, considering the gold ring.

Something clanged on the kitchen floor, and Will said, "Drat!"
Rebecca smiled conspiratorially at Beatrice. Beatrice remained
stony-faced.

"Do you know how I imagined you?" Rebecca asked. "I thought
you'd be the scholarly type. I don't know why, but I used to picture
that Will would have a son who was very studious and scientific.

Tristram, I decided his name was. And then when he said he had a daughter instead, I sort of turned you into a female Tristram. I imagined you'd wear a long muslin dress and this meek, old-fashioned hairstyle."

She attempted a light laugh that came out sounding tinny. Beatrice didn't laugh herself, but she seemed to be listening. Her eyes, for the first time, rested on Rebecca's eyes, and she stopped fiddling with her fork.

"I had this vision of you reading aloud to him in front of the fire," Rebecca told her. "I thought you'd have these serious philosophical discussions."

"Well, we don't," Beatrice said flatly.

"No, I can see that."

"End of the day? We're not speaking."

Rebecca misunderstood her, at first. Accustomed though she was to young people's turns of phrase, she thought that Beatrice meant they didn't say good night to each other. Then she said, "Oh. You don't speak *ever*?"

"This supper's an exception. But I'm not here because I want to be."

"Well . . . still, it was nice of you to come."

"I'm here because he promised me my own e-mail account if I came."

Rebecca said, "Oh."

Will barged through the swinging door, carrying a Pyrex casserole in both hands. "Ta-da!" he said. He set it on the table. Rebecca sprang to pick it up—she expected it to be hot, although he'd carried it in bare-handed—but she discovered it was lukewarm, nowhere near a temperature that would damage the varnish. She sank back down, feeling silly.

"This is a complete-in-one-dish, whole-grain meal," Will told Beatrice. "Entirely vegetarian."

"Actually, I eat meat now," she said.

"You do?"

His shoulders drooped. He looked over at Rebecca.

"We could *all* stand to eat more grains from time to time," she assured him.

"Okay, well . . . I'm not serving anything else because this is complete in one dish. Oh. I already said that."

"Have a seat," she told him.

He sat down across from her and stared glumly at the casserole. It was Rebecca, finally, who lifted the lid. Chunks of broccoli and cauliflower dotted what looked like oatmeal. A serving spoon was submerged almost the length of its handle. Rebecca plucked the spoon out with the tips of her fingers. "Beatrice?" she said. "Care to pass me your plate?"

Beatrice rolled her eyes, but she obeyed.

"Will? Some for you?"

He held out his plate. A fleck of something green clung to his lower lip. Rebecca resisted the urge to brush it off.

She served herself last, and then wiped her fingers and picked up her fork. "Mm!" she said once she'd taken a bite. The other two were already eating, chewing crunchily and steadily, and she couldn't think how because the dish was downright disgusting. The vegetables tasted raw and rooty, and the grain was so undercooked that she imagined it swelling up in her stomach and exploding. She looked around for water. There was none. Amazingly, Beatrice lifted another forkful to her mouth.

"I'm afraid I'm not much of a chef," Will said.

"I just think you're wonderful to make the effort," Rebecca told him. "There are lots of men who would serve TV dinners, in your situation."

He ducked his head shyly and said, "It's not as if it's all that complicated a recipe."

Beatrice said, "So, do many men have you to supper, Rebecca?"

"Um . . ."

"Do you do a good bit of dating?"

Will glanced over at Beatrice, looking alarmed. Rebecca said, "Well, no, I—"

"Because you actually seem pretty normal, on the surface. And

I'm just wondering if you realize what kind of a guy you're eating with, here."

"A very *nice* guy," Rebecca said firmly. "I've known him since he was a toddler."

"This is the guy who kidnapped our dog when Mom asked him for a divorce," Beatrice told her.

"Your dog?"

"Our little dog Flopsy Doodle."

Rebecca looked at Will. He swallowed. "I didn't kidnap her," he said. "I only . . . borrowed her. I happened to be upset."

"He stole her when we were out and didn't even leave us a note," Beatrice said. She spoke pleasantly, almost perkily; she was the cheeriest Rebecca had yet seen her. "We came home and called, 'Flopsy?' No Flopsy. So my mom phoned my dad; we knew it had to be him. She told him she was calling the police, and do you know what he did? He lied and said he hadn't the least idea what she was talking about. Then he opened his door and let Flopsy run off on her own, when everybody knows she's got a terrible sense of direction. It's lucky she wasn't killed."

"I was sad, all right?" Will said. "I was having a difficult time."

"Like it wasn't difficult for Mom and me."

"Look: it was a momentary lapse. I already said I was sorry. How many times can I apologize? I went looking for her myself, in the middle of a rainstorm; I was out half the night hunting her; I brought her back in my new car even though she was covered with mud—"

"Well, just so you realize," Beatrice told Rebecca. Then she rose and slid her chair neatly against the table. She gave her father a scornful stare down the length of her studded nose. "You can call me tomorrow about the e-mail account," she said.

She walked out, clicking briskly in her hard-soled black leather boots.

After they heard the front door shut, Will and Rebecca looked across the table at each other. "I guess that wasn't very successful," Will said.

"Nonsense; it went fine."

"Oh, I don't know, I don't know, I don't know," Will said, shaking his head.

"Girls that age are impossible," she told him. "*My* daughter? When she was your daughter's age? Her most cherished dream was to grow up to be a bartender."

Will didn't seem impressed. Rebecca went further; she said, "And she always fell for the scariest boys. Boys you wouldn't trust in your house, even! I worried what would become of her. But then she married the nicest man possible. Several nice men, in fact."

"I don't know, I don't know," Will went on saying.

"Will. Believe me. She's going to be fine."

He glanced up, then, from under his white eyebrows. "About the dog," he said. "I'm sorry to say she was right: I behaved very badly there, for a while."

"Well, no wonder! You were distraught."

"What Laura said first was, she just needed a little space. To do some thinking, she said. I accommodated her in every way; moved out immediately. I was so agreeable! Then she called me on the phone and announced she was making it permanent. It kind of . . . floored me. I went over to talk about it, and when I found they weren't at home, why, I must have gone a little nuts. But it was only that one occasion."

"And you did bring the dog back," she said.

"Yes, you should have seen the state of my car seats!" He grabbed another handful of his hair. "Well, enough of this. Can I offer you more to eat?"

"No, thanks. I'm stuffed," she said.

"Let's go into the living room, then."

"Can't I help with the dishes?"

"Absolutely not," he said.

She didn't argue. The undercooked grain was making her feel sort of logy; she envisioned dragging her stomach like a watermelon from table to sink.

He rose and came over behind her and slid her chair back. When she was standing, he took her gently by the shoulders and turned her to face him. Then he kissed her. This was not the light kiss they normally exchanged. It was more pressing and intense, more insistent, and she didn't know why she felt no response. Mainly, she felt embarrassed. She drew away. She reached up to touch one of her barrettes. "Well!" she said. "Gracious!"

"Rebecca," he said, still holding on to her shoulders.

But she said, "I should be going, I guess. It's getting late."

"Oh. Right," he said, and he released her.

In fact it was not yet seven o'clock, but he didn't point that out.

They walked through the living room, skirting newspapers. At the front door, Rebecca turned and gave him a brilliant smile. "Thanks so much for dinner," she said.

"It wasn't very good, I'm afraid."

"It was delicious. Really."

"If I'd only known Beatrice had gone back to eating meat," he said, "I could have served my chili. I have several extra containers now from the times when I've eaten at your house. I could have used them tonight and had the week's supply come out even again."

She laughed as she stepped onto the landing. But later, driving home, she was grim-faced and preoccupied, and when she parked and got out of her car, her body felt so heavy—so unspeakably burdensome—that she knew she couldn't blame it solely on the casserole.

S he saw now what she was up against: he was still mourning his marriage. He was grieving every bit as deeply as if he'd been widowed. That explained the missteps in their first few conversations, and his tendency to talk on and on about Laura, and his sad, unconfident manner. A man who kidnapped his wife's dog was a man who still felt connected.

Not that he was aware of it himself, Rebecca supposed. For he called her two days later to ask, "Seeing as how you've met *my* family now, what little of it there is, don't you think I should meet yours?"

"Mine? Well . . ."

"So far I've bumped into, what? Two or three of them," he said, "but I'd love to meet the others."

"Well, I guess I could have everyone to dinner."

"That would be great!" he said.

His eagerness was so uncharacteristic that she suspected he might be forcing it. She imagined his steeling himself before he picked up the phone to call her—squaring his shoulders, gathering resolve. "You know," she told him, "the Davitches can be kind of daunting, taken in a bunch. You could meet them just a few at a time, if you'd rather."

"No! I think this will be fun!" he said.

She recognized that glittery tone of voice. She had used it herself, many a time.

. . .

They settled on the coming Saturday. It could have been Thursday instead, but Rebecca didn't want one of those haphazard Thursday potlucks—some chaotic free-for-all where Will could be overwhelmed. No, this would be organized and sedate. People would arrive at a prearranged time and talk about civilized topics. She considered hiring Alice Farmer to serve, but Alice Farmer was fully capable of sitting down to interview Will—interrogate him, really, making sure he passed muster—while Rebecca herself did the serving. She decided against it.

Min Foo was the first one she called. "I'm inviting you to dinner this Saturday, October second," she said. "Just you and Hakim. No children."

"No children!"

"At eight o'clock sharp. And dress up."

"Why can't we bring the children?"

"It's a grownup affair. I want you to meet the man in my life."

This was the phrase she had selected ahead of time—so much more dignified than other terms she might use. It rolled off her tongue fairly easily, she felt, but was met by a silence as sharp as a crack at the other end of the line.

Min Foo said, "You have a man in your life?"

"Right," Rebecca said.

"You never told me that!"

"Well, you must have heard a man was coming around, now and then."

"I thought that was just a friend! Why are you springing this on me *now*?"

"Min Foo! I'm not springing anything on you! It's not *about* you!"

This wasn't going at all the way she had planned.

With NoNo, the focus was different. She wanted to know why a Saturday. "Is business really that bad?" she asked. "You're never free on a Saturday! Is the Open Arms going under?"

"No more than usual," Rebecca said.

"And haven't I already met this person?"

"Yes, but this will be his, sort of, formal introduction to the family as a whole."

"Oh. Okay," NoNo said.

She didn't seem impressed by that part about *the man in my life*.

Before Rebecca could place the next call, the telephone rang: Patch, in high dudgeon. "How come you invited Min Foo to dinner and not me?"

"Well, I was just—"

"Is this because she's your real daughter?"

"Patch! For heaven's sake! I'm inviting all of you!"

"And I have to hear it through the grapevine," Patch said. "I've a good mind not to come."

"Well, if you'd stay off the phone long enough for me to call you in the first place!" Rebecca snapped. And she slammed down the receiver.

Only Biddy reacted as she was supposed to. "A man in your life! Really?" she said. "Oh, Beck, I didn't realize. Is this the one who was there when I stopped by the other evening?"

"That's him," Rebecca said.

"Oh, this is so exciting. Tell me what food to bring."

Sometimes Rebecca thought that the whole point of having lots of daughters was, the law of averages said at least one of them might behave right at any given time.

Saturday turned out warm and humid, more like July than - October. This was a pity, because Rebecca had bought a fall outfit expressly for the occasion. It was a tailored gray straight-skirted suit, very subdued—unnoticeable, even. (And certainly nothing a hippie would wear.) She put it on anyhow, along with her flight-attendant pumps. She was plain on the surface but fancy underneath, because she had also bought new lingerie—sheer black lace that would have to be washed by hand. She didn't care. Also, it was killingly expensive. She didn't care at all. She had plans.

When she went downstairs to the kitchen, where Biddy and Troy were unwrapping food, Troy did a double take. "Why! It's Joan Crawford!" he said. Rebecca struck a model's pose, nose raised snootily in the air, and Biddy stopped work to say, "Are those *shoulder* pads? Goodness." Then she told Poppy, "Quit that!" because he was picking at a pie crust. She herself wore a ruffled blue sundress, which looked a little too froufrou on her spare frame, and Troy and Poppy wore coats and ties. Rebecca felt a rush of affection. It was nice of them to go to the trouble.

Will rang the doorbell precisely at eight. He was in a charcoal wool suit and his upper lip shone with sweat, either from the heat or from nervousness. "Don't you look stylish!" Rebecca said. When she kissed him, she smelled aftershave—something spicy—and all at once she felt lit up and optimistic, as if this were her very first party rather than her millionth.

"Am I early?" he asked. "Am I late?"

"You're right on time," she told him. "Come out back while we see to the food," and she took hold of his arm.

"Now, Biddy you've already met," she said as they entered the kitchen, "and you know Poppy, and this is Biddy's, um, Troy. Troy, this is Will Allenby."

"How do you do," Troy said, shaking Will's hand. Troy had extremely vivid blue eyes, and when he was introduced to people he often gave the impression of peering into their souls, drilling them with his hundred-watt gaze. Will responded by leaning forward determinedly and meeting Troy's stare straight on, so that for a moment they seemed to be butting heads.

Poppy said, "Why, hey, there! Good to see you again!" This could have been a bluff, but when Will said, "Good to see *you*, Mr. Davitch," Poppy said, "Please. Call me Poppy."

Which wasn't something he allowed just everyone. (Barry, for example, had recently been told that they weren't on close enough terms yet.) Rebecca sent Poppy a grateful smile.

She said, "Once you get to know the Davitches, Will, you'll realize we don't have a prayer of expecting them when they're due; so I suggest we make ourselves comfortable while we're waiting. Can I offer you a drink?"

"No, thanks," Will told her, but Poppy said he'd like a Scotch, and everyone else wanted white wine.

In the parlor, Rebecca lit the candles while Troy saw to the drinks. Biddy was asking Will where he came from, what he did for a living, how long he'd known Rebecca—the usual small-talk questions, which Will answered dutifully. "Church Valley, Virginia," he said, "but now I live in Macadam. I'm head of the physics department at Macadam College. I can't say for certain when I met Rebecca. Fifty years ago? More?"

"Fifty years!" Biddy exclaimed.

"I'll never adjust to the sound of that," Rebecca said. She accepted a glass of wine from Troy and sat down on the couch, close to Will but not touching. "Telling people I did such-and-such half a century back, or haven't seen so-and-so in forty-five years . . . I think, What am I saying? Can I really have been alive that long?"

"And so now you and Beck are getting acquainted all over again," Biddy told Will. She spoke in an indulgent tone, as if she found their story . . . cute, Rebecca thought. "It must be complicated, living in two different towns, though."

"Yes, my odometer's taken something of a leap," Will said. He turned to Rebecca and confided, "Little cough in my engine lately."

"Cough?"

"Kind of coughing noise when I accelerate."

Troy gave an abrupt laugh. "I would expect a physics professor to use a more technical term," he explained when everyone looked at him.

"No, Troy, I'm not in the least conversant with automobile engines," Will told him. "I have to put myself in the hands of strangers—mechanics who charge me a fortune and then, half the time, don't fix the problem."

"Oh, you should go to Aldo," Rebecca said.

"Aldo?"

"The man who coaxes my Chevy along. He's very gifted. And such a nice person! Biddy, *you* know Aldo."

"Oh, Aldo's great," Biddy said. "He solved my squeak when nobody else could."

"Aldo is forever bragging about his wife," Rebecca told Will. "How pretty she is and how talented and how she makes everything from scratch. Even the slipcovers. Even the rugs. Tanya, her name is. Tanya this, Tanya that, all the livelong day. Tanya and he are learning ballroom dancing. Tanya and he are planning a trip to Hawaii. Tanya and he got professionally made up and had their photograph taken as Bonnie and Clyde. The Man Who Loves His Wife, I call him. 'Doesn't that sound like the world's most incredible marriage?' I'm always asking people."

Will said, "This is your . . . mechanic?"

"Yes, and then last month he told me Tanya was at the doctor's. I said, 'I hope it's nothing serious.' He said no, she just needed to increase her medication. It turns out she's subject to these demented delusions and always has been. She thinks he's plotting to leave her; she swears that he's unfaithful; she once showed up on a woman's porch waving a souvenir Japanese sword. Two of their sons won't come home anymore. The oldest son asked him once, 'How can you put up with her?' and Aldo told him, 'Because it's somebody else. It's not the real, true Tanya.'"

"This is the man who repairs your car," Will said.

"Right," she said. "I just think he's so . . . admirable. He still believes his wife is amazing after all that's happened. He still boasts about her hooked rugs and gets made up like Bonnie and Clyde."

Will started to say something, but just then the front door slammed open. "Oh! Finally!" Rebecca said, and she went out to the foyer.

Min Foo stood there with Hakim, who was lugging one of those infant car seats that made parents appear to be returning from a successful trip to the farmers' market. Abdul slept soundly inside, curled over like a little cashew with a knit cap partially covering his eyes. "I know! I know! You said adults only," Min Foo told Rebecca.

"But what do you expect? I'm nursing! What do you expect me to do? Watch it, Hakim. Don't bang him into the wall."

She was wearing an elegant black silk pants set and every holy medal she owned, but a distinct circle of dampness darkened the tip of each breast. Inwardly, Rebecca sighed. All she said, though, was, "Hello, dear."

"Don't set him there!" Min Foo squawked, spinning toward Hakim. "The next person walking in is bound to step on him! Really, the man is hopeless," she told Rebecca. "This morning at seven—seven o'clock on a Saturday!—he asks me to brew him coffee."

"I only asked if coffee had been made, Min Foo," Hakim said mildly. He was stooping over the infant seat, trying to raise Abdul's cap off his eyes.

"You could have checked for yourself and *seen* that it wasn't made! 'It's not that I'm demanding,' he said, but what could he demand, pray tell, considering I've always brought him every little thing?"

"Now, now," Rebecca said, "I'm sure he didn't mean—"

"Naturally you would stick up for him," Min Foo told her. "You believe men are . . . What is that you're wearing?"

Rebecca looked down at her outfit. (Maybe it was not so unnoticeable after all.) Before Min Foo could deliver an opinion, though, the door swung open again. "It's us!" Patch cried.

It was not only Patch and Jeep but NoNo and Barry as well—Barry holding one of NoNo's famous fall-foliage arrangements—with Zeb bringing up the rear. "Did you all ride together?" Rebecca asked, and Jeep said, "Nope, just got here together by happenstance."

Rebecca had been hoping to spread the introductions out more, so that Will wouldn't feel too confused. "Well, anyhow," she said, "come on in and meet—"

"*What* is that you're *wearing*?" Patch asked.

"It's my brand-new suit that I bought on Thursday, and I like it; so don't say a word."

Patch blinked.

Rebecca reminded herself that it was crucial to stay calm.

When she led them into the parlor, Will and Troy both stood up. Will's arms were dangling docilely at his sides, which for some reason gave her a pang. "Everybody!" she said. "I'd like you to meet Will Allenby, the . . ."

It seemed redundant to refer to him once more as the man in her life. (And maybe Will would find it presumptuous, besides.) ". . . the person I invited you here to meet," she finished lamely. "Will, you remember NoNo, and this is her husband, Barry; and Patch and *her* husband, Jeep . . ."

"How do you do, how do you do," Will said, shaking hands. It was one of those situations where so many people might have spoken that everyone expected someone else to, and Will's voice was the only sound in the room. So when Poppy cried, "A toast!" Rebecca gladly took it up. "Yes, a toast!" she said. "I think we'll need a new bottle opened, Troy."

She helped him pass out the wine—a glass for Will, even, which he held awkwardly by the rim, his hand poised crablike above it. Min Foo insisted on club soda, another of those modern notions. (Rebecca, in her own breast-feeding days, had been ordered outright to drink lots of beer.)

"A toast to my birthday!" Poppy said when everyone was served.

Biddy said, "No, Poppy, wait."

"Oh, don't we all have drinks yet? *I'm* sorry."

"It's not your birthday, Poppy."

"Oh. Not my birthday."

He looked at Rebecca. "I guess I made a mistake," he said.

"That's all right, Poppy," she told him. Then she stepped closer to him and whispered in his tufted ear, "A toast to welcome Will."

"Will! Yes!" He raised his glass. "A toast to Will! To welcome Will!"

"To Will," everyone murmured—everyone except Barry, who sang out a ringing "Hear, hear!" in what Rebecca could have sworn was a British accent.

"Thank you," Will said, lifting his glass a few inches. He gave a slight cough. "And a toast to Rebecca, too; is that okay? To Rebecca, for being so lovely and gracious and cheering up my life."

Rebecca felt her face growing pink. She was conscious of everyone's eyes on her, and she felt a brief silence spreading around her before the others chimed in.

It was more than she had even thought to fantasize: her entire family, gathered in one room, hearing for the first time that somebody thought she was lovely.

.   .   .

At dinner, Will said, "I see you're taking good care of my plant."

"*You* gave her that plant?" NoNo asked.

Rebecca broke in quickly to say, "It's doing well, don't you think?"

It had grown at least a foot and put out two enormous new leaves, even though it was hidden away in the dimness of the dining room. (She had moved it there in the hope that it would attract less attention.)

Mercifully, NoNo just raised her eyebrows.

Rebecca's original plan was to seat Will on her right. But Poppy seemed to have a case of clinginess this evening, and he plunked himself there first, scooting his chair close enough so his knees could keep a reassuring contact with hers underneath the table. And Barry was already settled on her left. She had to point Will toward a spot several spaces away, down between Patch and Biddy.

"Oh, what a treat!" she told Barry. "I get to have you next to me." (Why did she always have to say the opposite of what she was thinking?) "Tell me," she said, picking up her fork, "do you find you're feeling at home with us yet?"

"Yes, absolutely," he said, but he was shaking his head instead of nodding, she noticed.

Biddy was saying to Will, "I trust you have nothing against hearts of palm."

"Is that what these are?"

"I thought they'd make a nice symbolic touch; don't you agree? But I see you've moved yours to the side of your plate."

"Well, I wasn't sure, you see, exactly what they were."

"They're the innermost core of the cabbage-palm stem. Very high in vitamin C."

"Palm trees have been cut up for this?"

"Well, yes."

"Is that a fact!"

"Broccoli plants are cut up, after all; asparagus shoots are cut up . . . Don't tell me you're one of those food avoiders."

"No, no, I just, I'm not all that much for experiment."

"Hearts of palm aren't an experiment!"

"To me they are."

"*Sea urchins* are an experiment. Hearts of palm are just salad."

"Yes, but, at home, you see, I generally have chili."

"Chili."

"I make this really excellent chili on Sunday afternoons—that would be tomorrow—and I divide it into seven containers for the seven nights of the week."

Biddy sat back in her seat and looked at him without expression.

Poppy was beginning a story. "In the fall of 1939," he told Hakim, "I experienced a dental emergency."

Jeep was discussing football with Troy, who was nodding attentively although his eyes had a sort of glazed look.

NoNo was talking to Zeb about . . . ballpoint pens, it appeared. "Once a week, almost," she said, "he tells me he needs ballpoint pens for school. Or maybe once every other week. In any case, way too often. I say, 'What did you do with those pens I just bought you?' He says he must have lost them."

Rebecca leaned forward a few inches to check on Will. He seemed to be dissecting a strip of roasted red pepper. Each tiny dot of char was set carefully to one side.

Min Foo was nursing Abdul, which flabbergasted Patch. "Min Foo! Do that in the other room! You can't breast-feed at the table!"

"Why not? I'm decently covered. I'm not sitting here undressed."

"We've got company! What must he think?"

Min Foo turned a placid gaze on Will. "I'm sure you've seen a woman nursing a baby before," she told him.

"Well," he said, "yes. But not at the table."

Patch said, "See there?"

Min Foo stood up, with the baby a squirming bulge beneath the hem of her tunic. She spun on her heel and strode out of the room.

Will said, "Oh, dear."

"Go after her," Biddy told Patch.

"I will not go after her! She's finally off in the parlor where she should have been all along!"

"*I* shall go," Hakim announced, and he rose with dignity and laid aside his napkin. A pause followed his departure. Then voices came from the parlor, and the cranking-up sound of the baby fussing. Hakim started singing in a low, cracked, rumbling voice. Some Arab lullaby, no doubt; something wandery and plaintive that Rebecca couldn't quite catch.

She looked brightly around the table. "Will has a teenaged daughter; did I mention that?" she asked.

Nine faces turned in her direction.

"The most intriguing person! Seventeen years old."

"She's very difficult," Will said.

"Difficult in what way?" Biddy asked him.

"Well, for one thing, she detests me."

"Yes, that *would* be a drawback," Barry said with a snicker.

But NoNo, dead serious, looked across at Will and said, "You know what, Will? I get that she's going to be fine."

"Excuse me?"

"I get that within the next eight months, she's going to develop a liking for you."

Will looked helplessly at Rebecca.

"NoNo sometimes . . . sees into the future," Rebecca told him. "That's what she means when she says she 'gets' something."

"It's genetic," NoNo explained.

"Genetic!" Will and Rebecca echoed together. Rebecca had

never heard this before. "Who supplied the genes?" she asked NoNo.

"Dad's second cousin, Sophie. You knew that."

"I didn't even know he *had* a second cousin!"

"Sophie was the family oracle," NoNo told Will. She was spearing a slice of ham as she spoke. "Nobody made a move without consulting her. Marriages, job changes, major purchases . . . They would come to her and ask, 'Should I? Shouldn't I?' She always knew the answer."

Poppy said, *"That's* who you take after?"

"Why, yes."

"Cousin Sophie Davitch?"

"Yes."

He started laughing. NoNo said, "What?"

"Oh, nothing."

"What's so funny?" she demanded.

"Okay: first, Cousin Sophie was three times divorced. And this was back in the 1920s, when *nobody* got divorced."

"So?" She reached for the mustard.

"So if she was so good at predicting, how come she couldn't predict that her three husbands would be mistakes?"

"Well, that I couldn't say," NoNo said. "All I know is, Grandmother Davitch told me I inherited my abilities from Dad's second cousin."

"And furthermore," Poppy said, "consider the woman's method. Do you happen to know *how* Sophie made her predictions?"

"Well, no."

"You'd come to her and ask, oh, should you take an ocean voyage. Then she'd turn it around and ask *you* questions. Had you ever traveled before, where had you gone, how had you enjoyed yourself. Let's say you told her you had so far only been on a train trip, and that was only to Philly, and you hadn't thought all that much of the place. Cousin Sophie would ponder a while, pull on her lower lip, stare into space; and then she'd say, 'My advice is, don't go. The ocean voyage won't be a success.'"

NoNo waited, fork poised in midair, but Poppy seemed to have finished. "When is dessert?" he asked Biddy.

"In a minute, Poppy."

"Oh, good." He dabbed his mustache with his napkin.

"But what was her method?" NoNo asked him.

"Hmm?"

"Cousin Sophie's method. What was it?"

"Why, everything that you told her had happened in the past, she just turned it around on you. Claimed it would happen again. If you could really call that a method."

"It would do," Will said. He was smiling; he seemed genuinely amused.

But NoNo said, "I'm sure there must be more to it than *that*," and she popped a bite of ham into her mouth.

Out in the parlor, Hakim was still singing. Rebecca suddenly recognized the tune. It was "O Danny Boy," of all things. "*O Abdul boy*," he rumbled, "*the pipes, the pipes are calling . . .*"

"At any rate," NoNo told Will, "I get that your daughter's about to start liking you. Take my word for it. And *I* didn't ask a thing about your past, now, did I."

"No," he said, still smiling, "you didn't. Well, thank you very much. I'm encouraged."

The others were smiling too, all around the table. Rebecca had one of those moments when her family seemed extraordinarily attractive—the girls with their animated expressions and black silk hair, the men so handsome and intelligent-looking, Poppy lending an air of distinction with his stately mustache. She let her eyes rest on each face in turn, feeling privileged and nourished, while Hakim sang softly in the parlor. "*'Tis I'll be here! in sunshine or in shadow*," he sang. "*O Abdul boy, my Abdul boy, I love you so.*"

. . .

It was a sign of how well the evening had gone that everybody stayed on after dinner. Min Foo got over her snit and agreed to accompany people on the piano; Troy and Biddy did their Nelson

Eddy–Jeanette MacDonald routine; and Barry turned out to be a wonderful tenor, although perhaps "The Lord's Prayer" was not the piece Rebecca would have chosen. It was nearly midnight before they all left.

Then she led Will to the kitchen—"Just to keep me company while I see to what can't wait till morning," she said—because she figured that would jog Poppy into going to bed. She was hoping she and Will could have a little privacy.

But no, Poppy came along with them, claiming he needed warm milk in order to sleep, and while he was waiting for it to heat he took it into his head that Will should be shown the family album. This came about because of a chance remark that Will made to Rebecca. "I had a little trouble," Will said, "sorting out who was who. Why is that one stepdaughter Chinese? And that person Troy: is he Biddy's husband? He seemed, er, not the husband type."

"Boy, have you got it wrong!" Poppy crowed, pivoting from the stove on his cane. "Min Foo is not a stepdaughter; she's Beck's daughter. And she isn't Chinese, either. I guess you were fooled by her name. And Troy for *sure* is not Biddy's husband; he's queer as a two-dollar bill."

"Three," Rebecca said.

"Huh?"

"Queer as a—"

Oh, Lord, she was turning into her mother. "Poppy," she said, "aren't you exhausted?"

"No, not in the least," he told her. "I believe I'll go get your friend the family album."

"Oh, that's not necessary," she said. "Basically, he's seen the album."

She meant the refrigerator door, with its multiple layers of photos. But Will couldn't have known that; so when Poppy asked him, "You have?" Will said, "Why, no, I don't think so."

"I'll be right back," Poppy said, and he left the room.

"Now you're in for it," Rebecca told Will. She switched off the gas beneath the milk. "Did you enjoy the evening? Did you like my family?"

"Yes, they were very interesting," Will said.

"You didn't see Min Foo at her best, I'm sorry to say. She's not usually so short-tempered. I'm worried she's beginning her same old pattern: have a baby, ditch the husband."

"Of course, they're all of them quite . . . outspoken," Will said.

"It's kind of like those nature programs on TV, where the female does away with the male after he donates his sperm."

"Pardon?"

Poppy said, "Here we are!"

He wasn't even in sight yet, but they could hear his cane pegging rapidly down the passageway. "Every light in both parlors was turned high as it could go," he told Rebecca as he entered. "You seem to think you have to siphon off excess electricity in case it might explode or something."

The album was clamped under his free arm—an ancient cardboard scrapbook bound with a tasseled string. He set it on the table and lowered himself, stiff-legged, into the nearest chair. "Sit down, sit down," he told Will, patting the chair beside him. "We should start with my late wife, Joyce. She passed away in 1969. I miss her to this day. Now, where are we. Let's see. Trouble is, there's no order here. Everything's jumbled up."

Rebecca poured Poppy's milk into a mug and placed it next to the album, using the excuse to set a hand on Will's shoulder as she leaned past him. He looked up at her and smiled.

"What I'm hoping to find is the picture of Joyce when we met," Poppy said, turning a page. "She wore the most fetching hat. It resembled two bird wings."

"I bet this is the one you call Patch," Will said. He was looking at a snapshot of a child with a bunch of balloons. "I recognize her freckles."

"Oh, then we're way too recent," Poppy told him. "I met Joycie long before Patch came along."

"And this is the one you call NoNo, I think."

Rebecca wished Will wouldn't refer to the girls as "ones," as if they were specimens of something. She settled in the chair across from him. "Yes," she said, peering at the upside-down picture, "that's NoNo at a birthday party. And here is Biddy. Doesn't she look cross? She used to hate to dress up, is why. She said dress-up dresses itched."

"So many *parties*," Will said.

"Isn't that the truth," Poppy agreed. He reached for his mug and took a loud sip.

"Everywhere I look," Will said, "—the refrigerator, the album—everybody's celebrating. We just get through drinking a toast and then you sit me down and show me pictures of other toasts, years of toasts. Even the children are drinking toasts! Do you really think that's wise?"

"We give them only a sip," Rebecca told him.

Poppy said, "Why am I not finding Joycie? That picture of her when we met. I hope it isn't lost."

"And after all," Rebecca told Will, "these are photographs. You don't usually photograph people reading books or playing chess, although we do those things too."

Poppy looked up from the album. "Chess?" he asked. "We don't play chess."

"Well, Dixon does, sometimes."

"I see your point," Will said. "It's just . . . maybe you have an unusual *number* of parties, don't you think? Why, any time you and I try to get together, we have to work around all your social events."

"Social? Those are professional!"

"Yes, but . . . it seems you're the social *type*, you know? Hobnobbing with your mechanic, for instance; sharing a stranger's marital secrets."

"Aldo's not a stranger!"

"Ah. Well. Truthfully, I must say I'm not sure I find the man as laudable as you do. To me, his attitude toward his wife shows a lack of responsibility."

"Responsibility for what?" Rebecca asked.

"He had a duty, in my opinion, to set some standards. Both for his children's sake and his own. And he neglected that duty."

"Oh, piffle," Rebecca said.

She may have been more forceful than she intended, because

Will drew back slightly. Rebecca drew back too, and pressed her fingers to her lips.

"Here we go!" Poppy said. "Joycie when we met." He slid the album closer to Will.

"Ah, yes. Very attractive," Will said, hunching over it.

"She was a cutie, all right."

Will's right hand rested on the top of the page, his thumb rubbing the corner with a repetitive, whiskery sound. Rebecca remembered him, all at once, seated at the library table: his papers laid out just so, his books in stacks, his colored pencils in rows.

With a little stretch of the imagination, she could have glanced toward the dark kitchen window and seen Joe Davitch's laughing face.

Poppy tugged at the album till Will released it, and then he studied Joyce's picture. "She had the brownest eyes," he said. "You think the Davitches' eyes are brown; you should have seen Joyce's. Hers were more like black."

He picked up his mug and drank off the last of his milk. "Well," he said. "I'm beat. I'd better haul myself off to bed."

Rebecca slid her chair back and stood up. She said, "I should say good night too, I guess."

"Oh," Will said. "All right."

He stumbled to his feet. He stood waiting while she went around to Poppy's chair and helped him up, handed him his cane, placed an arm round his waist; and then he followed them down the kitchen passageway.

"Feet ache, ankles ache, knees ache . . ." Poppy intoned. In the foyer, he turned to Will. "Good seeing you," he said. "Don't forget my birthday party."

"I wouldn't miss it," Will told him.

Poppy started up the stairs. Rebecca crossed to the front door and opened it. "When *is* his party?" Will asked her.

"Well," she said, "it's December."

"What date in December?"

She faced forward, gazing out. In the light from the street lamps, everything had a soft, gray, blurry look, like a memory. She felt she had been through all this before; she *knew* she had been through it: that dampening of her spirit; that tamped-down, boxed-in feeling; that sense she had in Will's presence that she was a little too loud and too brightly colored. And now she recollected that he was the one who had brought things to a halt that long-ago night on the sofa. She had been rushing ahead, ready to fling herself recklessly over the edge, and then he had pulled away and suggested they show more restraint.

She said, "I don't think we'll be seeing each other in December."

Even the distant traffic sounds seemed to come to a stop.

"Or before then, either," she said.

He took a ragged breath.

"Why?" he asked her.

And when she didn't answer, he said, "Was it something I did?"

"No, Will, you didn't do anything."

"Was it your family? Did they not like me?"

She felt a stab of pity. She said, "Oh, I'm sure they liked you!"

"Or Zeb, then?"

"Zeb?"

"He's obviously my competition."

The pity faded. "The fact of the matter is," she said, "this just won't work, Will. I'm sorry."

Then she stepped forward and pressed her cheek against his. He stood woodenly, not responding. "Goodbye," she told him.

He said, "Well. Yes. All right. Goodbye, Rebecca."

She watched his ungainly, angular figure set off down the front walk, and she waited until he'd climbed into his car before she shut the door.

The house had a muffled sound that seemed lonelier than silence. Coffee cups sat abandoned in the parlors, and the dining room looked half stripped and disheveled, and Aunt Joyce smiled wistfully from the album on the kitchen table.

It turned out that Rebecca was the one who was still in mourning.

t e n

A woman named Mrs. Mink called to organize a baby shower. "My friend Paulina Garrett recommended you," she said. "I told her I wanted someplace elegant. Someplace like a mansion."

Rebecca said, "Well, the Open Arms is just a row house."

"It doesn't have to be *really* a mansion, but it should have that atmosphere. That upper-class, elegant atmosphere. And then I'll want it decorated in baby blue and white, with a cloudlike effect in the dining room."

"Cloudlike?"

"Yes, ethereal; know what I mean?"

"We can decorate however you like," Rebecca said, "but our dining room is papered in a maroon-and-gold stripe and the furniture is some dark kind of wood; walnut, I believe. So I'm not sure—"

"Oh, you can do it! I know you can! Paulina Garrett told me their party last spring was wonderful. Everything so joyous, she said; you made it such an occasion that nobody wanted to leave."

Rebecca remembered the Garrett party all too well. A torrential thunderstorm had sprung up and somehow, by some process that she still didn't quite understand, caused the front-parlor chandelier to start raining on the guests. Nice to hear that the Garretts didn't hold it against her.

"The reason I want blue and white," Mrs. Mink was saying, "is we know this will be a boy. They've had that special test. And we know he's not going to live very long."

"Excuse me?"

"He's got some kind of disease they can diagnose in the womb."

"Oh, that's terrible!" Rebecca said.

"So I want this party to be perfect, don't you see? Every last detail. I want his *life* to be perfect. Because he gets to experience it for such a little while."

"Well, of course," Rebecca said.

But while she was discussing the fine points—the folding paper parasol, the white-clouded blue cotton tablecloth she'd seen advertised at Lust for Linens—she was reflecting that really, this baby's story was just a shortened version of everybody's story. Get born; die. Nothing more to it than that.

"And flowers?" Mrs. Mink was asking. "Paulina tells me you can recommend a florist."

"Yes, NoNo," Rebecca said.

"Pardon?"

"My stepdaughter, NoNo Sanborn. She could set out white asters and those pale-blue flowers, those what-do-you-call-them . . ."

In fact, Rebecca couldn't think offhand of any flowers that were blue, except for those chicory blossoms that grew wild along the highways and closed up in tight little winces if you picked them. She said, "I can't remember. I don't know. I don't have any idea."

"Well, that's all right, we'll just ask your—"

"I don't know. I just don't know. I'll have to call you back," Rebecca said, and she replaced the receiver, which all of a sudden weighed too much to hold on to any longer.

.   .   .

Lately, she'd been feeling so . . . What was the word? Blank. Low in spirit, flat as a desert; and now she grew more so every day.

Getting up in the morning was like hauling a dead body. Food lost its flavor. Conversation required calling upon every muscle, summoning her last particle of strength. She kept noticing how very little there was in this world to talk about. It was turning into a beautiful fall—clear and mild, the leaves staying on the trees much later than usual—but the brilliant colors hurt her eyes, and the meditation center's banner flapping in the breeze made a sinister, leathery sound, like bat wings.

Not a person in the family asked where Will had disappeared to. Well, except for her mother. ("Oh, Rebecca," she said sadly, once she'd heard the facts, "you were a fool thirty-three years ago and you're a fool today.") But the girls behaved as if he had never existed. She suspected they were trying to spare her feelings—taking it for granted, no doubt, that she had been jilted.

One night when she had nothing to do she got in her car and drove to Macadam. She parked in front of Mrs. Flick's house and gazed up at the second-floor windows. All of them were dark, though. Which was lucky, she supposed, because really it was the romance she missed; not Will himself. Still, she sat there a long, long time before she started her engine and drove home again.

She told Zeb, in one of their bedtime phone talks, that she thought the human life span was too long. "Really, I've finished my life," she said. "I finished it when the girls got grown. But here I am, just hanging around, marking time, waiting for things to wind down."

Zeb said, "Rebecca? Are you all *right*?"

"Define 'all right,'" she told him.

"Where is your man friend?" he asked.

"He's gone."

"You ditched him?"

"Yes, but that's not the problem. The problem is, I've outlived myself."

"Well," he told her, "remember what George Eliot said."

"What did George Eliot say?"

"Or maybe it wasn't George Eliot. At any rate: 'It's never too late to do what you want to do.' Remember that."

"What?" Rebecca said. "Well, of all the—Why, that's just plain *wrong*! Suppose I wanted to . . . I don't know; suppose I wanted to get pregnant! That's just plain *ridiculous*!"

She was so outraged that she hung up, not knowing she was planning to. Then she regretted it. When the phone rang a few seconds later, she lifted the receiver and said, "Sorry."

"I just remembered," Zeb said. "It wasn't 'do what you want to do.' It was 'be what you want to be.' I think."

"I'm just feeling a little tired," Rebecca told him.

"And I don't even know for sure that it was George Eliot."

She said, "Thanks for trying, Zeb."

.   .   .

She might have thrown herself into work, but business was very slow these days. Three different people had called to ask if the Open Arms was in a safe neighborhood, and although she had assured them it was—with reasonable precautions, she said; using normal common sense—they told her they would have to think it over and get back to her.

Besides, how often could a person celebrate? How many weddings, christenings, birthdays could she applaud, for heaven's sake? What was the *purpose* of it all?

Her *New York Times* collected in stacks and gradually turned yellow, untouched. Her *New Yorkers* drifted to Poppy's room and she never asked for them back. She passed her *New York Reviews* on to Troy without giving them a glance; she told him she thought there was something perverted about book reviews that were longer than the books they were reviewing.

One morning the library phoned to say that her interlibrary loan was in, and she made herself walk over to collect it. But it turned out the book was so rare—a crumbly brown leather volume edged in flaking gold—that she was not allowed to take it home with her. She had to read it there in the reading room, the librarian told her. (This was the same librarian who'd arranged the loan in the first place, but she issued her edict in such a disapproving voice, with such a humorless, raisin face, that Rebecca couldn't imagine why she'd once seemed a kindred spirit.)

She did try. She did settle at a table and pluck the cover open with the very tips of her fingers and leaf obediently through the brittle ivory pages. *A Baltimorean's Experience of the War for Southern Independence*, the book was called. The author was a lawyer named Nathaniel Q. Furlong, Esq., who claimed to have known Robert E. Lee when Lee was still a private citizen. Years before the War, Mr. Furlong maintained, Lee had confided to him that he could never support a cause that would allow the slaves—the "heathen Africans," in his words—to return to their native land and forfeit their one chance for Christian salvation. But when Rebecca managed to locate this passage (which was, she saw for the first time, of dubious credibility, written by a man whose boastful, unreliable nature revealed itself in every line), she wondered why she had found it so momentous back in college. She had just wanted to believe, she supposed, that there were grander motivations in history than mere family and friends, mere domestic happenstance.

She returned the book to the librarian, and she brushed the crumbs of leather off her hands and left the building.

.   .   .

Everything struck her as unutterably sad—even the squirrel with half a tail she saw bustling cheerfully down the sidewalk. Even Poppy's daily routine: his ritual round of activities, straightening his room and brushing his hat and tuning in his TV shows, all intended to keep himself from sinking into hopelessness.

She knew her mood had something to do with the season. Autumn was when Joe had died. She couldn't look at the poplar outside her bedroom window—the leaves so yellow that she would think she had left a light on, some cloudy days in mid- or late October—without recalling that shattered morning when she had emerged from the hospital in a stupor and taken forever finding her car and then driven bleakly, numbly down streets lined with radiant trees in every shade of red and gold and orange.

As a girl she had often said, about some potential disaster, "Oh, that can't happen; it's too *bad* to happen." But Joe's death had been too bad to happen, and it had happened even so. She had felt stunned by that all through his funeral—through the thready whine of the organ and the uncertain, off-key hymns and the peculiar poem Zeb had read called "Not Waving but Drowning." She had sat through that funeral white-faced with shock. It appeared that nothing was too bad to happen. How had she ever thought otherwise?

Grieving had turned out to be not unlike falling in love. She had pored over Joe's photographs, searched for the innermost meanings of his calendar notations, traced his dear signature on canceled checks. She had found any excuse to mention his name: "Joe always felt . . ." and, "Joe used to say . . ." It had troubled her that she could summon up no specific, start-to-finish memory of their lovemaking; only generalities. (He was a morning man. He liked to kiss her eyelids. He had a way of almost purring when she touched him.) She prayed for random moments to resurface. Once, driving along in her car, she was thrilled to recollect that he used to talk to the mirror while he was shaving. ("Ah, there you are, Joe. Ready for another glorious day of helping strangers get drunk together.") She received this image like a gift, and clung to it, and waited greedily for more.

Her life, as she saw it back then, had begun on an April evening when she had stood on the sidewalk peering at the sign overhead: *The Open Arms, Est. 1951.* And now her life was finished, but here she was, still circulating among the guests, a solitary splinter of a woman in the crowd.

"Well, you know what they say," Zeb had told her. (Zeb at twenty-two, full of callow assurance.) "God never gives you more than you can handle."

"Who says that? Who?" she had asked in a fury. "Who would dare to say that?"

"*I* don't know," he had said, taken aback. "God, maybe?"

Causing her to start laughing, even while the tears were streaming down her face.

Joe's November dental appointment, noted in his own jaunty hand with his stubby-nibbed fountain pen, came and went without him. His battery-run watch went on ticking in his drawer.

The worst days had been the ones where she had time enough to think. She thought, *What am I going to do with all the years ahead of me?* The easier days were the chaotic ones, where she proceeded from minute to minute just dealing with demands. Soothing the children, cooking their meals, helping with their homework. Standing stolid and expressionless when NoNo pushed her away and ran sobbing to her room, or when Patch asked, "Why couldn't *you* have died, and Daddy gone on living?"

Some people, she often noticed, had experiences in their pasts that defined them forever after, that they felt compelled to divulge to any casual acquaintance at the outset. The loss of a child, for example: almost anyone who had been through that had to mention it first thing; and no wonder. With Rebecca, it was the fact of her instant motherhood. That had been the most profound change in her life; it had made her understand that this *was* her life, for real, and not some story floating past. Which may have been the true reason that she still used the term *stepdaughter* long after the girls themselves, come to think of it, might have allowed her to drop it. And when she had become their one and only parent (for no one seemed to count Tina), she was all the more aware of the unpredictable, unimaginable shape her life had taken.

Once, introducing "my stepdaughters," she had happened to include Min Foo with a thoughtless wave of her hand. Min Foo had never let her forget it. "I'm sorry! It was an accident!" Rebecca told her, but privately, she had suspected that it revealed something significant. Min Foo was just as much her own separate self, just as different from Rebecca, as the other three were. And in some ways, she was less of a comfort, because she was the youngest and her memories of Joe were fewer. As the years went by, the older girls would reminisce with Rebecca — "Do you remember the time we all got on the train to D.C. and just as we were pulling out, we saw Dad standing there on the platform with the pretzels he'd gone to buy?" Rebecca would nod and laugh, and Min Foo would look from one face to another like someone seeking admission. "Did he ever sing to me?" she asked once. "I think he did. I seem to remember him singing to me while I was lying in bed."

"I don't believe so," Rebecca said, "but I know he read to you."

"What did he read?"

"Oh, just the usual. *Winnie-the-Pooh* . . ."

But you couldn't reconstruct a person from bald facts. Min Foo would never experience the details of him—the fine-grained skin on the backs of his hands and the curly corners of his eyes when he smiled. (One time a man invited Rebecca out, a year or two after Joe's death, and she accepted but then was filled with despair at the sight of the wiry red hairs on his forearms. He wasn't Joe, was the problem. He was a perfectly nice man, but he wasn't Joe.) And to the grandchildren, Joe was no more distinct than those names you see on nineteenth-century headstones. Joseph Aaron Davitch. He used to exist, was all. And now did not.

Oh, he would have made a fine old man. A *fine* old man. Sixty-six this past September; imagine. Rebecca was older now than he had even been, although she continued, to this day, to think of him as her senior. And he would have loved having grandchildren.

She used to assume that the bereaved were actually mourning for themselves, and of course that was partly true. But what she hadn't expected was the sorrow she felt on behalf of Joe. She ached to think of all that he was missing—the various landmarks in the girls' lives and the daily pleasures and the minor family triumphs.

At first she had thought, *I wish I could tell him such-and-such,* and, *He would have enjoyed so-and-so.* Then the years began to telescope, so that if he came back today and asked, "What's happened since I've been gone?" she would say, "Oh, well, I don't know. This and that, I guess." Like someone long dead herself, she would see that none of her little world's events had really been that important.

"How come the front parlor's cream now?" he would ask. "Where did you put my tennis racquet? What became of that big old oak that used to stand on the corner?" And she would say, "Oh! You're right: the parlor used to be gray. Your racquet? You played tennis? I'd forgotten there was an oak. I think it was struck by lightning." She would feel unaccountably guilty; you would think it was Joe she'd forgotten. Although it wasn't, of course.

Now she braced herself against autumn as if it were a buffeting wind that she had to endure with her eyes tight shut and her jaw clenched, holding on to the nearest support for all she was worth. October, heartlessly dazzling. November, dropping leaves like a puddle of gold beneath the poplar. Sometimes, when nobody was around, she spent half the afternoon gazing blindly out the window. Or she let the telephone ring and ring while she sat listening. The sound was a satisfaction. It was an even greater satisfaction when the ringing finally stopped.

.   .   .

"I suppose you're going to insist on some kind of brouhaha for Thanksgiving," Min Foo told her.

Thanksgiving?

Well, yes: November. She couldn't think how it had slipped her mind.

Thanksgiving was the one holiday when Rebecca did all the cooking. This had developed after a famous Thanksgiving when Biddy served braised pheasant and steamed quinoa in white truffle oil. There had been a sort of revolution, and Biddy had stalked out in a huff and Rebecca was put in charge forever after. Which was fine with her. She didn't mind the hard work; she welcomed it, in fact. But she dreaded the socializing. All that merriment! She would have to be so cheery! She wondered what would happen if she simply didn't bother. If the girls started one of their quarrels and she just let it happen. If the moment for the toast came and went and she just slugged her drink down in silence.

Still, she made out her grocery list. Went to the store. Baked the cornbread ahead for the stuffing. Had Alice Farmer come in to give both parlors a good going-over.

Alice Farmer planned to celebrate Thanksgiving at her sister's. "You know my sister Eunice, the one who's blessed with the gift of healing," she said. Rebecca folded her hands across her stomach and looked down at them. More veins crisscrossed them than she had ever noticed, knotted and blue and gnarly. Alice Farmer stopped dust-mopping and said, "Miz Davitch?"

"I'm sorry; what?" Rebecca asked.

"Maybe you ought to take this remedy that my Aunt Ruth takes," Alice Farmer told her. "It's real good for your nerves, but you can only buy it in Georgia."

"Okay," Rebecca said after a pause.

"Okay *what*? You want her to get you some?"

"No, that's okay," Rebecca said.

She thought that if she were shown a photograph of these hands, she might not even know they were hers.

. . .

Everybody attended except for Patch and her family; they were spending the holiday with Jeep's parents. And everybody, of course, was late, which caused no particular problem because Rebecca had counted on that when she put the turkey in. Zeb showed up first, then Min Foo and her brood, then NoNo with Barry and Peter. It had been sprinkling all morning, and most of them wore raincoats that dripped across the foyer. Underneath, though, they had on their best clothes. They always dressed up for Thanksgiving—much more than for Christmas, to which the youngest children wore pajamas. Rebecca, though, was not dressed up. She had sort of forgotten. She was wearing the sweatshirt and flounced denim skirt that she had put on when she got out of bed. "Shall I watch things in the kitchen while you run and change?" Min Foo asked her.

Rebecca said, "Oh, thanks," but then the door slammed open again, letting in Biddy's contingent, and Rebecca stayed where she was.

Biddy had good news: her book for senior citizens, *The Gray Gourmet*, had been accepted by a small press. She announced this even before she took her raincoat off, with Troy and Dixon beaming on either side of her. The first to offer congratulations was Barry. "That's great!" he said. "I've got an author for a sister-in-law!" Then Zeb asked what the publication date was. She didn't know yet, Biddy said. Then everybody looked at Rebecca.

Min Foo said, finally, "Maybe we should break out some champagne."

Rebecca said, "Oh. I'll go get it."

In the kitchen, she took two bottles of champagne from the refrigerator. Then she peeked in the oven to check on the turkey, and she lowered the flame beneath the potatoes, and after that she fell into a little trance at the window. The fog outside was made denser by the foggy panes, which were clouded with steam from the stove. Raindrops marbled the glass.

NoNo walked in and said, "Beck, I wanted to—Oh!"

She was looking at Will's plant, which had migrated to the kitchen and grown another six inches. "Good heavens, it's a tree!" she said. "I've never seen anything like it."

"I'm thinking of moving it out to the yard," Rebecca told her.

"Oh, I wouldn't do that in November. The first frost would probably kill it."

"What happens happens, is my philosophy," Rebecca said.

She expected NoNo to argue, but NoNo was busy going through her purse—a shiny little red-and-black box that matched her red-and-black dress. "I wanted to show you something," she said, and she pulled out a folded sheet of paper.

Rebecca opened it and found a list, computer-printed.

> 1. *Dry cleaner*
> 2. *Make dental appointment for Peter*
> 3. *Find someone to clean gutters*
> 4. *Buy my bro. a birthday present*

Till the mention of a brother, she had assumed the list was NoNo's. She looked up questioningly.

"Barry wrote that," NoNo told her.

"So . . ."

"He wrote that for *me*. These are the things that I was supposed to do last week."

"I see," Rebecca said.

"Beck. When you and Dad got married, did you ever . . . Don't take this the wrong way, but did you ever wonder if he'd married you just so he would have help with us kids?"

Rebecca opened her mouth to answer, but NoNo rushed on. "I'm trying not to think that of Barry, but look at this list! And he's always saying, 'Boy, married life is great.' He says, 'Things are so much easier now. I don't know what we did before you came along,' and while naturally I'm flattered, still it does cross my mind that—"

"Are you saying you don't think he loves you?" Rebecca asked.

"Well, I know he *says* he does, but . . . these lists! And the car pool, and the PTA meetings! Everything falls to me, which of course makes sense in a way because he does work longer hours, but . . . it's like he's saying, 'Oh, good, now that I have a wife I don't have to bother with any of that busywork anymore.' It's like I'm so useful."

"But, sweetie," Rebecca said, "isn't he useful, too? Before, you were all alone in the world. I remember once I asked you why you never took a vacation, and you said if you had a man in your life, someone to travel with, you said—"

"Beck, you know how I get these pictures sometimes," NoNo said. "Pictures behind my eyelids about the future. Well, the morning after my wedding, I was starting to wake up but my eyes weren't open yet and I got the most distinct, most detailed, most realistic picture. I saw myself walking up Charles Street, that part where it splits for the monument. I was wheeling a baby carriage and I was wearing a maid's uniform. Gray dress, white apron, white shoes, those white, nurse kind of stockings that always make women's legs look fat—"

Rebecca laughed.

"I'm glad you find it amusing," NoNo said bitterly.

"Maybe the point was the baby carriage. Did you think of that?"

"The point," NoNo said, "was that I was wearing servant clothes."

"Well, maybe the picture was wrong. It wouldn't be the first time! After all, you predicted Min Foo would have a girl, didn't you? And then something else, what was it, some other mistake—"

Too late, she realized that she was thinking of what Patch had said: that NoNo couldn't be very clairvoyant if she'd chosen to marry Barry.

"At any rate," she said, "doesn't it seem to you, really, that all of us love people at least partly for their usefulness?"

"No, it does not," NoNo said. "I would never do such a thing! Never! I fell in love with Barry because he was so gallant and romantic, and he had that kind of eyebrows I like that crinkle up all perplexed."

"Well, I don't mean—"

"Forget it," NoNo told her. "I knew I shouldn't have mentioned it. So! Shall I take these bottles out? Will two be enough, do you think?"

"Oh. Maybe not," Rebecca said, and she went over to the refrigerator. "What I meant was—" she said, but when she turned around, a third bottle in her hand, she found that NoNo had already left the room with the first two. Her purse remained on the table, with the list beside it. Rebecca picked up the list and studied it again.

"Min Foo says to remind you she's having club soda," Biddy said, walking in. "Shall I pour it? Is there any in the fridge?"

"Yes, there should be," Rebecca told her absently.

"What's that you're reading?"

"Oh, nothing."

Biddy peered over her shoulder. "Barry's list," she said.

"You've seen it?"

"Everybody's seen it. But it was tactless of her to trouble *you* with that, just now."

"Tactless? Why?"

"Oh, no reason," Biddy said hastily. "Never mind me; I'm just babbling."

"I don't know why people in this family are so unhappy," Rebecca told her. "Look at Min Foo! I'm worried to death she's going to get another divorce."

Biddy merely shook her head and removed the ice bin from the freezer.

"Last week," Rebecca said, "she told me this long-winded tale about something unforgivable that Hakim was supposed to have done. You'd think he'd committed ax murder! And all it was, was they were driving someplace together and Hakim took the wrong road and insisted on staying on it."

"He didn't like the inefficiency of a U-turn," Biddy said. "That's what she said he called it: the inefficiency."

"Oh, she told you this, too?"

"He wanted to keep on the way they were headed and just sort of *meander* in the right direction at some point in the future."

"But that's the way men are," Rebecca said. "It's nothing to get divorced about."

"I said the same thing, exactly." Biddy dropped ice cubes into a glass. "I said, 'Min Foo, you two should go for some help. Ask Patch for the name of her marriage counselor,' I told her."

"Patch has a marriage counselor?"

"I thought you knew."

"All these *problems*!" Rebecca said. "Thank goodness for you and Troy, at least."

Biddy stiffened. "Just because Troy is gay doesn't mean we don't quarrel like other couples," she told Rebecca.

"How reassuring to hear that," Rebecca said.

She'd intended to sound witty, but her words fell dully, and Biddy didn't smile.

They left the kitchen—Biddy with Min Foo's club soda, Rebecca with the champagne. In the dining room they passed Peter and Joey, who were seated at one end of the table. Peter was demonstrating some kind of game. "First you take a ballpoint pen and lay it flat," he said, "with the little air hole facing up. See the little air hole? Then you hold another pen exactly a foot above it, and you aim at the air hole and stab. Like this." He jabbed the second pen downward, rattling all the place settings. "The winner is whoever's the first to break the pen on the table. Your turn."

Rebecca felt slightly cheered by this scene. (Joey, four years Peter's junior, was hanging worshipfully on Peter's every word.) She dropped back to watch for a second, putting off joining the others.

When she arrived in the parlor, NoNo was setting out glasses while Zeb poured the champagne. Biddy was discussing her book. "Recipes for old people can be difficult," she was saying, "because they tend not to eat much. Also they're often arthritic, which makes peeling and chopping and stirring just about impossible. Not to mention they've lost all sense of taste."

"Oh, what's the *point*, then?" Rebecca burst out.

Biddy stopped speaking and looked at her.

"I mean . . . it must present quite a challenge," Rebecca said after a moment.

"Exactly," Biddy told her. "So what I've tried to do . . ." And on she went, while Barry circled the room handing each person a drink.

Poppy had the couch to himself, having stretched his cane the length of it to keep everyone else away. "Psst!" he said to Rebecca. "Come here; I saved you a seat." He waggled his cane invitingly.

She sat down without removing the cane, perching on just the front of the cushion.

"I was thinking people might like to hear my poem," he told her.

"Mm-hmm."

"Shall I recite it?"

"Why not," she said.

He hesitated.

"I can't seem to think of the words," he said. "Let me have a minute, will you?"

Someone pushed a glass of champagne into Rebecca's hands. Lateesha, helping out. "Thank you, dear," Rebecca said.

"I just need to get some kind of running start," Poppy was saying. "Otherwise, it won't come to me. How does it begin, again?"

"I don't know," she told him.

She really didn't, she realized.

She was conscious of a lull in the conversation, and she looked up to find everybody turned in her direction, each person holding a glass, waiting for her to propose the toast. She assembled herself. She got to her feet and raised her own glass. "To Biddy," she said, "and *The White Gourmet.*"

"Gray! Gray!" they corrected her. Someone gave a quick bark of a laugh.

"Sorry," she said. She sat down.

There was a brief silence. Then everybody drank.

.   .   .

Not counting the baby, there were thirteen at the table. This was one more person than could comfortably be seated, but a separate children's table with only three children—or four, if Dixon was exiled as well—would have seemed too puny. So Rebecca had everyone scrunch together, and she put Poppy next to her at the head although there wasn't room. He was still trying to remember the words of his poem. He said, "This has never happened before."

Rebecca patted his hand, which was practically in her plate. "Could you scoot about two inches the other way?" she asked him.

"Then I wouldn't even be sitting at the table anymore, Beck."

"Oh, all right."

Biddy seemed to have taken over the serving duties. Actually, Rebecca might have let things lapse a little, there. Biddy kept coming out of the kitchen to ask things like, "Don't you have any more butter?"

"Try the door shelf in the fridge," Rebecca said.

"I already did. You don't have anything! I can't find more salt for the salt cellars, either. You don't have any backups in the pantry!"

Barry was carving the turkey, Rebecca was glad to see. Zeb always made a mess of it. NoNo and Min Foo were passing plates around, and Hakim was jiggling a squirmy, whimpery Abdul on his shoulder. "I think this little man has gas," he announced, and Latee-sha said, "Ooh! Gross!" and crumpled into a cascade of giggles behind her fingers.

Biddy asked, "Where's the sauerkraut? Did you not remember the sauerkraut this year?"

"Back in 1923," Poppy began, "when folks still thought that squirrel meat was good for chronic invalids . . ."

Joey was eyeing Peter across the table, trying to get his attention, and Troy was discussing music with Zeb—or singing notes to him, at any rate. "Dah, dee dah-dah," he sang, holding up one index finger instructively.

Barry said, "Oh, no!" He stopped carving, his knife halfway through a thigh joint. "I didn't wait for the blessing!" he told Rebecca.

"Never mind," she said.

"I just started right in on the carving! I wasn't thinking!"

"Um, actually, we don't normally have a blessing."

"You don't?"

He got that rumple-browed look that NoNo seemed to find so fetching.

"Not even a moment of silence?" he asked.

"Well, I suppose—"

"Or, I know what!" He brightened. "We could do what my college girlfriend's family used to do. They went around the table and people each said one thing apiece that they were thankful for."

This struck Rebecca as a terrible idea. She was relieved when Zeb gave a groan.

But Barry didn't seem to hear him. "What do you say, you guys?" he asked. And then, when no one spoke up, "Well, *I'm* not shy. I'll go first. I'm thankful as all get-out to have my beautiful NoNo."

NoNo looked at him. She lowered the basket of rolls that she'd been about to pass to Dixon, although Dixon was still reaching for it, and, "Why, Barry," she said softly. "I'm thankful to have you, too."

Joey made a gagging sound, but Min Foo frowned him into silence. It was clear, from the way people started stirring in their seats and clearing their throats, that they were bracing themselves to go through with this.

Rebecca looked beseechingly at Zeb. He grinned. All very well for *him*; she supposed he would say he was thankful for some kind of Child Welfare Act or something. And here was Hakim, plainly intrigued by this unfamiliar American custom but putting his own stamp on it; for he rose to his feet, still jiggling Abdul, as if he were preparing to deliver a formal speech. "I personally," he said, "am thankful for my wife, Min Foo, and for my son, Abdul. And also for my other son, Joey, and my daughter, Lateesha. In addition, I would like to take this moment to—"

"Enough!" Min Foo said. She was laughing. "Time's up, Hakim!"

Which, for some reason, set the baby off. He let out a sudden wail, and although he might have settled down again, Rebecca recognized an opportunity when it came along. She stood up and reached for him. "I'll take him," she said. And the instant she had him, she made away with him, out of the dining room completely.

Out of the dining room and through the parlors, toward the stairs. But in the foyer, she paused. She hoisted the baby higher on her shoulder and opened the front door. It wasn't raining anymore, although a thick mist still hung like veils. The air was soft and mild, a kind of non-temperature against her skin. She stepped outside and shut the door behind her.

The baby, who had been uttering chirps of protest, abruptly stopped and raised his head from her shoulder to look around.

She walked down the front walk and turned right, passing the meditation center and the blue-gable house. The mist was so dense that the baby started making small gulping sounds, as if he thought he was underwater. She figured he must be warm enough, though, because he was swaddled in a receiving blanket. His little body felt compact and solid, much heavier than the last time she had carried him, and he held himself in a more organized, more collected sort of way.

She crossed the street toward a maple sapling that still had a few of its leaves, red as lipstick. "See?" she told the baby. "Red! Isn't it pretty?" She turned him slightly so that he was facing the sapling. He blinked and let his gaze travel across it, his head bobbling slightly with the effort of concentration. He no longer had that squinchy newborn look; he was wide-eyed and alert. His cheek, when she set hers against it, was so silky that she almost couldn't feel it.

They had so far had the street to themselves—they'd had the whole world to themselves—but now a bus loomed out of the fog and stopped beside them. The doors opened with a wheeze, letting off two dark-eyed young women, one of them obviously pregnant. They were followed by a tall young man in glasses, and the three of them stood at the bus stop a moment laughing and interrupting each other, riding over each other's words, talking about a party they had been to the night before. Then they moved off down the street, and as their voices faded, Rebecca noticed the quiet surrounding her and the baby. It was that cottony, thick, enclosing quiet that often descends with a fog, and it made her long, all at once, for the clamor of her family.

Anyhow, Abdul must be getting hungry. He was nosing hopefully into the crook of her neck. She turned and started home.

The mist was settling on her hair. She could see the glints in the strands that fell over her eyes. The hem of her skirt was growing heavy with moisture. The baby's mouth against her skin felt like a cool little guppy mouth.

Had it ever crossed her mind that Joe had married her for her usefulness? Yes, it had crossed her mind. And never more so than after he died; just up and willfully died and left her to cope on her own.

Now, though, she saw what he had rescued her from: that ingrown, muted, stagnant, engaged-to-be-engaged routine that had started to chafe her so. Oh, he had been just as useful to *her*; no doubt about it. What she'd told NoNo was true.

And while she had once believed that she'd been useful only in practical matters (tending the little girls, waiting on Mother Davitch), now she saw that her most valuable contribution had been her joyousness—a quality the Davitches sorely lacked. Not that she herself was joyous to begin with. No, she had had to labor at it. She had struggled to acquire it.

Timidly, she experimented with a sneaking sense of achievement. Pride, even. Why not? It didn't seem all that misplaced.

She carried the baby home jauntily, striding straight through the puddles, wearing jewels of mist in her hair and holding her head high.

eleven

As luck would have it, Poppy's party fell on a day when two paying events could have been scheduled instead. One was just a small luncheon, but the other was a Christmas party for a brokerage firm, and Rebecca was very sorry to have to turn it down. A promise was a promise, though. She had told Poppy they would celebrate on his actual birth date. Enough of these second-best, orphan compromises—major milestones observed midweek or shoved into the next month so as not to interfere with more important people's arrangements.

So: December 11th, a Saturday. The plan was to begin at two in the afternoon, for the little ones' sake, and extend into early evening. Presents were not discouraged. (Poppy had been firm about that.) Food would be served from the very beginning; none of this waiting around for the toasts. Lots of desserts, but no savories, no hors d'oeuvres or crudités, certainly no main dishes. And the centerpiece would be a towering cake, really more of a wedding cake, prepared by Toot Sweet in Fells Point. Poppy had done the research: Toot Sweet was the winner. Fortunately, Biddy didn't take offense. "Fine with me," she said. "I have enough on my hands with all those pastries he wants."

The guest list—saved these past six months in the pocket of Rebecca's calico skirt, where it had gone through the laundry twice and emerged as soft as blotting paper but still comparatively readable—consisted mostly of family, plus two of Poppy's old friends, plus some incidental acquaintances like his physical therapist and Alice Farmer. (It was ironic, Rebecca often reflected, that by definition those family parties that were largest and most demanding were the ones to which Alice Farmer had to be invited as a guest.) There had been more people on the list, but many of them were dead. A few others were too frail to attend, and a few had simply dropped out of sight at some unnoticed point in the past.

Rebecca's mother and Aunt Ida had accepted, much to Rebecca's surprise, with the understanding that they would leave the party early on account of the long drive home. Also they would arrive early, they announced, in order to help out. Privately, Rebecca began thinking up tasks that would keep them harmlessly occupied. Sorting through the napkins, inspecting the stemware for water spots . . .

Because it was December, the decorating scheme would be Christmassy. Already a slender tree stood in the front-parlor window, diminutive white lights twinkling tastefully from each branch. Now Rebecca set up another tree in the dining room, chunkier and messier, smothered in decades' worth of construction-paper chains and Polaroid photos of the children pasted on paper-doily snowflakes. Some of the photos were faded past recognition. Many were interchangeable, since Davitch babies tended to look fairly much alike below a certain age. (All those little clock faces, wisps of dark hair, squinty mistrustful eyes.) On top she put a gold foil star with seven different-sized, unevenly spaced points, brought home from kindergarten long ago by one or another of the girls; no one knew which anymore. She draped a huge banner across the rear-parlor mantel reading HAPPY 100th BIRTHDAY POOPY—a mistake she hadn't noticed until she got it home—and she lugged the TV and the VCR down from the family room and plugged them into an outlet in the front parlor, because Hakim (in love with Western technology, like every immigrant Rebecca had ever known) was

bringing as his present a professionally produced videotape assembled from the family's home movies. This was supposed to be a
secret, although Poppy had to have suspected something. On the
morning of the party, when he went in to watch cartoons, all he
found was a rectangle of dust on the TV stand. He didn't say a word
about it, though; just grunted and laid out a game of solitaire
instead.

The day was bright and unusually cold, which meant Rebecca
could wear her Bedouin costume. Although of course she didn't put
it on first thing. No, first she put on baggy pants and one of Joe's old
flannel shirts, and she raced around the house picking up and vacu-
uming and cooking Poppy a special breakfast. Nothing but sweets—
waffles and cocoa. (The man would contract diabetes before the
end of the day.) A little blue birthday candle flickered on the top-
most waffle. *"Happy birthday to you . . ."* she sang, all by herself,
standing over the table with her hands clasped together in front of
her.

Poppy said, "Why, thank you, Beck," and calmly blew out the
candle. It amused and touched and exasperated her, all at the same
time, how he accepted this fuss and bother as only his due.

"Just think," she told him. "One hundred years ago today, you
were just the tiniest bundle nestled in a cradle. Or maybe in your
mother's bed. Were you born at home? Did your mother have a
doctor?"

"She had a midwife," he said, cutting into his waffles. "Mrs.
Bentham: she came to the house. We lived on North Avenue then.
She was just starting out in her practice, and we were her first set of
twins."

"Oh, yes, twins," Rebecca said. "I'd forgotten that." Briefly, she
laid a hand on his arm. "It must make you sad, celebrating your
birthday without your brother here to share it."

"No, not really," he said matter-of-factly. "I've had a lot of years
to get used to it."

He took a much too large mouthful of waffles, dotting his mustache with beads of syrup. He was wearing his red plaid bathrobe

over striped pajamas. Bristly whiskers silvered his face, and his white hair stood on end, unbrushed, raying out like sunbeams.

"Eighteen ninety-nine," Rebecca said. "I don't even know who was President then!"

"Beats me."

"Your family wouldn't have had a car, I suppose, or a telephone . . ."

But he was pursuing another train of thought. He said, "I've wondered, from time to time, if I've had added onto my life all those years my brother didn't get to use."

He spoke as if his brother had had no choice—as if it hadn't been his own decision not to use those years. Rebecca said, "Well, I imagine he would have been glad to see you enjoying them."

"Not necessarily," Poppy told her. "He always did believe I got the best of the deal."

"How was that?"

"Oh, you know . . . he wasn't a naturally happy person. Some people, they just have a harder time being happy."

"Would you say Joe was naturally happy?"

Poppy took another bite of waffles, either considering her question or stalling.

"When I met him, he was laughing," she prompted him. Then she recalled that in fact, she was the one who'd been laughing. But she continued. "He said, 'I see you're having a wonderful time.' His very first words to me. Because Zeb was clowning around; you know how he does, and so I started . . . And when I decided to marry him, *then* he was laughing, for sure! I saw him laughing in the library window and I decided at that moment."

Poppy said, "Hmm," and blotted his mustache on his napkin.

"And don't forget," Rebecca said, "by profession, he was a party-giver."

"But he never felt party-giving was really his true life," Poppy reminded her.

"Well, no."

"And that's where he and I differed," Poppy said. "Because I was always telling him, 'Look,' I said. 'Face it,' I said. 'There *is* no true life. Your true life is the one you end up with, whatever it may be. You just do the best you can with what you've got,' I said."

"But he had a *fine* life!" Rebecca said.

"He certainly did."

Poppy folded his napkin and laid it beside his plate. "So what I tell myself," he said, "is I'm observing our birthday for both of us. That's how I like to view it."

Evidently, he had swerved back onto the subject of his twin brother. Rebecca took a second to realize it, though. That was what happened when you lived with someone confused: you became confused yourself, and one thing developed the oddest way of blurring into other things.

. . .

Her mother and her aunt arrived shortly before noon. Her mother wore her dressiest pants set and a fluffy mohair jacket that made her look smaller than ever. Her hair had been crimped into ridges as evenly spaced as the rows of tufts on a bedspread. Aunt Ida was all ruffles and froth—a pink rosebud print, despite the season— and she must have gone to the same hairdresser, although her curls were already beginning to wander out of formation. Between them they carried a large, flat package, beautifully wrapped and ribboned. "It's a portrait of William McKinley," Aunt Ida confided in a whisper.

"McKinley," Rebecca said.

"He was who was President in 1899."

"Oh, we were just discussing that at breakfast," Rebecca said. "McKinley! Is that who it was!"

"We thought it would remind Mr. Davitch of his youth."

"I'm sure he'll love it," Rebecca said. "Have you two had lunch yet?"

"Oh, we don't want to be any trouble."

"It's no trouble. I've got some cold cuts set out."

She placed their gift on the chest of drawers in the front parlor, and then she led them back to the kitchen. "Poppy's upstairs napping," she said. "He had a sandwich ahead of time and now he's trying to rest before the party."

"Law, he must be so excited," Aunt Ida said, but Rebecca's mother said, "I never did understand the notion of adults having birthday parties."

"Well, it's kind of our tradition," Rebecca told her. "And besides, this is his hundredth! He could have had his name read out on TV, if we had asked."

"*My* last birthday party was in 1927," Rebecca's mother said. "I was five years old."

Aunt Ida said, "Oh, that can't be right! What about when you turned eighteen and Mother gave you her pearls?"

"That wasn't a party, though, Ida."

"Well, you had a cake! With candles on it! If you don't call that a party, I'd like to know what it was!"

"Have a seat," Rebecca told them. "Who would like iced tea?"

"Oh, I would, darlin', if it's made," Aunt Ida said.

It was. (Rebecca knew that they always drank iced tea with lunch, even in the dead of winter, although at suppertime they would turn it down for fear of not sleeping well.) She brought the pitcher from the refrigerator and set it on the table. Aunt Ida was forking a mountain of cold cuts onto her plate, selecting each slice daintily with her little finger quirked as if that would make her portion seem smaller. Rebecca's mother was delivering a blow-by-blow account of their trip. "We took the old County Highway," she said, "because you couldn't pay me to drive on that I-95, all those truckers whizzing past blaring their horns at a person. I don't think I told you about Abbie Field's daughter having that awful accident on I-95 down near Richmond. She had gone to I think Heathsville, or Heathsburg, one of those places; was it Heathsville? Heathsburg? Went to visit her parents-in-law and was coming back on a Sunday after mass; her mother-in-law is Catholic, you know, one of those very devout Catholic widows, and she had invited Abbie to her ladies' bridge club luncheon on Saturday and then—"

"Wait; that's not possible," Aunt Ida said.

"Beg pardon? Of course it's possible. You can be a Catholic and still play bridge."

"You said Abbie went to visit her parents-in-law. Plural. But that her mother-in-law was a widow."

"All right; I misspoke. It's not a capital crime."

Rebecca said, "How's the move coming, Mother?"

"What move?"

"Your move to the retirement home."

"Oh, that. Well, I'm working on it, but first I have to sort my belongings."

Aunt Ida sent Rebecca a look. "Have a deviled egg," Rebecca told her.

"Why, thank you, hon. I really shouldn't, on account of my cholesterol, but you know I can't resist."

"Folks tell me I should hire help," Rebecca's mother said. "I'm too old to do all that sorting on my own, they tell me. But you know how *that* works. When Ida here tried to clean out my desk, would you believe what she did? Threw away a perfectly good sheet of three-cent postage stamps."

"Have a deviled egg, Mother," Rebecca said.

Then the phone rang, and she cried, "Whoops!" and raced off to answer it, even though the kitchen extension was no more than a foot away from her.

. . .

Rebecca's Bedouin costume was a long black woolen robe with broad vertical bands of purple, red, and turquoise running from shoulder to hem. It made her feel like Elizabeth Taylor in *Cleopatra*, she had told the clerk at Discount Dashikis when she was trying it on. In order to keep the bright colors from blanching her features, she applied a good deal more makeup than usual. Then she wound a splashy purple-and-black silk sash around her head. When she descended the stairs, the sash wafted out behind her like a bridal train. "Goodness," her mother said, meeting up with her in the foyer. Rebecca gave her a sphinxlike smile. (Nothing she would wear could make her mother happy.) But Aunt Ida, already seated in the front parlor, cried out, "Oh, my, don't you look cheery!"

"Thank you," Rebecca told her. In a majestically level, swift, flowing motion, she crossed to the hearth and bent for the butane torch hidden in the basket of pinecones at one side. She started lighting the candles she had set around the room—the Christmas candles and the Hanukkah candles and the all-occasion candles and even the pale egg-shaped candles ordinarily reserved for Easter.

"It's a regular conflagration!" Aunt Ida said gaily.

Rebecca's mother sat down in the rocker, first smoothing the back of her slacks beneath her as if she were wearing a skirt. "I laid out your cocktail napkins in a fan shape," she told Rebecca. "I don't know if that's the way you wanted them. I straightened up some in the kitchen, and I took the liberty of watering that poor dead plant out back beside the steps."

"Thank you, Mother."

"You'll find the leftover cold cuts on the top shelf in the fridge. I put them in one of those newspaper bags I found in the waxed-paper drawer, although I'm not entirely easy in my mind about letting foodstuffs come into contact with colored plastic."

"I'm sure they'll be finished off before the poison has time to take effect," Rebecca told her.

The doorbell rang. Her mother said, "Mercy," and checked her watch. "It's three minutes before two! Who do you suppose that is?"

"Not a Davitch, you can bet," Rebecca said. She went out into the foyer. "Company, Poppy!" she called up the stairs, and then she opened the door. J. J. Barrow, her electrician, was standing on the stoop with his twelve-year-old son. Both of them were dressed up— J.J. in a suit and tie, his son in a navy blazer and tan corduroys—and J.J. was holding a bottle of bourbon with a ribbon around its neck. "Come in!" Rebecca told them. "You two are so punctual!"

"Well, we didn't want to keep folks waiting," J.J. said. He was a large, bearded bear of a man, a type Rebecca had a weakness for, and she had invited him on impulse when he and his son came to fix the thermostat earlier in the week. Now she ushered them into the parlor, keeping an arm around the son's shoulders. "Mother," she said, "Aunt Ida, this is our electrician, J. J. Barrow, and this is his son, J.J.J." J.J.J. was what they called J.J. Junior, and she always had to stifle a giggle when she was saying it; it made her feel she was stuttering. "My mother, Mildred Holmes, and my aunt, Ida Gates."

"How do you do," Aunt Ida said, and Rebecca's mother smiled and tilted her head. "Are you . . . here as guests?" she asked.

"Yes, ma'am," J.J. said. "My wife would have come too, except her pastor dropped by unannounced."

"J.J. can handle anything electrical," Rebecca said, "and also some plumbing repairs as long as they don't require inspection. And his son knows nearly as much as he does; don't you, J.J.J.?" Oops, another giggle.

J.J.J. looked worried and said, "Well, I would still need Pop's help with some of the big things, though."

"Rebecca and me have been through a lot," J.J. said, falling into a chair. "She was my main support when my first wife up and left me. And I was around when her grandson Danny passed through that little shoplifting stage."

"Well, now!" Rebecca said, clapping her hands. (She hadn't mentioned Danny's shoplifting stage to her mother.) "Where's our guest of honor, I wonder!"

Her mother wore a blank expression. Aunt Ida just smiled and patted the sofa cushion beside her. "Why don't you come sit down, J.J.J.?" she asked. "Aren't you sweet, to attend an old man's birthday party!"

"I never met anybody who was a hundred before," he told her, and he crossed the room and settled next to her, admirably composed, hands folded loosely between his corduroy knees.

Now they heard Poppy on the stairs—cane, shoe, shoe; cane, shoe, shoe—and Rebecca went out to the foyer to meet him. He often woke from his nap extra stiff; she thought he might want help. But no, he was barely leaning on the banister, and his face looked rested and relaxed, not stretched by pain. He wore his gray suit and a narrow black bow tie knotted around a collar so high and starched that he seemed to have stepped directly from the year when he had been born. His hair was slicked down flat and his cheeks looked polished. "I thought I heard the doorbell," he said.

"Yes, J.J. and his son are here. You remember J.J.," she said hopefully.

He might or he might not. At any rate, he grunted and continued his descent.

"And Mother and Aunt Ida came while you were napping," she said. "You should see what they brought you!"

"I intend to open my gifts as they arrive," he told her. He reached the bottom of the stairs and started pegging into the parlor, passing her in a breeze of lavender cologne. "They won't get the proper notice if I just pile them in a heap and open them all at once."

"Fine, Poppy," Rebecca said.

Not that her permission was needed. Already he was reaching out a hand for J.J.'s bottle, holding it at arm's length to study the label. "Thanks," he said finally. "It'll make a nice nightcap." He turned toward the two older women. "Ladies."

"Happy birthday, Mr. Davitch," they said practically in unison, and Aunt Ida added, "You don't look a day over eighty!"

"Eighty?" Poppy asked. The corners of his mouth turned down.

"Yes, sir, it's not often I'm asked to celebrate somebody's hundredth birthday," J.J. told him.

"*How* often?" Poppy asked him.

"Well, now, I guess I would have to say never, in fact."

"Here, Poppy," Rebecca said. She took the wrapped package from the chest of drawers. "This is Mother and Aunt Ida's gift."

"Wait, just let me get comfy."

He chose a wing chair and lowered himself by degrees, first setting the bourbon on the table beside him. Then Rebecca handed him the package. "Nice paper," he said. He slid a trembling thumb beneath one taped flap. "Don't want to tear it; might as well save it for later use."

"Absolutely," Rebecca's mother told him, and she bit her lip and sat forward, concentrating, until he had lifted the flap without causing any damage.

William McKinley turned out to be a forthright-looking man in a high white collar and black bow tie nearly identical to Poppy's. Rebecca had worried Poppy wouldn't know who he was, but luckily a brass nameplate was tacked to the bottom of the frame. "William McKinley. Well, now," Poppy said, slanting the picture on his knees to study it.

"He was President the year you were born," Rebecca told him.

"Well, how about that."

"Got himself assassinated," J.J. offered out of the blue.

"How *about* that."

"It was McKinley who was responsible for us taking over Cuba," J.J. went on. "Also Hawaii, if I'm not very much mistaken."

Poppy lowered the portrait and turned to frown at J.J. "*Who* did you say you were?" he asked.

"J.J. is our electrician, Poppy," Rebecca said. "He just this week fixed our thermostat."

J.J. was nodding emphatically, as if urging Poppy to do the same, but Poppy kept his frown. Then suddenly his forehead cleared. "'All I Want for Christmas Is You,'" he said.

"What, Poppy?" Rebecca asked.

"That's what they were playing on the radio his boy brought along. 'All I Want for Christmas Is You.'"

"Whoa! Sorry if we disturbed you," J.J. said.

"Oh, it's better than some others I've heard."

He held the portrait out to Rebecca, and she stepped forward to take it from him.

"So! Mr. Davitch!" Aunt Ida said. "Did you receive a birthday greeting from the President?"

Poppy sent another frown in the direction of the portrait, which Rebecca was propping now on the chest of drawers. Perhaps he thought McKinley was the President in question. Instead of answering, though, he said, "Mr., ah, J.J., I wonder if you could settle a little argument for me."

"Be glad to if I can," J.J. told him.

"Those instant-on kind of lights. What do you call them? You know the kind. The ones that light up without blinking first."

"Incandescent," J.J. said.

"Now, I maintain that folks should turn those off whenever they leave a room. Because switching them back on doesn't require any particular burst of energy, does it? As opposed to a fluorescent. But Beck, here: oh, no, she has to leave a trail of lights lit anyplace she goes. A waste of money, I tell her."

"Yes, sir, you'd be amazed," J.J. said. "Why, a single hundred-watt bulb, left burning for an hour—"

"J.J.! Don't encourage him!" Rebecca said. "Poppy'd have us sitting in the dark, if he could have his way. Even the tree lights upset him! If we were to leave this room right now, just to go to the dining room and get ourselves a bite, he would turn off the tree lights first!"

"Oh," J.J. said. He looked unhappy. No doubt he felt he'd been put on the spot. "Well: tree lights. I mean, these dinky white things are not a major draw of power. And you have to figure the, like, decorative effect. They're more of a decoration, for people to see from outside too and not just inside the house."

"See there?" Rebecca asked Poppy. "Didn't I tell you? Oh, lights have a tremendous effect!" she said, turning to the others. "Like when guests are walking up the front walk for a party: it makes such a difference in their mood if they see all the windows glowing. They get . . . anticipatory. Switch on every light you own, I always say. Let them blaze for all they're worth! Let them set the house on fire!"

J.J. laughed, and his son grinned shyly. Aunt Ida said, "Yes, you would certainly want to give people a nice sense of welcome." Poppy, though, only grunted, and Rebecca's mother shrank back slightly in her seat.

"Well, anyhow," Rebecca said after a moment. "Drinks, anyone?" And she was careful to keep her voice at a decorous pitch.

. . .

It was so predictable that non-Davitches would show up before Davitches. Precisely fifteen minutes past the designated hour—Baltimore's idea of the proper arrival time—Alice Farmer rang the doorbell in a silver sharkskin suit and silver shoes and a black felt cartwheel hat, bearing a stunningly wrapped gift that turned out to be a prayer toaster. (A prayer on a bread-slice-shaped piece of cardboard popped out of the slot if you pressed the lever, one prayer for every day of the year.) The physical therapist, Miss Nancy, followed with a flock of Mylar balloons so numerous that they had to be nudged through the door in clusters. Next came Poppy's two friends, Mr. Ames and Mr. Hardesty. Mr. Ames brought a cactus with a bulbous pink growth on top that Poppy said reminded him of a baboon's behind. Mr. Hardesty brought nothing, which was understandable because he was in a walker for which he needed both hands, besides having to rely on a sullen niece for his shopping; so Poppy was gracious about it.

At a quarter till three the first Davitch arrived: Zeb, short of breath. "Sorry," he told Rebecca. "There was an emergency call from the hospital, and I went off thinking I'd come straight here afterwards, but I forgot about the gift; so I had to go back home first and get it."

He meant the gift that he and she were giving jointly: a framed reprint of Poppy and Aunt Joyce's engagement photo. He had bundled it clumsily in wads of white tissue and masses of Scotch tape. "I wish you could have seen it before I wrapped it," he told her. "They did a tremendous job with the restoration."

"Well, that's a relief," Rebecca said. She had been dubious when she first slipped it, stealthily, from the family album. Blooms of mold had destroyed most of the background, and a white fold line ran across one corner.

Poppy was getting rowdy, like an overstimulated child. "Well? What have we here?" he asked as Zeb entered the room. "Bring it on in! Let me at it!"

"Happy birthday," Zeb told him, and he laid the package across Poppy's knees. "This is from Rebecca and me."

"Well, thank you. Not much sense in saving *this* wrap, I don't believe." He ripped the tissue off one end and tugged the picture free. "Oh, my," he said.

Zeb was right: the restorers had worked a miracle. The background was unblemished now, and the couple seemed somehow more alive. Aunt Joyce, slimmer than Rebecca had ever seen her, wore one of those drapey 1930s dresses that appeared to have been snatched up at the midriff and given a violent twist. Poppy was startlingly black-haired and black-mustached, and he gazed out at the viewer while Joyce had eyes only for him.

"Isn't it amazing?" Poppy asked Rebecca. She thought he meant the restoration, until he went on. "There I am, watching the camera when I could have been looking at Joyce. I thought I had the rest of my life to look at Joyce, was why. I was thirty-nine years old. She was twenty-two. I thought she would outlive me."

"Oh, if *that* is not the truth!" Aunt Ida cried from the couch.

Rebecca's mother said, "Now, correct me if I'm wrong, Mr. Davitch, but wasn't I once told that your wife had always had a weak heart?"

"Weak hearts ran in her family," Poppy said. "But I never really believed that she would go first."

"Well, anyways, she sure was pretty," Alice Farmer said. She had crossed the room to peer over Poppy's shoulder. "How'd a plain old guy like you come to catch such a pretty young thing?"

"She used to work behind the pastry counter at her mother's breakfast place," Poppy said. "Finally her mother switched her to dishing out bacon and eggs, just so I'd eat more nutritiously."

"Very considerate of her," Miss Nancy said heartily, and J.J. chuckled, but Poppy just stared at the photo as if he hadn't heard.

Then the door slammed against the closet, and he straightened and said, "Ah, well."

First came NoNo with a sweater she'd been laboring over for months—a bulky white fisherman's knit, not really Poppy's style. He was nice about it, though. "You made this?" he asked her. "You hate to knit! You swore you'd give it up after you finished those baby booties."

"Well, this time I *will* give it up, I promise," NoNo said, and she bent to kiss his cheek.

Peter shook Poppy's hand and said, "I'm supposed to tell you happy birthday, and that me and the other kids are going in on one big present from the bunch of us."

"Well, that's all right, then," Poppy decided.

Peter was wearing his school blazer, the sleeves a good inch shorter than the last time Rebecca had seen him in it. It matched J.J.J.'s, she realized. They must go to the same school, for they seemed to know each other. J.J.J. made room for him on the couch, and they put their heads together over some kind of gadget that Peter pulled from his pocket. "I think the way I can get it to work is by differential friction," Rebecca heard him say.

Biddy arrived with still more pastry boxes — having brought most of the food earlier that morning — and headed for the kitchen, followed by Dixon, who first set a wooden keg just inside the front door. Troy, however, came straight into the parlor to hand Poppy a small, flat package. "Your old friend Haydn," he explained. "Biddy's gift is the food, but I wanted you to have something especially from me."

Poppy hadn't always seen eye to eye with Troy (he had suggested more than once that a timely stint in the Army would have set him straight), but he seemed pleased when he unwrapped the CD. "Oh, one of my favorites," he said. "The *Military* Symphony!"

Rebecca shot Troy a suspicious look, but he just smiled at her. "Why don't I put it on," he said, and he took the CD from Poppy and went over to the stereo.

Then Patch and her family arrived, and then Min Foo and hers. For several minutes, the foyer was wall-to-wall people. Children were struggling out of jackets; Abdul was cooing in his infant seat; Patch was having a tantrum over something insulting Min Foo had just said. (How had Min Foo had time, even?) "Come wish Poppy a happy birthday," Rebecca told them. "Emmy! Are you wearing *heels?* Hakim, let me take the baby while you . . . Patch, please, come on in and tell Poppy happy birthday. I'm sure Min Foo didn't *mean* whatever it was."

"Min Fool, is more like it," Patch snapped, but she trailed the others into the parlor, where Biddy had started circulating a platter of petits fours and Dixon was passing macaroons.

The party had changed to the stand-up kind, now that there was a crowd. Only the older ones stayed seated — Poppy receiving greetings benignly from his wing chair. Mr. Ames was telling Aunt Ida that he was choosing Poppy's birth date for his next lottery number. Mr. Hardesty was asking the room at large who on earth all these people were.

Patch handed Poppy a gift so heavy he almost dropped it. And no wonder: he unwrapped it to find ankle weights, shaped like big blue doughnuts. "For your daily walk," Patch explained. "They've just completed a study that proves . . ."

Then Dixon hauled in the keg, which turned out to contain the children's present—a giant collection of horehound drops, Jujubes, Allsorts, Good & Plentys, and other candies, some of which Rebecca had assumed to be obsolete. Dixon pried off the lid and held up various samples while Poppy made appreciative remarks. "*You* helped buy me this? And you?" he asked various youngsters, skillfully avoiding the use of any names. "Oh, my, sassafras balls. How did you know I love sassafras?" In fact, his enthusiasm was probably genuine; this may have been the most successful gift yet.

Hakim's videotape, on the other hand, bewildered him. He unwrapped it and peered at it doubtfully. "*Paul P. Davitch*," he read out, "*1954–1967*. What? I don't understand."

"Those are the years covered by the videotape," Rebecca told him. "Hakim took all our home movies to a shop where they turn reels into tapes. Remember Uncle Buddy's home movies?"

"Oh, yes. Yes, indeed," Poppy said.

Uncle Buddy was Mother Davitch's brother, the one technically minded member of the family, and when he died, in 1968, the movie camera might as well have been buried with him. Nobody had been certain how to work the projector, either; so this tape caused considerable interest. Children were called together and arranged on the floor, and chairs were dragged in from the dining room, and Mr. Hardesty's walker was placed to one side. Zeb, Dixon, and Troy—the three tallest—retreated to the back of the group. Then Rebecca started the VCR.

First there were the usual hurdles—a black-and-white snowstorm, a duel between the two remote controls until the snowstorm disappeared, a pause while a child was sent off to silence Haydn.

Eventually a white calling card came into focus with *Paul P. Davitch, 1954–1967* engraved in flowing script. The next card read *Photography: William R. "Buddy" Brand,* and the next, *Produced by Big Bob's Production Service*—all of these accompanied by a piano playing "Stardust." *October or November, 1954,* the last card read.

Whatever scientific advances had restored Poppy's engagement photo were evidently not available to Big Bob, because the people who filled the screen were bleached nearly white and shot through with darting white lines like slants of rain. Poppy stood on a brownish lawn with a plumper, dowdier Aunt Joyce, her knees like two underbaked biscuits below the cuffs of her long Bermudas. In front of them, hunched over the handlebar of a tricycle, was a small black-haired boy who would have to be Zeb. All three of them had their faces screwed up against the sunlight. "Would you look?" Poppy murmured, but he was the only one who seemed affected by this oddly unmovie-like shot. The younger children stirred restlessly, and a woman—perhaps Miss Nancy—was heard to ask, "Was there ever a less attractive fashion era than the fifties?"

A new card flashed on the screen: *Christmas 1956.* By now Uncle Buddy must have grasped the capabilities of his medium, for the scene was almost too animated. An electric train whizzed soundlessly around the base of a Christmas tree before it was obliterated by somebody's swirling plaid skirt. An out-of-focus child (Zeb again, suddenly taller) lunged gleefully toward the camera with a red metal dump truck in one hand. Then Joe (Joe! so young and graceless that Rebecca almost didn't know him, with his hair too short and his neck too thin) plucked Zeb up and removed him, and Mother Davitch advanced displaying a velvet-boxed bottle of perfume as if she were in a commercial, smiling a determined smile that was almost scary. She was followed, as if in a conga line, by Aunt Joyce vampishly modeling a pink angora sweater with a tag dangling from the top button, and then by Poppy holding a cellophane-wrapped bow tie in front of the bow tie he was already wearing. Last, a hairy arm was tugged into view by someone else's hand, and a shirtfront loomed up, and then a man's widely laughing, protesting mouth. "Uncle Buddy himself, in his one and only film appearance," Zeb had time to announce before the whole scene vanished.

The children were asking, "Where were *you*, Mom?" and their mothers were saying, "Just wait a minute. I wasn't even born yet." Poppy was telling Mr. Ames to take his word for it: this was not really the way things had been. More Christmases swam by—*Christmas 1957* and *Christmas 1958.* "Uncle Buddy lived in Delaware," Zeb explained. "He didn't get to visit more than once or twice a year." The train beneath the tree acquired more cars; Poppy acquired more bow ties; Zeb grew another six inches. "Stardust" went on playing languorously, although Mr. Hardesty pointed out that some sort of Christmas carol might have been more in keeping. As if to prove him wrong, the next card read *Spring 1961,* and when it was removed, Joe and a glamorous, cross-looking Tina were standing on the front stoop with a cylinder of pastel blankets. "That's me!" Biddy told the children, although she would have known that only because of the date. The clearest part of the picture was an arching bough of pink blossoms extending from the side of the screen where the front-parlor window would have been, and for some reason, this evidence of a long-dead, long-forgotten tree that Rebecca herself had never laid eyes on made her sadder than anything else. Poppy, too, gave a sigh. "Ah, me," he said, and he gently stroked his mustache.

Christmas 1962, Christmas 1964. Easter 1965 and *Christmas 1965* and *Easter 1966.* Biddy pushed a doll buggy and Patch learned to roller-skate and NoNo shook the bars of her playpen. Joe turned into the man Rebecca had married. Poppy's hair was gray but Aunt Joyce's was a yellower blond than ever. Mother Davitch's mouth started blurring around the edges.

Then *September 1966,* and who was this? A heavyset young woman standing in front of a picnic table, wearing a silly miniskirt that exposed her broad thighs. Her face was large and shiny. Rebecca felt embarrassed for her; she seemed like such an interloper, so presumptuous, beaming straight at the camera while other, more entitled people (Mother Davitch, Aunt Joyce) wrapped leftovers in waxed paper.

She slid a glance around the audience, but nobody made any comment.

Christmas 1967, and Min Foo scowled from her father's arms, her two clenched fists like tiny spools of thread. "There I am!" Min Foo said, hugging Lateesha on her lap.

As if Min Foo's arrival had been the whole point of the movie, a card proclaiming *The End* promptly filled the screen. A few people clapped. Then another card popped up listing family members in order of appearance. *Paul P. Davitch, Joyce Mays Davitch, Zebulon Davitch, M.D. . . .* Rebecca went on watching, transfixed, but the children were drifting away now and the adults had started talking among themselves. Biddy called, "Folks? Are you listening? Cake will be served in the dining room." Emmy and Joey were elbowing each other for space on the piano bench; Lateesha was chasing balloons; Poppy was telling J.J. that Joyce had been much prettier than the camera made her out to be.

The credits ended, followed by more snow. Rebecca bent to press the Rewind button, and then she went out to the dining room where a sizable group already stood admiring the mammoth birthday cake.

"My name wasn't on the card," she told Zeb.

Without turning, he said, "Hmm?"

"They didn't list me on the card when they rolled the credits."

Miss Nancy plucked Rebecca's sleeve. "Could I just say something?" she asked. "In view of Mr. Davitch's limitations, I'm not at all in favor of ankle weights for his walks."

From behind them, Min Foo said, "Didn't I tell them so? Didn't I tell Patch? 'The poor man can barely stagger around as it is,' I said, 'and now you want to tie lead weights to his ankles?'"

"I heard that!" Patch called from the other side of the room. "Criticize, criticize! Why don't you say it to my face, if that's how you feel?"

"I *did* say it to your face."

Meanwhile, Rebecca's mother was telling Alice Farmer how well the folks in Church Valley got along with the Colored; Haydn was resuming on the stereo; Emmy and Joey were playing "Heart and Soul" on the piano. Biddy was using the butane torch to light the candles on the cake—an actual one hundred candles, as Rebecca had insisted, plus an extra to grow on. They ringed each of the lower tiers and completely covered the top except for the center, where a little ceramic man stood—one half of a bride-and-groom set—wearing a black tailcoat and a tiny, bushy mustache very much like Poppy's. "Aww," several people said when they saw him. Poppy himself watched gravely, standing very straight with both hands on the crook of his cane.

Now Barry started singing "Happy Birthday," swooping his arms above his head like an orchestra conductor. It was good to have somebody else, for a change, play the part of cruise-ship director. Rebecca chimed in on the second note, and the others joined by twos and threes as the song continued. *"Happy birthday to you, happy birthday to you . . ."*

At the end, as always, a couple of the children went on singing. *"How o-old are you, how o-old are you . . ."* Their voices were so frail that Rebecca could hear, besides, Haydn on the stereo and "Heart and Soul" on the piano and "Stardust" on the VCR, which some-body must have started running all over again. The *Military* Sym-phony—at least this second section of it, whatever it was called—didn't sound military at all; it sounded delicate and sad. And "Heart and Soul" had always struck her as so haunting, such an oddly haunting melody in view of the fact that it was literally child's play. And anyone would agree that "Stardust" was a melancholy song. So that was probably why, in the middle of "How Old Are You?" she felt an ache of homesickness, right there in her own house.

But she brushed it aside, and, "Make a wish! Make a wish!" she chanted, until the others took it up. Poppy braced himself, sucked in a huge breath, and blew out every last candle.

Well, he did have help. Danny and Peter, whom he must have enlisted earlier, leaned forward at either side of him and blew when he did, which made everybody laugh. "It still counts, though!" Poppy said. "I still get my wish. Don't I?"

"Of course you do," Rebecca told him.

She stepped forward to take his arm, planning to settle him in a chair, but he resisted. Instead he stood for a long, silent moment watching Biddy pluck the candles from the cake. "Boy, that is kind of pitiful," he said finally. "A groom without his bride like that."

He was right, Rebecca realized. They should have thought how it would look: the poor little man all dressed up, all alone on his expanse of deforested icing. Well, too late now, for Poppy had already been reminded of his poem. *"You're given a special welcome when you get to heaven late . . ."*

Min Foo blamed Hakim. That blasted videotape, she said in a piercing whisper, with Aunt Joyce in every frame, just about, reminding Poppy all over again that she was dead.

Hakim said, "So? He would otherwise forget?"

Lateesha asked if she could lick the frosting off the candles. Mr. Hardesty's walker made a sound like *inch, inch* as he hobbled toward a chair. *"The journey may be lonely, but the end is worth the wait,"* Poppy finished. *"The sight of your beloved, smiling at the gate."*

And then, without missing a beat, "Why! That wouldn't be *fondant* icing, would it?"

"It would indeed," Biddy told him.

"Fondant icing! My favorite! Oh, my."

What Peter had said was right, Rebecca thought. You could still enjoy a party even if you didn't remember it later.

. . .

The champagne was a top brand; Rebecca had made sure of that. Ordinarily they'd have drunk something cheaper—just sparkling wine, to be honest—but not today. Barry gave a whistle when she handed him a bottle to open. "Pretty classy," he told her, and she said, "Well, we don't observe a hundredth birthday every day of the week." Even the little ones got the real thing. She poured a drop for each of them herself, over Biddy's protests that they would never know the difference.

"A toast!" she said when everyone had a glass. She raised her own glass. She was standing in the center of the front parlor, surrounded by so many people that some were all the way back in the dining room, and at the moment she wasn't even sure where Poppy was located. But she said, "To Poppy!" She cleared her throat.

> *"He's beginning to seem perennial;*
> *We're observing his centennial.*
> *So shout it from the chandeliers:*
> *We wish him another hundred years!"*

"To Poppy," they all murmured. And then, in the silence when the others were drinking, Patch said clearly, "Oh, Lord, Beck is back to those everlasting rhymes of hers."

Rebecca's eyes stung. She swallowed her sip of champagne and blinked to clear her vision.

From over near the fireplace, Poppy said, "Thank you, all."

He was standing next to Mr. Hardesty and grasping one side of the walker, so that at first glance it seemed the two men were holding hands. When he had everybody's attention, he said, "Well. This has been just what I dreamed of, I tell you. From the very start of the day, it's been perfect. Sunshine on my bedspread when I opened my eyes; radiators coming on all dusty-smelling and cozy. Waffles for breakfast, that puffy kind that are light inside but crispy outside, and one-hundred-percent maple syrup heated first in the microwave and then poured over in a pool and left a moment to soak, so the waffles swell and turn spongy and every crumb of them is sopping with that toasty, nutty flavor . . ."

Well, *this* would take a while. Rebecca downed the rest of her champagne and looked for a place to set her glass. Then she felt someone's hand on the small of her back. When she turned, she found Zeb just behind her. He said, "That was just Patch being Patch. She didn't mean anything by it."

"Oh," she said, "what do I care?"

But to her distress, the tears welled up again.

"The fact is," she told Zeb, "I'm a superficial woman."

She had meant to say "superfluous" (she was thinking again of the movie credits—how she might as well not have been present), but she didn't correct herself; so Zeb, misunderstanding, said, "They can't expect a Shakespearean sonnet, for heaven's sake."

"And another thing," she said, regardless of who overheard her. "How come everyone calls me *Beck?* Beck is not my name! I'm Rebecca! How did I get to be Beck, all at once?"

"*I* don't call you Beck," Zeb pointed out.

This was true, she realized. But she went on. " 'Beck's unrelenting jollity'—that's what Biddy told Troy this morning. I heard her, out in the kitchen. 'This party will be a breeze,' I heard her say. 'We've got Poppy's truckload of desserts, and enough champagne to float a ship, and Beck's unrelenting jollity . . .' "

"Why don't we find you a seat," Zeb said, and he increased the pressure on the small of her back and steered her through the crowd. "Excuse us, please. Excuse us."

People gave way, not noticing, still listening to Poppy's speech. He had traveled past the waffles now and arrived at his morning shave. ". . . anything nicer than soft, rich lather and a plenitude of hot water? The bathroom's warm and soapy-smelling; the mirror's a steamy blur. You draw the razor down your cheek and leave this smooth swath of skin . . ."

No chairs were free, but Zeb guided Rebecca toward the piano, where Emmy and Joey were sitting, and asked if they'd mind moving. "Your grandma's tired," he told them. They jumped up, and Rebecca dropped heavily onto the bench. She *was* tired, come to think of it. She buried her nose in her empty glass and remembered, unexpectedly, a long-ago childhood crying fit that had ended when her father brought her a tumbler of ginger ale. (The same spicy, tingly smell, the same saltiness in her nostrils.) Then Zeb's fingers closed around the stem of her glass, and she let him take it away to where Barry was pouring refills.

"The best thing about solitaire is, it's so solitary," Poppy was saying. "You're allowed to think these aimless thoughts and nobody asks what you're up to. You lay out the cards, *slip slip slip*—a peace-ful sound—and then you sit a while and think, and the mantel clock is tick-tocking and the smell of fresh hot coffee is coming up from downstairs . . ."

People seemed to have reached the conclusion that Poppy's speech was background music. They were discreet; they kept their voices low, but they were going about their own affairs now. Latee-sha was drawing a face on a balloon with a squeaky felt-tip marker. NoNo and Min Foo had the giggles. Mr. Ames had waylaid Zeb to tell him something medical—displaying a gnarled wrist and flexing it this way and that while Zeb bent his head politely.

J.J. sat down on the bench beside Rebecca and confided that he wasn't entirely at ease about his wife. "What seems to be the trou-ble?" Rebecca whispered, and he said, "I believe her pastor paid that visit because she asked him to. I believe she's starting to wonder why she married me."

"Oh, J.J., don't you think you're just anxious because of what happened with Denise?" Rebecca asked. "You've been a wonderful husband! You took her on that anniversary trip to Ocean City—"

"Yes, but I believe the more niggling things—the, like, wearing my socks to bed, which she hates . . ."

Lunch, Poppy was saying, had been precisely what he'd requested: a peanut-butter-jelly sandwich on whole wheat. "Oh, I know it's not foie gras," he said, "but there's something so satisfac-tory about a p.b.j. done right. And this was done exactly right: the grape jelly smeared so thick that it had started soaking through, making these oozy purple stains like bruises on the bread . . ."

Rebecca's mother and Aunt Ida tiptoed across the room with their purses tucked under their arms. They picked their way around a game of jacks on the rug and trilled their fingers toward Rebecca. "Don't get up!" Aunt Ida mouthed, but of course Rebecca did get up. She followed them out to the foyer, where they could speak in normal tones.

"I won't urge you to stay," she said as she helped them into their things. "I know you want to be home before dark." Already the light outside was dimming, she noticed. Both women placed soft, dry kisses on her cheek, and Aunt Ida said, "Thanks for a lovely party, darlin'."

"Thank you for coming."

"But I didn't quite understand about the guest list," her mother said.

"Sorry?"

"Who *were* some of those people? They seemed . . . beside the point."

Ordinarily Rebecca would have been annoyed, but something about her mother's wording struck her as comical, and so she merely laughed and said, "Drive safely."

"We don't want that Martin Luther King Boulevard," she heard her mother tell her aunt as they walked toward the street. "Don't want to get onto that ramp where the highways loop off like spaghetti . . ."

Other guests were stirring now. They were looking at their watches, sending meaningful glances toward the people they had come with. Oh, it always made Rebecca feel so bereft when a party hit that winding-down stage! The front parlor had a ragged look, with its empty chairs here and there and its scattered gift wrap. Instead of returning to her bench, she took a seat on the couch next to Peter. "Where's he got to?" she whispered—meaning Poppy.

"Nap time," he whispered back.

Nap time, and cool white sheets that warmed as they grew used to you. "It's like you've made yourself a nest the exact same shape as your body," Poppy was saying. "It's this body-shape of warmth, and if you find you're a little *too* warm, you just move your feet the least little bit and there's this fresh new coolness."

The person who kept replaying the videotape was Merrie; or at least Merrie was the person in front of the VCR at the moment, sitting tailor-fashion on the floor as close as she could get and studying one of the Christmases. Well, she was at that age, of course: seven. Still young enough to be interested in what kind of child her mother had been. In fact, Patch had been a downright homely child, as Rebecca recollected now that she watched her roller-skate across the screen. A spiky, knobby, wiry child, quarrelsome and thorny, not nurturing like Biddy or winsome like NoNo. But Patch was the first stepdaughter Rebecca had loved—or the first she'd become aware of loving. The night Patch's appendix burst she had been so ill, in such visible pain, lying there so white-faced and enormous-eyed with every freckle standing out; and Rebecca had been struck by fear as physical as a kick in the stomach. In some ways, she had never recovered.

Not that this lessened her irritation in the slightest when Patch said, far too loudly, "What's Poppy trying to do: set a world record?"

"Ssh," Rebecca told her.

He must be nearing the finish line now; he was dressing for the party. (". . . that crackly feel of starched shirtsleeves when you slither your arms inside them . . .") And anyhow, Rebecca was enjoying this. It was sort of like a report on what it was like to be alive, she decided. Let's say you had to report back to heaven at the end of your time on earth, tell them what your personal allotment of experience had been: wouldn't it sound like Poppy's speech? The smell of radiator dust on a winter morning, the taste of hot maple syrup . . .

Why, her own report might take even longer.

Zeb was wending his way toward her with that glass of champagne, finally. The jacks players were on their eightsies.

Peter was telling J.J.J. about scientists who made discoveries in their dreams. "And if you consider how many hours we spend dreaming," he said, "figuring, say, two hours a night, which is the national average; and say we live eighty years, and . . . let's see, two from ten, borrow the one . . . That would give me almost seven years of dreaming."

Maybe it was his mention of dreams, or maybe the way he was sitting—next to her but turned slightly away, so that all she saw was his profile—but Rebecca just then had the strangest thought. She thought Peter was the boy she'd been traveling with on the train. She smiled at him, even though he wasn't looking.

Poppy was describing the candles on his cake—"a wall of flame," he called it—and the wish he'd made before he blew them out. "I wished for an even bigger party *next* year," he said, "to celebrate my hundred and first. My palindromic birthday."

Several people sent Rebecca looks of sympathy.

The jacks players had reached their ninesies. Zeb placed the glass of champagne in her hands and planted a kiss on the top of her head.

There were still so many happenings yet to be hoped for in her life.

". . . and the icing was my favorite: fondant," Poppy was saying. "It melted in my mouth. I held a bite in my mouth and it sat for just a second and then trickled, trickled down my throat, all that melting sweetness."

On the screen, Rebecca's face appeared, merry and open and sunlit, and she saw that she really had been having a wonderful time.

Back
When We Were
Grownups

ANNE TYLER

A Reader's Guide

A Conversation with Anne Tyler

Q: What was the genesis of this novel? Did a particular character or situation come to mind first?

Anne Tyler: I plotted *Back When We Were Grownups* just after emerging from a year in which there had been several losses and serious illnesses in my family. I wanted my next novel to be full of joy and celebration, which is how I ended up with a main character who earned her living throwing parties.

That a sense of loss shows through anyway, at a later point in the book, is proof that the subconscious always tends to triumph in the end.

Q: Why did you choose this title for the novel? Were there others that you discarded along the way?

AT: It's one of my few organic, natural-born titles; it was always there, on its own.

Q: Has Rebecca really become the wrong person?

AT: Well, of course she's become a different person. But not the wrong one, as it turns out.

Q: Why is it so difficult for Rebecca to see that she chose Joe and the Davitches just as they chose her?

AT: Rebecca is no more astute—or less—than most of us about her reasons for doing things. If people were fully conscious of their motives, novelists wouldn't have anything to write novels about.

Q: Would you agree that Rebecca is unaware, on some important level, that she has become the center of the Davitch family?

AT: Yes. She's a very modest and unassuming woman; it wouldn't occur to her that she could be so important to other people.

Q: Has Rebecca finally come to terms with the family and the life she ended up with? Will she ever stop feeling like an outsider, like a not-a-Davitch?

AT: The point at which I decide a novel is finished is the point where I say, "My character has arrived, and I can picture him or her more or less settled there forever." So yes, by the end of the book she has come to terms with her life. (She's still not-a-Davitch, but that's immaterial.)

Q: Did Rebecca ever have a chance to truly mourn Joe, given the incredible responsibilities that were thrust upon her with his death?

AT: Even with all those responsibilities, she did mourn—but I think of it as a kind of stupor of mourning, unlike the more reflective kind of grief that she experiences toward the end of the novel.

Q: Poppy refuses to hide his grief over his dead wife, which perturbs many of the Davitches. Is his behavior, like the constant reciting of Aunt Joyce's funeral poem, troubled or simply honest?

AT: I certainly didn't mean to imply he was troubled. This is his particular response to loss—the opposite, or maybe the underside, of Rebecca's response to her own loss.

Q: Rebecca thinks she would have stayed with Will if Joe had not swept her off her feet. Was this a likely scenario?

AT: That's the kind of question I trust readers to know the answer to once they've read the novel.

Q: "Their [Rebecca and Will's] past was a bolt of fabric they had scissored up and divided between them." What do they gain from their exchange of memories?

AT: It's more a question of what the reader gains: a sense, I hope, of how fractured and subjective our interpretation of our past is.

Q: Could the Davitches—all of them—have helped Will open up to the world? Or is it too late for him?

AT: Some people really are not capable of change. I think Will is one of them. Any effort the Davitches might have made would probably have just overwhelmed him.

Q: Rebecca's treatment of Will—rejecting him for a second time after inviting him into her life—could be considered cruel. Do you agree?

AT: It was painful, yes. ("Cruel" implies too much of an intent to give pain.) I felt downright guilty when I wrote that scene. But for Rebecca to have stayed with him would have been even more painful. Sometimes, you just have to make that choice.

Q: We know how Zeb feels, but it is unclear how Rebecca feels about him. Might something romantic ever happen between the two of them?

AT: Someday, Zeb and Rebecca are going to marry. The Davitches will be taken aback at first, but they'll warm to the idea wholeheartedly as soon as they've adjusted.

Q: Rebecca reflects that "there were no perfect parties." Why are people, like so many of the Davitches, often unwilling to recognize how much hard work celebrations are?

AT: It wasn't the hard work of celebrations that I had in mind; it was the fact that there is no perfect event, period—that every human interaction is necessarily a mixed and mingled affair.

Q: Rebecca's disapproving mother continues to exert a powerful influence over her, as does Rebecca over her daughters. Is it possible to ever stop being your parent's child or your child's parent?

AT: Yes, on occasion. But for a novelist the people who don't stop are much more interesting.

Q: Do you ever find yourself getting angry at or having trouble writing for thorny and difficult characters like Patch and Rebecca's mother?

AT: In real life I might be very annoyed by some of my characters. I find it a great deal easier to be tolerant of them on paper.

Q: Once you have created a fictional universe, is it hard to turn it over to the rest of the world? Do you feel protective of your characters?

AT: I always have a spell of maternal anxiety when a manuscript is finally on its way to New York (where, for the first time, someone other than me will see it). I picture my characters riding the train, independent of me at last, excited and shy and unsure of themselves. But once they've arrived and been accepted, I tend to forget about them.

Q: If you had to choose a favorite character in this novel, besides Rebecca, which would it be and why?

AT: I'm very fond of Peter. I like his curiosity and his active mind; I think he's going to grow up to be a very interesting young man.

Q: What other books would you suggest for a reading group discussion?

AT: The most rewarding choice for reading groups would be a book that they could argue about passionately among themselves. Christina Stead's *The Man Who Loved Children*, for instance— people have always loved that book or hated it. It could make for a wonderfully lively discussion.

Q: Are you working on a new novel?

AT: I'm in the early stages of a novel about an unhappy marriage— a subject that intrigues me because it provides such a good opportunity to watch different types of characters grating against each other. It begins in 1941, and I'm finding it an unexpected pleasure to live in another time for a while.

Reading Group Questions and Topics for Discussion

1. "How on earth did I get like this?" wonders Rebecca at the start of the novel about the person she has become. Have you ever had a moment like this? Did you end up with the life you thought you would have?

2. While many people think longingly of the road not traveled, Rebecca decides to take it. Is this a good idea? If you were going to do so, what steps would you have to take?

3. Do you think that Rebecca would have stayed with Will if she had not met Joe?

4. Rebecca suggests to NoNo that "all of us love people at least partly for their usefulness." Do you agree?

5. Do you think Min Foo is going to discard Hakim as she has her other husbands?

6. Rebecca reflects that marriage leads to "knowing more than you should about the other person." Do you agree?

7. Tina's visit leads Rebecca to observe her life from the uncomfortable perspective of an outsider. Have you ever had that experience with a guest?

8. Rebecca describes Tina, Joe's first wife, as "the distant, alluring mystery woman whose edges had not been worn dull by the constant minor abrasions of daily contact." What has Tina gained and lost because of the distance she has placed between herself and her daughters?

9. Rebecca watches NoNo change as she takes on parenthood. Discuss how becoming a parent changes people and how it does not.

10. Both Rebecca and NoNo decide to take on instant parenthood. What are the challenges and rewards of choosing such a path?

11. Rebecca wants to believe that there are grander motivations in history than family and friends but concludes that there are not. Do you agree?

12. This novel explores the selective and faulty nature of memory. How accurate do you think your own memories are? What do you remember and what don't you remember?

13. Is the conditional and faulty nature of human memory a blessing or a curse?

14. Will reminds Rebecca that she wanted a big family with all of its rituals, something Rebecca had forgotten about the girl she once was. How could Rebecca have forgotten such an important piece of information about herself?

15. Why is Will so determined to see Rebecca as she is not?

16. How do you think Poppy's memory of Rebecca's first birthday party at Open Arms would compare with Rebecca's?

17. Zeb never married. Do you think he has been waiting for Rebecca all these years? What do you think will happen with Rebecca and Zeb? Who will have to make the first move if this relationship is ever to get off the ground?

18. Does Rebecca's family see her as a three-dimensional person by the end of this novel?

19. How do you think each of Rebecca's daughters would describe her?

20. Which is your favorite character in this novel and why?

21. If you could ask the author one question about this novel, what would you ask? And why?

22. Why did your group choose this novel? Are you happy with your choice? What book is up next?

© Diana Walker

About the Author

ANNE TYLER was born in Minneapolis in 1941 but grew up in Raleigh, North Carolina. She graduated at nineteen from Duke University and went on to do graduate work in Russian studies at Columbia University. This is Anne Tyler's fifteenth novel; her eleventh, *Breathing Lessons*, was awarded the Pulitzer Prize in 1988. She is a member of the American Academy and Institute of Arts and Letters. She lives in Baltimore.